Small Acts of Kindness

Small Acts of Kindness

BRONWYN DONAGHY

HarperCollins*Publishers*

The poem quoted on page 242–43 is attributed to
Henry Scott Holland (1847–1918), Canon of St Paul's Cathedral.

HarperCollins*Publishers*

First published in Australia in 2003
This edition published in 2004
by HarperCollins*Publishers* Pty Limited
ABN 36 009 913 517
A member of the HarperCollins*Publishers* (Australia) Pty Limited Group
www.harpercollins.com.au

HarperCollins*Publishers*
25 Ryde Road, Pymble, Sydney, NSW 2073, Australia
31 View Road, Glenfield, Auckland 10, New Zealand
77-85 Fulham Palace Road, London W6 8JB, United Kingdom
2 Bloor Street East, 20th floor, Toronto, Ontario M4W 1A8, Canada
10 East 53rd Street, New York NY 10022, USA

National Library of Australia Cataloguing-in-Publication data:

Donaghy, Bronwyn, 1948–2002.
    Small acts of kindness.
    ISBN 0 7322 6909 1.
    1. Female friendship – Fiction. I. Title.
A823.3

Cover design by Christa Edmonds, HarperCollins Design Studio
Cover photograph: Getty Images
Typeset in Bembo 11/14pt by HarperCollins
Printed and bound in Australia by Griffin Press on 50gsm Bulky News

5 4 3 2 1   04 05 06 07

To Anne St Quinton, my friend

Do not walk ahead of me — I may not follow
Do not walk behind me — I may not lead
Just walk beside me and be my friend!

Anon

PROLOGUE

On the day of the funeral, the sun blazed. Sensible mindless creatures slunk away in search of shade. Only the flies stayed, fat black bodies bashing against window panes and bouncing back to stick on lips and flick at eyes. The clouds climbed high, broke into slivers of fleece and disappeared. There was no rain. There was no release. The heat pressed in upon the people, raised sweat on their skin, soaked them with lethargy, removed all strength from the grasp of comforting hands, weighed down even the lids of their eyes.

Mothers, fathers, sisters, friends and brothers had to deal with death in heat as thick and wet as soup.

The men carried the coats of their suits over their arms and didn't pause to put them on until they stood just inside the portals of the church. It was a modern one, steel and soaring outside, creamy pine pews and sky-filled windows within.

The women wondered how long the flowers would last.

Everyone talked about them both. Talked and wondered. It was bound to happen; Jemma and Helen had been friends for so long, had shared their lives since childhood, while the town watched, waited, whispered. And now neither of them was here. Only the man, John Sullivan, the big bloke who had been with them all along. That's what people wondered about most.

Some people thought their story was unique, special; others decided that what had happened to them was inevitable, that their story was as ordinary as they come.

There's nothing new under the sun, as Jemma might have said.

Part One

TOM

The organ music consumed him. It droned in his ears, swelled in his nose, thundered behind his forehead, made his heart heavy, rolled through his arms and legs. It's weird, Tom thought, how organ music makes you even sadder than you already are.

Small, seven, the shortest person in the church, Tom kept his sprouty red head down. He could feel tears sitting behind his small bright eyes, waiting to squirt. He stared at his newly shined shoes, not blinking. If you didn't blink, the water stayed still. It was like carrying a cup of tea to Mummy when she was having her lie-in on Sunday mornings. You needed to move slowly.

Hamish had cleaned his shoes for him last night, using real polish, not the stuff you could paint on with the sponge at the end of the bottle. Hamish had cleaned everyone's shoes — his own, Tom's, John's and Poppy's as well. He had brushed on the polish and buffed them with one of Tom's old singlets, leaving them standing on the kitchen bench to dry. A line of black shoes. Empty but shiny bright.

The only woman not wearing a dark dress was Granny Babs, standing in the pew in front of Tom. Her coat was light blue, pale as the sky and long. It reached to her knees and made her legs, in matching pale blue trousers, look very short. Granny Babs' face was always covered with powder, tiny white particles flaking in the folds and frills of her skin. She was like the white moulds you could buy at the plaster painting shop in the school holidays. On this occasion she had been painted red, white and blue. Blue suit, red lips, white face, pale red circles where her cheeks should be. She could easily be a gnome at the Plaster House, thought Tom, but he would never choose her to take home. Her powdery smell clogged your nose and made you want to breathe fresh air. When she moved, little puffs of perfumed plaster floated in the air around her, as if bits of her cheeks and chin were breaking away.

Tom stopped thinking of a face breaking away, because that made him wonder what happened to people's faces when they died — some boys at school had once told him horrible things about bodies rotting and worms. He didn't want his face to be eaten by worms. When he'd told Mummy what the boys had said, she had brushed his sprouty red hair back from his brow and talked about angels and heaven, which sounded a lot more pleasant, although less believable. He had never seen an angel, not even in his dreams.

Thinking of this reminded him again that he was sad. Hamish had said this would be a Hard Day to get through. But there was nothing wrong with being sad on such a Hard Day, Hamish said, and it would be quite okay to cry. To Shed a Few Tears was how Hamish described it; it sounded like something Jemma would say. But Tom did not cry. None of the other men were Shedding a Few Tears.

Hamish had been so nice to him in the last couple of days, explaining things, answering all the questions that worried him most. Tom had fallen into his old habit of letting himself imagine what it would be like to have Hamish for a brother. Which would make John his father.

Tom glanced sideways at John's big arm, in the dark suit jacket, almost touching his. That would be Too Good to be True, another thing Jemma said.

Having John as his father was his favourite what-might-have-been story. Tom liked imagining what-might-have-beens. Often, when Mummy had finished reading him a story, he would say to her: 'Now let's think about what-might-have-been.' Like Prince Charming picking one of the ugly sisters because she was more interesting, and Cinderella's breath smelling like peanut butter. Or Snow White telling the wicked witch she didn't like apples, thanks all the same.

He was glad John was home again, even though he wasn't his usual self. Hamish had explained to Tom that John was angry with the world, not them. John didn't look angry today. Just sad. Like the rest of them.

Caitlin seemed the saddest. Without looking past John to see her properly, Tom knew she was Shedding a Few Tears. More than a few. He could imagine her face, a pale oval, and her long, fat plait of hair, reddish brown, darker than his, although people still said you could tell she was his sister. By sliding his eyes sideways he could see her hands, clutching a wad of white tissues, damp and falling to pieces, bits of them dropping to the floor. It was weird that Caitlin, who never cried, who always acted so fierce and cold, had been weeping very quietly all morning. The tears just kept running down her face. She made no sound. She just stood there, shedding tears and tissues.

Watching Caitlin made Tom's tears start to sting and poke their way through. He blinked very slowly so the water would not spill out of his eyes. When his vision cleared again he saw the caterpillar.

It was crawling along the pew in front, slowly, in time with the organ music, making its black and furry way towards Granny Babs' powder-blue bottom.

A tiny smile appeared on Tom's small mouth. He imagined Granny Babs sitting down in a minute and landing splat! On the caterpillar. Runny green caterpillar gizzards on the powder-blue suit. He had to press his lips together then, to stop the smile getting any bigger.

Caitlin had really howled at first. When Poppy told them about Mummy, she had uttered a great long scream of pain, like a cat that had been wounded.

Everyone had been surprised because Caitlin was usually so quiet. Tom was the noisy one. He was the one who asked too many questions. And today, on this Hard Day, he had so many questions but nobody looked as if they wanted to answer them. The organ was bellowing as if God Himself had arrived and now everyone was looking around to the back of the church . . .

Tom couldn't see past John, so he twisted his head right around and looked up.

On a verandah-like platform, at the back of the church, he finally saw the organ.

It was an enormous instrument, made of giant metal tubes, like massive wind chimes standing stiffly together instead of dangling free. And someone was playing it.

Not angels. Not God. Just a person. Someone he couldn't quite see, but still, someone real.

Knowing this made Tom feel better.

Tom kept his eyes fixed on the massive pipes. He didn't want to watch or think about the men in uniforms who were walking slowly up the aisle, carrying the heavy box on their shoulders, marching towards the banks of flowers at the front. He wanted to know how they got the organ up there. Would they have needed a crane? Did they take it up in parts and then put it together, like Lego?

He wanted desperately to ask his mother, but she wasn't there.

OUT WITHOUT A HAT

Of course her mother wasn't there. If she had been, chances are they would never have become friends. Never in a Million Years, as Jemma said later.

They met on a clear, hot spring day in 1959. No wind, but, in the early days of a Siren's Rock September, not too much humidity either. Helen, wearing her good black patent leather shoes and white socks, was out walking. She was exploring new territory, following the road that led her out of town, over the hill, past paddocks held back from the path with rusty knots of barbed wire and ribbons of weeds.

The walk had been Helen's own idea. She hadn't even told her mother she was going. She walked quickly, looking around her as she followed the snaking black road, trying to take in her new surroundings but really rehearsing excuses in her mind. Fresh air. Exercise. Finding the best way to her new school. A sensible thing to do. Afterwards she would know how to get there and how long it took; she would be better prepared for the beginning of the term. She had forgotten her hat. Sorry about that.

Sorry about that, sorry about that, sorry about the hat, the Helens in her head were chanting in time with her steps. She tried not to listen to them, tried not to think about Mummy too much. Tried to think about her walk and what she could see and how different it was to walking in the city suburbs, with their concrete footpaths and straight cracks, grimy gutters full of lolly papers and cigarette butts. Maybe her mother wouldn't mind that she had decided to go for a walk.

Nope. That's called wishful thinking. Of course Mummy would mind. Her thin voice would go on and on, hissing and spitting. A snake voice, uncoiling from her throat, rising, swaying, getting ready to strike.

Helen would be in trouble. There was no doubt about it.

The weird thing was that she had still decided to go. Had tried not to think about the trouble. Had blocked it out, pulled down a blind. In the years that followed, Jemma would often point this out to her. 'It's your strength and your weakness,' she would say. 'You can't pull a blind down on everything. Sooner or later someone raises the blind and if the terrible thing is still there and you haven't done anything about it ... well, you know. It's still a *problem*. It's still an *issue*.'

There was no need to find the road to school, her mother would scold. She would be driven to school in Daddy's nice car. The new Branch Manager's car, a black Holden with fat plum-coloured seats and a radio. That way there would be no risk of coming to harm.

Sorry about the hat, thought Helen again, trying not to listen to the two Helens in her head, giggling together as they mimicked her mother:

'. . . And why would anyone with any sense go walking in the hot sun? Now you'll get freckles. Big ugly brown spots on your face. As if having that sallow skin isn't a big enough handicap.

'It's not as if I don't try to make you look pretty. It's not as if I don't spend hours of my time setting your hair, making you nice

clothes. It's not as if I don't try to improve your looks. Such as they are . . .'

Helen was ten and slender, and her wispy hair, the colour of beach sand, was hooked back from her small face and wide brow with an Alice band. She had an Alice band for every day of the week and two spares. This one was blue, to match her cotton print dress. Polished cotton. Her shoes were polished too and neatly buckled. Her socks were trimmed with nylon lace. The socks made her feet smell but her mother made her wear them. Better than blisters.

All Dressed Up Like a Sore Toe, Jemma would say. Jemma would say that a lot. It was one of her favourite expressions. Sometimes, for a change, she would say All Dressed Up and Nowhere to Go. That would have been a better way to describe Helen today.

Helen was a nervous child. Already, after less than twenty minutes, she was worn out by this minor act of rebellion. The harder she tried not to think about her mother, the more she did.

What if Mummy was right? What if she came to harm? What if she met wicked people? How would she know if they were wicked or not? What if there was a fierce dog around the next bend? Or a snake? In this hot place at the top of the state, snakes were a definite possibility. It was so hot up here, much hotter than in Wollongong, down in the south, where they had lived before Daddy got his promotion.

Their old Wollongong neighbour, bossy Mrs Billings, had mentioned snakes. 'Wouldn't want to go up there meself,' she had said to Helen's mother, leaning on the top of the brick fence, her fleshy arms falling in folds over her elbows. 'Snakes and spiders. Too dangerous.'

'It's not as if we'll be out in the bush,' Mummy had said with a superior little smile. 'They're building a brand new house for us. Building it for the new Branch Manager. That's Douglas.'

Daddy was in charge now that he had been made Branch Manager. Daddy was a boss.

He had always been Helen's boss, of course. And Mummy's. And Baby Joy's, although she was too young to understand. What Daddy said, they all did. She pulled a blind down on Daddy and walked on.

When Helen heard the bushes beside the road start to swish and crackle, she slowed down. Voices. Chortling. Her heart began to thud. Worse than a dog. Boys.

Boys were big and rough. Keep away from boys, Mummy always said. They are rude and dirty. In Wollongong she had attended a girls' school and, of course, she had no brothers, so she had never had much to do with boys. With boys' games, someone always ends up getting hurt, Mummy said.

Daddy had once been a boy. Hard to imagine, until you thought about the hurting, the hitting. It was what boys did. And men. Once, Helen had heard Mummy telling someone she was glad there were no boys in the family, because there was a risk of Douglas belting them too hard. Mummy had said it like a joke, but Helen couldn't see how it was funny. She wondered how you could tell when belting was too hard. Or how bad you had to be. She would have liked to ask someone, but there was no one to ask.

Anyway, Daddy didn't use a belt. He hit her with the feather duster. The cane end. Or his hand, which was worse.

As it turned out, it wasn't boys in the bushes. Well, it was, but first to appear was a girl.

She burst from the bushes, crashing through the branches, crushing the leaves. With both hands on her hips, she flicked her hair out of her eyes and looked right at Helen — a curious and not unfriendly gaze.

Gave her a Good Once Over.

Helen stopped mid-step and, lowering her neatly shod little foot back to the ground, returned the girl's stare.

The bush had burped up a solid sprite with bare feet and dirty toes. A russet mane of tangled, twig-spiked hair, green eyes behind a scraped-back fringe, a plump and dusty olive-brown body, crammed into a tight white T-shirt and brief pink shorts. And then a huge white smile.

Thin, nervous, city-bred Helen, instantly enchanted, smiled back.

'Hello,' said Helen, still smiling, speaking softly so that she wouldn't frighten the sprite away. Not that she looked capable of fright. Though you could never tell; Helen had learned already that nothing was certain in this life.

She hesitated for a minute and then slowly put out her hand, the way her mother and father had taught her to do when she met important visitors from Daddy's work.

The sprite stared at Helen's hand and then continued her comprehensive inspection, taking in Helen's flyaway hair, her fragile body, her crisply ironed dress, those elegant shoes. Still staring, then grinning, she started picking some of the twigs from her hair.

'My name's Helen,' Helen said shyly, her hand still sticking out, as if she were a doll in the doorway of a weather clock.

'I'm Jemma,' the sprite said. A loud, confident voice announcing a strange but simple name that Helen had never heard before. A white smile that made Helen want to smile back forever. Her mouth felt strangely stretched. *'Our Helen's not much of a smiler.'*

Jemma didn't take Helen's hand and, after waiting another moment or two, Helen dropped it and put it behind her back. Her other hand nervously crept around to join it.

'You looked like a princess,' Jemma told Helen later. 'And you put out your hand like the Queen did when she came up here. I didn't know what to do with it. Nobody ever gave me their hand before. I was all dirty and you looked so clean. Like you'd never been dirty in your life.'

Behind the sprite, one by one, came the boys, six or seven of them. To Helen's relief, all but one of them were small; smaller even than Helen, and just as skinny. No Meat on their Bones, as their leader said. Rough, surly and grubby-looking, toenails clogged with dirt, shabby clothes stuck with bits of bush. The last one to emerge was taller and very brown. Brown hair, brown face, dark brown eyes, like Helen's. Brown clothes, bare brown feet. But he was still slightly shorter than the sprite, who now came closer.

'This is my gang,' said the girl named Jemma. 'We're called the Wildcats. We've got our own song and our own secret hideout.'

'We don't ever have to go home,' said one of the little boys. 'Not even to do a pooh.'

The other little boys all squawked with glee. Jemma ignored them. 'Where've you come from?' she asked Helen. She spoke clearly, with a broad Australian twang. Helen spoke softly and her voice was husky. Parents and teachers hated it, were always telling her to speak up. 'We just shifted here from Wollongong. I was finding the way to the school.'

'Wollongong?' asked Jemma, gazing pointedly at Helen's shoes. 'That's a coal city, isn't it? The trouble with cities is, city kids always wear shoes.'

Helen frowned with shame and put one patent leather foot over the other, covering it with dust.

'You want to get rid of those A.S.A.P.,' said Jemma. 'The thing is, you want to harden up your feet. My feet are so hard I could walk on broken glass.'

15

'Your hair was all floaty and fair,' Jemma told her when they became best friends. 'You were wearing that lovely dress, with the lace and puffed sleeves. And those beautiful shoes. I was so jealous. That's why I made you take them off. I couldn't stand you looking that perfect.'

'I could walk on spikes,' said one of the boys.

Jemma cast a derisory eye over his skinny frame. 'That's Robbie,' she said. 'Dave, Dennis, Gary, Derek, Flip.' They looked as if they had come off an assembly line: scrawny, squinty, stringy-haired, picket-toothed. 'And that's John, Robbie's brother. He's the vice captain of the gang. He takes over when I'm busy.'

Helen stopped frowning and smiled shyly at the all-brown boy. John nodded sternly and lowered his eyes. 'Let's go, Jemma,' he mumbled at the ground. 'Things to do.'

But Jemma and Helen were still gazing at each other with unabashed appreciation.

'I've lived in Siren's Rock forever,' Jemma declared. 'But my mum hasn't. She's German. And my dad is only half Australian, 'cos his mother, who is my grandmother, comes from Greece. So I'm a bitser. We got two dogs, one's a bitser, the other's pure labrador, and we got three cats and a bird. Maybe you'd like to come around and see the bird?'

'Not the dogs and cats?' asked Helen. She frowned again, frightened that she had sounded like a smart alec. '*Helen can be a real little smart alec when she puts on a turn. You'd be surprised. Butter wouldn't melt . . .*' 'I mean, would I see the smallest pet first and then . . .?' She felt her frown pulling down her Alice band as she muddled on. Jemma's white teeth flashed again and Helen was treated to a glorious peal of laughter. Relieved, Helen responded with a cotton-wool chuckle, low and thick in her throat. The boys didn't laugh. They stood behind Jemma, in the middle of the road, eyes screwed up, already bored, occasionally scratching themselves, shoving each other. Only John stood still, waiting.

'Anybody can see Rufus and Fox and the pussies,' explained Jemma. 'Seeing the bird is special. She's new.'

'Like me,' said Helen.

'Like you,' agreed Jemma. 'Pretty like you, too.'

'I'm not,' said Helen.

'Y'are.'

'Not like you.' Helen surprised herself: what a funny thing to say. 'I mean, I'd rather look like you.'

Jemma stared at her. 'Why?'

Why? Helen chewed her lip. She didn't know why.

What a pretty little girl Helen is. Where did she get those curls? Really? But they look so natural. Every night? My girls would pull them out. Lovely frock. She's a credit to you, Mrs Winter.

'You're not pretty,' Helen said anxiously, and then her cheeks burned with the realisation that, as usual, this was not what she had meant to say.

Jemma's grin disappeared. A hurt, sullen expression settled on her face. It made a huge difference, like the sun going behind a cloud. Closed, her lips were full and pouting. From the corner of her eye, Helen saw John frown.

'You're gorgeous, see . . .' said Helen, trying again. '*Helen's not much of a talker. Can barely string three words together at a time.*' 'Gorgeous. Not just pretty. Beautiful.'

The full fluorescence of Jemma's smile returned to light up her face.

'Gaw-juss!' sneered Robbie. 'She thinks you're gaw-juss, Jem! Why don't you kiss her then? Why don't you get married?'

'Shut up, dickwit,' Jemma said to him while she continued to smile at Helen.

'Jemma,' muttered John.

Jemma sighed. 'Things to do,' she said apologetically to Helen, but she didn't move. The two girls continued to look at each other. There was a painting on the wall of Helen's parents' new house: blue sky, purple mountains, brown cliffs and green waves. Jemma's eyes were the same sea green.

Jemma had never seen eyes so exactly the colour of honey. Blonde hair and brown eyes. Like Sandra Dee.

'Hey,' said Jemma suddenly. 'D'ya wanna join my gang?'

There was a chorus of objections behind her. 'You gotta arks us first,' said Robbie. 'We should have a meeting. That's the rules.'

'Shut up, Robbie Ratbag,' said Jemma. 'This is my gang. I make the rules. If I want Helen in, she's in. Right, John?'

Helen looked at John. He looked back and shrugged. 'Jemma's the captain,' he said, and looked away.

Helen took a deep breath. Her chest felt tight. Her face was hot with longing. Never in her life had she been asked to join a gang. Never had she had proper friends. They moved a lot, Helen's family. First there had been the dark suburb in Sydney which she hardly remembered. Then Wollongong. A coal town. Chimneys choking black smoke into the sky. Men coming home from work at the start of the day, blackened faces staring at her from bus windows. Now, the big move north. Three schools so far and it took Helen ages to articulate her way into friendships, always with neat, well-behaved little girls like herself; by the time she managed it, Daddy and Mummy would be talking about moving again.

'To be fair,' she said to Jemma, 'shouldn't we ask the rest of the, um, Wildcats?'

Jemma thought about it for a moment, then nodded. She turned around to her scrawny crew. 'Do you want her in?'

'Will she tell us we're all gaw-juss?' giggled Robbie. The boys laughed and shoved each other about, even John.

'Hurry up!' said Jemma. 'Yes or no?'

'What can you bring for the gang?' asked John.

'Cake,' said Helen quickly, trying to sound keen rather than desperate. But her chest felt tighter than a double knot. 'I can make cake.'

The boys looked at each other.

'I can bring toilet paper,' she added tentatively. 'For the cubby. We have heaps.'

That put the seal on it. She was in.

And Jemma set to work on her immediately: the shoes had to go. Helen willingly complied, and soon she was hobbling, her small white feet crunched up, on the hot tar. John wanted her to stop but Jemma, chewing Minties, was firm. 'Ten minutes,' she said. 'A little bit more tomorrow.' Helen wasn't complaining. Her small mouth was pressed tightly shut as they timed her with John's watch. The other boys were thrashing around in the bushes, emerging occasionally to check her progress.

'We'll have you walking on gravel by the end of the week,' said Jemma encouragingly, offering a Mintie as an inducement. The lolly was hot, squashed flat in the wrapping. 'Take two,' she said. 'What happens is, you have to chew so hard you forget the pain.'

A big black car loomed on the road and hummed to a stop alongside them. Helen didn't recognise her mother and father until they got out. The car was new.

When she thought about it years later, she wondered when their story really began. Was it the moment of the bursting bush, when Jemma bounced into her path, while Helen stood there, her small patent leather foot poised to take the next step? When for a moment, one long slow moment, there were just the two of them?

Or was it after her father caught her by the shoulder and yanked her towards the car, her mother fussing in her creased linen frock, tottering around in her high heels, picking up Helen's shoes and socks, squealing and squawking like a chook that had been shoved off its nest? When the little boys, taking one look at the big man with his dome head and his black-rimmed glasses, recognised punitive authority and raced off across the paddocks? When Jemma, flushed and grimly determined, strode up to Helen's father, grabbed Helen's hand and tried to pull her away from him? When John followed, horror and fear on his kind, thin face, put his skinny boy's arms around Jemma's waist and pulled as well?

Did it begin with the three of them, Helen being pulled two ways, Jemma and John trying to rescue her; was that when it was?

Helen remembered Jemma shouting: 'Leave her alone. She's our friend.'

Douglas Winter, incredulous, deep disgusted noises rolling around in his throat, didn't bother speaking to any of the children, didn't explain to Jemma and John that he was Helen's father. He unpeeled Jemma's hands from Helen's, shoved her away and raised his hand to clip John across the ear. Jemma screamed: 'Don't you dare! Don't you *dare*!' and leapt between them.

In the car, on the way back to their house, her mother clucked with indignation through her lipsticked beak. 'We were so worried — frightful little children, touching you, stealing your shoes. What were they trying to do, holding on to you like that? What were they thinking of?'

'Local scum,' said her father.

'We knew he was going to hit you,' Jemma said later. 'When he got you home.' Helen wondered how she knew that. Even on such short acquaintance she felt certain that no adult person ever struck Jemma Johnson.

Helen sat in the back of the car, suppressing a smile while a feeling like warm soup spread through her body. Thinking about it all. Forgetting to be afraid.

AN APOLOGY

The marks of the cane were still red on Helen's legs when they came to call that night. Jemma, showered and clean now — a sensible soapy smell doing its job on her firm brown flesh — and wearing a sleeveless green cotton dress, was with her mother. The magnificent Marte.

'Missus Winter?' said Marte in a voice even louder than Jemma's. 'I've brought my daughter round to say she's sorry for her rudeness to you this afternoon.'

Marte stood outside the Winters' wire door and beamed. 'And I have come to welcome you to our little town. Oh, Missus Winter. What a beautiful house! What a beautiful lady! Now I know what Jemma meant when she said to me: "Mum, I was bad. I was rude to a beautiful lady." So I brought her here to say she is so sorry.'

Marte spoke with an unusual hybrid accent which combined German, Greek and broad Australian. Lacking the patience for *t*'s or *th*'s, she generally substituted both of these sounds with a *d*, so 'that' became 'dat' and when she said 'daughter' it came out as 'dawder'. 'Beautiful' was 'beeyoodifooel', a word into which Marte managed to cram not only a sense of wonder, but a couple of additional syllables.

Helen could hardly believe Jemma's daring. Here she was with her mother, standing on the freshly concreted front porch of Number Ten Grand View Crescent, smiling through the brand new flyscreen, walking politely through the smartly painted portals of the Winters' lovely luxury home.

Marte was a big-breasted, big-boned, handsome woman with small blue eyes sparkling above massive cheekbones and a wide mouth. She wore an astonishing nineteen-forties hairstyle, rolled up with combs on top and curving down into a pageboy which hung to her wide shoulders like a brown velvet curtain. She carried a plate of pastries under a cloth, and her greeting smiled over a xylophone of teeth.

'Missus Winter! What a lucky thing it is for our town that you have moved here. Good people. People with taste! Sophisticated!'

Babs Winter untied her apron, flapped her hands helplessly, glared at Helen, glanced at herself in the mirror over the brand new French polished mantelpiece, patted her hair, sighed, had little choice. Marte and Jemma were invited in. Teacups were produced from the new walnut-veneer sideboard. The traymobile, patina gleaming, was pulled out and a sponge cake, two layers separated by a smear of jam, was brought in from the kitchen. The girls were given lemonade.

Douglas was out when they arrived, but he returned as Marte and Jemma were preparing to leave. Under his wife's frantic eyes and Marte's steady gaze he blustered and eventually sighed. Shrugged. Came Down from his High Horse, whispered Jemma to Helen. Marte silenced her daughter with a stern look. She said sadly that Jemma was a good girl underneath but she had to learn more respect when she was with important people; as she had just been saying to Helen's beautiful mother, the Winters were just the sort of people Siren's Rock needed to Put it on the Map. She and her husband, George — and next time Mr and Mrs Winter were down town, they should get some fish and chips from George's shop, on the house, to say welcome — had probably spoiled Jemma a little. But what could you do? One beautiful daughter. One troublesome son. Ah, the Winters had two daughters? How wonderful. Their Helen was going to be such a good influence on her Jemma.

The terrifying thing was, as Jemma often said in the years that followed, Marte had meant it all. 'My mother,' Jemma would say, 'is absolutely sincere!'

'Why do you always have to be so humble?' Jemma would rage at Marte when she was older, when she was sixteen, twenty-six, thirty-six. 'Why don't you hold your head up and be proud of what you are, of what you've achieved? God almighty, you're a German. Germans are supposed to be a proud people!'

'I'm proud of *you*, Jemma,' Marte would say. '*You* make me hold my head high. But for myself, okay, I'm just grateful that life has been good to our family.'

'But life *hasn't* been good to you, Mum,' Jemma would reply. 'Life has let you down. You were a *performer*, you were a *star*, people *cheered* you, knew your name! There were pictures of you on posters! *That* was when life was good to you. Then you gave it all up. To clean other people's houses. To sell fish and chips. To scrimp and save every cent. To live here. *Here*!' Jemma's voice would get louder, and her smoother, shinier vowel sounds would begin to twang. 'You gave it all up for this! And what good did it do?'

'Family is good,' Marte would mutter. 'You and Nick and Dad and me. That's what's good. Hard work don't hurt no one. And we have happiness too. Family is better than fame.'

And Marte would leave it at that, saddened because she could not make her daughter understand.

Arguing with Jemma wore Marte out more than cleaning fifty houses.

Even on that first night the contrast between her new friend and her mother amazed Helen. Jemma waited patiently for Marte's fawning speech to end, then looked Douglas Winter in the eye and apologised for her earlier rudeness, said, as she had never seen him before, she thought he was a kidnapper trying to steal her new friend away and hold her for ransom. Douglas Winter looked at Jemma and knew she was lying. Jemma continued to stare back at him. Jemma was not sincere. Jemma was not humble. She stood there with her chin tilted up, one hand on her hip and her fabulous white smile lighting up her face. Douglas hesitated and was compromised rather than conquered.

Nobody mentioned the shoes.

John waited outside in the warm, dark night. Invisible in his brown skin and brown clothes, he stood near the besser-brick fence, bare feet on cool, rich earth. No grass yet, but the house looked smart, deceptively comfortable.

John knew better.

He hung around out of sight when Jemma and her mother went inside, and stayed behind the fence until they came out again, Marte laughing softly, Jemma prancing about and chattering as they strolled away together.

Feet sinking in the soft soil, John watched the house for a while longer. He heard some shouting from the big man, then a small child cried and after that the house became silent. Jemma would be home with her mum and dad by now, safer than anyone else in the world. Helen would be in bed too, but still not safe. Not in that house.

Finally he walked home, to the small shabby cottage that shared his street with a straggly market garden and two cow paddocks. If anyone had asked John what he had been doing in Grand View Crescent, or what he could have done, he would have had no answer.

ROCKY ROAD

Considering their difficult beginning, it was a wonder they were allowed to see each other at all, let alone become friends. But then Babs Winter hired Marte Johnson to clean her house. You couldn't really say to a person: 'I'd like you to come Mondays and Thursdays, I'd like you to scrub out the bathroom and vacuum through and dust and polish the furniture and I might give you a bit of ironing as well and, by the way, I don't want your daughter to have anything to do with mine.' Not in classless Australia. Not any more. Siren's Rock was a small town; Branch Managers' wives with beautiful homes were generous and bountiful, especially to those of inferior origins, especially when those inferiors knew their place.

Within weeks the girls were constantly together. They vied for top of the class at school, Jemma having the edge but Helen coming closer with each test, though John could beat them both at maths.

Helen loved going to Jemma's place, a triple-fronted fibro house on a big flat block of land. The house was painted apple green and had two stone lions guarding the front gate. In the huge back yard was a comprehensive vegetable garden, neatly fenced off from a series of flower beds and fruit trees laden with spring blossoms. Rows of crimson, purple and pink azaleas lay in the dappling shade of an enormous jacaranda tree. It was a lovely place to play.

She met the bird, the cats, and Rufus, the panting black labrador, and Fox, the bitser. And she fell in love with the family. There was Maria, Jemma's black-eyed, black-garbed grandmother, who seemed to spend her life sweeping, and Nick, Jemma's young brother, who spent his life making messes and getting into trouble. But she especially loved George, Jemma's dad, with his bandy walk, his skinny, hairy legs, his missing front tooth, his broad grin and his huge eyes glittering above sacks of dark skin that stretched up into a million creases when he laughed.

When Helen and Jemma arrived at the Johnson house straight from school, they would sit down at the laminex kitchen table which was almost always laden with delicious pastries and buns. Marte always seemed to be pulling something crisp out of the ancient oven just as the girls raced through the flapping rainbow plastic streamers that hung over the back door. They sat on plastic padded chairs, curled their legs around the chipped chrome legs and ate as much as they liked, while Marte entertained them with stories of what she'd been doing that day, her 'chobz', the difficulty of cleaning this house or that, the astonishing behaviour of other people's animals (never the people).

Forties pageboy flying, sturdy limbs swaying, Jemma's mother clowned, she danced, she gesticulated, she mimed, she acted out her entire day for the girls and they laughed until they had to hold their tummies, although whether this was from laughing or too much food eaten too fast, they couldn't tell. It didn't matter. Marte never told them to stop.

On Friday afternoons Helen was sometimes allowed to go

down into the town with Jemma after school. They caught the clattery bus and jumped out right opposite George's fish and chip shop, screaming 'ta-ta' to the blubbery driver, whose massive bottom drooped down around the seat like shiny navy icing looping over a cake. She loved going into the shop, with its sizzling vats of fatty oil, and waiting with Jemma for George to see them, anticipating the huge grin breaking across his sweaty face. Within moments he'd be holding up two giant golden salted chips, popping them into their mouths.

Full of fat and giggles, burping — Jemma could burp better than a bull frog — they would walk down to the library, in the park at the end of the town, where they could further gorge themselves, this time on books — CS Lewis, LM Montgomery, Louisa May Alcott, the Secret Seven, the Famous Five, and tales about girls in the Upper Sixth and the Lower Fourth and their enviable experiences of midnight suppers and hockey matches in English boarding schools. At six o'clock George would shut the shop and drive them home in his ute.

When the summer Sundays became stifling, George and Marte took them to the beach, bouncing around in the back of the ute with the beach umbrella, baskets of food and bundles of towels. George and Jemma taught Helen how to ride the waves, how to recognise a shoot by the curl on each glistening mountain of water, when to start swimming like mad so that the wave would pick you up and hurl you like a spear towards the shore. Or if they stayed at home, Marte would put the sprinkler hose on in the garden and the girls would race through the spray, giggling and screaming and soaking themselves. Helen, her set curls reduced to lank straggles, loved the sound of mud and water slopping between her toes and the fresh smell of the wet grass.

Helen adored everything about Marte, especially the stories she told about the years she'd spent as a buck jumper in a travelling rodeo show — a brash, breathless procession of stories full of colour and climax and dust and noise. Marte could still leap feet into the air and click her heels, the way she used to do in the rodeo. She did it on the day she paid off the television. She did it on the day her Tante Traute back in Heidelberg won some kind of lottery. She did it on the day she paid off her car. Helen's mother said she found it extraordinary that a woman from a migrant family who had to go out to work was the only woman of her acquaintance who drove her own car. Whose family owned *two* cars? Strange priorities, said Babs, wrinkling her nice little nose.

Sometimes Helen and Jemma would sit and play jacks for hours, munching slabs of Marte's homemade Rocky Road. Jemma's solid fingers were astonishingly nimble, scooping and scattering the plastic knuckle bones; Helen's slender hands flashed as she learned to flip and rake. And they talked. They talked about the books they were reading and their teachers and the other kids at school. They talked about movie stars and the clothes they wore and how many times some of them had been divorced. Siren's Rock was not a place where people got divorced. They were born, they got married, they had children and eventually they died.

'That's not going to happen to me,' said Jemma. 'Soon as I'm out of school, I'm leaving. Going round the world. Having adventures. I'm going to be famous — a writer or an actress or a dancer. I might even get divorced myself.'

Helen loved listening to Jemma. More overwhelming, especially in the beginning, was the discovery that Jemma was prepared to listen to *her*. Jemma asked her questions, made her think, demanded some expression of her feelings. Slowly, gradually, Helen began to unpack the small, tightly wrapped parcel of her life and lay out the contents for Jemma to see. She didn't know she had so much to say.

Didn't realise she had been thinking about things. She certainly didn't understand why Jemma found her interesting, why sometimes she even sounded jealous.

'But your house is so lovely, see,' Jemma tried to explain. 'You have carpet on your floor. There's space. You don't have things everywhere. Everything matches.

'It must be nice moving to a new town before you get sick of people,' said Jemma. 'It would be great to live in all those places. Different houses, new schools, new people to meet.'

'It's awful,' said Helen. 'You don't make good friends. Just when they start to notice you, you move again.'

'They'd notice me straight away,' said Jemma.

John didn't miss Jemma at first. It was good, being leader. Though he didn't have the ideas for games that Jemma came up with, he was good at thinking of projects and things to make and build. But it wasn't enough to keep the younger boys entertained, and as their boredom grew, so did their willingness to listen and follow his orders.

What was missing were the stories Jemma told them. John could work out battle plans and spot an ambush at twenty yards, but he was short on story-lines. And he wasn't a hero. That was the main problem, really. Jemma was always the hero of her own stories — taller, stronger, smarter, more brilliantly attired and more glorious than the enemy or the members of her own army. Nobody questioned her authority or superiority. While John was — well, he wasn't glorious. He had enormous feet but his legs were skinny and he wasn't much taller than the other kids. He had funny teeth and his voice sometimes squeaked when he least expected it. His thick hair stuck up in tufts unless he put water on it and when he did that, Robbie held his stomach and doubled over with giggles. That was the other problem. It's hard to be glorious when your brother is in the gang. Your brother sees you sleeping with your mouth wide open, hears you farting in the toilet and listens to your parents going off at you when you are in trouble. Because of his legs and his feet, his voice, his hair and his brother, John had an image problem.

Sometimes Jemma and Helen came to the cubby and played for a while. On those days, Jemma immediately assumed control and John was glad to let her do it. Helen tried hard to fit in, but it wasn't the same. Sometimes she did things that embarrassed them all, even Jemma. But Jemma quelled any attempt to deride Helen with a compelling glare which reduced them to a muttering, scratching silence.

She told them stories, but Helen was always in them now, the princess to Jemma's prince, the lieutenant to Jemma's commander, usurping John, who rarely rated a mention.

Sometimes, for John, it was a relief when the two girls got up to go. But his freckled troops were not satisfied. They wanted more of Jemma and didn't know how to say so. They showed off, fought more, pushed each other into the murky creek water. When John went home to the ramshackle house in Fielders Road, where he and Robbie lived with their weary, limping mother, their silent, sour, mostly absent father and all their shy, shabby, frightened, finger-sucking sisters, he spent a lot of time thinking of ways to keep his troops happy. He had to — even without Jemma, the company of the younger boys was infinitely preferable to hanging around the house with his sisters.

John didn't have many friends his own age. Most of the boys in his class lived out in the country on farms and came in to school by bus, a long journey on lumpy roads. In the long summer holidays, they stayed on the land, helping their fathers with the crops and the cows. So, for John, his little gang was pretty much it, at least when he had free time of his own.

Every day after school John helped his mum. He swept the floors, scoured the bath, hung washing on the sagging line, went to the shop for potatoes and heavy food. He did all the jobs his mum couldn't manage sitting down. Meg Sullivan would have preferred to let John play with his friends more often, but with his dad away so much, she depended on him to be the man of the house.

When he was little, Marte Johnson and Meg Sullivan had been close friends. They took Jemma and John to the park and pushed them on the swings, changing their sagging nappies under the jacaranda trees that sprinkled tiny leaves or purple petals over them according to the season. But in the years that followed Jemma's mother only had one more baby and John's mother had many. One after another they came, and Meg Sullivan grew thinner, wearier and greyer with each one. She had no time for visits to the park, or friendly chats and cups of tea with Marte. All but John and Robbie were girls, scrawny, screaming infants who grew into scrawny, silent children. They were all afraid of their father, big Joe Sullivan, and clung to their mother when he came home, which was neither often nor regular. 'Just often enough to give her another kid,' said some of the people of Siren's Rock.

Joe was not an unkind man, but the burden of providing for an ever increasing family weighed heavily upon him. Beer made him feel better but diminished the pay he worked so hard to earn. His tolerance of his young family was low and he was slow with words and quick to whack them into submissive silence. But he swiped out rather than striking down.

Big Joe was an unhappy man but his skills and willingness to work hard commanded a degree of respect in the Siren's Rock community. Some of the locals said he could hardly be blamed for seeking a certain amount of solace from the bottle. He travelled throughout the district, building and repairing wooden bridges, wire fences and unimportant roads. Sometimes he was called upon to fix vehicles, or to repair pipes or tanks, or to put up verandahs and sheds. Though he had no formal qualifications, he was gifted with his hands and it was said he could fix anything.

Except his wife — slender, pretty Meg Kelly, delicate, dancing Meg, who was as light as tissue paper in his arms on the night he met and fell in love with her at a school social. After they married, the string of babies crushed the lightness and joy and pulled her down to earth. She was diagnosed with cancer shortly after giving birth to her seventh child and, although Joe Sullivan took her to the big hospital in Bridgetown to have an operation, she never seemed to recover from the surgery or the disease. The illness had affected her bones. She now had something badly wrong with her hip, and walked with a limp. These days she was more and more often to be found peeling potatoes or stringing beans while hunched in a chair, struggling to run the home her husband had never maintained and the family he rarely had time for.

Because of his oversized feet, John was sometimes told he would one day be as big as his father. He reacted each time with bewilderment and disgust. He hung his tufty head and saw his concave frame and his stick thin legs and he wondered at the stupidity of grown-ups.

At least after his mother's operation there were no more babies. In a way, said the people of Siren's Rock, the cancer had been a blessing. For John, who had never complained, there was nothing blessed about it. It was just the way it was.

GOODIES AND BADDIES

The best times of all were at the drive-in.

Funnily enough, the first time they went it was with the Winters. Helen could hardly believe it. It wasn't the sort of thing she would ever expect her parents to do. But it was hot — one of those hot, stuffy summer afternoons that sat on Siren's Rock like a suffocating quilt, making people want to lash out and throw it off, if only they could. And Helen had already observed that the silent, sodden heat of Siren's Rock sometimes made people desperate and strange.

In their shiny cream kitchen, her mother was taking a powder at the sink. Babs tilted back her small, neat head, perfect parallel waves gleaming, and flicked out her skinny red tongue, expertly curling the tip so that every fleck of the white powder was safely and tidily caught. She washed it down with a glass of water, turned and saw Helen looking at her.

'That's better,' said Babs, smiling brightly. 'Nothing like a powder to perk you up in the heat.' Her lipstick was very red and she wore a crisp cotton shirtmaker dress. She had just completed her late afternoon toilet — 'freshening up' she and her friends called it, followed by 'putting a face on', a necessary preparation for her husband's arrival home. New make-up, crisply ironed frock, a pretty organdie apron, sheer and useless, replacing the big pinny she wore during the day.

Babs started every day with a powder and, depending on the difficulties of her itinerary, topped up her supply of phenacetin again in the afternoon. Her headache seemed permanent. A couple of times Helen had asked her why it was that her head hurt so much and so often. Babs looked cross and said when Helen grew up and had a family to raise and as much work to do as she did, she would understand.

Lately Helen had looked at what Babs did at home — the washing, the tidying and the cooking in a house that was brand new and already clean — and compared it with what Jemma's mum did. Marte cleaned her own house, although it never looked as if she had finished, and she also scrubbed and scoured for other families. She washed and ironed, mowed the lawn, pruned unruly shrubs and bushes, grew vegetables, baked quantities of cakes and pastries and went shopping, lugging huge amounts of fruit and vegetables and groceries home in her car, unloading and unpacking them.

Helen's mother bought her groceries from Mr Campbell, the wavy-haired, seriously smiling man who owned the local store and came on Tuesday mornings in his rattly green Holden, wearing nicely pressed shorts and long socks. As Babs dictated, he carefully wrote down the Winters' order, then returned in the afternoon with a box of neatly wrapped packages. The fruit man, brown and hairy, came once a week in his truck and carried the fruit up their back steps, sweating and cursing under his breath. He always apologised as soon as Babs opened the door to him and allowed him to step briefly into the cool of the kitchen.

Marte also looked after Jemma's wild eight-year-old brother, Nick, who was loud and boisterous and always fully armed with sticks, toy guns and rubber daggers. Nick could be seen on any afternoon having sword fights with trees, leaping over small shrubs in a single bound while brandishing a rifle, or dancing on dusty feet, fists raised. Although he never seemed to make actual physical contact with any of his enemies, real or imagined, he was inclined to knock into things and he was always falling and hurting himself. Marte was continually putting either Nick or her furniture in for repairs. 'Boys!' she would shout, rolling her eyes at Helen and flinging her strong brown arms heavenwards. 'What can you do with them?'

Helen's mother had to look after Baby Joy, of course, but Baby Joy was four now and almost as quiet as Helen, although much sweeter- natured, as her mother was inclined to point out. But then Marte was big and healthy, while Babs was famously delicate. Uncertain of the meaning of this, Helen assumed that delicate people wore organdie aprons and took powders, while people who were not delicate ate well, laughed loudly and occasionally jumped into the air and clicked their heels.

She could see already that she was destined for delicacy.

And then suddenly, on that particularly hot afternoon, her dad was in the kitchen doorway, *smiling*, and announcing that they were going to the drive-in pictures!

'But the chops!' said Babs, overcome with surprise but twittering with excitement all the same.

'Put them in the fridge, Mother, we'll have them tomorrow,' said Douglas Winter. 'It's not every night that the breadwinner comes home from a hard day at the office and offers to take his girls to the pictures.'

It certainly wasn't. In fact Helen could not think of one night in her life when this had happened. It had taken a hot day, the prospect of a hopelessly sticky, suffocating evening, and the opening of a drive-in film theatre to make this miracle possible. And there was her father planting a kiss on her mother's white cheek, his balding dome gleaming with sweat and oil, his big black-rimmed glasses glinting, just as Jemma appeared at the top of the back steps. Before she even thought about it, Helen gabbled: 'Can Jemma come too?' And to her astonishment and joy, her father consented, though her mother's twitters took on an anxious tone as she looked doubtfully at Jemma in her favourite shorts, pink and tight, and her big bare feet.

'But that's the idea, Mother,' boomed Douglas, full of good humour and strange twinklings. 'That's the whole idea of the drive-in! You don't have to get dressed up. In fact, if they want to, the girls can wear their pyjamas!'

Jemma was dispatched home to change into her purple pyjies, as Marte called them, and Helen and Joy were duly bathed and put into their pink baby-doll pyjamas with the white broderie anglaise trim and matching cotton bloomers.

That first night at the drive-in was unforgettable. There were the attendants, like soldiers, wearing white overalls and maroon berets and huge gloves, waving them to their spot on the tiers of humps in front of the giant screen. There was wonderful fatty food in striped cardboard containers, handed out at the refreshment bar — dagwood dogs, scallops and chips. And then, with their hands covered in grease and salt, there was the ecstasy of sitting together in the back seat of the car, balancing on towers of pillows, craning to see through the front-seat gap between Douglas and Babs.

Up on the giant screen were Technicolor cowboys, lantern-jawed, eyes smouldering beneath big hats, handsome as gods. Then there were the horses. Jemma kept wishing aloud that her mother could see them.

'My mum loves horses *so* much,' she told them. 'My mum would rather be a horse than human.'

And the Indians. Hundreds of them, wearing feathers and leather, led by a warrior with noble cheekbones and a massive headdress, whooping and wielding a flaming torch.

'That would be me,' said Jemma loudly, and Douglas Winter snorted, already starting to regret his generosity. 'I would be the Indian chief,' said Jemma, 'leading the battles. Helen would be an Indian squaw.'

Douglas didn't deign to comment, but Babs, in her snake voice, said, 'Jemma, you're a *girl*. Girls don't lead armies. You would probably be one of those ladies in the frilly dresses,' then added sardonically, with a little sideways look at Douglas, 'no doubt entertaining the men in the bar.'

'Look at their lovely frocks,' Babs sighed a little later. 'I wish women still wore bustles. They give us such a nice feminine shape.' But Helen watched the thin-faced squaws with their oiled black plaits and their soft brown clothes and decided she'd rather be married to a big brown man in feathers than wearing a false bottom for a cowboy who needed a shave.

When Joe Sullivan hit John or Robbie, he usually clipped them over the head with the flat of his hand. But if they had done something really bad or if he had been drinking, he would smack the backs of their legs, having first ordered them to stand still so that he could be sure his aim was true. Meg would hunch in her chair, flinching.

'They didn't mean to be naughty,' she would whisper. 'They're good boys, really.'

The little girls would huddle behind her, keeping out of their father's way, although he generally reserved corporal punishment for the boys. He hardly ever looked at the girls and certainly never had a conversation with any of them. Sometimes John thought that at least while his father was

39

hitting him and Robbie, he was acknowledging their existence. It was usually after a hiding that he seemed to recognise that raising sons also required him to take an interest in them. These were the times when he spoke to them most, especially John, asking him about how he was doing in school, talking a little about his own work. Engines. Bridges. Tools. John answered in monosyllables, listened, focused every fibre of his skinny frame and his busy brain on absorbing what drops of information he could get. He didn't realise how much he liked and looked forward to those times. He never asked himself how many hidings he was willing to endure in order to experience the rare times when Big Joe remembered to be a father.

When Douglas Winter hit Helen he used a stick. Sometimes it was a ruler, but usually it was the cane end of her mother's pink feather duster, which wasn't really made from feathers but some soft, fuzzy nylon stuff.

She was usually punished for not eating her dinner, or for getting home later than expected from school, or for being rude or answering back — although this was a grey area and difficult to work out. Answering was okay. Answering back was not. Not answering at all was considered sulking and was also forbidden.

The initial thwack and sting would bite sharply into Helen's skin and the resulting red swelling was very painful. She was always relieved that her father only hit her and never Baby Joy, whose legs were white and plump and could never have stood it.

Sometimes she understood why her father had to hit her, when she had done something that even she could see was thoughtless or stupid — like breaking one of the best china cups or knocking a precious ornament off the mantelpiece. Or the time she had been sent to the shop and spent the change on sweets, an unthinkable crime for a Branch Manager's daughter.

As the summer gave way to autumn and then a balmy Siren's Rock winter, Jemma became increasingly enraged about the regular punishments Douglas Winter inflicted on his elder daughter.

Helen didn't have to tell Jemma that her father had hit her; she knew. Although Douglas Winter was careful to aim for the tops of her thighs and Babs was careful to conceal any bruising with a skirt of the appropriate length, Jemma could see it in her eyes.

'But why?' she asked over and over again. 'What do you do that's so wrong? You're the best behaved person at school. You couldn't even be bad if you tried!'

But there was one aspect of the punishments that Helen could never reveal to Jemma. There were worse things than having her legs caned.

When he was in a certain sort of mood, Helen's father beat her in a different way. He would lie her across his thighs, straining in their shiny black trousers, so that her head hung down, making her brain all swimmy and hurting her neck. Her thin blonde hair would fall forward, hiding her reddening face, while her father pulled down her pants and hit her hard, many times, snapping the cane across her bottom.

And sometimes he used his hand instead of the cane. These were the worst times, not because it hurt more but because she hated the feel of her father's hands on her most personal places. Sometimes his fingers went a little bit *into* the places and that did hurt. Horribly. And the only thing worse than *that* was afterwards, when he made her stand between his legs, her little panties still down around her ankles; when he took her small blonde head in his sweaty

41

hands and stared into her pain-saturated eyes and ordered her to say she was sorry.

Whichever way he beat her, he always made her apologise.

He would pull her in tight to him and put his face very close to hers, holding her face tightly so that her cheeks were squashed forward around her lips and she looked like a squirrel. She could see the holes in his skin from which each whisker was beginning to sprout and she could smell his hair oil and his onion breath. And she could feel the bulging bundle in his trousers pressing against her, and she hated this more than anything. So she would say: 'I'm sorry, Daddy,' as quickly as she could, leaning back as far as she dared — but it was never far enough to escape the bulge that wriggled against her belly. Sometimes she couldn't get the words out without choking, because the tears made her throat swell and thicken. He would keep her there, squeezing his legs around her, pressing her skinny body against his, demanding that she stop crying. 'Stop that stupid noise now or I'll give you something to cry for,' he would say. Often he made her repeat her apology — '*What* are you sorry about? You're just sorry you've been smacked, is *that* all you're sorry for?' — keeping her pressed up against him until she had said enough words for his satisfaction.

Saying what she meant or how she felt was always hard for Helen. People to whom words came easily were incapable of understanding the demons that held her tongue. Sullen, was the verdict. Sulking. Shy was the gentlest comment anyone ever made, although that wasn't strictly true either.

Sometimes he told her to stop behaving like a child.

Once, just before Douglas became a Branch Manager, standing in her Wollongong bedroom, with her pants still tangled around her feet, she had sobbed: 'But I *am* a child, Daddy.' Apparently it was the worst kind of answering back. Her father's face had grown red and pulpy, and he had narrowed his magnified eyes behind the glasses and slowly reached between her legs. He had thrust his hand down between her small white thighs and roughly grabbed her soft and naked little crotch, gripping her there to pull her back across his knees. He had smacked and smacked her bottom while his other hand clutched the most private part of her, his fat fingers hurting her while his right hand slammed down onto her buttocks. Finally her gabbled, frenzied screaming — 'I'm sorry, Daddy! I'm sorry, Daddy! I'm sorry, Daddy!' — had brought her mother running in from the dining room.

'Doug, Doug, the neighbours,' her mother had gasped.

He had stopped then, shoving Helen quickly away from him and stomping from the room. Followed by her twittering, frightened mother in her fresh lipstick and her organdie apron, wasted that day because Douglas didn't give his wife a second glance.

Helen had hardly been able to sit down for days.

SHARP AS A TACK

Helen felt a lot better having a champion on her side, even though Jemma's outrage was never going to affect Douglas Winter. Besides, one of the best things about living in Siren's Rock was that her father was often away. Every couple of weeks he had to travel to the bank's three sub-branches, in towns much smaller than Siren's Rock. This was why the bank had given him such a good car. Because of the distances involved, he was often away for two or three nights, staying in hotels and motels and not coming home until Thursday or Friday. Helen was enjoying a freedom she had never experienced before — hours to play with Jemma and sometimes with the gang. There were wonderful evenings at Jemma's house when her amazing, handsome, noisy Greek relations came to visit and celebrate around a table groaning with tender lamb and gravy-soaked potatoes. There were succulent strips of souvlakia and hunks rather than slices of bread, which you ate with oil instead of butter. There were capsicums and tomatoes stuffed with rice and olives, and fat purple vegetables Helen had never heard of before and had no trouble eating — if only her parents could see how she cleaned her plate at those gatherings.

· Helen's mother, too, had found friends at Siren's Rock. These were elegant, tidy ladies who played canasta and occasionally tennis, and who lunched in the dim dining room at Vale's, the town's department store. They talked to Babs on Sundays after church and made plans for Wednesdays, when they gathered at each other's elegant, tidy houses to play cards and nibble scones and pikelets and drink tea from bone china cups. There was Mrs Violet, the doctor's wife, and Mrs Egan, who was married to a solicitor, and the formidable Mrs Basingstoke-Brown, the undertaker's wife; the undertaker's family was reputed to be the richest in town. The Basingstoke-Browns had three daughters, all with hyphenated Christian names as well, so people got them muddled up. Instead of calling them Cindy-Lou, Mary-Anne and Cathy-May, Jemma always referred to them as Violet-Crumble, Peach-Melba and Fish-n-Chips, which made Helen laugh until her cheeks ached.

When Babs was happy she was less inclined to find fault with Helen. And she was happier than she had been for a long time.

Two good things happened in the winter months. First, Jemma and Helen started playing regularly with the boys again, which cheered everyone up. The bush was safer now, with less danger of snakes and spiders, and the cool days were perfect for building forts and new cubbies. They could stretch out on the flat sun-warmed rocks and listen to Jemma's stories, which grew wilder and more fascinating with every telling.

'Helen's with us. Like It or Lump It,' she told the Wildcats. At first they sneered and stood apart, watching her with cynical, squinting eyes, chewing paspalum, hoicking spit balls, chucking rocks that just missed the spot where she was standing. Eventually they realised they liked it. In fact, Helen was kinder to them than Jemma. She asked them about insects and fish and trees and blue tongue lizards and even manure, and what they dreamed about at night. It was John who started answering her first and when they saw that she really wanted to know, the others came around.

And whenever she was with the Wildcats, Helen took off her shoes.

The second development was the arrival at Siren's Rock Primary School of a new teacher — a young man in his twenties with an enormous black moustache and matching hair, which looked as if it was glued to his head. Mr Paterson had come from his city teachers' college determined to make the most of his required period of purgatory at a country school. He won the boys over with his cricketing and football prowess; and being stocky, dark and handsome, he didn't have to work too hard to gain the girls' attention.

He noticed Jemma straight away. Only two days later he picked out Helen, lurking as always in her friend's shadow. And somehow, during a vigorous game of football in the paddock beside the school, he discovered John. How he knew so much about them all after one footy match with John and a brief conversation with Jemma and Helen on the steps of the town library, nobody could ever work out. But within weeks of his arrival, a subtle competition for the previously withered academic stakes at Siren's Rock Primary was in place. Spelling, maths, story writing — Jemma, John and Helen were spending a lot more time with their books open, their heads down and their HBs sharpened.

'Mr Paterson's Sharp as a Tack,' Jemma confided to Helen. What she didn't confide was that Mr Paterson had said she could beat John at arithmetic and geometry with her brains in a bucket, if she just put her mind to it. She put her mind to it. John did the same. Mr Paterson told Helen she should write books when she grew up. Helen told Jemma and Jemma wondered why he hadn't said the same thing to her.

'I'm good at stories too,' she told Mr Paterson, standing beside him under a jacaranda tree as she sucked lukewarm, lime-flavoured milk at recess.

Mr Paterson looked at her. 'I'm sure you are,' he said. '*You* can do anything you set your mind to.'

Jemma sucked for a while, digging a little hole in a patch of dirt with her big toe. 'D'you mean Helen can't?' she asked.

'Hmm,' said Mr Paterson. 'What do *you* think?'

Eventually she looked up at the teacher, flicked her fringe out of her eyes and put her hand on her plump hip. 'Because she always *thinks* she can't. But I always think I *can*.'

Mr Paterson looked straight through her fringe and held her eyes with his. 'I wonder what we can do about it?'

In the end it was Jemma who dropped her eyes, shrugged and swayed away, tossing her milk bottle into the crate with another flick of her red-brown hair.

'Mr Pat thinks you're really smart too,' she said to Helen, lying down beside her in the playground grass.

'Only at stories,' said Helen.

'No, you could be good at anything, if you put your mind to. That's what he says.'

'That's you. Not me.'

'Anyway,' Jemma stretched her arms and legs and turned herself into a star, 'he might be right. You might be famous too. Not as famous as me, of course. But famous.'

'I don't think so,' said Helen. And she laughed. 'I hope not.'

Helen and John never discussed their beatings, but on the days when one or the other of them was recovering from a punishment, distress hung in the air between them like a curtain.

Helen would look at John's thin, brown face, with its ugly bruise or swollen eye; she would feel his hurt and hang around him, stand helplessly beside him, inarticulate with sympathy he did not want. She would have liked to touch his hand, but didn't dare.

Jemma sometimes ranted and raved to the gang when Helen had had a caning from her dad. The younger boys would look shifty and wander off until she calmed down. But John would stay. He'd listen to Jemma's arguments, nodding quietly, looking at Helen to see if she understood. John wanted Helen to know that she didn't deserve to be beaten. Helen was a good girl, a bit dumb maybe, a lot less interesting than Jemma, of course, but that applied to everyone. Certainly she didn't deserve to be caned. Jemma even pointed out that John, being a boy, sometimes got up to something and had to be Kept Under Control, so John probably *deserved* to be hit by his father from time to time. In a way, it proved his father cared about him. But with Helen, it was different. She was never up to anything.

And she was small, and frightened, like his sisters, thought John, so how could hitting her prove anything? At least Joe Sullivan didn't hit little girls.

John sometimes fantasised about growing very big, as big as everyone said he would when they looked at his feet, and hitting Douglas Winter. Hitting him hard in the middle of his big shiny red face. Smashing the glasses and the face in one blow. Showing him how it felt, how Helen felt.

When John could see that Helen was getting embarrassed by Jemma's tirades, even tearful, and that she just wanted to forget it all and get on with a game, he would speak up about something else altogether. A plan. A project. A question. He would steer Jemma in a new direction. John was good at that. Redirecting Jemma's energetic torrents of talk was no small feat. Helen was never sure if he did it on purpose, because he felt sorry for her, or just because he was bored. Sometimes she offered him a little smile of gratitude and wondered if he noticed.

If John's distraction worked, Jemma would go off on a new tack. And Helen would pull down the blind, block out despair, and follow her friends into the sunshine.

There was always a steady stream of books and films that Helen could lose herself in. Venturing into other worlds, other lives, took her mind off her own. The drive-in remained her favourite place of escape and, after that first time, she and Jemma went often, sometimes with the Winters, but usually with Jemma's parents. George would park his ute backwards so that the girls could lie on mattresses in the back, sucking on milk shakes and free to choose between watching the film or the stars in the sky. They went in summer, spring and winter. Only their pyjamas changed with the seasons, from baby-dolls to fleecy-lined ski-style pants and sweaters.

They never had to get All Dressed Up Like a Sore Toe for the drive-in.

These nights at the open-air theatre were the nearest thing to heaven in Helen's childhood. Bellies full, gums sticky with sugar and salt, the roofs of their mouths coated with fat, the girls waited impatiently through the Movietone news for the cartoon to come on, before settling down for the two feature films, which they would discuss endlessly afterwards. Doris Day, Rock Hudson, Frank Sinatra, Dean Martin, Jerry Lewis, Janet Leigh, Ethel Merman, Marilyn Monroe, Alan Ladd, Cary Grant, Grace Kelly and the new starlet, Sandra Dee — films full of falling in love and never-failing families, handsome men and glorious women wearing rainbow clothes, singing songs they'd never forget. There was dancing down stairways and on ceilings, Technicolor sunsets and Americans in sensational uniforms, winning wars over and over again; magnificent horses, magnificent houses, battles and romance, and the sort of panoramic lives and deaths which would never happen in Siren's Rock.

Never in a Month of Sundays, as Jemma would say.

Part Two

CAITLIN

They were playing her mother's favourite hymn.

All around her, thin voices faltered, focused on the familiar, then swelled into the song. Sad but loud, buoyed up because they knew most of the words. Like a pop concert, thought Caitlin. The devout fans appreciate the special arrangements, but there is a communal sigh of recognition and relieved applause when the band belts out one they all know.

The Lord is my shepherd, they warbled, although chances were that most of them had little regard for the Lord and no confidence in His ability to round them up and keep them in a safe fold. *In pastures green, He leadeth me . . .*

Pastures, beaches, bedrooms, you name it, someone certainly led her mother through them all, though nobody ever seemed quite sure *who* was leading her. Or screwing her, for that matter. Only God and her mother knew, and, as Jemma would say, God's not telling. Of course, under the current circumstances, it wouldn't be politically or even morally correct to blame her mother for being easily led astray. So why not blame God? The inefficient Lord, carelessly losing another lamb. They worshipped Him when life was good and they blamed Him when things were bad. That was the way it worked.

Must be hard, thought Caitlin, being God.

Tall, slender as a silver gum, dressed in grey, her oval face pale as porcelain, her copper hair twisted into a plait which hung like a rope down her long, straight back, Caitlin wept.

Damn them, she thought. Damn the tears. Block them. If only they could be stored in an orbiting reservoir until they were really needed. What had happened to her, to the person who for eighteen unemotional, independent years had been Caitlin Connor?

She had prided herself on never crying, and had always regarded indiscriminate weeping as an indulgence of the shallow and sentimental. A gut reaction to emotional manipulation. Helen and Jemma had been champion weepers. Typical of their generation, they didn't even realise how easily their strings could be pulled.

Caitlin desperately wanted to find the way back inside her walls. Where survival was possible because it was cool and private. Only she could no longer find the door. She was trapped, groping in a dim, unfamiliar corridor like Alice in Wonderland. No longer self-contained, no longer calm, confident, proud.

Pride Goes Before a Fall, Jemma would say. It would be horrible to have to accept that cliches are correct, thought Caitlin. That life, for people as blessed as Jemma — and she *was* blessed, even Caitlin could see that — could be that predictable, that straight. Pride punished with a fall. Leapers looking. People in glass houses sensibly resisting the urge to chuck a stone or two. Sea-green eyes alight with clear, unambiguous truths.

Caitlin clutched her damp and disintegrating tissue and wept some more.

Hamish looked along the line of mourners and saw her driving a fist into her eyes, the futile, angry gesture of a child. Ferocity, protest, misery, clenched in slender fingers. He watched her, willing her to look up, to turn her head and meet his gaze. Hamish, eighteen months older than Caitlin, tall too, but slightly hunched, his black hair cut close to his head, his skin olive and sallow with sorrow.

Look at me, said his sad, dark eyes. Acknowledge me. Acknowledge my grief and I will recognise yours. Let's share.

Even when they were small children, raised in the same house, playing with the same toys, Hamish had understood the concept of sharing, had offered her his toys, his favourite puzzle. His mother. Anything.

Caitlin felt his eyes on her and kept her own on the ground.

'No,' she said, under her breath, and Hamish saw her lips move around the word, and looked away.

So what the *fuck* had her mother been doing in Ireland? Why wasn't she at home, in the kitchen, whipping up a nutritious salad, grilling a steak, ironing a shirt, even having a row with her daughter about what time she came in last night? Driving Tom somewhere. Buying Caitlin a dress.

Caitlin, taut with guilt and unbearable grief, didn't wear dresses. Didn't eat salads. Hated steak. Knew she was being unfair. Hated the world and everyone in the hot church and herself most of all. Wanted her mother. But, of course, her mother wasn't there.

TWO BIKINIS

'Should we phone your mum?' asked Helen. 'She always says just ring and she'll come if we need her.'

Jemma, flat on her back on a beach towel, lifted the lids of her eyes only as far as she needed in order to focus on her friend. 'Julie baby,' she said softly, in the sultry Italian accent of her favourite film star, 'are you saying you *want* to go home?'

Helen sat on her own towel, hugging her knees, and hung her head so that her blonde bouffant cone of hair hid her face from view. 'It's just ... it's late and we've missed the last bus and they'll be getting anxious and that makes them cranky ...'

Jemma tried not to sound annoyed. She was happy. She was comfortable. Despite Marte's cooking, and with a gigantic effort of will, she had lost seven pounds this summer and she was feeling rather pleased with her body. Her firm young breasts rested like peaches in the cups of her brand new burnt-orange bikini. Her stomach was flat, especially when she was lying down, her long legs were already lightly tanned. Funny how a tan looked darker in the late afternoon, Jemma thought.

She was entertaining a wonderful fantasy about being a beautiful movie star who had just surprised the world by writing a brilliant Pulitzer-Prize-winning novel. The descending sun was warm on her golden skin; the sand was soft, the ocean was lapping contentedly just a few yards from her feet. Best of all, not too far away was a group of boys who she felt certain had been looking at her and Helen all afternoon. They were big boys, with broad shoulders and narrow waists and long hairy legs. Men, really. If they hung around the beach just a little bit longer — well, you never knew. You never knew your luck in a big city. Nor at Mermaid Cove. Especially if you were wearing your new bikini.

'I don't want to go home,' she said.

Helen's bikini was the same colour as the sand. They had read in a magazine that blondes should wear beige or cream; these shades suggested nudity. They had laughed themselves silly and Jemma said it was a load of old rubbish but, nevertheless, Helen felt terribly daring in her new two-piece cozzie.

Strictly speaking, it *was* a two-piece. She had got around her mother by pointing out that a two-piece must be quite respectable since there was a photo in their family album of her mother wearing one when she was a young woman. Babs had pursed her lips, sighed, and taken Helen to Vale's department store to try some on.

Babs had chosen pink first, and then blue; Helen didn't care. All that mattered was having a bikini like Jemma's. Babs had cast a critical gaze over her daughter's slender frame and clicked her tongue against her tiny teeth. Why couldn't Helen cover herself decently with a nice navy one-piece? Helen had begun to panic when Jemma arrived by arrangement and immediately found a tiny shiny black bikini that Shocked

Babs to the Marrow. She wouldn't even let Helen try it on. Jemma had then made a point of sighing with resignation as she produced the sand-coloured two-piece she had spotted as soon as she walked in. It fitted Helen perfectly and Babs shrugged and started looking for her purse.

'It's a bit boring,' Jemma had said offhandedly.

Helen's mother had sniffed. 'Nice girls don't draw attention to themselves.'

'You're right, Mrs Winter, nobody will notice Helen at all in this one,' Jemma had said earnestly, treating her to one of her fabulous white smiles. And as usual Babs had a problem working out whether Jemma was being agreeable or rude.

Naturally, neither of the girls had said anything about nude colours to Babs. But the thought was uppermost in both their minds this morning when they had dressed up — or rather down — for a day at Mermaid Cove. Both bikinis were masterpieces of construction, boned and padded so that their breasts were at once supported and angled to point in the same direction as their chins. 'Lift your head up high when you walk or sit,' Jemma had instructed. 'If your chin is high and sticking out, your boobs will stick out too.' They both knew that in Jemma's case, the advice, the bones and the padding were redundant. But Helen needed it all.

'We can ring Mum when we're ready,' Jemma said, lazily closing her eyes again. 'But think about it, Julie. Back home it's hot and there's homework to do. And it's nearly Monday morning and school. Right here it's cool. There's nothing to do but lie on the beach. And it's still Sunday afternoon.'

Helen raised her head and smiled affectionately at her friend, resting her chin on her knees.

'Okay,' she said.

'Are they still looking?' Jemma asked.

Helen turned her head slightly. 'Yep.'

Jemma smiled, kept her eyes closed and stretched luxuriously from her shoulders to her toes — a movement studied carefully on the silver screen. It worked. The boys nearby looked on with even greater interest, and now a second group of young men, who had been tossing a football around in a desultory way, stopped and gazed in their direction.

An elderly couple stomped past, sand streaming through their sandals as they lugged their beach umbrella and bags towards their car. The woman, plump, permed and salty, flickered a glance over Jemma and Helen as they passed. Helen smiled shyly. The woman nodded at her, then leaned towards her husband's ear. 'That's the new girl with the hoity-toity mother,' she whispered. 'The other one's the Johnson girl. She's growing up fast.'

Her husband, still looking back, had noticed without help.

When they disappeared over the dunes, only the boys and the two girls were left on the beach.

Five years after arriving in Siren's Rock, Helen and her parents were still the new people. Douglas sometimes found it bad for business; Babs rather liked it. A new home, carefully acquired vowel sounds and a veneer of sophistication — to Babs, being new smacked of superiority. Helen said her prayers every night, begging God to help make her daddy good at being a Branch Manager, so that they could stay in Siren's Rock. Staying was infinitely better than going, whether they were accepted by the locals or not.

'Why would you want to be?' asked Jemma reasonably. 'Look at how they think they have the right to know all about your life. Look at how they point and stare.'

Helen knew that Jemma didn't really mind being stared at. They both knew that being subjected to pointing and staring was part of Jemma's destiny. She was setting out on the road to fame. And Helen, self-conscious as she was, tagged along. Just being with Jemma made her feel more adventurous, and over the past year the pursuit of glamour had become their shared goal.

At fifteen, from Monday to Friday, in their school tunics and white blouses, Jemma and Helen looked like the high-school girls they were. At weekends, after spending Saturday afternoons doing some serious shampooing and setting, after hours under the ballooning plastic hood attached to Jemma's electric drying machine, after intense make-up and fashion sessions, they'd emerge as sixties swingers.

'All Dressed Up Like Sore Toes,' Jemma had said excitedly, when they'd completed their primping for their first town hall dance. 'We look twenty-one, easy.'

'D'you think?' Helen had asked, always the doubter. They were both wrong. Strapped into their jutting bras, matt-powdered, with white lips and legs encased in ivory nylon, Jemma looked thirty and Helen looked like a ten year old in her mother's clothes. However, Jemma got one thing right: they both looked easy.

Every fourth Saturday night, in their big hair and tiny dresses, bouncing on the back seat of Marte's Austin or sprawled in the dim and roomy luxury of Helen's father's Holden, they were driven to the town hall, where a supervised dance was held for teenagers. Here, during the early part of the evening, they'd dance demurely with the boys who came in from the farms, scrubbed and wearing jackets, their ham hands always in exactly the right position for the Pride of Erin, all of them good steady dancers who knew how to lead.

They'd zig-zag their bodies to the Twist and stamp to the Stomp and later in the night, when the pubs closed and older boys slid like oil into the hall, they'd pray desperately that the sleepy, superior gaze of these desirables would result in an invitation to join them in some seriously slow dancing.

The last dance of the night would invariably be the Hucklebuck and they would perform it in a business-like fashion, their eyes open and rolling with boredom, because by then their fathers would have arrived to pick them up. The Hucklebuck was the price they were required to pay for dreaming their way through the second-last dance (assuming someone had asked them) which was always slow and played to dimmed lights. Songs and dreams from the other side of the world, Merseyside love songs in particular.

Sometimes they went to the pictures and waited afterwards for their parents to pick them up at the Coffee Pot, their eyes glued to the doors, hoping some senior boys from school might come in and choose a table near theirs. They sipped milk shakes and picked at raisin toast; the butter ran between their carefully manicured fingers and they giggled and licked it off daintily.

On other Saturday nights, as long as a love story was on the bill, they went to the drive-in theatre with Marte and George. Douglas and Babs had long ago tired of the novelty, preferring now to impress by dining at the Working Men's Club in Turner Street, with its white cloth-covered tables and pretentious plastic flowers.

Jemma and Helen loved films about love. They would sit through the songs, the scenery, the action and any amount of interminable dialogue, waiting for the kiss. Their eyes would brighten, their toes would curl, their hearts would pound and sometimes, if the scene teased and prolonged their anticipation, their stomachs seemed to drop and they would unconsciously moisten their candy-pink lips and clutch each other's hands. When it came it was always wonderful. The kiss. The kiss was everything.

'You wonder how they can breathe,' Jemma had said one night, 'with their mouths stuck together for that long.' And when they got home they'd each practise on their hands in private, seeing how long they could hold their breath.

The girls themselves had become their own screen idols — Julie Christie and Sophia Loren.

Helen's eyes were the wrong colour and a liberal amount of pancake make-up was needed, in tandem with a heavy fringe, to hide the spots on her forehead. But apart from that, Jemma assured her, she was an almost perfect clone. After two hours in giant plastic rollers, followed by a prolonged session with the teasing comb, her fine hair became a huge, fragrant blonde mass. Her mouth, with its intriguingly narrow top lip and fuller, softer lower one, was painted pale. Her cheekbones were gaunt, her body slight but lithe, her limbs graceful and fine. Her voice was husky and low, her laugh a velvet delight. Jemma said she was Julie with a capital J.

But if Helen could have worked as a double on the set of *Billy Liar*, both girls were convinced that Jemma could probably take Sophia's place at a premiere and no one would know the difference.

From her mane of russet hair to her ocean eyes and generous lips — 'we've both got good mouths,' Jemma told Helen complacently — to her astonishing figure, she was already every inch a star. Even at fifteen, the combination of her Mediterranean and Teutonic genes gave her the bearing and impact of a warrior queen.

Without her hourglass assets, Jemma might have been just another migrant's daughter, a buxom girl with nice eyes and heavy hair. If she had simply exuded sexuality, it would have been only the men whose attention she attracted, but women liked looking at her too. There was something about the proud, joyful way she carried herself that made people of both sexes and all ages turn their heads to follow her proud progress along the paths of Siren's Rock.

But there were two problems with this.

First, although women who looked like Sophia Loren were generally regarded as beautiful, schoolgirls who looked like Jemma were generally regarded as tarts — and some of her classmates whispered just that behind her back, or ridiculed her chin-up, boobs-out posture. But Jemma was neither a woman nor a tart. She loved being looked at; she lit up, preened, glowed in the reflection of admiring stares, but, as she sometimes remarked to Helen, she didn't much like being touched.

So the boys looked. And whistled. And came closer. And she smiled and flirted and told them stories — and led them along, as she had always done. When they tried to touch she backed off. She ran away, laughing. Was not easy at all, in fact.

The second problem was that despite her lush curves, Jemma's body had not reached its state of near perfection without effort. Marte's generous servings of calorie-rich food threatened that hourglass shape, and looking good to her potentially adoring public was a battle Jemma frequently despaired of winning. 'I get fat,' she often told Helen, then and over a lifetime.

Meanwhile, Helen could eat huge portions of bread, meat, chocolate and ice-cream without ever changing shape at all, an injustice which annoyed Jemma more than she dared to admit. Luckily, as she frequently pointed out to Helen (and Helen readily agreed), her willpower was a lot stronger than Helen's. And not only with regard to food.

★ ★ ★

Despite its name, Siren's Rock was about half an hour's drive from the coast, and how any siren could have made her way to a place quite so far from the sea, and whether she had any luck luring sailors to their doom from there, was a mystery. It was a sprawling town in a shallow, humid valley, a collection of brick bungalows and older wooden houses built on stilts to catch the occasional cool breeze from the ocean. Since the Winters had come here, the town had sprawled a little further, and the ratio of 'new people' to 'locals' had increased a little, but it was still small, still a world of its own.

The Rock itself sat atop an unimpressive hill that rose up behind the town, ambitiously called Rocky Mountain by the locals. It had a lookout, with a smart white-painted wooden arch announcing to anyone interested enough to care that this was Bob Snell Memorial Park. From there the distant sea could be glimpsed in the form of a tiny blue triangle, wedged between the hills of the east coast. A rumpled green blanket of pastures draped over the land to the north, south and west of the town, and in the distant hinterland, crouching like gigantic versions of the lions that guarded Jemma's front gate, lay the real mountains of the Great Dividing Range.

At weekends, an ancient creaking bus took families and noisy groups of adolescents from Siren's Rock to Mermaid Cove, which offered a patrolled surf beach, a kiosk, a rickety old hotel and not much more, apart from a string of faded fibro holiday cottages straggling behind the dunes.

Jemma and Helen had been allowed to travel by bus to the cove since turning fourteen.

Marte thought it was good for the girls' independence, and Babs reluctantly went along with it. But her fears of something dreadful happening to Helen in Jemma's company had diminished over the past year: the girls went to the beach, to the pictures, to the dances and, though Babs was often disapproving of her daughter's fashion choices, nothing terrible had happened. In fact, as Jemma pointed out to Helen, nothing happened at all. Ever. And it was their responsibility, Helen's and hers, to do something about this sadly neutral state of events.

But now, in the late afternoon, Helen was worried. They should have left on the last bus. It would have been wiser to leave when they were safe, knowing the boys were interested, without having to do anything about it.

It wasn't that Helen didn't believe in Jemma and her ability to master any situation, however difficult. Jemma, she knew, would always emerge unscathed.

It was herself she had no faith in.

Finally they came.

The sun slipped out of sight behind the dunes and the beach became pale. The sea was silvery, the waves small and murmuring, the sky had assumed the light blue-grey of early evening. The air was fresh and cool.

Back at Siren's Rock, most families were sitting down to Sunday night tea. So why were the girls still here? That was what the boys asked them — the two who came first, followed at a decent distance by four others.

They really were men. Wide brown shoulders, slightly scabby from sunburn, broad chests, tiny swimmers, strong, well-muscled legs — what Jemma and Helen called Aussie legs. English legs were long, white and thin. Greek legs were short, brown, hairy and solid. These blokes were a lot older than the boys at school, maybe eighteen or even twenty. Boys who shaved and owned cars. What the girls classified as Hunks with a capital H.

The ones who did the talking were strangers but a couple of the faces in the background looked familiar — possibly big brothers of the boys from the farms.

Jemma sat up slowly, pretending to consider their question. Why *were* they still here? She drew her legs up gracefully and held her stomach in. The orange triangle between her legs and the boned cups provided a slash of colour on the faded beach.

She imagined the cameras rolling.

She glanced up at the two boys, tossed her mane, and dusted the fine sand from her legs. 'We're here because we want to be,' said Jemma. This provided her with the ideal opening to the script in her head. 'Don't you think this is the most beautiful time of the afternoon to be at the beach?' she asked dreamily, opening her eyes very wide and leaning back on her elbows so that her hair hung back and her chest lifted in a way she knew would draw attention. 'You know, when the crowds are gone and the sun isn't so hot?'

Helen stifled a nervous giggle. She could never get over Jemma's confidence, her ease with words, the normal, natural way she could speak to anybody. Even to hunks like these who were easily the oldest and cutest guys they had ever spoken to.

Right on cue the second boy smiled down at Helen. They were both just standing there, legs apart, easy in their skins. Helen loved the way boys stood, comfortable in their bodies. Only the talk was awkward; they needed some more cues from the girls.

'What's the joke, Miss Pretty?' the second one asked Helen.

'Nothing,' she said quickly; she could never think of anything to say.

Jemma glanced at Helen, green eyes telegraphing a message: he's yours, I'm happy with this one. She would be,

Helen thought. The first one had inky black hair, black eyebrows and a square jaw. His mate was sandy, nice but not divine. On the other hand, at least he thought she was pretty.

The two sat down beside them in the sand, which was a sign for the others to join them. There were introductions. Jemma's was Bill. Helen's, incredibly, was Sandy. There were other names that Helen remembered and Jemma instantly forgot.

'How will you girls get home then?' asked Bill. He was gazing at Jemma's chest which was pointing at the sea. He didn't seem to want to look at the sea. 'You come from Siren's Rock?'

'Oh, we'll probably phone a friend,' said Jemma casually, carefully avoiding the second question.

'And what do you girls do?' Bill asked Jemma's breasts. 'You nurses?'

'We're on holidays, actually,' lied Jemma.

She ran half-shut eyes over Bill's broad shoulders. 'I guess you guys do something where you use your muscles a lot,' she said, smiling. 'I can tell, because you are all such a great shape.'

They laughed, looked down, looked out to sea at last, went redder than their sunburn. Despite their size, they reminded Helen of the little boys who had been in their gang. Scuffling and kicking and scratching with embarrassment. Desperate for Jemma to notice them but not letting on.

'You mean *in* great shape,' said Bill, continuing his deeply meaningful conversation with Jemma's chest.

'No, I mean *a* great shape,' grinned Jemma. 'Your bodies are like triangles. Broad like that at the top ...' she drew a triangle in the air, 'and coming down to a point like this at the bottom.'

They all laughed at that, and asked her again and again what she meant, loving it, loving to hear how great they looked, loving the hint of dirty talk, loving the look of her, loving the relationship their eyes were having with her burnt-orange bikini.

Meanwhile, Sandy and Helen were having a wordless conversation of their own.

The first time they all laughed Sandy moved closer to Helen, so that his legs were parallel with hers — although, of course, they were a lot longer. The second time they laughed he casually slung an arm around her hunched, anxious shoulders. Her cone of hair brushed his red-brown arm. The third time, he curled his fingers firmly around the top of her arm. Helen sat in the curve created by his arm, wanting him never to take it away. She felt safe there. Protected.

Helen had seen Marte hug Nick and Jemma a thousand times. She had watched George wrap his arms around his daughter and close his eyes with pride, enjoying the pleasure of cuddling her. Jemma would hug them back in a desultory way. More often she shoved them off, looking sheepish or annoyed.

Helen looked with longing at any demonstration of affection. Imagined warm flesh on warm flesh. Wondered how it felt to be cradled in loving arms. To be held by someone who would keep you safe.

Sometimes she hugged Jemma. But Jemma didn't hug back. Didn't sling her arm around her shoulders like some girlfriends did. Not even on her birthday. As soon as Helen's arms slid around her, Jemma would stiffen. 'I just don't enjoy cuddling,' she said to Helen once, embarrassed but firm. Marte had been trying to make them entwine their arms and legs for a photograph. She did what her mother wanted but broke free as soon as the Brownie clicked. 'Friendship is about being soul mates,' Jemma had said. 'Anybody can cuddle. Not everyone can be a soul mate.'

Now, while the Hunks with a capital H flirted with her soul mate, Helen soaked in the warmth of the strange boy's encircling hug. Felt his skin against hers. Time, beach, buses, beatings — all faded, failed to matter.

With his free right hand the boy drew patterns in the sand. Now and then his fingers brushed Helen's. After a little while longer, while the others were still talking and laughing with Jemma, he drew a question mark in the sand, turned his head and looked very deeply into her eyes. Helen felt hollow, as if the only thing inside her body was a tight tube stretching from her crotch to her throat. She understood that something more was required of her and stared into his eyes, looking for a clue, blocking the others out. His eyes were very blue. She could see grains of salt on his peeling nose. There was a faint smell of beetroot and meat on his breath.

According to all the movies she'd binged on, he was about to kiss her.

Not yet, she thought. Not in front of everyone. Where then? How would they get away from the others?

He didn't kiss her. Instead his right hand left the sand and came to rest on her stomach.

They dropped their eyes at the same moment and watched his hand together, as if it had nothing to do with either of them. A broad red-brown hand, sprinkled with sand and salt. Fine straw-coloured hairs sprouting from the strong, stubby fingers, cupped slightly and lying gently across her small, flat, golden belly. Hiding her navel. Warm.

It was the most heavenly sensation Helen had ever experienced.

Slowly, eyes lowered, she smiled.

Slowly, eyes lowered, his fingers began to spread. The thumb slid over her belly, pointing up. The fingers spread out and down, just touching the top of her bikini pants. Just touching. And lay still.

Stop now, she thought. Fingers frightened her. Let's just stay like this, she thought, sitting in the circle of his left arm, with the warmth of his right hand on her belly. She could sit like this forever.

He would kiss her soon, she knew, and now she didn't care about the others. The kiss was everything.

There was another burst of laughter. Sandy didn't laugh this time. Nor did Helen. He was looking at her face again. She looked up into his. His left hand stroked her arm. Her small sweet mouth opened slightly as she imagined how it would taste. Delicious boy's lips.

The hand on the belly spread, the fingers pressed softly a little further down. If Helen had been looking at his hand instead of his mouth, she would have noticed that the tips of his fingers were beneath the elastic of her pants.

Inside her sand-coloured bikini, something damp and hot was happening. It had happened before, at night when she was alone and in bed. And once when she was at the pictures, watching *Where the Boys Are*. It had never happened in the daytime. And now there was a hand, creeping like a crab towards the damp place.

Without taking her eyes from his, Helen dropped her own skinny fingers on his wrist. Lightly, almost as if she was taking his pulse.

If only he would kiss me, thought Helen, acutely conscious now of the course the crawling fingers were taking. If only he would kiss her, a long, soft kiss, just like the one James Darren gave Gidget in *Gidget Goes Hawaiian*. If he kissed her she would melt into his arms, *both* arms . . .

Only, there had to be a kiss first.

Instead there was Jemma. Suddenly standing up. Standing over them. Clouds over her stunning smile. Her face twisted with revulsion.

'How about you get your dirty hand out of my friend's pants?' she said loudly. A telegraph pole, driving big, ugly words into Helen's gut.

Jemma was between her and the boy, shoving him away, her strong brown hands pushing him back into the sand, grabbing Helen's hand, pulling her to her feet.

Sandy, sitting back in the sand and laughing. Around them, the other boys laughing too. Bill, looking embarrassed, at last looking away from Jemma's tits.

'Get your stuff,' Jemma hissed at Helen, who did as she was told, picked up her towel, wisps of hair straying into her hot face as she groped for her bag, looked around for her beach coat, her shoes.

'Hey, don't go,' said Sandy. He grinned up at them both. 'We were just starting to have some fun.'

'We are not interested in that sort of fun,' said Jemma coldly. Helen had found her things. Her face was burning so badly it hurt. She stood behind Jemma and stared at her feet. She didn't want to look at any of them. Especially not Sandy. Snap! the elastic had gone when Jemma wrenched his hand away. A humiliating, horrible, embarrassing noise.

'I'm not so sure about that,' said Sandy, slowly getting to his feet. He was still smiling but there was a nasty expression on his face as well. 'Your little friend here was lapping it up. Weren't you, gorgeous?'

Everyone was standing up now. Jemma pulled herself up to her full height and buttoned her orange beach coat over herself. Helen kept her eyes on the sand and tried to do the

71

same, holding her beach bag with one hand, fumbling to find the button holes.

'What d'ya reckon, fellas?' drawled Sandy, grinning at his mates. 'I think it's time we had a bit of fun with these girls who don't want to go home.'

Nobody moved.

Belatedly Helen sensed the danger. Embarrassment was instantly swallowed by fear. A familiar fear.

'Get lost,' said Jemma. 'We're leaving. Come on, Helen.'

Sandy blocked their way. They were now encircled by the boys. Helen finally raised her eyes from the sand and scanned the beach desperately for someone who might help them. The other boys looked bemused rather than threatening, but you couldn't be sure. Bill wore a hunted expression. But Sandy, still smarting from the ignominy of being pushed aside by a girl, wanted trouble.

'What's your hurry, little Miss Big Tits,' said Sandy softly, walking up to Jemma and standing horribly close to her. 'Don't tell me you weren't asking for it just as much as her.'

A thick sob of terror grew in Helen's throat. But he didn't touch Jemma. Something about the way she stood, with her head up and her eyes full of disgust, kept his crab hands under control.

'You know,' said Jemma, 'we actually thought you guys were smart. We actually thought you were capable of conversation. We didn't realise you were just like every other dickwit on the beach.'

There was a rumble of protest from them all and Helen was convinced Jemma had gone too far.

Jemma took a deep breath. 'What?' she said, glaring at them all. 'You want to screw two fifteen-year-old virgins? Well, did you know Helen's dad's a cop?'

Sandy sneered and started to say something but the others

just opened their mouths and shut them again. Jemma grabbed Helen firmly by the arm and dragged her through their circle, which opened easily, and up to the road.

Behind them, someone shouted: 'Sluts!'

As soon as they were over the dune and into the car park, they started to run.

They rang Jemma's mum from a phone outside the kiosk, which was shut, shades pulled down behind the windows. They didn't speak to each other. Jemma's mouth was a sullen, angry, downward curve. Helen felt sick. They waited nervously near the phone box, looking around for people, feeling relieved when a man or woman occasionally appeared on the footpath and strolled past.

After a while an aging Holden roared past, coming from the direction of the beach. The girls tried to make themselves as small as possible behind the phone box but the car didn't stop. The horn blared and somebody gave them the finger out of the window. Helen thought it was Bill.

When the car was out of sight, Jemma finally raged at Helen.

'I can't believe you,' she said. 'All this good-girl talk, all this doing the right thing and worrying about getting home on time,' her voice grew rough and louder, 'and then you let a total stranger ... *touch* you like that. You hadn't even had a conversation with him for heaven's sake,' she yelled. 'You just sat there ... and ... *let* him!' She was shrieking now, and ugly. 'What is *wrong* with you, Julie?'

Tears shone in Helen's eyes but didn't fall. 'I don't know,' she whispered. 'I don't know. He put his arm around me ...' A little sob erupted from her. 'It felt good, and ... and I *thought* he was going to kiss me. I thought he was.'

Jemma glared at her. 'And would that have made it all right, do you think?' she asked scathingly, lowering her voice to normal. 'If he'd kissed you, it would have been all right for him to shove his hand down your pants?'

'Don't,' said Helen, closing her eyes. There was bile in her throat. She was afraid she might vomit, right there in the gutter. She swallowed hard. 'Don't.'

Marte's Austin appeared at the end of the street.

'You're bloody lucky I got us out of that, you know,' said Jemma, picking up her bag. 'You're lucky I knew exactly what to say.'

Helen's face was pasty white. '*Bloody* lucky,' she muttered. Low, sarcastic. Jemma, walking towards her mother's car, turned and looked at Helen in surprise.

'I'm *so* lucky to have you for a friend, Sophia,' snarled Helen. '*So* lucky to have a friend who can talk me into anything. *Bloody* lucky to have a friend who can make up such good *lies* to save me from the stuff *my friend* talked me into.'

Jemma stared at her, still speechless. The Austin pulled up beside them.

'Youse are naughty girls,' said Marte, leaning along the seat to open the back door for them. 'Where have you been all this time? Even Helen's daddy's been on the phone.'

'We were coming home but we met some boys,' said Jemma casually, looking away from Helen. 'We thought they were going to give us a lift home but they weren't going our way, so we had to ring you. I'm sorry, Mum, I didn't realise it had got so late,' said Jemma.

Lied Jemma, thought Helen.

If Marte thought it was strange that the girls sat in silence all the way home, she didn't say so. Jemma stared out of her window and chewed her bottom lip hard to keep the questions from spilling out. She couldn't get over it — that moment when she had looked across at Helen to give her a wink of triumph ... *they like us, they're interested* ... and had seen what he was doing with his hand. It was so dirty. It was so horrible. How could Helen let a boy *do* such a thing to her? What was she thinking?

And then, unbelievably, Helen had turned against her. Her! Jemma! Helen had been nasty. Sarcastic even. To her!

Somewhere, a long way back in Jemma's consciousness, a persistent, nagging voice was suggesting that Helen's resentment was justified, that part of the responsibility was hers. That she had wanted the boys to come and talk to them. That she had done everything physically possible to bring them across the beach. That she had talked about bodies. That she had contributed to the trouble. But I just wanted them to talk to us, she thought. To like us. To ask us out on a date maybe. To give us a lift home. And people would see us, in a car with boys like that.

Jemma hadn't done anything dirty.

What Helen had done, had let him do, was dirty.

I'm not saying I'm sorry, she thought. She's the one who should be sorry. She must know this is all her fault.

Suddenly Jemma felt tired and too old to be only fifteen. It seemed she had been teaching and protecting Helen for years. How to walk in bare feet. How to make a grass whistle. How to build the best cubbies. How to catch a shoot. How to dive. How to dress. How to dance. How to make friends. How to handle parents.

How to survive.

John had helped, but the main responsibility for Helen had always fallen squarely on Jemma's shoulders.

How to get other kids to like her. Without Jemma, Helen would have had no friends at all. How to get on with boys. First, little boys. Now, big ones. What to do. What *not* to do. What was wrong with Helen anyway, that she didn't know these things?

Helen sat in an invisible cell of silence, breathing softly, preparing herself for her arrival home.

You'd think Jemma would be happy now, she thought dully. Something had finally happened. But neither Jemma nor Sandy, nor any of the boys with the triangle chests, were uppermost in her mind.

The Helens in her head, who had apparently been rendered speechless by the boy's creeping fingers, were talking to her again. She was back in her own private and frightening place.

'Even Helen's daddy's been on the phone.'

BECOMING A WOMAN

He had stopped hitting her when she was thirteen. She remembered the night well, because it was when she had started to bleed.

It was weird that she started getting periods before Jemma. They had talked about it; had even looked forward to it. 'I hope we get them together,' Jemma had said. 'Imagine us both racing off to Miss Dempster, imagine her face if we told her neither of us could do P.E.'

They'd shrieked with laughter, clapping their hands over their mouths to suppress such shocking mirth about a subject so serious.

They knew they probably *wouldn't* get their periods together, because Jemma was obviously better developed. Marte had told Jemma what to expect. Helen was relieved that Marte was so full of information; her own mother offered none. Babs talked about growing up in terms of hair-setting, judicious use of lipstick and the amount of material in Helen's skirts. 'I'll make you a straight skirt,' she told her daughter. 'But they look best on ladies with a bit of shape.'

And yet it was Helen who was the first to see a silky, golden-brown fuzz growing beneath her arms and around her vagina, and to feel her breasts ache a little from time to time. She had been trying to find the courage to ask Marte whether this was normal. Had not yet managed to find the words on the night her period came.

She'd noticed the pain down low in her stomach after dinner, but when she'd asked her mother if she could take an aspirin, Babs, who was setting Joy's hair before bed, had said it was probably indigestion. To Helen's great relief, her mother had given up on *her* hair; she had let it grow long enough for a ponytail. Jemma said it looked nice hanging straight down, a bit like Mary Travers'. Jemma's hair was cut like Cilla Black's, a thick curtain that swung into her mouth when she moved.

Joy was nearly seven by then and turning out very differently to Helen, as their mother frequently pointed out. Apart from being plumper and prettier, she was much more cheerful, full of giggles and chatter, a twinkling pink and white child who drew approving glances from mothers and fathers and glum resentful stares from many of the string-haired, sunburnt children of Siren's Rock. Babs adored Joy; it showed in the way she smiled at her younger daughter, in her habit of lightly touching the top of Joy's golden head. Daddy called Joy his Little Princess, and she would light up with excitement whenever he came home. She would wrap her arms around his leg and he would walk a few steps with her clinging to him, then untangle her little hands and swing her off the ground.

Sometimes he would dance with Joy. Helen had come into the lounge room one day because she could hear her own record, 'Blame it on the Bossa Nova', playing on the radiogram. Daddy was holding Joy in the classic dancing position, except that she had placed both of her little feet, in their white lacy socks, on his big ones. Helen watched them sway and twirl, both of them smiling and laughing.

As far as Helen knew, Joy had never done anything wrong. Naughty, yes, but not wrong. Not like her. Joy was never rude. She was never cheeky, never answered back. She didn't recognise sarcasm. ('She's not smart enough,' remarked Jemma.) She always ate all her dinner, punctuating her mouthfuls with 'yum yum' and 'dee-lishus, Mummy'. ('Joy sounds like a television advertisement when she eats,' Jemma said.) It was true that she wasn't as clever as Helen; wasn't in the A class at school. But Mummy said brains were not the be-all and end-all and being a sweet person was more important.

Mummy said that's second children for you. More popular. More personality. Less inclined to sulk. 'You fail with your first,' she told her friend, Edna Egan, who always wore a hat that looked exactly like a meringue, 'because you learn as you go along. And you succeed with your second. It makes sense.'

Helen could never think of anything to talk to Joy about. She loved her, of course; it was natural to love your little sister. But no matter how hard she tried, Helen's well-intentioned words would get stuck in the silly, sugary smile that Joy always wore when Helen tried to speak to her. 'It's like trying to have a conversation with a cake,' she said to Jemma, who laughed and shook her head. 'I don't know why you try,' she replied.

Sometimes Helen wondered that herself. Once she heard Joy asking permission from Babs to give her sister a little woven mat she had specially made for her at school. Would it be all right, wondered Joy, or had Helen been too naughty for Joy to be nice to her?

But Helen felt very protective of her little sister. For years she had been worried that Daddy would hit her. Joy was little, a baby. She trusted everyone in the world. Joy was small and round and sweet. Helen couldn't bear to think of those soft little limbs flinching and quivering as the cane cut into them. She didn't know how she was going to protect her if it happened. She had imaginary conversations with her father, in which she said to him: 'Hit me, I'm used to it.' Wondered if she would be brave enough to say this out loud.

Anyway, it wasn't true. Although it had been happening less often, with Daddy being away so much and Mummy increasingly contented and less inclined to report her failings to him, she never got used to it. Her heart would still seize up in fear every time she heard the handle of the feather duster slice the air before it hit her legs or her bottom. Her stomach would still heave when she lay across her father's lap with the smell of his trousers in her nose and the feel of his big hands on her bottom and worse. Her throat would still thicken with disgust when he stood her between his thighs, when she tried not to feel the bundle of genitals pressing into her through the shiny serge, as he waited for her to say she was sorry.

The stupid thing was that the older she became, the more difficult it was to apologise. It became obvious to her that she never did anything so terribly bad. Jemma's influence stirred her up. Sowed seeds of doubt, as Jemma said. It did her no good. Taking a long time to apologise only meant she had to stand for longer in that awful place.

For as long as she could remember, her mother had never been present or even close by while the punishments were going on. There had just been that one time back in Wollongong when she ran in at the end, worrying about what the neighbours might hear and think. But after the final beating, Mummy had come into the bathroom while Helen was running warm water into the tub, in order to bathe away her pain, and hissed in a thin, high voice: 'All you had to do was say you were sorry. That's all you had to do. Anyone would think you enjoyed being smacked.'

Helen, leaning over the bath to test the temperature, had stared up at her. *Smacked*? Is that what Mummy thought it was?

Her mother had glanced down at the angry welts on the back of Helen's legs. Her lips tightened. She was unscrewing the lid from a large salt shaker.

'Put some of this in the water,' she said. 'It helps.'

Helen stood up, and for the first time realised that she was almost the same height as her mother.

'Nothing helps,' she said softly.

Babs pulled her lips into an even tighter line and put the salt shaker down on the edge of the bath.

'Now you know why he hits you,' she said as she left the room.

Helen couldn't bear to think of any of this happening to Baby Joy.

And then, miraculously, suddenly, wonderfully, it had stopped happening to her as well.

Of course, she could never be sure. From time to time her mother reminded her that she would have no compunction at all in letting Daddy know if she thought physical punishment had again become appropriate. But Helen didn't really believe her. She was pretty sure it was her mother who had told him he had to stop. Because of the blood. Because blood, in some way Helen didn't understand, made life more complicated for both men and women.

It had been two years now since the last hiding. He hadn't used the cane that time. There had been less pain than usual from the blows he managed to land on her bottom. But there had been more of the other thing. The thing Helen never mentioned. Not to Jemma. Not to John. Not to herself. Even the Helens who lived in her head remained silent.

On that particular night, the unfamiliar ache that had been hovering low in her stomach all afternoon had diminished and she was hunched over her little white desk, studying for a history exam, when she heard him come in. The night was warm and balmy; she was wearing a T-shirt and shorts, her hair up in a ponytail. The desk lamp cast a yellow glow over her book, but the rest of the room and the house was dark. Her mother and Joy, neatly pinned, were in bed asleep, but Mummy had said she could stay up until she finished summarising the chapter.

When he loomed in her doorway the first little lick of fear flickered in her throat. He had been drinking. She could tell now. He had finished off his week on the road with a few drinks at the inaccurately titled Working Men's Club. When she was little she hadn't understood about such things as 'having a few drinks'. When she heard her parents use the expression, she had imagined a line of glasses filled with lime cordial, cherry cheer, lemonade.

It was John who had told her about grog and what it did to grown-up people. They'd been lying on their backs on a river rock, guessing shapes from the drifting clouds. For no particular reason — it wasn't as if the clouds had looked like beer bottles or anything like that — John had told her that without alcohol, his father would be the best father in the world.

John was also thirteen at the time. He had finally started to grow. He was taller but still skinny. 'When he lies on his back the sparrows think his chest is a bird bath,' Jemma said.

He had a nice face. Helen liked the way his brown eyes crinkled when he smiled.

'I know my dad is proud of me,' John had said to Helen. 'I know he wants to be a good dad. It's grog that mucks him up.'

Helen had thought about this a good deal, and a few days later asked John how you could tell whether a person had been drinking alcohol. John told her some of the signs, and added, in his slow, thoughtful way, that if an adult had been drinking, it was best to keep right out of their way. Even if it meant going out of the house.

'What if it was night?' Helen asked.

'You could still go,' John said. 'You could go round to Jemma's.'

Helen chewed her plump bottom lip and frowned. 'What would you say to Jemma's mum?'

John thought for a while before replying: 'You could come to my place.'

Helen fell silent at that. First they had been talking about 'a person'. Now, 'you'. As if he knew what might happen to her. As if she might need to leave the house at night.

John seemed to have read her mind. 'Mum is always wishing my friends would come around,' he said. 'It's a bit of a mess — but nothing bad would happen if you were there.'

Well, that was true of course, of all parents. All of them were good at being nice when other people were around. Putting On An Act, as Jemma said. Helen's parents were masters of the art. Especially her mother.

'Come if you need to,' John had said.

The conversation with John was in her mind as she turned and saw her father swaying against the door frame.

'Hello, Daddy,' she said. 'Did you have a good trip?'

'Why aren't you in bed, young lady?' asked Douglas Winter.

Helen turned back to her book. 'Exams, Daddy,' she said quietly. 'I'm studying. Not going out. Having no fun at all.' A little smile. Suddenly unable to resist, she murmured softly: 'You'll be pleased to hear.'

Douglas stared at her. The light reflected on his glasses and she couldn't see his eyes.

'Get undressed, you sarcastic little bitch,' he said, 'and get to bed. Now.'

Her smile slipped from her face. What had she been thinking? How much Jemma would laugh at her last remark when she told her about it tomorrow? But it was not yet tomorrow and Jemma wasn't here. There were just the two of them here now. Just Helen and Daddy.

'Okay,' said Helen hastily. 'But Daddy, I wasn't being sarcastic. I thought you would be pleased to hear how hard I've been working.' She was starting to babble so she took a breath and slowed down. 'I was just finishing off summarising this chapter. Mummy said I could. Because I borrowed this book off Sarah Perkins and I have to give it back to her in the morning. So can I just ...?'

'Didjyou hear what I shed to you?' he slurred. The lick of fear turned into a fat tongue of fright and she thought she might choke on her own stupidity. Too late now she knew she should have obeyed him the moment he managed to get the words out. And the smile had been a big mistake.

In two strides he was beside her at the desk, yanking her up out of her chair by the front of her T-shirt. While she quavered and gabbled, 'Please Daddy, *no*, I was just going to bed, I was going straight away, I'm sorry, Daddy ...' he hauled her towards her narrow bed, sat down heavily, opened his legs wide and pulled her towards his bulky body, wedging her between his thighs. He groped clumsily at the button of her shorts as she tried to grab his hands, tried to pull them away, started to cry. Then he pushed down her shorts and her panties and tipped her across his fat knees.

He grabbed her ponytail with his left hand, yanking her head down against his legs, while with his other hand he slapped her bottom. The alcohol made his aim poor and the slaps were not too hard. 'I'll ... teach ... you ... to ... disobey ... me.'

Tears ran down Helen's cheeks onto the carpet but they were tears of fright and humiliation rather than pain and she made no sound. Eventually the slaps petered out. After one last sloppy slap he spread his hand over her bottom and squeezed her flesh. Helen stiffened. The only sound in the room was her father's wheezy breathing. Long loud breaths.

What followed was the worst thing.

Nothing he had done to her before had hurt as much as this.

For too many long, agonising, never forgotten minutes, his fat fingers penetrated her vagina. Penetrated that most intimate of flowers, probing and peeling back the small, moist petals, digging in, hurting her in the most horrible way. She thought she screamed, but his left hand remained clamped around her ponytail, holding her upside-down, face hard against his serge shin. She tasted bile, which choked her sound into an ugly croak.

Then, as the tearing pain became unendurable, very suddenly he stopped. He pulled his fingers out of her and shoved her onto the floor.

It was something he had never done before. Usually, after a hiding, he made quite a production of uprighting her again, holding her between his legs until she apologised. But this time Helen landed with a thud on the carpet.

She lay very still, and heard him walk out of the room. She waited with her face in the carpet, curled up like a caterpillar, her T-shirt rucked up around her ribs, her small white bottom bare, her vagina sore and trickling fluid. Wondering if she had wet herself. Not caring.

She heard the floorboards creak as he went down the hall to his own bedroom. Heard her parents' voices whispering, her mother's sibilant whine, her father's low rumble.

She knew she should get up but she was too tired. Low in her stomach the pain had returned, nasty, spreading down to her thighs. Her hips ached; her shoulders, her knees, even her elbows were sore. Her limbs felt heavy. Something was happening to her; she felt ill. She wondered if she might be dying, whether what he had done to her could kill her.

Papyrus reeds, she thought. Half an hour earlier she had been reading about the Egyptians writing with papyrus reeds.

'Get up,' said her mother's sharp voice as she snapped on the overhead light. 'You should be ashamed of yourself, lying there with your bottom naked for all the world to see.'

Helen jerked as if she had been shot. The ludicrous words wounded her a second time. Penetrated the private place in her mind. She reached behind her to cover her bottom with her hands. *Whatever we do, we mustn't let the world be shocked,* said one of the Helens in her head. She wasn't sure if it was the cynic or the saint.

She began to uncurl herself. She must have been crying all that time because her eyes were so swollen and stuck together she could hardly open them. When she did, she saw the blood.

It was on her hands. There was some on the carpet. When she staggered to her feet, mute with horror, it ran down her legs.

'What has he done to me?' she choked.

'Don't be ridiculous, Helen,' said Babs coldly. 'Your pain has arrived, that's all. It means you've become a woman.

'Go and get washed,' she added, crossing the room to put something on Helen's desk. 'Here's one of my belts and a sanitary pad. Put it on before you go to bed.'

It was sad but apt, Helen thought years later, that her mother's term for becoming a woman was 'pain'.

THE BAN

Jemma didn't become a woman for another six months but when she did, as she said herself, it was all on for young and old. It was a slow on-again, off-again process, involving false alarms, mess, cramps and complications. Jemma was embarrassed, sore and resentful. Once a cycle of sorts finally became established, she felt her body had turned on her, violating her previous trust in its potential; she felt trapped in deceitful flesh and blood, a lumbering heavy swollen presence that kept her off the beach, out of the bush, even off the dance floor. For at least one week in every four — and sometimes more — Jemma hated to go out in public at all.

She took up playing jacks again, and ate large quantities of Marte's homemade Rocky Road.

Helen sympathised and stayed inside with her. But for Helen, the arrival of her periods had been a blessed release. Not only did her father stop caning her, he stopped touching her altogether. He'd pull himself in when she passed him in the hall, step out of range when her mother ordered her to peck him good night. The closest he came to physical contact with his elder daughter was when other people were around on special occasions, like Christmas and birthdays. It was as if Helen's menses was an infectious disease and he was afraid of catching it.

As if becoming a woman had made Helen's physical presence repugnant to her father.

It was the best thing that had ever happened to her.

But she never stopped worrying about Joy.

With the termination of corporal punishment, responsibility for keeping Helen under control had passed entirely to Babs. As Helen grew shapelier and prettier (although not a lot taller), Babs had risen to the challenge of turning her into a credit to her parents. Becoming a credit meant being polite, keeping clean and wearing proper smart clothes. Babs loved it when people congratulated her on her quiet, well-groomed girls. Helen and Joy were the Branch Manager's daughters. And always would be. No matter what.

The 'what' in question was Jemma.

To Babs Winter, Jemma Johnson presented a conundrum. While her garish clothes were often frightful, the girl's behaviour could not be faulted when she was visiting; Babs had never heard her speak a cheeky word or forget her manners. Yet she frequently heard rumours from her friends in the canasta club — Edna Egan and Mrs Basingstoke-Brown — that young Jemma Johnson was a tart, a hot little piece, a disgrace to the town.

'Keep your Helen away from her,' warned Mrs Egan. 'She's trouble. Runs wild, you know. Those foreign parents let her do anything she likes. God alone knows what she gets up to in the bush with those dregs of boys that hang around her like flies.'

Sometimes the stories were quite specific. More than once Babs had listened avidly to the details, while being fully aware that on the days under discussion Jemma had been in

Babs' own lounge room, watching 'Bandstand' with Helen, or sitting in her kitchen, carefully cutting Helen's fringe with the assistance of strips of sticky tape.

One hideously embarrassing day, to her own surprise, Babs heard herself defending Jemma. Mrs Egan and Mrs Basingstoke-Brown were discussing the likely prospect of Jemma Johnson becoming pregnant at an early age through her association with some of the local louts. 'You can see it on their faces when they watch her walk past,' said Mrs Egan. 'Drooling, practically.' A small bubble of drool appeared on Mrs Egan's own crimson lip as she remembered the scene. 'I saw her yesterday, in those tight shorts, with her middle showing, giving some boys the come-hither look. Goodness knows what went on behind the toilet blocks.'

'Jemma was at my place yesterday, actually,' said Babs nervously. 'She and my Helen were doing an assignment together. But she did arrive with John Sullivan, because they had come on the bus from town. From the library. With books for the project.'

Her two friends looked at her over the edges of their teacups and sipped in unison. There was an uncomfortable silence.

'And how do you know what she and young John Sullivan were doing before they arrived at your place, Babs?' smiled Mrs Basingstoke-Brown.

Babs flushed. 'I don't. I just mean they were here at eleven in the morning and I don't really think Jemma ...'

'You're a good Christian soul, Babs,' said Edna Egan silkily, 'and good on you for always thinking the best of people.'

Babs smiled gratefully.

'It might have been Tuesday I saw her,' added Mrs Egan.

Babs stopped herself from volunteering that Jemma had been at her place on Tuesday as well.

'Babs dear,' said Mrs Basingstoke-Brown, 'don't let your own purity of spirit close your eyes to what goes on in this town. If you want a word of advice from me,' she sipped again, leaving a thin red lip line on the Royal Doulton, 'and remember I have three lovely girls of my own, I'd be keeping a close watch on the quality of person you allow your girlie to associate with.'

Both Babs and Edna Egan knew it was far too late for that. But a little turn of the cake fork made Mrs Basingstoke-Brown's day.

Babs found herself meditating on the fact that at least her girlie was slender, blonde and smart, unlike the double-hyphenated Basingstoke-Brown daughters, who were shaped like meat pies and probably had brains as small as peas beneath their naturally curly hair.

All the same, was Jemma a tart or was she just an over-developed lass of New Australian descent who wore tight clothes? From what Marte told her as she wielded the iron or heaved the hoover around, it sounded as if Jemma, like Helen, did her homework at night, rather than touting her wares around Siren's Rock.

That was the other difficulty. Marte Johnson was still cleaning Babs' house. And the Jemma Marte talked about so volubly was not the slutty piece that the canasta club discussed. Marte's Jemma was another person altogether, a hard-working, respectable girl of whom any mother and father would be deservedly proud — but even so, a girl who worried her parents for very different reasons.

'You know what she wants?' Marte said to Babs, down on her knees, scrubbing the floor of the cream kitchen. 'She wants to be a star! Can you understand that, Mrs Winter?

Show business? I been in show business. I was with the horses, you know. I got out as soon as I met George. Show business is not for families, that's what I'm telling my Jemma. Being famous doesn't make you happy. Family is what makes you happy. Husband, kids, nice house, good food. Mrs Winter, are any of them stars as happy as you and me?'

Babs, standing with a doily in one hand and an empty vase in the other, shook her head.

'I'm saying to Jemma, you grow up, you meet a nice boy, you get married and have a family of your own. Helen too. Two lovely girls, two families. That's what we want for them, hey Mrs Winter? That's what will make our girls happy.'

But these days Babs didn't spend much time thinking about Helen and her happiness. She had developed a life of her own at Siren's Rock and she enjoyed that life much more when Helen wasn't in it. If Helen was off with Jemma, Babs no longer had to waste her time worrying about how she was turning out or, for that matter, how she wasn't.

It was easier these days for Babs to block out the image of her elder child — and of her husband. Thinking of them together was the picture she avoided absolutely.

Whenever Douglas had punished Helen, Babs had kept herself as far from Helen's room as possible, so that the image of Helen doing whatever she did for her father during her cowardly pleas for forgiveness would not force itself, flickering like a faulty neon, into her unwilling imagination.

The sounds had been more difficult to ignore.

There would be all that childish gabbling, followed by the crack of the cane. Then came the inevitable screams, the splash of flesh on flesh, and the whimpering. What Babs hated most was the long pregnant pause, punctuated by low-pitched growling from Douglas and followed by Helen's pathetic little whines, which Babs assumed were Helen's required apologies.

There were the other noises too; the ones Douglas made when he came to bed after punishing Helen. Horrible noises, escaping through his open mouth, just before he fell asleep. Humiliating for her to hear, embarrassing for him.

It had been a huge relief for Babs when Helen became a woman, and she and Douglas had decided she was too old for hidings.

Not that this had made any difference to Helen herself. Even now, two years after Douglas had last molested her, when she wasn't with Jemma, Helen sat around the house, silent, sulking, rarely speaking. When she did speak, there was always a sarcastic tone in her voice. She never talked to Babs about nice girlish things, the way Joy did more and more these days. It annoyed Babs that Jemma Johnson was apparently the only person capable of squeezing smiles and even prolonged laughter from her daughter's tight little face.

There was one fact relating to Jemma that all three of them understood well. It was in Babs' power to separate Helen and Jemma. This would be the best, the most effective, the most cruel punishment she could inflict on Helen, should the need ever arise.

'She's keeping it up her sleeve,' Jemma had said one day to Helen. Helen knew it too.

But the irony was that when Babs finally activated the ban, the girls weren't speaking to each other anyway.

Cerise lipstick coloured the small, determined bow which Babs wore for a mouth on the balmy spring evening when she stood in her kitchen, waiting for Helen to come home from the beach. Douglas stood behind her, large, the fluorescent light glinting on the black frames of his glasses.

Helen stood in the back doorway, salty, her sun-bleached hair starting to collapse, her hand clutching her beach coat closed, her heart thudding so hard she was sure they could hear it. They both stared at her. She knew they were waiting for her to start apologising, to start grovelling. She was so tired. It all seemed so pointless. They would punish her anyway.

One thing she had already decided on the journey home in Marte's car: if her father hit her — or touched her — she would run away.

The problem was where to go. She couldn't go to Jemma's. Not now. But she couldn't go to John's either, as he had suggested a long time ago, because the Sullivans no longer lived in Siren's Rock.

Standing just inside her mother's kitchen, Helen decided that, if necessary, she would steal money from Babs' purse and catch a bus out of town.

But no. It wasn't necessary, because she was not going to be beaten. Instead it was the ban. The long-anticipated total ban on her friendship with Jemma. No longer up her mother's crisply ironed sleeve, but issuing from her red bow lips.

Never to be together again.

The worry the pair of them had caused. The embarrassment of having to ring the Johnson house, the cleaning woman knowing more about their daughter's whereabouts than her parents.

Never to be together again.

The trouble the friendship had caused. The rudeness that had resulted from Jemma's influence. The cheek. The answering back. The common behaviour.

Never to be together again.

A girl with a bad reputation. Not what they wanted for Helen. No discipline. Never liked her, not from the first day. Bare-footed. Gutter child. Dago.

'Half German,' said Helen. 'One quarter Greek. Her father's Australian. Like you.' She saw her father's hand involuntarily jerk and took a step backwards, felt her bottom bump into the squeaky screen door.

Never to be together again.

Daddy and I have decided. The time has come. Always a bad influence. Forbidden from now on. Find some nice friends. Decent girls who know there's more to life than chasing after boys.

Shower and go straight to bed. Perhaps an empty stomach will remind you of the sacrifices your parents make to keep you clothed and fed and in return this is the thanks they get.

Never to be together again.

Helen wondered how her parents, who knew so little, had found out about the boys.

THE LOUISVILLE LADY RIDER

Jemma told everyone she didn't give two hoots.

She was alternately revolted by Helen's wanton behaviour, which she mentioned to no one, and stung by her friend's sarcasm, which she snarled about to some of the girls who now hung around with her at school.

Helen generally reserved irony for conversations about her parents. Certainly, during the five years they had been friends, Jemma had never been the subject of any form of attack from Helen. How could she talk to her like that, Jemma asked her new acolytes, who shook their heads and wrinkled their freckled noses in disgust.

Helen was going to have to apologise, said Jemma, and they all agreed. Jemma said it was Helen who had behaved badly and then been nasty about it, even though Jemma had saved them from ... what? The faces around her waited breathlessly for details. Jemma paused. From something horrible, she mumbled. Rape or worse, she thought, but didn't say. It was up to Helen to show some appreciation, some remorse.

Helen, in fact, was saturated with remorse, shame and guilt. As damp and depressing as the inevitable but familiar humidity that was beginning to settle on the town, her self-loathing sickened her stomach, thickened her head. She was inarticulate in her misery. Not only had she behaved like a slut and put both of them in danger, she had been nasty to her friend — the girl who had been kinder to her than any other person in her entire life.

All she needed to do was to go to Jemma's house and say: 'I'm sorry.' She couldn't. She no longer felt worthy to be Jemma's friend.

Jemma couldn't understand why she missed Helen so much. There were plenty more fish in the sea, she joked to the schools of them now swimming eagerly in her wake.

Everyone noticed Jemma and almost everyone liked her. Men, women, boys, girls, Jemma had a way with people. Well, most people. Not counting a few old cows who lived on the posh side of town, a few of the cattier girls at school, and some of the teachers who tried to pull her into line when, secure at the top of most of her classes, she distracted those who needed to be concentrating harder on the blackboard.

So why would it matter so much if she lost her shadow? How could the absence of her little fair friend, as her grandmother called Helen, make such a difference to her life?

Groups of girls at school now actively competed to get Jemma into their circle. The softball team wanted her to sit with them at lunchtime. So did the athletics group. Her friends in the debating club tried to seduce her with Cherry Ripes. The drama club begged her to try out for the part of Titania in the school's end of year production of *A Midsummer Night's Dream*. She responded to all the invitations. She thumped balls into the distant paddocks around Siren's Rock High with alarming vigour, she broke the school record for the hundred yards dash. The debating club won the summer competition with Jemma as a commanding first speaker. Only the drama club held disappointment when she tried out for the fairy queen and instead was cast as Bottom.

'Anyone tall can play Titania,' the drama teacher said earnestly. 'Nobody else can play Bottom the way you will. You'll have them rolling in the aisles.' Jemma thought about it for two nights and finally agreed. It was tempting to play a role where she could stride around the stage looking beautiful, she decided, but to be famous it was also necessary to crowd those aisles with rolling fans.

What bothered Jemma was that despite her busy days, she was often on her own.

She couldn't remember ever feeling lonely. She had always enjoyed being with her friends and family, but she also liked her own company, unlike Helen, who thought it would be wonderful to be like that. Alone, Helen felt rejected, was tortured by self-doubt. In the past, when Jemma was unavailable, her only refuge had been provided by the pages of a good book.

In the weeks that followed their break-up, Jemma's nights were long and silent. You couldn't run or bash balls about at night. You could learn your debating points and rehearse your lines, but Jemma was not used to doing this sort of thing alone; for years now she had always had a guaranteed audience of at least one.

She watched a lot of television. She read piles of love comics and *Seventeen* magazines. Her mother made Rocky Road and gleaming pastries and Jemma ate for comfort, knowing as she reached for another one what havoc the healing cakes would wreak on her hips.

'Why doncha ring Helen?' said Marte, looking at her daughter with sad and anxious eyes. 'Her mother will come round, you just see. Do you want me to say something to her?'

'No,' said Jemma. 'I couldn't care less about her mother.'

'Who *could* you care about?' asked Marte. She was puzzled and upset. Babs Winter had every right to ban her daughter from going to the beach or anywhere else for that matter. But to ban her from seeing Jemma? Marte didn't understand it. The girls had always been so good for each other. And they were both smart; they egged each other on to do well at school. What was the problem?

Okay, so they had stayed out too late one afternoon. They could have got into trouble. But they didn't. And that was weeks ago now. Hadn't the girls paid the price?

Babs had taken to going out when Marte came to clean. Marte knew she was embarrassed. What could she say, poor woman? She was only doing her best to bring up her daughter. We all want the same thing, thought Marte.

The most surprising thing was that Helen, too, found herself in demand.

A studious group of girls, the ones who ran the school magazine, the sort of girls who were always asked by the teachers to run errands, shyly approached Helen and invited her to sit with them at lunchtime. To Helen's surprise, she learned that, like her and Jemma, these girls had lives away from school too. They had jokes and histories and trouble with their parents and sisters and brothers. Helen thought of the fun she and Jemma had made of these girls, whom Jemma had dubbed the Goody Gollies, and felt ashamed.

Jemma's glance flickered across the tarred quadrangle. She noticed the bent blonde head and the cluster of others around it, talking, gesticulating, laughing in moderate bursts from time to time. She imagined the reaction of the Goody Gollies if they discovered what Helen had done at the beach. They wouldn't have a bar of her then, she told herself. A few words in the right ears from Jemma, and Helen wouldn't have a friend in the world. She'd be right back where she was at the beginning, when her prissy mother and fat-bummed father brought her to town in their big black car.

Before Jemma had saved her.

'Con artist,' thought Jemma. 'She cons everyone into thinking she's quiet and sweet.'

At first everyone wondered what had happened to split up a friendship so strong that it had aroused resentment and jealousy in many a schoolgirl heart. Helen and Jemma sat with their new friends at opposite ends of the quad, and felt eyes burning into their backs. But as Helen refused to discuss Jemma at all, and Jemma flung out tantalising but vague allusions to having saved an ungrateful and sarcastic Helen from 'something horrible', most of the girls grew tired of asking.

Trust John, thought Jemma. Trust John not to be around just when we need him most.

She couldn't remember when the thought had presented itself to her, like a single skinny candle flame, flickering quickly and then going out. John. John would know what to do.

John was her friend. But as Jemma knew, Helen had also talked to John more than anybody else, apart from herself. He knew them both well.

Only John no longer lived in Siren's Rock. Somehow the Sullivan family had come into money. Enough money to have brought Big Joe back to Siren's Rock to make arrangements for John and Robbie to be sent away to boarding school. St Patrick's was in Bridgetown, a difficult two-hour drive on a notoriously bad road winding south-west from Siren's Rock. Too far to come home very often.

In any case, their mum had become too sick to look after her children any more. She had gone into hospital and an aunt had come to look after the girls while Joe Sullivan was away on his travels. Meg was in and out of hospital a lot after that, getting thinner than a bunch of sticks, Marte had reported, after visiting with one of her huge parcels of food. Eventually, even Big Joe had stopped going away.

'I don't know why John couldn't come home at weekends,' Jemma had grumbled to Helen. 'Bridgetown isn't that far away. And he could bring home his friends and introduce us to the St Pat's boys. They're all good looking and they wear those beautiful blazers.'

Last year, when Jemma, Helen and John were fourteen, Meg Sullivan died.

Jemma came home from school and found her mother sobbing at the kitchen table, her head resting on her meaty arms. 'She used to be my friend,' Marte sobbed, when Jemma, frightened, put a tentative hand on her arm. 'I should have helped her more. I should have made the time to go and see her more. And now it's too late.

'She was worn out with it all, with him and all those babies. That's when the cancer got her. That's what cancer does. It takes the tired ones. I should have seen it coming. I could have helped. And now all those little girls. Without a mother to love them.'

Jemma saw John and Robbie at the funeral. John stood beside his father and she was surprised at how tall he had grown, how wide his shoulders were. Tall, quiet as always, sad and remarkably grown-up and smart in the maroon college blazer and long grey trousers. His face was still brown. His hair was shorter and thicker. He was a lot bigger, Jemma told Helen, who hadn't been allowed to go. 'Ladies and children don't attend funerals,' Babs said.

Marte and George offered their condolences to Big Joe Sullivan and Robbie, who was also taller and almost unrecognisable in his uniform, but Jemma, embarrassed, for once could not think of anything to say to John, this tall, neat-haired person who looked at her so sadly, waiting patiently for her to speak. She couldn't imagine this awkward young man in his long, pressed trousers lying on a rock in the summer sun, watching for blue tongues, or leaping through the bush, a medieval knight on an invisible horse. He made her feel uncomfortable.

She lowered her eyes so that she would not embarrass him with her tears. And he, too, finally looked away, and then moved off to take one of his weeping sisters by the hand.

The next day he was gone.

The aunt took John's sisters away to live in Sydney. Big Joe climbed into his truck and headed out of town.

Helen and Jemma were walking past the cemetery a few weeks later when Helen suggested that they try to write to John at St Patrick's, telling him how sorry they were that his mother had died.

'Why?' Jemma said. 'I told him at the funeral.'

'Anyway,' she added after a while, 'John was never one for writing. And we probably won't see him again for yonks.'

'I know, but ...' Helen frowned. 'I dunno, I wasn't at the funeral. I'd like him to know that sometimes I ... we ... you know. It would be ...' As usual she wasn't able to find the words.

Jemma took pity on her. 'What?' she asked. 'A small act of kindness?'

Helen's rare sweet smile lit up her face. 'Yeah. Yes.'

So Jemma agreed to write the letter to John. Marte helped them find the address of the school and they worked on the letter together. 'Say we know he must be sad,' Helen suggested, 'but we think about him. Tell him, you know, we miss him.'

'But we should give him some news about us as well,' said Jemma. 'So he doesn't think we've turned out weird.'

So the letter was duly written, stamped and posted. No reply ever came.

John would have talked some sense into both of us, Jemma was thinking as she sat at the kitchen table, stringing beans on newspaper for her mother. Suddenly she put her head down on her arms, overcome by a sense of loss.

That night, Jemma finally cried.

George heard her on his way to bed. He went into her room and touched her gently on the shoulder. Jemma sat up, and surprised him by burying her face in his neck. He patted her back helplessly and felt the warm tears trickle onto his skin. He didn't know what to say.

'I miss John, Dad,' she sobbed. 'Why did he have to go away?'

'Don't worry, my darling girl,' said George softly. 'He'll probably come back one day. And if he doesn't, someone better will come along.'

Ah, boys, George thought. Girls had been breaking their hearts over boys since the world began.

But Jemma wasn't crying over a boy.

She cried again the next night. It was as if once she had given the tears permission to flow, they wouldn't stop coming. She opened her mouth very wide in a great howl of sorrow, but kept the pillow stuffed between her lips. Even so, Marte heard the muffled, painful noises she was making, and came in to sit on the bed with a sympathetic sigh.

'I hate this stupid town,' Jemma wept into her pillow while her mother patted her heaving back. 'Stupid boring girls, stupid people who talk about you behind your back, stupid boys who want to be disgusting, stupid schools, stupid houses ...' She paused, having run out of stupids, and as the hopeless nature of everything about Siren's Rock overwhelmed her, she lifted her head from the pillow and burst into loud and uninhibited sobbing.

Nick appeared in the doorway, a deep scowl on his thirteen-year-old face — looking ready to defend rather than attack his big sister for a change. Marte waved him away.

'This is a bad time for you,' Marte said at last. 'I know it is. But it will pass, believe me, it will.'

'No, it won't,' wailed Jemma. 'Nothing's right. Everything's wrong.'

Marte sighed. 'When I was your age I thought the bad days would never pass but they did. You'll feel better when you make up with Helen.'

Jemma sat up and wrapped her arms around her knees. 'It's nothing to do with her,' she said with a congested snarl. 'It's this whole town. I hate it here, I hate it.'

'There are nice things about this town,' said Marte. 'Nice people. Nice shops. Look how close we are to the beach. You love the beach.'

At the mention of the beach Jemma began crying again. 'I hate the beach,' she said. 'And I hate growing up. It spoils everything.'

'You can do a lot more interesting things when you're grown-up and settled,' said Marte.

Jemma took her head out of her arms and stared at her mother. 'How can you say that, Mum, when you had such a fantastic life when you were young?'

'When did I ever tell you I had a fantastic life?' asked Marte, exasperated.

'You travelled all over the country with the horse show,' said Jemma, 'and all those men came to watch you and you wore that wonderful white leather costume with the fringes on your skirt and the big white hat and they cheered you and cheered you . . .'

'You know what else I had to do?' asked Marte crossly. 'I fed the horses and brushed them and looked after the equipment, and I drove the big trucks which scared me stupid, and the men would come around, wanting to do rude things with me, and I would have to hide or tell the boss, because he had promised my father, "no men".

'I never got any friends, you know?' said Marte. 'We never stayed in any town long enough. Once I went in the buck jumping at a rodeo in a town where we were putting on our show. And I won. I won lotsa money and they wrote about me in the paper. But that same night we were back in the trucks and on our way to the next town. The boss kept my prize money,' she shrugged, 'and I never even saw my name in the paper. Fifteen years old, working with the horses, hiding from dirty men, no friends . . .' Marte stroked Jemma's hair. 'You haven't got it so tough.'

Jemma watched her mother with swollen eyes.

'People knew who you were,' Jemma said enviously. 'You were the Louisville Lady Rider. They paid money to see you. And you told me you loved working with horses.'

'I loved the feel of them,' said Marte, dreamily stroking Jemma's hair, 'and the smell of them. I used to wish I was a horse. To me they were better than people.'

'Why?' asked Jemma softly.

'I told you,' said Marte, but Jemma never tired of hearing the story, so she continued, because this was better than listening to her daughter cry. 'My mother and father had eleven children and I was the fifth girl in a long line of girls and they didn't want me,' said Marte. 'I heard my mother say so. There was a long tablecloth on the dinner table and I was hiding underneath it one night when I was little. Some people came over to eat with my parents and that's what my mother told them. "I coulda done without Marte," that's what she said.'

'Little Pitchers have Big Ears,' prompted Jemma. 'You left that bit out.'

'Yeah,' grunted Marte. 'Little pitchers. Then the boys started coming after me,' she continued, 'and my mother was too busy to care what I was doing. The man on the farm next door, he let me ride his horses. I rode them bare-back because nobody could afford a saddle.'

She was staring out of Jemma's window, blind to the lazy moon and the mess of stars tossed out into the night sky. She saw the horses. Their kind, understanding faces. She smelled them. She remembered the warmth of them beneath her.

'And you got to be such a good rider you were asked to join the horse show,' sighed Jemma. 'The Louisville Lady Rider. Your name in the papers.'

'You're not listening to me, Jemma,' said Marte, moving her frank eyes from the window and gazing helplessly at her daughter. 'That's your problem, you know. You only hear what you want to hear.'

Jemma's wide mouth drooped in a sullen curve but her mother continued.

'You are a lovely girl, Jemma, but you don't know how lucky you are,' said Marte. 'You have a mum and dad who wanted you more than anything else in the world, and a brother who loves you too, though he probably don't know it himself yet, and you have good friends, especially Helen, who you should get back as soon as you can.

'You have love and a safe home and a happy family,' said Marte, raising her voice over Jemma's when she started to argue. 'That's everything. That is our gift to you. That is what you need to give your own children.

'What is fame and fortune?' asked Marte. 'People clapping? People knowing who you are? People clapped me, yes, for one night. Then they went on with their lives. And my family, they didn't care about me.'

Jemma frowned. 'I don't want to be ordinary,' she muttered. 'I hate it. Everything in this stupid town is ordinary.'

Marte flung up her hands, stood up in the dark, walked across the bedroom floor, then returned and sat down on the bed again. She took Jemma's face in her hands. Jemma flinched and stiffened, but Marte did not release her.

'Fame!' said Marte fiercely and blew a raspberry through her xylophone teeth. 'Fame don't make for happiness, Jemma. Be happy with what you got.'

Jemma had never heard her mother speak for so long about such serious things. Had never heard Marte suggest that everything about her beautiful daughter was not absolutely perfect. She rolled her eyes, flopped back on her pillow and tried to squeeze out some more tears but she was all cried out.

So that's what I'm supposed to aim for, is it? A family living happily ever after in Siren's Rock? Never in a Month of Sundays, said Jemma to herself.

SET AND MATCH

The only bright spot on the horizon was the play.

When Jemma pranced onto the stage with her legs wide apart and her hands in her pockets, stuck out her stomach, stuck out her jaw, rolled and crossed her eyes, and sputtered to her fellow honest artisans: 'Are we all met?', everyone at the rehearsals stopped what they were doing to watch and laugh. Even Mr Brennan, the drama teacher, relaxed his expression of permanent anxiety and made notes on his clipboard with a self-congratulatory smirk.

There was no doubt that Jemma wiped the dusty floor of the school stage with all the other players, even Derek Sweeney, a thin-faced boy who had carved himself a reputation as a public speaker in the rough but by no means dead wood of Siren's Rock High, and was suitably officious in the part of Peter Quince. As the leader of the motley collection of tradesmen who would put on a play for the King and Queen of Athens, unctuous Derek was a perfect foil for Jemma's self-centred, dominating, bumbling Nick Bottom, who wanted to play all the parts and was convinced of his superiority to everyone else on the stage. As one teacher remarked, a brilliant piece of casting.

The only person who wasn't pleased with Jemma as Bottom was her mother. Marte railed and wrung her hands. 'Whoever heard of a girl playing the part of a great big man? A stupid man?' she said to Babs Winter, who had arrived home early to find her cleaning lady still polishing the door handles. 'I could have made her such a lovely dress if she was Titania. Or Hippolyta — she would have made the perfect Queen of Greece. Who better than a girl with Greek blood, and tall and holding herself like royalty? But Bottom! She's wearing a brown sack. The craft class are making her a donkey's head to wear!'

Babs pursed her lips and rehearsed again the lines which would terminate Marte's service. The words would never come. Babs was perfectly aware that the moment she let Marte go, she would be snapped up by one of her envious friends. Besides, the ban no longer seemed to matter. Helen had nice friends now, girls from sensible families, and Babs no longer had to torture herself with the Jemma question. Even Cindy-Lou Basingstoke-Brown had been around for afternoon tea this week. Someone should have told Cindy-Lou to stop at one piece of cake, thought Babs. However, as long as she averted her gaze from Helen's moping form, everything in her own garden was looking rather lovely. And looking lovely was Babs Winter's idea of heaven.

Babs had been disappointed that Helen didn't get the part of Helena in *A Midsummer Night's Dream*. Fair and delicate, she would have been ideal. Helen explained that she needed more than a similar name to have a starring role in the school play. The desire and ability to act, for example. Babs decided that Helen was jealous of Jemma's strange success, but she couldn't have been more wrong.

★ ★ ★

About a week before the first of the two scheduled performances of the *Dream*, the school was rocked by some astounding news. The drama club had been invited to stage an extra performance at St Patrick's College in Bridgetown. The sixth form students there were studying the play and the principal, Father Benedict Brennan, brother of the Siren's Rock drama teacher, had heard nothing but good things about the quality of the impending production.

The girls in the cast, who outnumbered the boys about five to one, were hysterical with anticipation. They were going to perform in front of a school full of gorgeous, previously unattainable males! Boys who wore smart blazers and long trousers and shirts and ties, boys who were as different to the juvenile drongos at Siren's Rock as elusive butterflies are to blowflies. Not only that, the entire cast and crew were invited to join the staff and senior students for supper after the performance! Never in the history of the high school drama club had there been such possibilities for romance and excitement.

To avoid taking junior members of the drama club to Bridgetown, Mr Brennan approached Helen and the Goody Gollies and asked them if they would volunteer for a few crucial jobs behind the scenes. They accepted eagerly. Even Helen's new friends were not oblivious to the appeal of the males of St Patrick's College. Helen agreed to be props mistress, thinking that here at last was a chance of seeing John. She attended the last week of rehearsals and silently marvelled at Jemma's performance — it was even better than she'd imagined.

Fancy putting Helen in charge of props, thought Jemma. She was neither tidy nor organised and she was bound to go off into a daydream and forget what she was supposed to be doing. Jemma was sure she could handle the job as well as the role of Bottom, but Mr Brennan sighed and said no. 'Just concentrate on being the best Bottom Siren's Rock High has ever produced,' he said gravely.

Still, she kept her eye on what Helen was doing. She began wishing Helen's eyes would just once meet hers. But Helen's head was always bent over her clipboard with its scratchy little props list, her hair falling thinly over her face.

Helen didn't have good hair any more, Jemma thought. Helen's hair was only good if it was properly set and dried and teased. She was tempted to tell one of the Goody Gollies how to do it. Helen needed all the help she could get.

They went to Bridgetown in a hired bus. Their performance was scheduled to begin early as they were travelling back the same night. Even so, they wouldn't be home until almost midnight. It was all terribly thrilling.

Jemma sat in the front seat behind the driver and flirted outrageously with Lysander, who was unable to believe his good fortune. A lanky Egan cousin with oily black hair, vaguely oriental eyes and effeminate waving hands, he nevertheless made the most of the curving road out of town by leaning against Jemma each time the bus took a bend. Eventually she folded her arms tightly over her alluring chest. Lysander sighed and studied his feet.

There was no chance to glimpse the college boys before the show, as the Siren's Rock students were ushered out of the bus and down a series of gloomy, echoing corridors. 'Why on earth were we dying to go to a boarding school?' Jemma wanted to ask Helen, but Helen was bringing up the rear with the backstage people, and anyway they still weren't speaking. They were directed into a large room with temporary cubicles created by curtains, where they had to put on their costumes and make-up.

When the play began, the St Patrick's students were visible only as a sea of white faces, drifting on waves of appreciative silence as Helena and Hermia pouted and panicked in front of them. They broke into tides of laughter each time Jemma and her foolish team of thespians stumbled onto the stage.

Helen peered from the wings into the audience, running her eyes along each row of maroon blazers in search of someone skinny and brown with tufty hair. But from there all the boys looked much the same.

Quite a few things went wrong during the play, notably Puck not being able to find the ass's head seconds before she had to ram it over Jemma's. 'I knew she would muck it up,' muttered Jemma as Helen, blushing and apologetic, suddenly appeared with the missing object, but Mr Brennan said in the interval that it would be all right on the real opening night as long as they all learned from their mistakes at this performance.

The cheer they received at the end was strangely subdued, Jemma thought, for two hundred boys who had just been allowed to feast their girl-starved eyes on a number of shapely young bodies from Siren's Rock. If that was discipline, fully grown boys being forced to clap politely (where was the whistling and the stamping of feet?), she was glad she didn't have it.

Still, the supper was yet to come. Jemma had high hopes for the supper.

At first she had been mortified at the thought of appearing in her costume, dressed like a burly working man, with all her best features totally covered with padding and make-up — even her smile, because two of her teeth would be blacked out. But, inevitably, Jemma had decided to make the best of it: she would give the performance of her life, be as ugly as possible, and then dazzle them at the supper with her transition into Sophia Loren. (*'No! No, I don't believe it. Nobody as beautiful as you could possibly have been . . .'*)

She wondered if John was out there in the audience. They had been told that only the sixth form boys would be coming to the supper, so she knew already she wouldn't see him there, wouldn't get a chance to talk to him about her rift with Helen. Besides, she was bothered by the possibility that the vice captain of the Wildcats was greatly changed. A strange, silent, funereal John could easily cramp her style.

In the dressing room after the performance, everyone was in a tizz. People lost their underwear, couldn't find bags, made a mess. Cast members were running around with great bundles of white tissues in their hands, wiping off their grease paint, removing their crimson lips and looking for their silver-pink instead. Girls were trying to wriggle into their bras through the arm holes of their frocks so that the boys in the cubicles at the other end of the room wouldn't see them in their underwear. Boys searched for socks while girls pulled on stockings, clipped suspender belts into the wrong snaps, found bums in their faces, lost shoes. The room was full of shrieks, bangs, bumps, gasps of hair spray.

St Patrick's College had never seen anything like this.

Even after she had done her best to remove the make-up and unblacken her teeth, it took Jemma longer than anyone else to get out of her ponderous costume, the thick woollen tights, the boots, the pillows roped around her waist. She saw Helen across the room, nicely dressed already in a pale pink shift with a keyhole back. The single advantage of being a member of the backstage crew, rather than a star, was that you could get dressed at home without an audience. Helen was helping Peter Quince to remove his dangly beard, which was caught in his belt. Her hair was fat again tonight, Jemma observed quickly — someone must have shown her how to do it after all — and she experienced a stab of intense jealousy. Helen should have been at her own side, the patient handmaiden she had always been. She would have made Jemma's transition from Nick Bottom to Sophia Loren so much easier. And if Helen looked nice it should have been because Jemma had helped her.

Jemma's dress, sewn lovingly by Marte, was exactly right for the occasion and not unlike Helen's. It was sleeveless, to show off her arms, but had a high, demure neckline, as befitted supper in a religious school. The back, however, plunged down into a deep and generous U. Marte had helped her buy a strapless bra — Jemma's first. It had a stiff bodice, supporting pale pink satin cups, strongly engineered and firmly wired to clasp Jemma's generous breasts, and the back was cut very low. Anyone standing behind Jemma would be treated to the sight of most of her smooth, tanned back.

Hurrying now, Jemma clipped herself into the bra and looked around for her dress. Everyone else seemed to be ready. They were all leaving, heading out into the corridor and up the stairs. Jemma shoved the short turquoise shift over her head, yanked it down over her hips and picked up her shoes. She raced after them all, still struggling into her shoes, stretching on tip-toe on her way through to check her face in a high, dim mirror that hung near the door.

She overtook most of the other cast members en route, gracefully coiling her way past a knot of them hovering nervously in the entrance to the sixth form common room. Helen was leaning over the banister on the main stairway, watching lines of boys filing out of the hall below. 'How obvious,' thought Jemma.

At one end of the huge common room there were tables covered with snowy cloths, bearing jugs of icy orange punch, plates of striped sandwiches and cakes covered with pastel icing. Small groups of St Patrick's sixth-formers stood nearby, munching with undisguised relish and talking with a handful of the more courageous Siren's Rock students. They were jovially supervised by priests in long black robes.

Inside now, Jemma paused, took a deep breath, and walked slowly towards the food, her head high, her body swaying. Around her, people started to stare. She let a small smile play around her lips. '*No, you couldn't be the girl who . . .*'

By the time she reached the first of the white tables, everyone in the room seemed to be looking straight at her. This was more than even Jemma had imagined. She bestowed the full white magnificence of her smile on a tall, gawping St Pat's boy, whom she had correctly identified by his badge and stature as the school captain and said: 'Hi. My name's Jemma. What's yours?'

'Well, how do you do, Jemma,' said a polished voice beside her, and she turned to find herself gazing into the frankly admiring eyes of a priest.

'Father Brennan,' he said, offering his hand. 'I'm the poor soul who is in charge of all these young ratbags for the better part of the school year. You, I assume, are a member of the very talented cast.'

He had incredibly blue eyes, a tanned leathery face and wavy white hair. And quite the most delightful smile Jemma had ever seen on an older man.

'Yes,' said Jemma, trying to include the captain in the breadth of her returning smile, glancing past the priest, who wasn't much taller than she, and up at the boy, running her eyes admiringly over his lanky shoulders. 'I am. And is this one of your favourite students?'

(*Did you see Jemma Johnson at the St Pat's supper? The school captain never left her side all night. They're going out together now.*)

'Oh yes,' said Father Brennan. 'David is everyone's favourite student. Now forgive me ... Jemma, wasn't it? Yes, Jemma.' To Jemma's annoyance, he had manoeuvred himself between her and David so that David could not see her properly any more — although he was still gawping. 'Forgive me, Jemma, but I don't seem to ... exactly what role were you playing?'

This was the moment when she was supposed to reveal the miracle of her transformation. She didn't want to waste it on the school's headmaster, no matter how sweet his smile happened to be. He was old. She hesitated.

'Now let me guess,' said Father Brennan heartily. 'Not Titania, surely. She was a smaller girl than you. Not Hermia. She was exceptionally short and you are a tall girl. Not Helena either. As I recall, Helena was ...' he paused.

'Thin,' said Jemma. She put her head on one side to see if David was still looking and listening. He was, and now a number of other boys, all tall, all wearing prefect badges, had gathered beside him and were peering over the priest's shoulder.

She took a deep, deep breath. For a moment, she thought she heard one of the boys whimper. 'As a matter of fact ...' Jemma began, and then she saw Helen.

She had appeared, quite suddenly, on the other side of the priest, neat in her short pink dress, big hair bobbing. And she was smiling in the strangest way, her candy-pink mouth stretched over her two neat rows of pearly teeth, but her eyes were not smiling at all, just fixed on Jemma's, and she was talking, talking, talking. *Helen was talking.* Jemma was so surprised that she stopped what she was saying herself to listen. Helen moved right in front of her, reached up, put her skinny hands on Jemma's shoulders, stood on tip-toe and gave her a little peck on the cheek.

'She was so good, wasn't she?' gabbled Helen, keeping her hands on Jemma's shoulders, speaking to Father Brennan and the boys. 'She was so good as Bottom, didn't you think? Would you ever have guessed a girl could play Nick Bottom so well? Good on you, Jemma, we all knew you would be wonderful.'

'No!' said Father Brennan. 'Surely you couldn't be . . .'

But Jemma missed what he was saying because, in an extraordinary movement, Helen turned around and faced Father Brennan, squeezing herself between him and Jemma, standing so close to Jemma that her hair tickled Jemma's nose. But then, when Jemma tried to take a step backwards to make more room between them, Helen stepped back too, stood on her toes, in fact, stood on them hard.

And Jemma said 'Ow!' at the same time that Father Brennan raised an eyebrow in astonishment and said: '*Bottom*?'

'Bottom,' said Helen, nodding her head vigorously and leaning back against Jemma. 'Would you believe it?'

Months later, when she was able to think about it without feeling nauseous, which even then was not often, Jemma remembered the feeling, weird and strange, of her bare chest against Helen's keyhole back.

Jemma looked down.

There wasn't much to see, with Helen squashed up against her in that extraordinary way. But she understood.

She was wearing her dress back to front.

The deep U which should have been showing off her back was plunging towards her navel. Her breasts, thrusting enthusiastically from her boned pink satin bra, were on display to the bemused headmaster and appreciative students of St Patrick's Catholic College.

Jemma was never certain how much time passed between the moment she looked down and witnessed her disgrace and the moment she slipped her arms around Helen's slender waist, keeping her carefully positioned in front of her, and said breathlessly: 'Would you excuse us, Father Brennan? I think it's time Helen and I visited the ladies.'

He nodded, relieved and intrigued, his eyes still twinkling away like lights on water. Jemma could have said to him: 'Look, I put my dress on backwards by accident. I just have to go and turn it around.' He might have understood, even though he was a priest. But she knew the boys would not. And she realised far too late that he had been trying to protect his unsullied students from a sight they normally saw only in two dimensions, in the calendars they kept hidden beneath their mattresses.

Or perhaps, like Helen, he had been trying to protect *her*. She would never know.

The girls hurried off across the room, a conga line of two, Jemma keeping her eyes firmly averted from those of the ogling boys as she held onto Helen's tiny waist.

In the toilets, when she was properly dressed again, Jemma sobbed and sobbed. How could she ever face any of them again?

'Well,' said Helen practically, offering bundles of toilet paper to mop up the mascara, 'you probably won't see any of them again anyway. And I don't think anybody from our school even noticed.'

'Of course they did,' wailed Jemma. 'My boobs are huge. *Everyone* noticed. I want to die. I want to die. What am I going to do? I'll have to leave the play and ... and ...' the full implications of the tragedy struck her with a rush, 'if I leave the play it will be *ruined*!'

'Exactly,' said Helen. Two pairs of eyes, one of them ringed with smudged mascara, met in a washroom mirror which had only ever seen schoolboys cleaning their teeth and examining their chins for whiskers.

'That's why you have to go on,' said Helen quietly. 'That's what stars do.'

Jemma looked pathetically at her reflection.

She started to sob again. 'I want to go home.'

'Let's go and get your things and then we can sit and wait in the bus,' said Helen.

At the toilet door, Jemma stopped. 'I'm sorry I was horrible to you,' she croaked.

Helen stared at her. 'Don't,' she said. 'I'm the one . . .' Her voice crumbled away.

'Let's not talk about it any more,' said Jemma.

They waited in silence in the bus. A long time later Jemma said, 'Did you see John?'

Helen shook her head. 'No. But I bet he saw *you*.'

When the others finally came, the talk was mainly about the St Patrick's boys and how gorgeous they were and how much cake everyone had eaten. A few girls smirked at Jemma as they made their way up the aisle of the bus, and Lysander raised an oily eyebrow and said, 'Set and match to Bottom,' out of the corner of his mouth, but nobody else said anything.

Jemma was tempted to believe that Helen was right and not many people had been looking at her. She was unaware that Mr Brennan, informed by his brother of Jemma's humiliation and alarmed at the prospect of losing his star performer, had issued a stern warning to his cast and crew.

The boys of St Patrick's could not be similarly gagged, but by the time they were free to compare notes, Jemma was on her way back to Siren's Rock.

Whether a lot of people had noticed or not, Jemma was hotly aware that Helen had cut short a demonstration of tartiness which, however unintentional, could have been recorded on the tongues of Siren's Rock for an eternity.

As the bus rolled slowly home, Jemma reached for her friend's hand and squeezed it gratefully.

The *Dream* opened at Siren's Rock High to a full house, parents and families cramming the school's splintery hall. Oberon and Titania, in black and silver sequins, were wonderful against a background of forest painted in four shades of green by the fourth form art class. The warring lovers frustrated and entertained and Lysander, waving his limp hands expressively, managed to brush both Helena's and Hermia's breasts with his languid fingers without anyone suspecting him of anything other than overacting.

Only Puck, entwined in a costume of green satin streamers, which had reduced her mother's fingers to strips of flesh as she sewed long into the night, left a lot to be desired. Puck was rather tall for the part and inclined to scratch her eczema between lines.

Helen — who had persuaded Mr Brennan to retain her services for the opening night — didn't forget any of the props.

But the night belonged to Peter Quince, Francis Flute, Tom Snout, Robin Starveling, Snug and the brilliant, blundering Bottom, who reduced the audience to fits of laughter with every line.

In her triumphant final scene, Jemma held five hundred people in her hand as she led the company in a silly dance, bowing and flouncing and even plunging one of her brother Nick's old plastic swords into her heart.

'The roar of the crowd was deafening,' Jemma told her grandmother when she finally got home, her face sore from smiling, her cheeks wet from kisses, her back and shoulders having been thoroughly and constantly clapped.

The roar had been the best moment. The second best was when she finally left the stage, her heart pounding. Helen was standing in the wings, clapping so hard her hands were almost numb. When Jemma walked towards her, she stopped clapping and held out her arms. Jemma walked straight into them.

She was all padded up, pillows roped around her waist under the brown serge tunic, thick grease paint in layers on her face. But Helen hugged her tightly and Jemma didn't push her away.

'You're a star!' Helen shouted over the applause which was still continuing on the other side of the curtain.

'Did I rock them in the aisles?' Jemma shrieked.

Helen laughed. 'Rocked them and rolled them over.'

Out on the stage, Puck, tripping over her trailing tails, exhorted the audience to settle and be kind:

'Give me your hands, if we be friends,
And Robin shall restore amends.'

Jemma and Helen stood in the wings of their lives and grinned at each other.

Part Three

JOY

Jemma and Helen, Jemma and Helen, Jemma and Helen, yes of course, she should have realised that's how it would be. Especially today. And hot. She should have remembered the thick, sticky heat of this damn town. Warm, wet, sticky heat, ruining her hair, oozing through her nice clothes, no matter how straight she sat.

Fancy choosing Hamish to do the eulogy, thought Joy, smoothing her navy linen dress over her tight-together knees. Would he make it through without breaking down? He was standing in the pulpit, talking in a feeble, disjointed sort of way. Of course you had to make allowances, but really. Helen and Jemma, Helen and Jemma. Yes, yes. But what about Jemma and *John*? What about *Helen* and John? Did Hamish know anything about Helen and John, wondered Joy.

Did anybody?

Poor Hamish. Such an unattractive boy, so tall and awkward, those red girl's lips and that awful haircut, spiky, shapeless. How disappointing for Jemma, who had kept her looks, to have produced such a plain son.

How fortunate she and Warren were to have three such beautiful children. Warren often said fondly that he could take no credit — they all looked like their mother. A small smile played around Joy's red ribbon lips as her glance hovered over Paula, Peter and Sharon, her slender, white-haired, even-featured children. They were perfect in every detail, she decided, apart from their eyes, which were weak like Warren's and just a tiny bit too close together. It was a shame they all wore spectacles, but they were coming into adolescence now and contact lenses were just around the corner. That would make everyone happy, especially Mummy, who had trouble keeping it a secret that she considered glasses to be an impediment to prettiness. Especially for girls.

Warren didn't like it, thought Joy. All of them sitting at the back of the church, as if they were poor relations — whereas they were actually the well-to-do relations from out of town. They should have been sitting down the front with Mummy. It had been Joy's decision to be as close as possible to the exit. She had been nervous at the possibility of having to escort one of the children out of the church before the completion of the service. Some of the people of Siren's Rock would almost certainly have said she was trying to draw attention to herself.

Whereas, as usual, the attention was all on Jemma and Helen.

What about Helen and Joy?

Life was really all about making choices, thought Joy. What goes around comes around, as Jemma would say, and in the end Joy had made the right choices, and Helen had not.

Helen had chosen the wrong man. Men really. She should have waited for someone who would respect her and love her for life, the way Warren loved Joy. Instead, it had become increasingly obvious over the years that Helen chose men purely for sex.

Joy could not understand that at all. Sex was a relatively small part of a permanent relationship. It was obligatory, of course, if you wanted children. But how much of your daily life did you spend having sex? Probably less than the time you spent ironing! And it was considerably less rewarding at that.

Helen had also chosen the wrong job. She should have done something that took her away from Siren's Rock. Joy had been to teachers' college at Wentworth, then worked at a school in Bridgetown, and finally made a move to a private school which attracted a nicer class of child.

While teaching at St Ursula's Joy had met Warren, a solicitor trapped in a crumbling marriage to a girl he'd been stuck with since high school. An ugly, liberated, bra-burning woman who wore shapeless clothes and never used make-up. Warren couldn't believe it when he met Joy. Sweet, scented, sympathetic Joy, with her blonde curls, her wholesome prettiness; compliant, gentle Joy, who helped him sweep away the crumbs of his disastrous first marriage so that together they could start a fresh, clean life. A house in Bridgetown. Nice furniture. Good jobs. For Warren, a partnership. And quite soon, quite quickly really, Paula, Peter and Sharon. Their owl-eyed but otherwise perfect family.

Helen had chosen not to show respect and gratitude to their parents. Joy had chosen to be obedient and gentle with Mummy and Daddy, whereas Helen, despite being six years older, had no idea how to handle them at all. Throughout their childhood, it apparently never once occurred to Helen that if you showed Mummy and Daddy some appreciation, they would do anything you wanted. Wrapping Them

Around Your Little Finger, Jemma called it. 'That's what you do, isn't it, Joy?' she had said once, when Joy was about sixteen, and Joy had giggled and simpered and looked up at Jemma from underneath her eyelashes, in the way that worked so well with adults as well as boys. It didn't work with Jemma, of course. Nothing like that worked with Jemma.

'Jemma's too honest to play the sort of games other people play,' Helen had told her years ago.

But what was wrong with wrapping parents around your little finger if it made everyone happy? Where had sulking and sighing got Helen?

Had they let Helen go to teachers' college? Had they given Helen a complete set of silver cutlery as a wedding present? Had they lent Helen money to put a deposit on a dear little Federation cottage? Renovated kitchen, in-ground pool, new bathroom, walk-in robes. Mummy had even given Warren and Joy the money they needed to add the extension, including a lovely flat, which meant Mummy would be close to them all now that Daddy had passed on.

A small frown disturbed Joy's smooth forehead. Warren wasn't *too* keen on having Mummy so close to them all. It had been Warren's idea last year to put Mummy's name down beside a handsome deposit at a good nursing home, ensuring a place when the time came.

They hadn't quite got around to telling Mummy about that yet.

Of course it had been taken for granted that Helen would accept no responsibility for Mummy. Everyone knew that Helen was never capable of looking after anyone properly, not even her children — not even herself, as it now turned out. She let Jemma look after her.

Jemima was all she ever wanted. Joy glanced down the pews at John's bulky form in the front row and wondered what he thought about that.

Poor Hamish. He had been reading something. He read quite well, really; he had a nice voice. Now he was staggering back to his seat all red in the face with the effort not to cry. What on earth had he been saying to upset everyone so much? Joy quietly opened her white clutch bag and took out a handkerchief.

Helen had chosen not to be sweet to Daddy. Even in the face of incontrovertible evidence that being sweet to Daddy got you a good deal. Helen said Daddy was cruel to her, but logic said that if Helen had been sweeter to Daddy the so-called cruelty might never have happened. Not that it *did* happen. Not the way Helen said.

But there was one night in particular which Joy had the most trouble not remembering. It was the night they had forgotten to close the bedroom door.

She had been about ten. Daddy had just finished reading her a story. He was still sitting on the edge of her little pink bed and she had run across to her cupboard, with its transfers of Jemima Puddleduck on the doors, to put her storybook away. It was her favourite: *Pookie Believes in Santa Claus*. She'd skipped back to give Daddy a good-night cuddle and he had opened his legs and squeezed her between them while she wound her little plump arms around his neck and hung on tight, mashing her cheek against his while he held her as close as could be.

Helen, who must have been about sixteen at the time, was padding past on her way to the toilet. She had come barging into the room.

'Don't you dare!' she had screamed at Daddy. 'Don't you *dare!*'

For a minute, Joy had thought Helen was actually going to hit Daddy. But she stopped in the middle of the bedroom, her arms rigid at her sides and her fists clenched. Even Daddy, who was never short of a word, was speechless, sitting there with his hands around Joy's little waist and his mouth hanging open with shock.

Nobody in the house ever spoke to Daddy like that.

Joy pulled herself out from between her father's legs and ran to get Mummy. When the two of them came back into the room, Helen was still standing in the same place. She had her back to them but she was still standing as stiff as a flagpole, with her fists in balls. Daddy was still sitting on the bed, staring at her. Mummy looked at the two of them for a few seconds and then took Helen's arm and turned her around. Helen's face was red and streaky, and her eyes were sort of blank, as if she couldn't see Mummy at all.

That was what Joy couldn't forget. Helen's face that night.

Still nobody said anything. And then Mummy did a frightening thing. She raised her hand and slapped Helen across the face. Hard.

Joy had let out a little scream.

Helen had just stood there and let her do it. And Daddy just sat there and let her do it. Only Joy did something to stop it. She started to cry. Her whimpering little sobs set everyone into motion again, as if someone had turned off a film projector for a minute or two, but had now set it rolling again. Helen walked out and went back to her own room. Daddy got off the bed and went to the door. Mummy gave him a strange look as he passed her. Joy saw it as she was standing right there, beside both of them. She had never seen that look on Mummy's face before, or heard that tone in Daddy's voice. Never ever. He sounded like a little boy. A naughty little boy. 'I didn't,' he said to Mummy. 'I didn't.'

Nobody took any notice of Joy at all. Nobody mopped her tears or gave her a cuddle or told her everything would be all right. Everyone walked away, leaving her alone with Jemima Puddleduck and Pookie and her signed photograph of Annette Funicello.

The incident was never mentioned again and Joy had remained confused. Until just a couple of years ago, when Helen made the worst choice of all.

She told everybody.

With Daddy in his grave and totally unable to defend himself.

All Joy could think at the time was thank goodness she had escaped. Thank heavens she and her children and even Mummy were no longer living in Siren's Rock. It had been so *unnecessary*, thought Joy. And after all, even if it was true, which Mummy said it wasn't, it was all so long ago. It was *over*!

Helen's story was so sordid that people never dared to mention it to Joy on the rare occasions when she came back to Siren's Rock. They just looked at her with uncomfortable and sometimes sympathetic faces.

She tried not to wonder how many of them believed what Helen had said.

She didn't.

Joy and Daddy shut the door at story time because it was their special time together.

After the story, Daddy always made her get up and put her book away herself so she would grow up to be a tidy girl.

Daddy squeezed her between his knees for their good-night cuddle because he loved her so much.

No matter what Helen believed, Daddy had loved her. Daddy had never hurt Joy.

He had promised.

All Helen had needed to do was be nice to him, thought Joy as the music started. How hard would it have been, she thought, signalling to her children, smoothing her skirt, getting up to sing.

There was never any music in our house, thought Joy. Or noise, she remembered suddenly. There never was any noise.

Instead of the organ, a sweet clear song reached out with strings: 'The Wind Beneath My Wings'. Soaring from some hidden sound system.

An ugly, broken sound was wrenched from Joy's perfectly drawn lips. She sat down again, her skirt twisted beneath her. Her children stared at her, shocked. Sharon emitted a nervous giggle.

Nobody else had stood up.

The song seemed to split her head in two. She wrapped her hands around her temples to shut out the words. She saw Warren's horrified stare. Years of self-discipline failed to kick in. Joy sat helplessly in the pew, tears sliding down her cheeks.

Of course. How typical. Obviously Jemma had produced this show, even if she hadn't been able to make it here to see it being staged. *One performance only! Absolutely no extended season!* Jemma and Helen *would* see themselves as Bette Midler and her beautiful, unremembered friend. Jemma and Helen *would* be so wrapped up in themselves that, right to the end, they were deluded into thinking their lives were movie material.

Life and Death! Starring Jemma and Helen and nobody else. That's how it had always been.

THE PLAN

They should have bought a three-man tent. According to the pimply boy in the camping store, a two-man tent would be pretty cramped. Especially, he said, in nasal cockney tones, if they were planning to live in it for six months or more.

But they were not flush with cash and, as Jemma said, they weren't two men, they were two girls, and they didn't take up much room.

They bought the tent in an army disposal store off Oxford Street, not the most practical place to invest their hard-earned savings in enough camping equipment for a long-term trip, but they hadn't been in London long enough to find the best bargains and at least they knew how to get to Oxford Street; they had gone there on their first day, to buy their warm coats. Since then they had seen Buckingham Palace, taken a full-day bus tour around London and another longer one to Windsor, and they had walked miles around a city already familiar from endless sessions of Monopoly. They waited for hours at crossings wider than the entire shopping centre of Siren's Rock, travelled in the tube, and clutched each other's hands with excitement when they sat in nose-bleed seats up in the gods and saw John Gielgud and Derek Nimmo live on stage in the West End. Or heard them, as Jemma pointed out, and watched the tops of their tiny heads.

They had left Siren's Rock in March and headed straight for London. After finally finishing her four years of university Jemma couldn't wait for the European summer. She and Helen had saved their money, made their bookings, had their injections. They were ready and raring to go, Jemma said, and you could wait a lifetime for England to get warm.

They had also been to their respective doctors and arranged to take the Pill.

'What about The Plan?' Helen had asked dubiously.

'It's just that you never know,' said Jemma. 'What if we meet our one true love?'

'Well,' said Helen, 'it's just that I thought you said . . .'

'You never know your luck,' said Jemma, 'in a big city.'

The photographs in their passports showed off their new short, easy-care hair. Jemma's mane, lopped and layered, had sprung into short thick curls which hugged her head and made her carefully outlined green eyes look large and exotic.

Helen morosely announced that her newly cropped head resembled the back of a poodle.

'You look elfin,' lied Jemma. 'It'll grow back. Stop whingeing. Vanity is a curse.'

So Helen had bought a soft grey hat with a floppy brim, and waited obediently for her hair to grow.

'We can't stop you going,' Helen's mother had said. 'You're twenty-one. But girls who go looking for trouble usually find it.'

'Don't expect to come back to the cushy number you've had here,' said Helen's father. 'I'm in line for a promotion, you know. We may not even be here when you come home.'

'I'll try to cope with the disappointment,' said Helen, to Jemma, not to her father.

'Always remember you never have to do anything you don't want to do,' George reminded them. 'Have a good time.'

'Stick together,' said Marte. 'It's harder for a man to attack two girls at once.'

'Look after each other,' George said.

'We always do,' Jemma had assured them, winking at Helen and silently mouthing their secret code word: The Plan.

It was the end of winter, but in their ugly little room in Earl's Court the central heating brought the daily temperature up to midday under a desert sun. They sprawled in their underwear on the room's twin beds, which were covered in vomit-coloured chenille. No-one had warned them about England's love affair with central heating. They had brought no suitable clothes. They had expected to be cold.

Helen, cross-legged on the bed, was scanning the London papers for a place to buy a car. 'The Pushbike Song' was playing for the fourth time that day on their small transistor radio. They'd come all the way to England for the Beatles, the Stones, for Gerry and the Pacemakers, and an Australian pop song was on top of the English charts. It was as disappointing as the chenille which they had thought was exclusive to the beds of Siren's Rock.

Helen said it would be good if they had some boys to go with them to the car places, because boys knew about engines and things.

That was all it took. 'I wonder why neither of us has ever had a really serious boyfriend,' said Jemma dreamily. They were in a different hemisphere but they were listening to the same song and talking about the same old thing.

'Well, because we've had The Plan of course,' said Helen, who was tired and so hot her throat hurt.

'Yes, but The Plan only works when we're together,' said Jemma. 'And we've been separated for years.'

'That's true,' muttered Helen.

'I really thought I'd have a passionate affair with someone while I was away at uni,' mused Jemma. She lay splayed out on her back, fanning herself with the classifieds. 'Everyone kicked up their heels so much, you know, especially in the first year. Girls who had never been interested in boys at all, like all those Goody Gollies, they just went berserk while they were staying in the colleges.'

'But they weren't all madly having sex,' said Helen, who hadn't gone to university but had heard all this before. 'Not the Goody Gollies. I don't believe it.'

'No, probably not, but there were plenty of wild parties with lots of drinking and groping,' grinned Jemma. 'I don't know, maybe they were having sex. None of them got pregnant, anyway.'

In Siren's Rock, girls who had sex before they were married almost invariably became pregnant and quietly disappeared for months or even years. 'You always know which girls go all the way,' Helen had told Marte whom she'd visited frequently while they were both desperately missing Jemma. 'They're the ones who wear leopard-skin boots. At school they were the ones who sat up the back of the bus on sport days and let boys feel them up through the pockets of their shorts. They thought the rest of us didn't notice.'

Helen, lolling in her undies on the bed, wished they didn't have to talk about sex. It had all been said already and all the talk in the world made no difference in the end.

'At least with The Plan,' said Helen, 'we've never had to worry about wearing shorts with pockets.'

★ ★ ★

They had both learned a valuable lesson from the episode at Mermaid Cove. In the months following their reconciliation Jemma had talked around it from time to time, stalking the subject like a cat prowling around a grounded bird. Confused. Wondering.

Helen was uncomfortably aware that Jemma couldn't let it go; that Jemma was desperate for a reason for Helen's behaviour on the beach, so that she could continue to love her and be her friend.

'I like it when boys cuddle me,' Helen told Jemma when they were sixteen. 'I like being touched.' It had taken her six months to unwillingly work it out for herself and another six months to find the courage to say it out loud.

Jemma was shocked, as Helen knew she would be. She stopped walking — they were on their way to Helen's, to do some history homework together — and folded her arms around herself as if she had felt a cold wind.

'You could get yourself into trouble feeling that way,' Jemma said anxiously.

'I know,' said Helen. After a while, she added: 'It's not as if I *want* to feel like it. I just *do*.'

There was a very long pause while Jemma absorbed and classified this information.

Finally, Helen said hesitantly, 'You give boys the wrong impression too, you know. By looking at them the way you do. And walking the way you do. I know you don't mean to, but you do. Like me. It's just the way we are.'

'I know,' said Jemma. 'I'm trying to stop.'

Helen was surprised. 'You know?'

Jemma looked embarrassed. She started walking again, very fast. Helen had to skip a bit to keep up. 'I was looking at the way ghastly Gail Farthing walks . . .' said Jemma. 'And I thought she reminded me of someone . . . and I realised it was me. And I talked a bit to Mum as well. What do you think I should do?'

'It's not really your fault,' said Helen. 'It's your shape. You have such a beautiful body. People get the wrong idea. Because you're so . . . you know . . . so Sophia.'

Jemma knew.

That was the day when she came up with The Plan.

They were in Helen's room, homework completed and so free to talk for one more hour.

'It's funny how I understand the effect boys have on you and you understand the effect I have on boys, but neither of us understands ourselves,' said Jemma.

'Hilarious,' said Helen, who didn't think Jemma had the faintest understanding of the effect boys had on her or she on them.

'I've thought of a plan,' said Jemma. 'We should put it into action now and follow it until we get married.'

'This sounds serious.'

Jemma took a deep breath. 'I'll save you from yourself if you'll save me from the boys,' she said.

Helen didn't know what she meant.

'I'll give you the signal if I think you're doing too much snuggling and heading for trouble,' said Jemma. 'Or I'll just say: "Hey, Julie! The Plan!" And you mustn't get hurt or offended. You have to remember I'll be doing it For Your Own Good.'

Helen made a small doubtful noise.

'And you can tell me if I'm being a tease. Leading boys on. Looking tarty. You know what I mean. Remember how you saved me at St Patrick's? All you have to say is: "Sophia! The Plan!" '

Helen was dubious. But Jemma always had the best ideas.

'Okay,' said Helen.

'Give me a hug,' said Jemma. 'That'll make it official.'

Helen laughed. 'You don't like hugging.'

'Well, I'd rather hug than slit a vein and mix our blood.'

Helen relaxed against the warmth of her friend's soft bosom and strong arms. Jemma felt tense, clasping her friend's skinny frame, uncomfortably aware of her breasts squashed against Helen's, but she hung in there and held on for a decent interval. Gradually, and with difficulty, Jemma was beginning to understand Helen's hunger.

From then on, at the town hall dances, at the movies, at beach parties, even at their high school farewell formal, whenever Helen talked to a boy for too long, Jemma would hover into view, opening her eyes very wide, soundlessly mouthing 'The Plan', sucking in her lips over the capital P. Or she would simply smile. And Helen would be reminded of her weakness and would meekly move away, out of range, out of danger.

In return Helen would sometimes say to Jemma: 'Not that skirt, I don't think.' Or: 'Check the back view in those pants.' But on almost every occasion, Jemma would look so hurt that Helen hated herself for saying anything at all and she soon gave it up.

In any case, time and nature combined forces to save Jemma more effectively than Helen. As she grew taller, her curves became softer and more subtle. Jemma's appearance would always be teasing to men and pleasing to women, but while she still walked as if she owned the world, the strut slowly disappeared from her stride.

Helen, too, moved more gracefully now. Her little-girl stick figure had filled out and softened. She rarely hunched her narrow shoulders; she had a neat, compact frame and her small waist accentuated her breasts and bottom. When the two friends walked into the school hall to have their photos taken before their farewell formal, Helen in pink chiffon, Jemma in tangerine taffeta — 'All Dressed Up Like Sore Toes,' Jemma had whispered to Helen out of the side of her mouth — a murmur of admiration rose from the knot of teachers and parents who had gathered to congratulate the graduating class.

SEPARATION

'Why?' asked Douglas Winter, when Helen asked him if she could go away to university.

'University costs money,' said her father, swollen in his armchair, squinting at Helen through a stream of smoke. He had become much thicker and wider during his years at Siren's Rock and he had recently begun smoking cigars. Even Babs wrinkled her elegant nose at the smell, which seeped into the rose-patterned carpet and hung around in the curtains for days.

'We never suggested you should go to university,' he rumbled, picking bits of cigar off his tongue, examining them, finally glancing back at Helen over his glasses.

'I've been in the top five in my class every year,' said Helen. 'I've won a Commonwealth Scholarship. It will cost you nothing.'

'Don't speak to me as if I am an imbecile, young lady,' said Douglas. 'Who would pay for your food and accommodation? Are you seriously suggesting your mother and I should continue to keep you for another three years?'

'A lot of parents do,' said Helen.

'A lot of parents don't,' said her father.

'I could get a job,' said Helen. 'I could work my way through. Pay you back as I went.'

Douglas chuckled without moving his eyes. 'Tell me about your wide work experience,' he said. 'Tell me when you have ever earned your own money, not counting stealing my change.'

'Daddy, I was *eight*,' said Helen, failing in a feeble effort not to sound desperate.

'Yes,' said Douglas, 'Now you're what — seventeen? And not much smarter from what I've seen. Until you're twenty-one you'll do as I say.

'Girls don't need a university education,' he added, raising his newspaper, shutting her out with a shake and a crackle.

'Jemma's going,' said Helen. '*Her* parents can afford it.' She looked straight at her mother and took a calculated risk. 'Even though her mum is our cleaner.'

She lost. Her mother looked straight back at her. 'That's the best reason of all why you shouldn't go,' she said coolly.

Helen couldn't think of anything else to say.

'Daddy has already agreed with me that you should do a secretarial course at Miss Sweeney's here in town,' Babs continued. She was sewing some lace onto the collar of one of Joy's frocks. 'A year of that and you'll be able to earn your own living.'

'And then you certainly can start paying us back for all that we've done for you,' said her father from behind his newspaper.

'So all that studying was for nothing,' said Helen.

'It was your choice,' said her mother. 'We never expected you to be clever.'

Helen hated it when her mother was right.

★ ★ ★

On their last afternoon together before Jemma left for university at Wentworth, on the other side of the Great Dividing Range, she and Helen went to Mermaid Cove. Summer was preparing to leave and autumn was mumbling around, ready to move in with its little puffs of cool wind and moody squalls of rain.

'Remember when your oldies said we could never be friends again?' said Jemma, as they set out for a walk along the shore. 'And then we made up and they hardly noticed?' she went on. 'Now it's changed *again*. Your mother likes me now and *my* mother can't stand me any more.'

'That's ridiculous, Sophia,' smiled Helen. 'Your mother adores you and you know it. And my mother *doesn't* like you — she *endures* you. She's thrilled that you're going away. She knows that will make me unhappy. That's, you know, her idea of bliss.'

'I'm sure she loves you deep down, Julie ...' Jemma stopped, for once short of anything else to say.

'I know it's one of God's commandments,' Jemma resumed when they had walked a bit further. 'Honour thy father and mother. But it's getting to be a real challenge. If it wasn't for leaving you, I'd be glad I'm getting away for a while.'

Jemma often talked about God when they were at the beach, as though He lived in a heavenly weekender near the sea. Jemma's God ran the world according to the commandments she had learned in Sunday School. As Jemma and her parents only went to church at Easter and Christmas, and occasionally for weddings, christenings and funerals, Helen often wondered how Jemma's faith in God had become so strong and, considering her cynicism on so many other subjects, so unquestioning.

'I'll show her,' Jemma went on. 'I'm going to have a brilliant career and everyone is going to know who I am and if Mum and Dad don't like it they can lump it. They can lump *me*.'

Helen nodded solemnly. Helen and Jemma both knew quite well that whatever Jemma did, her parents would always adore her. Lumping was not an option.

'If God can really see everything,' said Helen, 'He would know why I hate my father. He would understand.'

Yes, thought Jemma, and He would want you to forgive him. But she kept quiet.

Everyone thought Helen was such a sweet girl, thought Jemma. But she wasn't really sweet at all. Intelligent, considerate and incredibly loyal, yes. Tolerant and an excellent listener, certainly. But not sweet and not simple. And she was becoming increasingly inflexible about the things she believed. She had even argued with George and Marte about the Vietnam War. Not rudely of course. Helen was never loud or rude. But in her soft husky voice, she made no bones about the fact that she thought the Australians had no business being there. Helen was nobody's sweet girl.

Jemma had decided to major in English literature and philosophy, and chose psychology as one of her additional courses — a subject which gave her startling new insights into character and personality.

In September, after her first semester, she came home confused. 'With your history, you should hate men,' she told Helen.

'Life's a riddle,' said Helen lightly. She had read some of the psychology books on Jemma's study list and her conclusions were that self-analysis was a self-indulgent activity from which she had learned nothing that common sense had not already told her.

But Jemma absorbed it all like a sponge. That first year she joined the university drama club and the debating team, and consumed every book she laid her hands on. And each class, each new opportunity to learn or shine, fuelled her ambition. Somehow in the future she would combine it all — her acting talent, her speaking and writing ability, her interest in psychology and philosophy. She wasn't sure how it would all come together, but it would. Recognition was waiting just around the corner.

Jemma's new academic interests directed her intelligence away from the subject of boys and falling in love. She made many friends of both sexes at Wentworth, but apart from some amorous scuffles at the end of uni balls and some occasional groping when everyone had drunk too much at Flaherty's bar, her early sexual potential remained unfulfilled.

Meanwhile, Helen had made friends with the other girls in her secretarial course. Occasionally she went out with them but she spent most evenings reading in the poor light from the frilly lamp in her room. Unless Jemma was home, she avoided boys and men altogether. Going out was no fun without Jemma and, besides, nobody asked her.

Occasionally, when Jemma was home for the holidays, they borrowed Marte's indestructible Austin and drove up the coast to Berry Beach, a resort two hours' drive from Siren's Rock, which had a couple of motels and a night club. They sunned themselves on the beach in the day and did a little dancing at night. Boys approached them, bought them drinks, asked them to accompany them onto the beach or up to their bedrooms. But Jemma and Helen, true to The Plan, chatted and flirted but returned to their rooms alone.

They still liked the drive-in best.

After a year, Helen finished her course, passing her examinations with ease, and found a job as secretary to a man who made curtains and covered furniture, doing the correspondence and the books. She paid her parents board and lodging and spent the rest of her meagre salary on movie tickets and books.

She read history, biographies and whole collections of classics, often going all the way to Bridgetown on the bus to raid the library there — the trip took an entire Saturday but she had nothing else to do. A lonely eighteen-year-old girl waiting for time to pass, she escaped into those other worlds, gratefully leaving herself far behind.

Jemma didn't fall in love at university, but in the middle of her third year, Alex Kouros, with his single luxuriant eyebrow and liquid-velvet eyes, fell in love with her. 'It's the Greek connection,' she explained to Helen when she brought him home during the holidays. 'He thinks we have something in common, because of my grandmother.'

'He's lovely,' said Helen. 'I'm so happy for you.'

'Good grief, don't say it like that,' said Jemma. 'You sound as if we're going to get married or something.'

'Are you?'

'Don't be stupid, Helen,' said Jemma crossly. 'You know I'm not marrying anybody until you and I have been around the world and I've done everything I want to do.'

Helen hated herself for feeling relieved.

'How's The Plan going?' Helen asked.

She was sitting on the edge of the bath at Jemma's house, while Jemma perched on the closed toilet seat. The girls were keeping their voices low to prevent the hapless Alex from hearing his future being discussed over the guest towels and fish-shaped soap in Marte's frantically tiled bathroom.

'We're fine with that,' said Jemma, very pleased to be able

to provide a one hundred per cent pure report. 'He knows the rules.'

'Which are?'

'The same ones I gave you. No tongue. No touching the boobs or anything below the waist. No lying down.'

'And Alex has agreed to all this, has he?' asked Helen, incredulous.

'Yep. Do you really think he's lovely? I am trying to think of a nice way I could suggest he could shave between his eyebrows. What do you think?'

Helen started to laugh and slid helplessly into the empty bath, her legs sticking up in the air over her head.

'I think it's a good thing you're not going to marry him,' she spluttered, making such a terrible noise that Marte came to the door to see if she was choking.

After fourteen frustrating months, Alex eventually dropped Jemma for a girl without rules. When Jemma came home she didn't seem too distraught. What it amounted to, she said, was that you could only do a certain amount of kissing and hugging before it all got a bit boring.

Helen was quieter than usual that summer. She didn't ask many questions about Alex, seemed to be consciously avoiding the subject of love and romance. Jemma assumed this was out of deference to her own wounded feelings and was grateful.

In any case, they talked of little else other than their trip. It was to be their last Siren's Rock summer and they were working hard and saving every cent they could. Jemma worked for her Uncle Theo at his fruit shop. Uncle Theo, who looked just like George, only scaled up by two sizes, said his profits soared every university holidays because people would come in just to watch Jemma weigh the fruit and see her smile.

When Theo told Jemma she could have the Australia Day weekend off, she suggested to Helen that they go to Berry Beach, and was surprised when Helen angrily refused.

'We're supposed to be saving up,' snapped Helen, knowing that no matter how much Marte and George would miss Jemma, they would dip into their precious bank account if she couldn't save enough. 'And anyway, we're too old for that now, Jemma.'

'Too old to go to the beach?' asked Jemma innocently.

'Too old to chase boys,' said Helen, 'especially when we're not offering anything.'

Jemma frowned. 'That's a funny way of looking at it,' she said. 'At uni I had heaps of boys who were just *friends,* you know. I never even had sex with Alex and . . .'

'And he dropped you for someone who did,' said Helen.

Suddenly, surprisingly, Jemma's eyes filled with tears. Helen was ashamed. Taut with remorse, she moaned and put her arms around Jemma, trying to hug away the hurt.

'I'm sorry, Sophia,' she said. 'That was a horrible thing to say. I just meant — it's just not worth it.'

'What's happened to you?' said Jemma, sniffing loudly and wriggling out of Helen's arms.

But Helen just shook her cloud of hair and, wiping the back of her hand vigorously across her runny nose, said again: 'It's just not worth it.'

THE TWO-MAN TENT

Exciting as it was to be in London, they were soon keen to leave. The income from their casual jobs was barely enough to live on, let alone augment their holiday savings. The traffic worried them and the streams of people depressed them, as did the grey skies. They were not city girls.

On a misty May morning, with their jacket collars turned up against the stiff spring breeze and the skin on their faces marbling with the chill, they watched their lumpy little car being lifted in a sling onto a ferry headed for Stavanger. They were on their way. The European adventure had begun.

Norway literally took away their breath. In Sweden, the darkly forested mountains gave way to cultivated slopes and tidy cities, where blonde men and women with glowing skin impressed them almost as much as the Scandinavian fjords. Eventually they steered Horace the Morris onto the sleek black motorways which led them into the heart of Europe.

They took it in turns to drive as they made their way through Germany, the Netherlands and Belgium into France, enjoying a succession of glorious picnics. When they arrived at each new campsite, they would pitch their tiny tent, set themselves up and wash out their underwear in a variety of sinks and tubs ranging from ancient stone to stainless steel. Then they would cook, look, learn, talk, eat, drink and often sing — Neil Diamond, Simon and Garfunkel, Seekers songs and, sooner or later, 'House of the Rising Sun'. Often the talking and drinking and singing lasted into the early hours of the morning.

Sometimes, depending on the amount of wine or beer or sangria consumed, they would tangle arms and legs with the guitar players or the occasional eager local boy. But there had been no night yet when they had not ended up back in their two-man tent without a man. Just Jemma and Helen. The way it had always been.

Helen saw him first, loping from the toilet block to his battered van, just before midday in a huge and crowded campsite outside Paris. They had been there for a few days, having decided to stay as long as it took to see the world's most beautiful city.

'Look at that,' Helen said to Jemma, as they stood side by side over a broad concrete tub, vigorously scrubbing their jeans in the sunshine. 'You'd swear that specimen was straight out of Siren's Rock.'

Jemma followed her gaze. 'My God,' she said. 'A blond-headed, stompie wompie, real gone surfer boy.'

Grezza was bone thin and brown as beer, the sunburnt skin on his skinny arms, legs and chest punctuated with scaly patches of peel. His shabby singlet and loose shorts were far too big for him. His stiff, matted yellow hair had not seen a comb for many months.

Sensing their stare, he glanced over at them, stopped and changed direction, loping towards them with a grin of delight. He had white teeth, although not enough of them, and wide, pale blue eyes, the irises framed by roadmaps of red, the lashes astonishingly thick.

'Gidday girls,' said Grezza, staring at Jemma. 'What are two beautiful birds like youse doin' in a place like this?'

'We were just saying you had to be Australian,' said Jemma.

'Like us,' said Helen reassuringly.

Grezza smiled briefly at Helen but returned his gaze to Jemma and was hooked. To give him credit, she said later, it was her face he kept staring at, and not her boobs. Which made a change.

In fact Grezza was from Perth, or a small country community a few hundred miles away, which on the other side of the world seemed like almost the same thing. He had been on the road for more than a year, he told them, travelling mainly on his own, although he had recently hooked up with a bunch of wankers who also came from Western Australia.

'They're morons,' he said amiably, 'but they're my mates so I have to look after 'em. And what about youse girls?' he asked, scratching pieces of peeling skin from his concave chest. 'Do a bit of surfin', do ya? Been down to Biarritz yet? That's where I'm headin'. Haven't got high hopes for a decent wave, but. Youse are lookin' pretty brown,' he continued thoughtfully. 'Both of youse,' he added, finally turning his gaze from Jemma to Helen. 'Yep,' he said, reassured by his inspection. 'Youse'd both be a glorious sight on any beach. Tell ya what. Come over to me van and have a beer. I'm as dry as an Arab's fart.'

They went, because it was nice to hear an accent from home, and because he amused them. They introduced themselves as Sophia and Julie and were impressed when he remarked that Helen looked just like the bird in *Doctor*

Zhivago, had anyone told her that before? As it turned out, the 'morons' were all sleeping off a large night on the vin rouge, so the girls and Grezza ended up on the banks of the Seine, drinking their beers on a stone wall, their faces tilted up to catch the sun. Grezza entertained them with tales of his travels, which were all the more appealing because of what Helen called his quaintly antipodean turn of phrase — 'Jeez, Julie, did you swallow a dictionary when you were a kid?' — and his old-fashioned manners, a legacy from life in a rural community.

Gradually, during the following days and weeks, Grezza, with his awful hair, his gap-toothed smile and his constantly moulting skin, somehow crawled beneath their guard and became their friend. Crazy, crass, but oddly courteous, he had a way of gazing frankly into their eyes and telling them about his family, his father's farm or some adventure he had just had, with a beguiling enthusiasm neither of them had any desire to resist.

As they drove down through France, the sight of his battered blue and pink Kombi, with its curving boomerang painted on the rear window, was a sight they always looked for when they drove into a camp, particularly in the larger cities. Occasionally, after a night at the campsite bar, he became sentimental with Helen ('I think I'm in love with Sophia, Julie, but I'm not in her class') and tried on many of these occasions to persuade Helen to comfort him. 'Jeez, Julie,' he whined, 'what's the harm in a bit of a kiss and cuddle?' But unfortunately for Grezza, he was not the sort of boy for whom The Plan was needed.

Jemma and Helen were as happy as they had been during their first long hot summer in Siren's Rock. Happier, as there were no rules, no restrictions, no parents, no punishments. Nothing could detract from the excitement of being free and on the road. Not frustration, nor fatigue, nor their occasional disagreements; not sudden floods nor limited funds.

Their only real problem, as it grew warmer, was the two-man tent. By the time they had crossed into Spain and come out on the Mediterranean, summer was spreading a clear sheet of intense heat across the European continent and Jemma's claustrophobic thrashing about nearly drove them both crazy at night.

'I've never been this hot in my life,' said Jemma crossly, 'and I never want to be this hot again.'

They found refuge in a camping ground above Cannes, where they pitched their tent in a sloping vineyard in the path of a cooling breeze. It was pleasant and quiet — there was no sign of Grezza and they both slept soundly for the first time in many nights.

On their last evening there they became involved in a long and intense debate about women's liberation with a group of American girls, two of whom unsettled them by holding hands all night and occasionally nuzzling each other's necks.

While Jemma kept her gaze rigidly averted, and Helen looked on with interest, they argued about a variety of issues, including not only equal pay and a woman's right to have a career, but abortion on demand, women who loved women and the advantages of divorce.

Jemma was uncomfortable all night. She agreed with almost nothing the Americans said and she was far from oblivious to their scorn when they discovered she had not yet read *The Female Eunuch*.

But worse than any of this was the revelation that neither Jemma nor Helen had ever gone bra-less.

After all, Helen tried to point out, they came from Siren's Rock, a town where you could get a reputation by wearing shorts with pockets.

'My *God*!' shrieked the loudest American, who said her name was River. ('I bet she made it up,' said Jemma later.) 'Next thing you'll be tellin' us you're *virgins*!'

They had all doubled up with laughter, even Jemma and Helen.

'I want to ask you something,' said Helen the next morning, carefully negotiating a curve. They were heading towards Monaco on a dappled coastal road, fringed and shaded by delicate foliage and dignified trees. 'With Alex . . . did he ever make you feel, you know, out of control?'

'Nope,' said Jemma. 'I was tempted with Alex, but I had good willpower and he knew the rules.'

'Always?'

'Yep,' said Jemma. She was embarrassed at the incredulity on Helen's face. 'Why would I want to be out of control?'

Helen said nothing.

Jemma sighed and hugged her breasts tightly. 'Okay, Julie,' she said softly. 'You mean what would it be like for us if there was no Plan? No *thinking* all the time about what might happen? I don't know,' she admitted with a sigh.

'It might hurt,' said Helen.

'Not if you're really, truly in love,' said Jemma, 'as opposed to pashing on with guys who stick their tongues down your throat.'

'Experienced a few tongues, have you, Sophia?' Helen smiled faintly.

Jemma sat up and pulled a face.

'Haven't you noticed it's the first thing they try?' she asked. 'As if they think we actually enjoy having a bit of their floppy wet flesh in our mouths? And we've both had our tits groped. I know yours aren't as big as mine,' she

152

added, 'but they're a lovely shape and I bet plenty have tried. It's the next thing they do after the tongue.'

Helen no longer looked amused. 'I mean,' said Jemma, noticing the expression on Helen's face, 'we're over twenty-one now. We're not innocent little Siren's Rock girls any more.'

'Well . . .' said Helen.

'Alex was nice to cuddle,' Jemma went on. 'I just didn't love him enough to have sex with him. But one day we'll both meet one special boy — man really — and with him it will be different.'

'That's what you've decided, is it, Sophia?' asked Helen.

'Yes it is, Julie.'

'*Neither* of us likes all that sexual stuff?'

'No, we don't. I know you're more tactile than I am. But *neither* of us really enjoys overt and unsolicited sexual pressure.'

'*Tactile*, Sophia?' said Helen. '*Overt* and *unsolicited* sexual pressure?'

'Tactile, yes,' Jemma was defensive but firm. 'And unsolicited sexual stuff.'

'Well . . .' said Helen.

'When we're truly in love, we'll be mad for it,' said Jemma.

'That's what will happen?' asked Helen.

'That's what happens,' said Jemma. 'That's why we're on the Pill. Just in case we do find true love and we have to abandon The Plan.'

'Well . . .' said Helen.

'Forewarned is forearmed,' Jemma added.

Self-consciously they both glanced down. They had begun the day's journey out of harness, their breasts free beneath their T-shirts. Jemma, who was in a considerable amount of pain, was relieved that it was Helen's turn to drive. At least she could sit in the passenger seat and fold her arms.

'It feels quite nice,' said Helen after a while. 'The way the cotton brushes the nipples. It's sort of sexy.'

'God, Julie, is there anything in the world that doesn't turn you on?' asked Jemma, wincing. 'Every time we go over a bump it hurts.'

Helen slowed down and pulled over with a small spurt of gravel. 'I know,' she said. 'It's even hurting me a bit. Put your bra back on.'

'No, I think we should stick it out for at least a day,' Jemma said bravely. 'We can hardly say we've gone bra-less if we put the bloody things back on again after an hour.'

Helen made no move to start the car. They sat for a few seconds in silence.

'Helen,' said Jemma suddenly, quietly, sounding unusually feeble. 'Can I ask *you* something now?'

'Of course,' she said.

'Do you think we're *normal*?' asked Jemma.

'Of course we're normal,' said Helen as she glanced down at the string of beaches clinging like a necklace to the cliffs below. 'What on earth do you mean?'

Jemma's cheeks grew red. 'Helen,' she said, staring ahead, 'did you ever wonder if we might be ... lesbians? I mean, without either of us realising it?'

Helen stared at her friend for a second before she tipped her head back against the seat and shrieked with laughter.

'All right, all right,' said Jemma, crossly. 'It's just what those girls were doing last night ... and I was thinking just then about how I *did* get bored kissing Alex and how I *could* always stop him from going too far ... and Grezza keeps throwing himself at us and we always turn him down.'

Helen looked across at Jemma's flushed, unhappy face. Her hair was sticking to her neck. 'That's because Grezza has as much sex appeal as an old shoe and frequently smells like one,' she said.

Jemma still looked miserable, so Helen arranged her face into an expression of sympathy. But it was too hard. She was overcome with laughter once more.

'All *right*!' said Jemma.

Without warning Helen reached over and slowly slid the back of her slim brown hand over the swell of Jemma's breast.

Jemma flinched and pushed the hand away. 'Don't!'

Helen grinned. 'Doesn't turn you on, Jem?'

'No.'

Helen shook her head and turned the key in the ignition. 'Jemma, for pity's sake,' she said in exasperation as she steered Horace the Morris back onto the road. '*Think* about it.'

After a while, gathering speed and hitting the potholes again, she muttered: 'You *really* need a man.'

After a while, Jemma replied: 'Well, anyway, *that's* not true. I like being free! I don't care if we *are* the only two virgins over twenty-one in the whole world!'

Helen kept her eyes on the road.

THE DRIVE-IN

It was the first secret she had ever kept from Jemma, if you didn't count that business between her and Daddy. And as for that, the older she got the more she wondered what she'd been so hung up about anyway. She'd read enough now to realise that lots of girls and even boys had been touched — and much worse — by men. Even men in their families. *Usually* men in their families. Not that Jemma would have understood that.

Touched, that's all it had been with Helen, anyway. It wasn't as if she had been raped.

And sooner or later, when you grew up, just about everyone got screwed as well.

It was no big deal, she thought, pulling down the blind.

Well, for Jemma, it was a big deal. Jemma truly believed that sex was something sacred to two people who had vowed before God to be together forever. But Jemma's God was the sort of God whose rules you would *want* to respect. Anyone lucky enough to be loved by Jemma would be grateful to God for the rest of their lives. Helen had always known that.

Anyway, for most people, sex is just something you do. Like eating or drinking. You do it and then it's over and that's that. That's what Helen the cynic told Helen the saint.

John had come back the year before, because his dad had died.

The Sullivans still owned the house in Fielders Road, which had stood empty for years, with the windows boarded up and slabs of corrugated iron coming off the roof and thrashing up and down with an awful eerie sound whenever there was a strong wind. The aunt had sent him to have a look at it with a view to selling it if he could. His father had been dead for less than a week when he left the city and headed for Siren's Rock, and the grief and strain did not begin to affect him — hurting his eyes, squeezing his throat — until he stood outside his old home, in the middle of the empty street. Other parts of Siren's Rock had grown and changed over the years he'd been away, but here in Fielders Road it was as if time had stood still.

For a while he thought about his father. But not long after he stepped warily into his past she was there, bursting into his memories in full colour, turning the images of his family into silent sepia.

Jemma.

He went to her parents' house, looking for her. She was in Wentworth, of course, and so were Marte and George. They had gone up to see her in a play at the university and were spending a few days there. Helen had been invited to go too, but she had to work — that particular Saturday she had been called in to do a stocktake. Babs and Douglas had taken Joy and a friend to see a show in Bridgetown, to celebrate Joy's birthday the week before. Helen had just arrived home when the doorbell rang.

She opened the front door with her neat black shoes in her hand.

She didn't recognise him, but he knew her straight away. Her small face was framed by a fat cloud of fair hair, her short black skirt revealed her pretty legs, her white shirt was crisp and smart. She was as neat as she had been as a child. And in her brown eyes was the same wariness, the same impenetrable sorrow.

The locals had been right after all. He had grown into a very big young man. Tall, broad-shouldered, solid, handsome, he filled the front doorway and blocked out the sun. He still looked all brown, even in a white open-necked shirt and black slacks. He stared at her and she smiled politely and said: 'Can I help you?' She thought he might be a Jehovah's Witness. Or a Mormon who had wickedly taken his jacket off.

It was only when he said: 'Helen?' and smiled and his eyes crinkled up that she realised who he was.

She didn't know whether to hug him or to hold out her hand. He stood there, smiling at her, his arms hanging awkwardly at his sides. Eventually they had left it too long to touch, so she told him to come in and he stepped into the Winters' carpeted hall.

'I don't believe it,' Helen kept murmuring as she took him into the kitchen and poured him a glass of lemonade. She felt her heart ricochet in her chest. 'You're so huge!' she said, smiling at him.

'You're so pretty,' said John in a deep voice which he had not acquired when he left town at the age of thirteen. She was pretty! He thought she was pretty! But she had a cold sore on her lip! She put her fingers over it and raised her eyes to his face. What had happened to his funny teeth? Now they were so straight and white.

'And what about Jemma?' said John. 'I bet she is absolutely gorgeous!'

Helen's heart lobbed slowly back into place and was still. Her legs steadied and became flesh and bone again. She smiled at him and took her hand away from her mouth.

'Yes,' she said. 'She *is* beautiful.'

And after that they sat on the verandah and watched the sun go down over the roof tops of Siren's Rock, and talked about Jemma.

When she had finally finished telling him all that he wanted to know, but felt she had still not satisfied his desire to know more, to know *everything,* she offered to cook him dinner. Instead he suggested they find somewhere to eat down in the town. 'Is there anywhere these days?' he asked. 'Other than the Coffee Pot?'

They decided to go to the new Chinese restaurant in Malley Street. Helen had not been brave enough to ask for time to get changed, so she went in her work clothes. She put her shoes back on as they were leaving, and John laughed.

'Remember the day we met?' he asked. 'When Jemma made you take off your shoes so she could train you to walk bare-footed? And she made you do it there and then, on the boiling hot tar?'

'I can't believe you remember that.'

'I remember everything,' said John. 'I remember everything I ever did with Jemma.'

John drove them the short distance to the restaurant in his Holden; it was an old car, but well kept. When they arrived they ordered chicken chow mein and sweet and sour pork and John asked the waiter to bring the wine list. Helen was astonished and impressed. This was a degree of sophistication not common in Siren's Rock. John poured them both a glass of spumante straight away. The bubbles went up Helen's nose. She wasn't used to it.

'I can't believe you were that skinny kid,' she said. 'John Sullivan. Vice captain of the Wildcats.'

But he looked suddenly sadder now and he only smiled a little. 'I can't believe it either,' he said.

They looked at each other for a while without speaking.

'Do you want to tell me about your dad?' she asked.

'Not really.'

But he did. With his eyes on the tablecloth at first, but eventually looking up more often, he told her everything.

Big Joe had been killed in a road accident. His was the only car involved; it was found rammed into a telegraph pole. All those years on the road and it was the first accident he'd ever had. John looked at the tablecloth and fidgeted. Helen waited. Actually, there had been a post mortem. His father had had cancer. Not in his bones, like John's mother, but in his stomach. It had cast some doubt on the cause of death. He looked at her.

'He was a Catholic,' he said defensively. 'He wouldn't do that. No matter how ill he was.'

'No,' said Helen. 'Of course not.'

John drank a glass of wine in one go and put the glass down loudly on the table. He met her eyes again. So he was more distressed about his father's death than he had seemed earlier. Well, obviously. The man had only died on Monday. Today was Saturday. She wondered why he hadn't stayed in the city, with his family, his sisters, his aunt. Why come tooling all the way up here?

Surely not to find Jemma? What did he think Jemma would say or do to help him? After all these years?

He changed the subject suddenly, asked her how her parents were and how they were treating her 'these days'.

She looked into his face to see what he was really asking. Remembered with a slightly nauseous feeling how much he knew about her own life as a child. How much he knew and how much he had guessed. She had forgotten all that. Pulled down the blind. Turned out the light.

We're just pretending, thought Helen. This is not a nice normal reunion of two childhood friends.

She remembered what he had said about his father being a good man, except for the alcohol. That was the difference between his father and hers. What she didn't know was whether John was sad because his father had been cruel to him, or because he had loved his father and now he was dead, or because his father might have killed himself. How could she know that?

All she knew was that John was hurting. She recognised it, felt it, almost smelled the hurt in him. Knew the effort he was making to keep it under control.

The pleasure of his company cut out. She had always been inarticulate under pressure. Now she had no idea what to say or how to talk to him. He was looking at her desperately, waiting for a reply. There had been a question. She couldn't remember what it was. Oh yes. How her parents were treating her 'these days'.

She lowered her head and fiddled with her cutlery — chopsticks were unheard of in Siren's Rock. 'My parents are fine,' she muttered. 'They don't ...' She stopped. What should she say? They don't cane me any more? They don't like me very much? They don't ... what didn't her parents do? They had fed her, clothed her, and paid for her to spend a year learning how to be a secretary. Her father had spoken to the man in the curtain shop about considering her for a job. Her mother was teaching her to sew. Why should she allow John to go on suspecting her parents were monsters when in fact they were perfectly normal people? When the only one in the family who was a bit strange was Helen herself?

'What's wrong?' asked John. 'What don't they do?' But then the food came.

They began to eat in silence. John kept filling their glasses with the fizzy wine. After a while he began talking again. He told her what he'd been doing, what it had been like at boarding school and how much he had hated it at first. Football had saved him, in the end, football and growing too big to be bashed or teased.

'Did you see Jemma in the play?' asked Helen. 'Did you see her as Bottom? She was so wonderful.'

He smiled. 'I saw her,' he said. 'She was wonderful all right.' But that was all he had to say on the subject.

He told her he was studying engineering at Sydney University. He shared a house with some other students because his aunt had her hands full with the girls. She was a good woman who had done more than her Christian duty, taking on all of his sisters. Robbie lived in a flat, but not with John. He had gone off the rails for a while but seemed all right now. Rob was at uni too. In his first year of engineering. It must be in the blood.

The more he talked, the faster he ate and the more he drank. He ordered another bottle of wine and swigged it like water. Their eyes, two shades of brown, moved around over their food and up again, their gazes shifting, colliding, shifting again. It seemed that no matter how hard they tried not to, they couldn't help looking helplessly at each other. He wants to get finished and get out of here, Helen thought. He wants to get away from me. He doesn't want me to see how sad he is. He doesn't want to know how sad I am. That's not why he came.

John gulped down the last of the wine and went to pay the bill at the big glittery cash register beside the fish tank. He swayed a little and Helen pretended not to notice. She went to the toilet and had trouble focusing on the mirror over the small sink. She realised she was drunk. Her face, surrounded by her circle of blonde hair, looked ashen. Her cold sore seemed to be bigger.

'Will I take you home now?' he asked, when they were both back in his car.

Now she couldn't bear the thought of leaving him. In Jemma's absence, she felt responsible. Jemma would not have sent him off alone on the night after his father's funeral.

But where to go? What to do?

'I don't know,' she said.

'There's never been much to do on a Saturday night at Siren's Rock, has there?' said John with a thin laugh.

'Just the drive-in,' said Helen. Oh God, what a stupid thing to say.

John turned on the engine.

They drove there in silence, arriving just as the second feature was beginning. John parked in the very back row, a long way from the other cars, with a curtain of bushland behind them.

He turned off the ignition and pulled on the handbrake. Didn't bother with the speaker box. Slid down in the bucket seat, turned his head, looked at her.

Shyly, Helen looked back. Slid down a little in her own seat, leaned her head back on the nice-smelling leather, her face turned towards his. Listened to herself breathing. It seemed to Helen that as each breath escaped from her lips it became a small fluttering creature, hovering between them. She wondered if he wanted to cry. How to tell him it would be okay. She would understand.

The moon made her blonde hair silver and her eyes were in shadow. 'I'm so sorry you've lost your dad,' said Helen at last in her husky, uncertain way. 'He was a good man underneath.'

John didn't answer or move. He just sat there, slumped in the seat, staring at her face, his eyes black in the dark. Tentatively, and without any idea why, she leaned across the gap in the seats and put her head against his chest.

'He loved you,' said Helen.

I'm not good at this, she thought. I don't know what to say.

When he began to shake, she slid her arms around his enormous shoulders and held him gently while big, heaving sobs were torn out of his body. He buried his head in her small shoulder and she held it there, made soothing noises, stroked the back of his neck. She felt his tears wetting her own neck and her chest pressing against his. She felt the gear stick jamming into her thigh and hurting like hell.

She held him until the sobs slowed and he was quiet and still.

In the years that followed, when she allowed herself to think about it again, she could never explain to Helen the cynic what she had had in mind when she suggested to him that they should get into the back seat.

Her motive was entirely pure. In the beginning she was convinced of that. The boy's heart was breaking, for pity's sake. She was incredibly uncomfortable, he was so heavy, the gear stick was sticking into her flesh ... there was nothing sensual in what they were doing. He hadn't kissed her ... she couldn't let him, even if he wanted to, because of the cold sore. Anyway, he didn't want to. He had simply clung to her and wept. And she, dry-eyed, had held him.

But then she had whispered: 'Let's get into the back.' Why had she done that?

She just wanted to be able to put her arms around him properly and hold him for as long as it took. Because he was so big, and the gear stick . . .

Sure, said Helen the cynic.

He sat up slowly and looked at her, and without waiting to discern the expression on his face — which was impossible anyway, because it was so dark — she opened her door, stepped out briefly into the night and moved into the back.

This is going to be really embarrassing if he doesn't get in here too.

But he did.

This time, without speaking a word, it was he who held her, wrapping his big arms around her. She realised he was going to kiss her and quickly turned her face away. He put his tear-damp face into the curve of her neck. His breath was warm and moist but he had stopped weeping.

After a while he slid his hands under the back of her white shirt where it had come untucked from her skirt. He sighed. I've made him feel better, thought Helen, and sighed too. He stroked her back, long fingers, grown-up hands that made her skin sing. A wonderful, unfamiliar song.

Beneath his hands, the skin on her back and shoulders hummed. His fingers were like a musician's on her flesh; the rest of her body begged to join in, clamoured for a part.

Gently he pushed her down and all she could feel were his hands, and all she could see were the shadows that hid his face as she lay back on the clean-smelling leather and wound her arms around his neck, sighing, skin singing.

He stroked her neck and the rest of her yearned to be touched that way as well, but she knew she mustn't let him kiss her. She had a cold sore and besides ... she couldn't let him anyway.

She had no idea how much time had passed, or when she became aware that his other hand was unbuttoning the front of her shirt. But she knew exactly when his hand slipped into her bra and touched her breast, because she was waiting for it, wanting to feel his fingers there. He caressed her gently. *You mustn't let him do that,* said Helen the cynic, as she raised herself up beneath him and pressed herself against his body.

She felt him shudder. He was sobbing again or perhaps he was just breathing very heavily. His hand spread across her back but her breast was left alone again. She wanted his hand back there. *Where has the hand gone?* His arm was down between them now, doing something to the front of his trousers.

It was only when he reached under her short black skirt and pulled down her panties in one quick, smooth movement, sliding them right down and over her feet — *How did he know how to do that? He's done this before* — that she knew it was time to stop. That she realised she didn't want this part of it at all. The top of her was singing but her lower body wasn't ready, her naked genitals were singularly unrehearsed. She didn't want to do this any more, not this way, not with this boy, someone she hardly knew any more. Not this boy who was pouring his grief into her because he couldn't find her friend.

'You save me from the boys and I'll save you from yourself,' the voices in her head chimed Jemma's words.

But how could she say no now? When it was she who had suggested getting into the back seat? When one of his arms was around her and the other was between her legs, a warm, sensitive, stroking hand, not digging, not punishing, not an uninvited crab crawling ... this was the hand of a friend who thought he was welcome. What should she say? How could she stop him without making him feel even worse than he already did?

He doesn't seem to be feeling quite so bad at this moment.

It's Jemma he wants, not you.

Jemma would never let him do this.

It's too late, thought Helen, as she panicked and stiffened. John didn't seem to notice. He was opening her up and easing himself in, and helplessly she let him enter her small private body, let him hurt her, gritted her teeth, held on to him tightly with both hands, desperate for the words that would stop him, biting her tongue so that she wouldn't cry out.

Nothing she had read in any book had prepared her for the pain of it, the force of it, the size of it, the time it took. When would it end? Would it ever end? Perhaps she would die here in agony, flat on her back in the back seat in the back row at the Siren's Rock drive-in theatre. A squaw, impaled beneath a big man.

'You're so huge!' That's what you said to him.

Agony, on and on. And only when he slid his hands from her back down to her bottom and, clasping each cheek, kneaded the soft flesh in time with each thrust, did she finally whimper: *'No'* and begin to cry.

He was drunk — had been drinking even before he arrived on her doorstep — but he was not beyond feeling. He heard her sob, and paused, finally stricken. Took one enormous breath and, with a terrible effort, forced himself to be still. For a few seconds the only sound in the car was Helen's stifled sobbing. Then he pulled away and there was a small sucking sound followed by Helen's gulping sigh of relief. The pain stopped immediately, but he was as heavy as lead and she was small and crushed beneath him.

Quickly he pulled up his trousers, sitting up to zip his fly. She took a huge breath. She heard herself whimper again.

John looked down at her, lying on the seat beside him, her legs now clamping tightly together. Gently he reached over and pulled her skirt down so that it covered her.

'My God, Helen,' he said in a cracked voice. 'What have I done?'

She tried to get up. He put his arms carefully around her, as if she were an invalid, and helped her into a sitting position.

'I'm so sorry,' he said. 'I'm so sorry. I never meant that to happen.'

The terrible, ridiculous, stupid thing was that as soon as his arms went around her again she wanted to cling to him. Wanted to feel his hands again. Wanted him to hold her and stroke her, to put his hands under her shirt again, *but not under the skirt*, wanted to feel his warm skin against hers.

But her crotch felt dry and sore and she didn't want any part of him there.

What is wrong with you?

He got out and went back around to the driver's seat. There was a long and terrible silence while she groped for her panties and pulled them on. Then she, too, climbed out of the car, stiffly, wondering if she could walk. She opened the front passenger door. As both car doors slammed, first the back one, then the front, a few wags tooted their horns. Helen felt sick.

They sat up straight and stared at the screen. She still had no idea what the movie was.

'You must hate me,' said John.

'No,' she replied. 'It was as much me as it was you.'

'I didn't mean *that* to happen,' he said. 'It was the last thing I had on my mind when I came to see you. I hope you believe that.'

'I believe you,' said Helen. 'Neither of us wanted that. It was just because ...' she sighed and her voice quivered. 'It was because we were both feeling sad.'

'You'll be all right, you know,' he said nervously. 'I didn't — I stopped in time. Before — you know.'

'I know,' said Helen.

He wouldn't have, though, said Helen the cynic. *He wasn't thinking about stopping at all — he only stopped because you bawled.*

Which was kind of him, said Saint Helen. *He was always kind.*

They sat in silence. Tears ran down her face. She wiped them away but they kept coming.

On the screen a man and a woman in evening dress were locked in a passionate embrace.

'Maybe we should just pretend it never happened,' said John at last.

On the screen the man and the woman drew apart, gazed into each other's eyes and then fell hungrily into another long and lingering kiss.

John started the engine. People hooted again. They left the drive-in as quietly as John could manage and then drove to Helen's house.

He stopped the car and, with an obvious effort, offered her his crinkly-eyed smile.

'Friends?'

'Friends,' she agreed softly. She opened the door and got out. She turned and poked her head back inside. 'Next time, come in the uni holidays,' she said. 'She'll be here then.'

He looked embarrassed. 'I don't know if we should tell her ...'

Helen forced a bright smile. 'You were never here.'

Now he looked even more uncomfortable. 'Um ... Helen? Could you write down her phone number for me? It's a long way if she's not around.'

Oh, I don't know. You could always screw her little friend rather than waste the trip.

He opened the glove box and pulled out a stained envelope with his own name and an address on the front, written in a childish hand. He smiled sheepishly. 'It's a letter she wrote to me when I was at St Pat's, just after my mum died,' he said. Helen held on to the car door and stared in. 'I never answered it,' John told her. 'The Brothers read everything we wrote. Anyway, I didn't know what to say. But I've kept it ever since.'

Helen took the envelope. 'For seven years?'

He sighed. 'Jemma said she thought I might be lonely. God, she was so right. I was sick with loneliness. I was like a fish out of water at that school. Jemma was the only one who understood.'

Helen leaned the envelope on the bonnet of the car, took a pen from her bag and wrote the Johnsons' number on the back. Her vagina felt raw and sore. She was desperate to get into a warm bath. 'It was kind of her,' she said. 'Jemma's a wonderful person.'

She walked stiffly up the steps to her house and opened the front door. It was unlocked; her family had come home. When she turned back to wave, the car was already pulling away from the kerb.

She stood in the hall in the sleeping house. Carpet on the floor. Soft lamp light on the table. Joy's cardigan tossed onto a chair. Ordinary life. Still going on.

You were never here.

She waited there, listening to the sound of his car fading into the night.

Part Four

GEORGE

Please rise, said the minister.

George Johnson stood. A big grey boulder in his bulky best suit, clasping his wife's hand. Marte, the magnificent woman he had married, was somehow shrunken now after her recent stroke. Her shoulders were shaking as she stood beside him, leaning heavily on her stick.

Small tremors of movement beat against his palm as Marte stifled her sobs, forcing her grief to remain at an acceptable level. They were all doing it, thought George. All through the church, soft, civilised sniffing punctuated the Reverend's remarks. Quiet Anglo-Saxon sobs, damp but muted, resonated around the pews.

George had been to many Greek funerals. This was not one of them. He was glad his mother had not lived to be here today. Maria had always grieved openly, loudly, passionately. George would have liked to mourn like that.

But George had done his weeping. He had wept for hour after hour. Today he felt empty. Bereft.

On the opposite side of the aisle, standing very straight, her puffy chest squeezed beneath her pale blue coat, her aged, powdered face white and dry, Douglas Winter's widow wasn't weeping either.

George tried to remember if Babs had shed any tears at her husband's funeral, fifteen years before, when Douglas Winter's life had been cut short by a massive heart attack.

George stared at Babs. How does she live with it? he wondered. What does a woman do, thought George, when she realises she is married to an evil man?

He pulled his eyes away from her, squeezed them shut, took himself away into the corridors of his memory, where comfort lay in the pictures that hung there. Happy pictures, all of them, despite the years of struggle. His wedding day, his wife, his children, parties, pets, smiling friends.

Only one picture made him open his eyes.

The trouble at the Working Men's Club had occurred almost thirty years ago now. George remembered it still, although in his mind it had faded like an old film.

George normally did his drinking at the Victoria Hotel, a pub on the corner where he could lean on the counter and chat at his ease to the real working men of Siren's Rock; he had been at the club that night because a visiting rep was trying to persuade him to introduce a line of ice-cream desserts. The rep was paying the bill when George heard a fuss breaking out in the corner of the dimly-lit dining room.

The manager in her little black dress was remonstrating with Douglas Winter, who was obviously the worse for drink. Two waiters were glowering. It was something about a waitress. *Touching* the young waitress. 'Little more than a child,' George heard the manager hiss in disgust. 'Asking for it,' he heard Douglas rumble. And then, to his horror, Douglas had spotted him. 'They're all asking for it, hey George?' he bellowed across the room. 'Even our own little bitches. Begging for it! And then they squeal when they get it!'

At the white shrouded tables the few remaining patrons were staring.

George pushed his chair back and hurried towards the entrance, belting the backs of chairs with his belly as he navigated his way out of trouble.

He had driven home with nausea in his gut. What was the man talking about? What did he mean?

But of course he knew.

Because it was too horrible to put into words, George hinted around the subject for days until Marte finally caught on. But her handsome face closed. Her wide mouth clamped shut as she slammed a mug of tea down on to the kitchen table.

'We should do something,' said George. 'What can we do?'

Marte unlocked her mouth. 'About some things,' she said, 'nothing.'

And when George began to protest, she talked him down. 'You tell and then what?' she asked. 'Scandal. Shame. Everyone in the family disgraced. Nobody wins. Helen is a big girl now. If it happened, she has put it behind her. I bet. You should do the same.'

'Jemma . . .' muttered George.

'Don't be stupid,' said Marte. 'As if she would let him.'

So George had put it behind him.

He had forgiven Marte, as he forgave her everything. He had never forgiven himself.

Babs had worn black to her husband's funeral, with a heavy veil hanging from her hat. The veil had small velvet spots on it. He remembered little Caitlin screaming, mistaking the spots for bugs crawling on her granny's face.

Jemma had stayed home with Hamish that day. But Helen was there with her three-year-old daughter, her face as white and still as the most tragic Madonna ever carved from stone. When Caitlin started screaming, George had picked her up in his doughnut arms and taken her outside. He had badly wanted to take Helen too, this lovely white-faced girl whom he loved like a daughter. He wanted to take them both home, Helen and her doll-like child, and leave them with Jemma and Hamish, who were working out jigsaws at the kitchen table and chomping biscuits and doing the safe, normal things that young mothers should do with their children.

Babs had been supported at Douglas Winter's funeral by a weeping Joy and the serious, lipless young man who was now her husband. So Joy's all right, George had thought with relief, when he heard about the marriage. George and Marte had sat with Helen, and John was also there. He stood beside Helen throughout her father's funeral and afterwards, occasionally placing his arm behind her back, shielding her from people who came too close.

A good friend, John, thought George. And a good husband. No matter what people were saying. No matter what they thought.

In the long run, thought George, what the people thought was rarely the real story.

REUNION

By the time they reached Italy, Grezza had given up all pretence of travelling alone and was following Horace the Morris along routes they discussed each night at the campsites. As his cumbersome bus rarely went far without developing a mechanical problem, Helen suspected that it would not be long before Grezza actually joined them in the Morris and so it proved to be. He sold his bomb at the campsite outside Venice, for a disgustingly small amount of lire.

'You can travel with us as far as Bologna,' said Jemma sternly, but he was still singing bawdy songs in the back seat when they were heading for Florence, leaping out to fill their petrol tank whenever they stopped for gas, getting drinks, chopping watermelons, pounding in their tent pegs with untiring enthusiasm.

Grezza could turn a tin of beans and some sausage into a good meal; he lined up at bars to get them drinks; and while he regularly reminded them that he would willingly go to bed with either of them — but preferably Jemma — he continued to treat them with his odd, old-fashioned courtesy. He was not, he told them, a bloke who would put the hard word on a bird. Every morning before they set off, he performed small essential services to make the Morris roadworthy for the day. By the time they drove into Florence, even Jemma had begun to wonder how they had managed without his itchy presence.

The campsite in Florence was on the edge of the town, rising in steep terraces and very pretty, with a view of the dark green Florentine hills.

Grezza offered to put up the tent and told the girls to go straight into town to have a look at the place where the Renaissance actually began. 'What do you know about the Renaissance, Grezza?' asked Jemma. 'We studied it at Warrabi High,' said Grezza. 'There was a lot of religion in it and some sex. All these wog cities are obsessed with religion and sex.'

When they arrived back at the campsite, they were hot and dusty and slightly shiny with perspiration. They were eating slices of watermelon, standing up and spitting the seeds onto the dry ground, when they saw the legs.

The terrace directly above theirs was already occupied by a large and very professional-looking tent, with a gleaming Volkswagen Kombi van parked beside it.

'Aussie legs,' murmured Jemma, jerking her head upwards.

Helen glanced up and saw two strong, brown, hairy legs emerging from white socks and sturdy tennis shoes. 'Absolutely,' she grinned.

'Yeah?' said Grezza, spitting enthusiastically. 'Oi, mate!' he bellowed, craning his neck to see the people standing above them. 'You Aussies?'

Helen saw the tennis shoes turn, heard the voice, 'Sure are, mate,' and watched the world around her go into slow motion as the owner of the sturdy legs hunkered down to lean over the terrace and have a look at them. Jemma, in a loose pink singlet and checked shorts, was standing directly below him, biting a chunk out of her smile of watermelon. She shook her hair back from her damp face and grinned up at the stranger.

There was a short silence while Helen waited.

'I don't believe it,' said John.

It seemed as though Jemma would never stop waving her arms up and down and saying: 'No, *no*, it can't be, oh my God, oh my *God*, John, little John Sullivan, *John!*' while John just stood there, outside their tent, with his arms hanging awkwardly at his sides, saying quietly: 'Jemma, I can't believe it.' Grezza kept talking at Helen: 'I take it they know each other. How well do they know each other? Do you think this means she'll never fall for me?'

Helen watched John and Jemma, together at last, and marvelled at the way they didn't touch each other.

Finally — and later she wondered where she had got the idea and the courage to do it — she walked slowly over to John's side and took his hand. It was a big firm hand, and she remembered it. The feel of it. Her own hand was wet and slightly sticky from the melon juice. John glanced down at her as if he had never seen her in his life, as if she was just a forgettable scrap of a girl. As if the last time he had seen her, he had not been overwhelmed with weeping. As if her body had never been impaled by his on the back seat of his car at the Siren's Rock drive-in theatre.

Helen gave John's hand a little tug, then she took Jemma's hand and placed it in his. They gazed in delight into each other's faces and, without any help from Helen, they joined their other hands as well.

Jemma gazed up at John. 'Wow!' she said, and her loud voice was suddenly as husky as Helen's. 'You're so huge!'

Helen looked down at her feet.

John looked at Jemma. Looked and looked. 'You're so beautiful,' he said. And his voice was the huskiest of all.

None of them would ever forget that night.

When John finally let Jemma have her hands back, they introduced Grezza, and Helen waited for John to say something to her. Only he didn't. He couldn't stop looking at Jemma. And she, Helen noticed with increasing interest, couldn't stop looking at him. *So that's what it's like*, mused Helen the cynic.

And neither of them could stop talking to each other. *So that's what happens*. They raced through the first essential details of how they had arrived in Florence, how long they'd been travelling, where they'd been already and where they were going. Then, armed with beer and coke, they sat on a rug in front of the tent and plunged into the stories of what had happened to them all after John's family had left Siren's Rock. Some of this Helen already knew, but there was no flicker of memory on John's face, even when he told Jemma about his father's sudden death. Or if there was Helen didn't see it, because she was sitting very still, cross-legged, staring at her toes. Jemma, on the other hand, couldn't stop fiddling with her hair, adjusting her clothes, waving her arms, clasping her hands. And John couldn't stop watching her. And laughing at her jokes. And listening. And talking. And watching. And laughing again.

It must be lovely, said Saint Helen.

They were well into the Wildcats when Grezza interrupted them to suggest that they should get showered and continue the reunion over a meal. Only then, when Jemma went into the tent to get her toilet bag, did John finally look properly at Helen.

She was horribly aware of her stringy hair, her face, sunburnt in patches, her baggy shorts and the tiny tank top sticking to her body. But he just smiled, very slightly, and said: 'Helen. It's great to see you again too. I mean it.'

She smiled, equally shyly, and tried to think of something to say. She wanted to say something to reassure him. Something that would make everything all right.

But no words came. Not even one.

In the end she just smiled again and, feeling frustrated and stupid, followed Jemma into the tent.

The girls raced to the showers and barely got inside before Jemma slammed herself against the wall, filled her cheeks with wind and blew out a massive breath.

'Julie!' she gasped. 'He is absolutely *gorgeous*. Tell me I'm not imagining it. He is absolutely *gorgeous*. Little John Sullivan. Big and brown and the most gorgeous man I've ever seen. And he's *huge*.'

'He's gorgeous, Sophia,' smiled Helen. 'And what is better still, he's bigger than you. At last.'

Jemma screamed with laughter. Then she hugged Helen, which was still unusual.

'And better even than that,' said Helen, 'he's in love with you already.'

Jemma screamed again. She grabbed Helen by the shoulders and gazed into her eyes. 'He can't stop looking at me, can he? I can't believe it. It's like a movie. God, I feel so *hot*! Why is it so *hot* all of a sudden?' She began tearing her clothes off, without even going into a cubicle.

'It's been hot for weeks,' said Helen, and smiled. It was no effort to smile. She hadn't seen Jemma so happy, so out of control and excited, since her night of triumph as Bottom in the school play.

It was enough, Helen thought. It was enough. To see Jemma happy. The friend who had saved her from her family, who had taken her away from Siren's Rock, who had kept all her promises. Jemma, who had made her happier than she had ever thought possible, was finally happy herself. *More* than happy.

This was right. That Jemma should be rewarded for waiting for so long for the right man.

Unlike me, thought Helen.

'Do you think it will last?' yelled Jemma from the shower. 'This amazing feeling? Do you think I'm falling in love? How could I fall in love with a little boy from Siren's Rock? What will I *do*, Julie?'

'For God's sake, Sophia,' yelled Helen through a spray of icy water. 'For once, don't *do* anything. For once, why don't you just let it happen all on its own?'

'He looks like John Gavin, don't you think?' said Jemma, soaping and scrubbing. 'Or is it Rock Hudson?'

'Definitely John Gavin,' said Helen, stepping out of her shower. 'And nothing will go wrong. Just enjoy it.'

'What do you mean, enjoy it?' called Jemma. 'I mean, he is absolutely gorgeous and I might have to let him kiss me very soon, if he keeps looking at me in that hungry way, but it will just be kissing. There's The Plan.'

Helen rubbed herself hard with her towel. One thing's for certain, she thought: this would be the end of The Plan.

NIGEL

They met as arranged, at the taverna on the outskirts of the campsite. John brought along his travelling companion, another Australian with an Irish name. Nigel Connor was extremely tall, even taller than John, but thin as a broomstick, a slightly built feline fellow with a supercilious smile. The boys were touring the continent together. They were away for only twelve weeks. After that, John had to return to Sydney, where a good job had turned up just days before he was due to leave on his adventure. 'Around the world in eighty-four days,' said Nigel.

'Gob full of plums,' Grezza muttered to Helen as they sat down.

They ordered huge white plates of tagliatelle and, abandoning their daily budget, drank four bottles of Chianti, chewed on baskets of crusty bread, and told every passing tourist and waiter about the incredible coincidence of their meeting. And talked. Talked and laughed and shouted with mirth and memories. Even Helen talked and laughed a great deal, surprising herself. Everyone, with the occasional exception of Grezza and Nigel, was happy. Grezza took one look at Nigel and pronounced him a ponce — not out loud, but Helen read his lips. Sympathetically, she squeezed Grezza's knee under the table. She thought he might feel redundant, which wasn't fair. Nigel should have been the odd man out, although it was obvious straight away that Nigel would never allow himself to feel out of place anywhere.

'Years of practice,' he told Helen much later. 'If nobody wants you, darling, you have two choices. You can curl up and feel small and miserable and undesirable, the way you do, or you can grow a very thick skin and force yourself on people of your choice, like me. Of course, being charming and witty helps. A bit of wit would do wonders for *you*, Julie.'

Nigel had thick copper-coloured hair waving over a narrow, foxy face. He had an impeccable accent, perfected at a number of Australian private schools during the years his parents spent trying to find an educational institution from which he would not be expelled. 'Anything rather than live with me themselves.'

He entertained them with stories of how he'd regularly escaped from these sports-obsessed schools by stealing, performing minor acts of vandalism ('the odd dead rodent, that sort of thing') and dabbling with drugs ('never underestimate the usefulness of chemicals, chicken — it's amazing how a little bit of substance abuse terrifies alcoholic headmasters throughout the land').

Helen was at first amazed and wondered how Nigel and John had become friends. What could they possibly have in common? Nigel camped it up, flinging his long thin fingers about in the air and tossing back his floppy wave of hair like a girl, and his sarcasm put both her and Jemma to shame. Even Grezza, with his laconic drawl, colourful vocabulary and affection for beer, seemed a better match for John.

He's probably a homosexual, sniggered Helen the cynic. *Maybe John is too. What if you did that to him?*

It seemed that Nigel and John had spent their final year at school together ('when my parents had exhausted every other avenue') and when Nigel began telling stories of what they had got up to at St Patrick's, John finally stopped looking only at Jemma and egged Nigel on. There was a great deal more laughter. Nigel was very witty in a clever, snide sort of way.

'So far up himself 'e's inside out,' muttered Grezza, but after a while, listening carefully, Helen worked it out. Nigel had been picked on and bullied at school; for some reason, John had saved Nigel in the same way he and Jemma had saved her.

She wondered why he'd bothered.

The boys had ended up at the same university. 'You're not an engineer too?' asked Jemma. 'Electrical,' said Nigel. 'Shocking, isn't it?'

John, like Jemma, had only just completed his university course and had been planning to wait a few years before seeing the world. But Nigel's parents had given him a round-the-world air ticket for his twenty-first birthday ('anything to get rid of their golden boy') and when he had invited John to come with him, John's ever-vigilant aunt had told him to go.

'It was one of the first spur-of-the-moment decisions I've made in my life,' said John, looking sheepish. 'One minute I was scanning the employment lists, looking for a decent job, and worried about making enough money to live on, and the next thing you know, I've got money to burn and I'm on my way to Europe.

'My aunt sat me down at the kitchen table and told me about this trust fund my dad started for me,' John explained.

'She talked me into having a trip. She said I'd done my share of looking after other people, it was time I started to reward myself.'

'Whereas I,' Nigel purred, 'have never stopped.'

'Two weeks later we were on a plane,' said John, flicking Nigel carelessly over the ear.

'Careful, careful,' murmured Nigel. 'Don't damage the merchandise. Women go mad for the hair.'

'How fabulous,' said Jemma. 'We planned our trip for years and years. How fabulous to just get up and go like that.'

'And now it's all worth it,' said John, gazing at her.

'Jeez, that was a great meal,' said Grezza, not sounding as if he meant it. 'I'm full as a boot.'

Nigel splashed wine into his glass, tipped it down his long throat and leaned over the table. 'Come along, my dears,' he said. 'The hour is late. Methinks these two would like to be left alone.'

Helen and Grezza got up together. Neither Jemma nor John objected. Grezza mumbled something about finding a card game and ambled off into the dark. A small knot of anxiety tightened in Helen's stomach and she fought the temptation to call him back. Nigel strolled beside her towards her tent. He was exceptionally tall and he had an oddly graceful, gliding walk. His long arms trailed at his sides. When they reached the tent she glanced up at him. 'Would you like me to boil some water for tea?' she asked without enthusiasm.

He smiled quite nicely. Narrow lips and beautiful small white teeth. 'No thanks, sweetness. Never touch the stuff. I think I'll just slide back into my canvas condominium and get my beauty sleep. After all, somebody has to drive tomorrow,' said Nigel, 'and I'm assuming that our friends won't be getting any tonight. Sleep, that is,' he added, raising his eyebrow, before he began to walk away.

Around them in the darkness the campsite murmured, sighed and snored. Nigel's words made Helen feel grubby on Jemma's behalf. And John's, too, for that matter.

'They've only just met again, you know,' she called after him. 'Last time they were together they were only kids.'

Nigel stopped and slowly turned around.

'You know,' said Helen. 'Um. I hardly think the first thing they are going to do is ...' she stopped. The irony of what she had been about to say took her breath away.

'What?' asked Nigel, walking back to her again. 'You don't think they're going to get it off? Why ever not?'

Helen glared at him. A horrible piece of work, Jemma would call him later. Helen tried — and failed of course — to think of the right words to cut him down.

'He has a whole lot of woman there,' said Nigel. 'She's practically falling into his loins. If he doesn't fuck her as soon as possible, she'll be very disappointed. And so will he.'

Anger boiled and spat. 'You're disgusting,' Helen hissed. 'It's not like that with them. Jemma's not like that.'

Nigel was watching her with interest in the dark. 'Really?' he said softly. Unexpectedly he broke into a fruity American accent: 'And believe it or not, folks, these words are being spoken in the Year of Our Lord nineteen hundred and seventy-one, by an inarticulate but beautiful blonde who is over the age of consent.' He stopped and Helen said nothing.

'What about you, fair Helen,' asked Nigel, softening his voice again. 'Are you ... um ... how did you so delicately put it ... in words that would induce poets to fall upon their pens ... are you ... *like that*?'

She didn't answer. Suddenly he stretched out a sinewy arm, slid his fingers around the back of her head, bent his long body down, kissed her on the mouth. Or rather, *in* the mouth. His tongue, very long and pointed, slid between her open lips and coiled around hers. She flinched and recoiled in shock, but Nigel held her head firmly. Helen stood still and closed her eyes. Eventually he completed his exploration and withdrew his tongue much more slowly than it had gone in. When he drew back his head so suddenly that Helen's eyes popped open, she was off balance and almost fell. Nigel lightly grabbed her by the elbows and steadied her.

Helen felt as if she had been kissed by a snake. She still couldn't speak.

'So now we know. Good night then, fair Helen,' Nigel said smiling, walking off into the dark.

Jemma and John's first kiss was much more satisfying.

When the others left the taverna, they stood up to dance, reached out, moved into each other's arms, smiled shyly into each other's eyes, moved closer. Shuffled together on the tiny dance floor while other couples flowed around them and the swarthy musician embraced his accordion. Eventually, when Jemma said they had lots of sightseeing to do the next day, they walked slowly out of the taverna, with their arms around each other's waists, and wandered along the darkened pathway towards the tents.

When John stopped and looked at her, Jemma raised her face and he kissed her softly, sweetly, as gently and as perfectly as the lover of her dreams.

Reaching the girls' tent, standing outside, in the same spot where Nigel and Helen had stood an hour earlier, they kissed again. A damp, deep chasm was opening up in Jemma's body and she realised her lips were open too. With an enormous effort and a little gasp, she drew away. John smiled at her in the dark, tightened his arms around her and again covered her mouth with his. For the first time in her life, Jemma didn't want to do anything about it at all except close her eyes and soak in John Sullivan's kisses.

It was John who stopped at last, and stroked her cheek and whispered: 'I've found you now, Jemma. I'm never going to let you go.'

Then he, too, walked off into the darkness, while Jemma stood staring at his broad retreating back.

After a few minutes, she bent over and slid into the tent. Curled up into a big tight ball. Kept her mouth tightly closed over a long, thin squeal of excitement which began in her throat and shot through her splendid, still quivering self. Kept it inside until she ran out of air. Finally breathed out, hugged her arms, and whispered to herself: 'Good.'

Lying on her back in the little tent, Helen pretended to be asleep. She had cleaned her teeth three times longer than usual but she couldn't scrub away the thought of Nigel's tongue.

Despite The Plan and Jemma's best efforts, Helen had tasted other tongues. But Nigel's kiss had seemed more like an attack. Helen tried desperately to sleep. She determined not to think about it any more. However, the alternative was to think about Jemma and John and she didn't want to do that either.

She wondered whether Nigel was right, at least about John. Was John in the habit of sleeping with every girl he picked up? Had John had so many girls that he had genuinely forgotten what had happened at the drive-in? Or had he just been very drunk? Had John been pining for Jemma for years? How would you know for sure? Neither she nor Jemma really knew him any more.

The memory of Nigel's tongue, forcing itself into her mouth, came back again. *Such a strong tongue*, said Helen the cynic. *Long and thin like him. And of course you just stood there and let him stick it down your throat.*

What is wrong with you? asked Saint Helen. *Why didn't you kick him in the balls?*

Helen's eyes snapped open. What sort of language was that from a saint!

Why do I give in so easily when men want to take control of me? Helen wondered. It's not as if any of them have ever loved me or cared about me. It's not as if I really love any of *them*.

It wasn't about love and caring at all.

Helen sat up, leaned forward, hugged her knees and took several deep breaths. It wasn't even about sex. It was all about control.

It was the wine, she thought. Wine had always made her weak.

Any excuse, said Helen the cynic.

Don't let Nigel or anyone else spoil this. If Jemma and John are falling in love with each other, that's a very good thing, said Saint Helen.

PERSUASION

They travelled in convoy through Italy, the girls driving Horace behind the boys' smart Kombi, while Grezza, devastated at losing any chance he had ever had of crawling into Jemma's sleeping bag, yet liking the man who had cut him out of the challenge, divided his time between the two vehicles.

In another hillside campsite on the outskirts of Rome, John and Nigel erected their five-star tent, as Jemma called it, arranging herself against a tree and distracting John disgracefully as he pounded tent pegs.

For Jemma, the journey to Rome and the time they spent in that most beautiful of cities passed in a haze of excitement and anticipation. Later she could barely remember what she'd seen or where she had been, only endless conversations, wild laughter, long, hot silences, secret smiles and hours of intensifying passion. Their kisses became longer, deeper and more desperate, and their partings from each other at night occurred later and later, leaving them both ratty and randy and, as Helen put it, madly in lust.

'No,' said Jemma defensively, 'not lust. That sounds as if we are doing something dirty. And we're not.'

'Lust,' said Helen. 'Pure and simple.'

They were getting dressed for their last day in Rome. It was unbearably hot, although Jemma and John had hardly noticed. 'You've run the rules past him then, have you?' asked Helen solemnly. 'You're sticking to The Plan, I hope.'

Jemma chewed her bottom lip. 'As a matter of fact, no,' she said. 'I mean, yes, I'm sticking to The Plan. But I haven't had to tell him the rules. He follows them anyway.'

'Good grief,' said Helen. 'You mean there's no touching? He's keeping his hands off your rude bits? No groping? No tongue?'

'Sort of.' Jemma looked sallow in the dim light of the tent. 'Certainly no groping. Anyway, I don't really want to talk about it. It's very personal.'

'Sorry,' said Helen.

There was a silence as they combed their hair and applied mascara.

'Are you putting up with Nigel all right?' asked Jemma.

'I keep as far away from him as I can,' said Helen. 'I'm enjoying Rome. That's where we are, by the way.' She grinned. 'And I'm helping poor old Grezza cope with his broken heart. All the same,' said Helen, 'he's very funny. Nigel, I mean. Very clever.'

'Do you think he's queer?' asked Jemma.

'Don't know. Been wondering.'

Helen became aware that Jemma was looking at her. She stopped fiddling with her eyelashes and looked back. 'What?'

'It's not normal, is it?' said Jemma in a much smaller voice than usual. 'John, I mean. You'd think he would have tried something by now. Even Alex tried eventually. I mean, any other bloke would have tried something by now.'

'Do you want him to *try something*, Sophia?' asked Helen.

'Well, it makes me wonder if he really likes me. And

sometimes I think he is going to, and then he doesn't and I know that he's being really decent because he respects me and everything, but I just ... Look, I know this sounds awful, Julie, but I *want* him to touch me. You know?'

'Yes,' said Helen. 'You know I know.'

Jemma looked at Helen sadly. *But it's different,* she wanted to say. *This is John.* Instead she said: 'Julie, I think I love him. And I thought he was falling in love with me, but lately I'm not so sure.'

Helen bent to crawl out of the tent. 'He loves you, Sophia. It stands out a mile.' She giggled. 'In every way.' And she wasn't quick enough to dodge the flying brush that hit her retreating bottom.

They reached the island of Corfu on a ferry which arrived in the late afternoon. It rained for the following three days and they all grew bored and restless. Helen snapped at Grezza, Jemma snapped at John. Nigel went off to annoy a large group of South African campers. When he came back he found Helen in the boys' Kombi, where she had tucked herself away to read *Anna Karenina*.

'Tolstoy,' he said. 'And who are you, Helen? Kitty or the lovely Anna?'

Helen looked at him steadily over the top of her book. 'I'm Anna, of course,' she said.

'Pulsating with love for a conceited bastard while your dear friend revels in the love of a good and steadfast man?'

'I'm not up to that yet,' said Helen. 'At the moment Kitty and Lenin are having trouble understanding how much they love each other.'

Nigel smiled. He had a very nice smile, thought Helen, when he wasn't trying to be smart. 'Would you like a coffee?'

'Thanks,' said Helen. 'Have you read any of Tolstoy's other books?'

'All of them,' said Nigel. 'And Dostoyevsky. Love those Russian authors, darling. The tragedies. The suffering.'

'Me too,' said Helen.

'Why does that not surprise me?' said Nigel.

The next day they all drove through Corfu, past the mirror of the bay, through a tangle of white streets lined with stone terraced houses, and along scrubby roads scattered with plodding land workers and children leading donkeys. At the port they boarded the ferry which landed at Igoumenitsa, on the mainland of Greece.

They drove for two hours to Ioannina, through olive-brown hills which became increasingly rocky as the road climbed higher. A pale sun came out, whitening the light around them. They passed small roadside shrines furnished with bottles of ouzo and often a lighted taper burning inside. All along the road walked peasant women, veiled and dressed in black, carrying urns on their heads and clutching lumpy bundles, some riding donkeys. When the sun disappeared into the shadows of the evening, they arrived at a beach on the edge of a lake. They sat on rugs near the water, smelled it and watched it lapping until the wind became too strong, then they all went to bed. John pulled Jemma away from the others but a few minutes later she joined Helen in their tent.

'What's going on?' asked Helen, sliding into her sleeping bag.

'You know what I think?' said Jemma. 'I think he's a virgin.'

Helen could think of nothing to say.

'I think he is a lovely bloke,' said Jemma, 'but he was brought up a Catholic, remember, and I think he genuinely has no intention of sleeping with anyone until he's married.'

'But,' said Helen faintly, 'neither do you.'

'So we shouldn't be cuddling so much,' Jemma told her, 'because it is driving us both crazy and sooner or later he might not be able to stop himself, you know? And I would hate to be responsible for, you know . . .'

'Eternal damnation?'

'Making him do something he thinks is wrong,' said Jemma.

'Well . . .' Helen sighed.

'But the real trouble is . . .' said Jemma, and Helen realised with surprise that tears were pooling in Jemma's green eyes, 'the trouble is that if he really is holding off until marriage and everything, that means it's just not going to happen at all.'

'What's not going to happen, Sophia? What's the matter?' Helen reached out and touched Jemma's damp cheek.

'I can't marry him, Julie,' said Jemma, her voice cracking with misery. 'Not that he's asked me, but even if he does, I can't. And that means we'll never properly love each other. And I don't know how much longer I can stand it.'

'Don't cry, Sophia,' said Helen softly. 'It is *so* obvious that he's *madly* in love with you. Anyway, *why* can't you marry him if you want to?'

'Helen, John is from Siren's Rock,' said Jemma, exasperated through her tears. 'I know he lives in Sydney *now*, but he's a Siren's Rock boy through and through and do you know what? He wants to go back there. He wants to settle down in that horrible little backwater — and you know I can't do that, Julie. I can't go home and marry a local boy and have his babies and be a housewife for the rest of my life.' She put her head into her skinny pillow and began to cry as hopelessly as a child.

'But, Jemma,' said Helen, rubbing her friend's back, 'if you marry him, think how happy you'd be. You might not even care about becoming famous any more.'

'I know *that*,' said Jemma, pushing away Helen's hand. 'That's what worries me. That I'll be tempted into it.'

'Into sex?'

'*No!*' sobbed Jemma, kicking one long leg and making the two-man tent quiver. 'Into happiness. It's so ordinary. Who wants ordinary old *happiness*?'

'Most people,' whispered Helen. But Jemma either didn't listen, or didn't want to hear.

The Acropolis silenced and separated them. They stood beneath the columns, dwarfed by the power and strength of the stone, and looked out over the city. Athens at close quarters was tacky, dusty, hot and vile. But from this height it was white and lovely, veiled by a golden haze which stretched north, east and west to the gaunt Hellene hills and south to the shimmering Mediterranean.

Helen skirted a column and came upon John, alone on a ledge, staring intently at the view. She followed his gaze. Then she looked at his handsome, sunburnt face and took the plunge.

Helen had decided to interfere.

Saint Helen understood, but was nervous. Helen the cynic was shaking her head in disbelief. But she was going to do it anyway. She was going to defy them both.

She had worked out the words.

'I have to tell you something,' said Helen.

John glanced at her. She closed her eyes, prayed to the gods to help her — surely there were lots of gods around this place — and dived.

'I suppose you know that Jemma's in love with you,' said Helen. 'No,' she said as he started to speak, 'let me say it. I've never seen her so happy, and I know her better than anybody. Except maybe you. So if you love her as much as

I think you do ... well, um, I think you had better show her.'

John now stared at her.

'I *have* told her,' he said. 'She knows I love her.'

'I don't mean *tell* her,' said Helen, shifting her gaze to the hazy view of Athens below. 'I said *show* her.'

John turned his face away too, looking again at the vista beyond. 'I've tried to do everything she wants,' he said dully. 'I treat her decently, I show her how much I respect her ...'

'She thinks you're a virgin,' snapped Helen.

John's face reddened. His fingers pressed down on the ledge, reddening too.

Helen got up and brushed the bottom of her shorts, still carefully not looking at him. She touched him lightly on his stiffened shoulder.

'Respect is not what she wants right now,' she said.

She walked away across the floor of the Acropolis and, when she was sure she was out of his sight, stopped and leaned her back against one of the columns. Rays from the glowing sun glanced off the sparkling stone. She slipped off one solid brown leather sandal and pressed the bottom of her foot against the pillar, feeling the smooth coolness of it through her toughened sole. Because she had closed her eyes, she jumped when she heard his voice close to her again.

'Helen.' John was standing in front of her, looking intently at her face.

'What?'

'That night when I came back ...'

'No,' said Helen.

He continued to look at her, confused, unhappy.

'You were never there,' said Helen. She closed her eyes again and kept them closed until she heard him walking away.

That afternoon they drove to Piraeus to board the ferry to the islands. Helen and Jemma couldn't wait to get there.

For five months they had driven hundreds of kilometres on the wrong side of the road, whispered their way through countless churches, museums and galleries, tramped endless paved and cobbled streets, eaten huge quantities of pasta, tuna and beans, pounded hundreds of tent pegs. They had seen, done and learned more than either of them had imagined possible when they set out from Siren's Rock. But they were weary from all the travelling and were now looking forward to a rest, a holiday within a holiday, a time when they could do what they were used to doing at home on long, hot, lazy days — lie on some sand, soak up some sun and dip themselves occasionally into cool water.

The girls had chosen the island of Lassos as their final destination. It was not one of the main tourist islands, but it was the place where Jemma's grandmother, Maria, had spent part of her childhood. Maria had shown them aged, cracking photographs of the island, which did it no justice at all, and they were jubilant when Lassos turned out to be as idyllic as if they had designed and painted it themselves.

Their first view of the island, from the bows of the ferry boat, revealed a wedding cake, white-iced tiers decorated with frills of lush green vegetation. On the peak stood a monastery, complete with a bell tower that might have been made from sugar crystals, and a rickety road had been slung loosely around the island's erratic coastline. The entire concoction was served on a plate of clear blue sea.

'Unbelievable,' murmured John, slipping his arm around Jemma's waist as the ferry nosed its way into the quay.

The village rose in tiers from a flat square. Shops and cafes crowded on three sides, with the fourth providing access down to the wharves and their fringe of fishing boats. The sun glinted on the whitewashed buildings of the little port. Olive-skinned women in black dresses watched sternly without interrupting their work; swarthy men with hairy arms and huge moustaches hurled parcels and shouted greetings; dogs ran in and out of the legs of small children. The smell of fish was tart and salty.

'Oh my God, it's just exactly right,' sighed Jemma, and she and John tightened their arms around each other's waists. 'I feel like Charmian Clift.'

They all climbed back into the two vehicles and drove off the ferry, winding their way with difficulty up to the village on a road which had never been designed for cars. Small children ran alongside, white teeth flashing, hands waving, offering souvenirs and sweets.

'Gorgeous,' said Helen, who had climbed into the Kombi with Nigel so that Jemma could be with John.

'Don't touch the merchandise,' snarled Nigel, slapping little hands away. 'I wonder when any of these little brats last soaked in Palmolive.'

John drove Horace while Jemma hung out of the window, laughing and trying to talk to the children, exchanging greetings with broadly grinning men. 'This is my country,' she said to John and Grezza, who had folded himself into the small back seat. 'I belong here. These men are so lovely. They remind me of my dad. Look at them all smiling! I think they know I'm one of them.'

Grezza followed the precise direction of the men's fascinated stares. 'Yeah,' he drawled, 'you're just like one of the family.'

When John and Nigel had changed their plans, deciding to visit the Greek islands instead of John's relations in

Ireland, Jemma had been thrilled, but Helen and Grezza had shared a grizzle about Nigel, who alternately lured them into shame-faced hysterics at his ridicule of others and depressed them with his acerbic and too often accurate observations of themselves.

Helen noticed that he was never nasty to John, though. And he had not attempted to touch her again. Small mercies, she thought.

They set up their tents in the late afternoon, on a flat slice of land leading to a sandy beach about five kilometres out of the village. There were no campsites on Lassos, but for a small fee the proprietor of a squat, ochre-coloured hotel permitted campers to use the basic but adequate hotel facilities. There were two other tents already erected among the trees. One was a blue igloo style and the other a small faded pink tepee. 'Americans,' sniffed Jemma, checking out the contents of a dusty van.

'Naked Americans!' said Grezza hoarsely, with the same subdued excitement that a movie cowboy might mutter: 'Indians!'

It wasn't wishful thinking: Grezza had spotted one of them on the beach below. When they all walked down with him to the water's edge, they were treated to the sight of a well-endowed, lightly tanned young woman, lying face down on her towel and wearing nothing but tiny bikini pants and a fat brown plait.

As they gazed at her with a mixture of appreciation, shock and awe, she looked up and smiled with delight.

'Well hi!' she exclaimed, scrambling up into sitting position, her plump bosoms bouncing around with an enthusiasm directly reflected in Grezza's eyes. Her honey-brown nipples were almost the same colour as her tanned breasts. It was impossible not to look at them. 'More people at last,' said the girl. 'Ah was jes gettin' really lonely here all bah maself. Ma name's Susan.' She put out a hand and Grezza was there in a flash.

Immediately the two started sharing travel tales, Grezza making no effort to avert his eyes from Susan's assets and Susan showing no objection whatsoever. Grezza remembered his manners long enough to make a quick round of introductions, and Susan told them that her friends Davina and Chuck were off on a trek somewhere 'but they'd prob'ly be back real soon'. John tactfully said that he and the others were going off for a swim before dark and that they should all get together later for dinner.

As they walked away Jemma looked at Helen with a wild expression in her eyes. 'Tell me she's not real.'

'Well hush mah mouth and cawl me nawty,' drawled Nigel. 'Ah thank she's the real thang, Jemma honey. Yo-all betta get yo gear off mighty quick or she-all may just outdo yew tew.' But while John and Helen laughed, Jemma just looked cross and shook her head.

'It's disgusting,' she said 'This sort of thing is very offensive to the local people. And with all this bush around, she could get *bitten*.'

'At the very least,' giggled Helen.

'No, by insects I mean,' hissed Jemma.

Grezza, in the seventh heaven of delight, stayed with his new friend — and they didn't see him, or Susan, for dinner.

'Isn't it wonderful,' Jemma murmured softly, feeling the midday sun warm on her skin, listening to the throbbing chorus of cicadas. 'To just stop at last. To just stop and let it all soak in.'

They were lying in a line on the sand, John beside Jemma, his head turned to look at her. Her autumn-toned bikini covered a lot more of her than Susan's skimpy 'one-piece', but could in no way disguise her voluptuous body, her melon breasts, her narrow waist and the unfulfilled promise of her thighs. She lay on her back, her legs stretched out in the sand. John reached out and stroked a few loose grains from her cheek. She didn't look at him but she smiled.

Hoping the gods were still on her side, and that Jemma's God was busy on a beach back home, Helen stood up and shook her towel. 'I'm hungry,' she announced. 'Let's walk into the village and get some stuff for lunch.'

'Oh, Helen,' groaned Jemma as the others got to their feet. 'I just got all comfortable. Are you hungry, John?'

'That's okay,' said Helen quickly. 'We'll bring something back for you two.'

The veil of pines around the cove threw shadows onto the sand and the water darkened into cobalt blue. John thought they would never go. What an amazing girl Helen was, he thought. Kind. Sensitive. Loyal. Forgiving.

And she knew Jemma well. He was counting on that.

John sat up on his towel and looked at the lush young body beside him. He swallowed. God she was beautiful.

GOOD LOVING

Jemma woke to the sound of cicadas tuning up for a new day. The early morning sun filled the boys' spacious tent with filmy light. She lay on the wide mattress that was John's bed and stretched like a big cat. For the first time in her life, Jemma Johnson was sumptuously, richly, wonderfully at peace.

She was satiated with sex.

Beneath a rumpled sheet with a pattern of racing cars, she was naked. Jemma couldn't remember sleeping naked on any night of her life. It was a lovely feeling. Sticky but nice. Another new and unanticipated pleasure she had never allowed herself to imagine.

The sheet was an old one John had brought from home. They had talked about it, laughed at the pattern when he pulled it out of a bag and covered her gently. That had been afterwards.

She lay tangled in the cotton sheet, absorbed in sensation. Cotton fibres beneath her naked skin. Stickiness between her legs. The damp, pleasant aching of her clitoris. The caress of the sheet against her nipples. The utter inertia of her sprawling limbs. She pushed down the sheet and watched her breasts rising and falling as she breathed. She touched them, brushed her fingers over her nipples. Smiled.

She had spent a lifetime studying this body. Had examined her face and figure for blemishes and blackheads, for faults, fat and follicles, for flab and floppy bits, but never before had she felt so intensely aware of her own flesh. And never had she contemplated the crop of intimately sensual pleasures that her body might yield, and had yielded during the long and turbulent night.

She was glad John wasn't lying beside her. She wanted to remember it all quietly.

The way they had stood alone together, kissing on the beautiful beach, shaded by the spreading shadows of the early afternoon. The way he had led her into the tent and kissed her again, her shoulders, her neck, her lips. The way she had wanted him never to stop.

How he had finally let her go and stepped back, looking candidly into her sea-green eyes. She had hesitated, knowing this was her decision and he was asking her to make it. She had slowly put her hands behind her back to undo her bikini top and couldn't manage it. Hadn't the strength to unfasten a simple clip. She had looked at him imploringly, embarrassed and shy, and he had moved towards her again, put his arms around her, kissing her as he undid the clasp and slipped her top off without touching her, even though she was longing for his fingers on her flesh. She had shivered when he put his big hands on her waist and slid them down over her hips, and she had helped him then, impatiently yanking down her bikini pants and stepping out of them. She had stood naked in front of him, her eyes on his face, waiting, watching the wonder in his eyes as he looked at her, wonder as naked as her body, wonder erasing any remaining doubt.

They had stretched out on the mattress together and Jemma had closed her eyes, waiting for the inevitable hands on her breasts. He didn't touch her for so long that she opened her eyes again. He was leaning up on one elbow, just looking.

'Don't laugh,' he had whispered, 'but I felt I ought to pray.'

She had smiled. 'Okay,' she whispered.

She remembered the way he had murmured: 'You are my miracle.'

His prayer had been cut short, though, because suddenly she couldn't wait any longer and had pulled his head down to hers.

She remembered the way he almost reverently held her heavy breasts in his hands and slowly put his mouth on them, warily, as if he were tasting some forbidden fruit. She remembered how he had stroked and caressed her, all of her, all the parts of her body which had formerly been out of bounds.

And even that was not enough, nowhere near enough, and she had thought she would go crazy and actually scream out loud in her desperation to have all of him.

Mostly, because thinking about it brought it back, she remembered the ache low in her belly becoming an agonising urge to be filled; how she had pushed impatiently at his swimmers, sobbing — had she actually been sobbing? — with desperate desire.

She stretched again. Remembered every sensation. Every kiss. Every gasping breath. Every driving stroke. And the two explosions, first his, then hers, carrying them both into a place beyond desire, where there was only wave upon wave of passion.

It had happened the way she knew it would. She had waited patiently for a warrior brave enough, kind enough, skilled enough, *big* enough, to come galloping across the screen of her life, to take possession of her body and her heart. It was absolutely right, she decided, that John Sullivan should be that man.

Afterwards, with the racing-car sheet binding them loosely together, they had talked.

They had been talking to each other for weeks but suddenly there was so much more to say. Things they had never talked about before. How they had been longing for each other. How they had been waiting for each other. How John was the tallest, strongest, most handsome man Jemma had ever seen. How he was the only man she had ever loved and the only man she had ever wanted. How John had realised he was in love with Jemma on the day of his mother's funeral; how he had dreamed of making love to her every day since. How everything about Jemma was perfect — her eyes, her lips, her skin, her breasts, her silky arms, her warm brown belly, her long legs, her glorious hair, her unbelievably beautiful body . . .

This brought the talking to an end and the lovemaking began again. And then they slept.

The first time she had woken up it was getting dark and he was asleep beside her. She could hear the others calling out softly to each other and laughing. There were the sounds and smells of dinner cooking. There was no moonlight in the tent. The flaps had been firmly zipped. The others would see the closed flaps and know not to come in. She didn't care what they thought.

The second time she had woken in his arms and he was gazing at her face. This time there was moonlight.

'I'm sorry you're not the first,' he had said quietly.

'I'm not sorry,' she whispered. He had stroked her breasts then, aroused her with his long fingers, and had plunged into her suddenly and urgently with a strength that had almost frightened her, until her body responded with an unexpected urgency of its own and she was rising and rising again on the intensity of her release.

Later they had to sneak out of the tent to pee. When they returned they had talked in whispers. There was so much more to say, to explain. Jemma thought they could talk into eternity and there would still never be enough time to say all they had to say. And do ...

John came into the tent, followed by a slash of morning sunshine, with his arms full of food. Jemma stretched her arms above her head and smiled at him. He gazed down at her, lying in his bed. 'My God,' he said in his Peter Sellers voice, 'but you're lovely.'

'Come here,' said Jemma.

John carefully put down the bread and fruit and lowered himself onto the mattress beside her. He brushed a thick lock of auburn hair away from her cheek. 'It's not fair,' he murmured, 'that one woman should be so beautiful.'

Jemma reached for him. The sheet slipped down and she didn't care. She smelled stale sweat and the fishy stickiness between her legs and she didn't care. All the things she used to worry about when she contemplated sex, like bad breath and sleeping with her mouth open and the way her body smelled in the mornings and being too big and heavy for the man, no longer mattered to her. She took his hand and cupped it around her breast. There it was, the delicious ache in her loins had returned. She sat up, pushed away the sheet and moved into his arms, pushing her breasts against his bare chest, winding her long brown legs around his waist and linking her ankles behind him.

'Hey,' said John, between kisses. 'We missed lunch and dinner yesterday. I thought we might have some breakfast. First.'

'No breakfast,' said Jemma, kissing and kissing, pushing him backwards and lying on top of him.

'No breakfast?' said John faintly, as she pressed her hips against his erection.

'Not yet,' murmured Jemma. 'First I want yesterday all over again.'

John uttered an ecstatic groan as she slid her hand into his shorts.

'Whatever you say, Captain Wildcat,' he said, putting his arms around her. 'You've always had the best ideas.'

In the months that followed, years, decades afterwards, long after his broad body had thickened and his shoulders had softened, when his tufty hair had receded and small pockets of flesh had appeared on each side of his comic book hero's mouth, when responsibility had furrowed his brow, John's memory of that day on Lassos continued to arouse him. He would recall, with titillating clarity, the moment Jemma Johnson, his captain, finally released him from the rules. When Jemma freed herself from ambition and inhibition and became his fiercely passionate, ecstatic, insatiable lover.

His dream come true.

For one whole glorious day.

More than twenty-four hours after they had first disappeared into the tent, Jemma met Helen emerging from a cubicle in the hotel's toilet block. Inexplicably, Jemma's eyes filled with tears. She held her arms out to her friend as if she were a small child who had been lost and had just found her mother. Helen put her arms around Jemma and hugged her tightly.

'Oh Julie,' she whispered.

'Just tell me,' whispered Helen, 'if it was wonderful.'

'More than wonderful,' said Jemma, rubbing her face on Helen's small shoulder. 'I never knew anything could feel like that, be like that, and it's all because John was so . . .'

Helen put two fingers against Jemma's lips. They felt skinny and bird-like compared with John's strong fingers, which had been in the same place such a short while before. 'I'm glad,' she said.

When she took her fingers away Jemma giggled.

'And now you should get into that shower,' said Helen, 'because you stink.'

As darkness dropped over their third day on the island they all sat together on the beach, listening to the water licking at the sand. They drank sweet wine that Nigel had brought from Athens in case they got tired of retsina, which had happened almost straight away. They ate sausages, eggs and beans, cooked over a fire by Grezza, who had been full of enthusiasm since his long-awaited fulfilment on his very first night on the island. He was also looking alarmingly clean, having treated himself to a haircut in the village. 'This barber guy had more gold teeth in his head than I've had hot dinners,' he said. 'That bloke could sell the metal in his mouth and buy himself a unit at Surfers Paradise.'

Everyone else was quiet and conversation around their small flickering fire was desultory. There was no moon. After they had eaten, Susan's friends, Davina and Chuck, quickly disappeared in the direction of their tent, then Susan yawned and stretched.

'Come on, honey lamb,' she smiled at Grezza, gripping the front of his T-shirt. 'This baby needs some good lovin'. Good night, yo-all,' she smiled sweetly to the others.

Helen couldn't resist flicking a quick glance at John, to see if he'd heard what she said, but John was kissing Jemma.

He was so totally absorbed in kissing Jemma, and Jemma, leaning against him, was so obviously responding to being kissed, that Helen couldn't tear her eyes away.

So that's what it's like.

'People might say they're in love,' said Nigel beside her.

Helen's head snapped around like a plastic doll's. That was how he made her feel. Like a doll that moved when the rubber band inside was pulled this way and that.

'People would be right,' she said.

Nigel sipped his wine and looked at her over the edge of the glass. He offered her some but she shook her head and looked away, looked straight at John and Jemma again and was obliged to look back at Nigel. He was still holding out the glass. She took it and had a big swig, feeling the sweet sticky muscat slither down her throat.

Helen had been very glad that Susan, Davina, Chuck and Grezza had been around while Jemma and John were exploring each other behind the tightly zipped flaps of John's tent. To have witnessed her friend's fulfilment with only Nigel for company would have been difficult. He was increasingly interested, she thought, in snapping her elastic.

Something had happened to Nigel since they had arrived on Lassos but Helen couldn't put her finger on what it was. She wondered if he was jealous or hungover, or both. Despite his snide asides concerning Jemma's tendency to tease and John's obvious frustration, perhaps he had preferred things the way they were. He was *really* jealous now, thought Helen. Nastier. Drinking more.

Now and then she had seen an expression on Nigel's thin, foxy face which was familiar to her. It was the way a kicked dog looks when a foot comes close. The way a small child looks when its mother walks away. The way she used to look when she met her own eyes in the mirror. And sometimes still did.

She didn't want to think about why Nigel looked like that. She didn't want to care.

He would have been a skinny little boy, she thought. Pretty, golden-haired. Different from most other boys. Easy meat. Until he was saved by John. And he had been hanging around with John ever since. What Nigel probably didn't know, thought Helen, and was too self-absorbed to have guessed, was just how long John had been waiting for Jemma. And what a difference their relationship would now make to the way John felt about *him*.

Nigel was missing John. That's what it was.

Or maybe it was nothing so subtle. Perhaps Nigel was simply cursing himself for not beating Grezza to the amazing Susan on their first day.

Anyway, thought Helen, whatever is wrong with him, what's happening between John and Jemma is more important.

I wonder if I did it, thought Helen. If my small act helped. Or would it have happened anyway, even if I hadn't said anything?

'You did it,' said Nigel.

Helen flushed in the dark. She hated the way he did that. Pulled off her head and looked inside. It made her feel transparent, easily manipulated. It undermined the few good feelings she had about herself.

The flames of the fire were flickering lower. The sea was black. John and Jemma had blended into a single shape in the dimness.

'I don't know what you did or what you said,' murmured Nigel, 'but you did it.' His tone was ambivalent. He was hugging his knees and staring at her. She wasn't sure if he was angry or amused.

'You're a girl with hidden talents, fair Helen,' continued Nigel. 'You're full of surprises. There are some deep secrets in that lovely little body of yours.'

Helen lifted the glass and drank some more wine. It really was very sweet. She didn't want him to know how uncomfortable he was making her feel. Jemma and John broke apart and helped each other up. Helen was relieved. It was one thing to be pleased that they were getting together in John's tent; it was much harder to watch them kissing, clinging to each other as if there was no tomorrow, as Jemma would say.

John smiled at Helen and Nigel in a glazed sort of way. 'We might turn in,' he said, only slightly sheepishly considering the understatement. 'You okay to sleep in the van again, mate?'

'Not tonight, no,' said Nigel, getting to his feet.

It was impossible to see John's expression in the dark, but Helen imagined it was as disconcerted as they all felt. Now what's he trying to do, she wondered. Surely he's not going to spoil it for them?

Nigel smiled, reached down, took Helen's hand and tugged. She finished off the wine and stood up slowly, wondering what was coming next. Nigel held her by the wrist.

'I'm sleeping in fair Helen's tent tonight,' said Nigel. 'She's tired of being left alone. Aren't you, darling?'

Was he joking? She tried to pull her hand away but he held on to her. 'Don't be silly,' she said. 'Of course I'm not. It's only been one night anyway.'

'But now there's tonight,' nagged Nigel. 'And who knows how many more nights after this? And I think everyone will feel much better if they know kind Uncle Nigel is taking care of little Helen in her tent, while John is taking care of Jemma in his.'

'Shut up!' snapped Jemma, suddenly loud and normal. 'Don't be so bloody stupid, Nigel. Helen doesn't want to sleep with you.'

'Well, ma goodness gracious,' drawled Nigel. 'Now who-all mentioned anything about *sleeping*?'

He was sliding his thumb in small circles around the softest part of Helen's wrist.

'Come off it, mate,' said John impatiently. 'If you want our tent, Jemma and I will use the van. Just leave Helen alone.'

'Stay out of Helen's tent,' said Jemma, stepping forward, 'and keep your dirty little claws off her.'

'Meeoww,' purred Nigel.

There was a tense silence. Nigel's thumb continued to trace a pattern on Helen's wrist. Helen tried to think of something to say. Her tongue was sticky from the muscat. No words came. They were all being stupid, even John. Laying down the law about what Nigel could and couldn't do with Helen the doll, Helen the elastic toy. Giving orders about Helen and now tugging at Jemma's arm, trying to pull her away.

'So let me get this straight,' said Nigel pleasantly. 'John and Jemma can fuck themselves stupid in the boys' big tent, but Nigel and Helen can't even think about it. There's one rule for the big people and another rule for us. What game are we playing here? Mothers and Fathers?'

'Helen,' said Jemma. 'Tell him to get knotted.' But she didn't move towards Helen; she stepped back to John's side.

Still Helen didn't speak. John muttered to Jemma: 'Helen's a grown-up. She should make her own decisions.'

Helen stared at his shape in the dark.

More than Jemma's fury or Nigel's thumb, John's words jerked painfully at the slender rubber band that was holding Helen together.

She turned away from them and followed Nigel through the trees to her tent.

Jemma collapsed on the mattress and stared at John with wild, worried eyes. 'She's so vulnerable,' she said. 'Boys take advantage of her. I don't know why she lets them, but if I'm not with her she has this ... problem. It's as if she can never say no.'

John looked miserable.

'What?' said Jemma crossly.

His face was full of pain. 'Jemma, I love you,' he said sadly.

'I know. I love you too. But I'm worried about Helen.'

'I've never loved anyone else,' said John. He looked desperate. 'But there's something I have to tell you.'

'John,' sighed Jemma, her voice softening. 'I know you've slept with other girls. You've told me, and you don't need to say any more. It's normal for a boy. Helen and I have talked about all that. It's okay.'

'Talked about all what?' said John.

'The rules,' said Jemma. 'It's different for boys.'

John was thoughtful for a minute, and then he said: 'Nigel was only teasing. He's jealous. But he won't hurt her. He just wanted to stir us up.'

They looked at each other, wanting to believe he was right.

INVENTION

Not even Helen could stand up in the two-man tent, so Nigel didn't have a hope.

They both remained on their knees, like supplicants awaiting forgiveness for sins they had not yet committed. *But you will*, said Helen the cynic, nudging and winking. *Not necessarily,* said Saint Helen. *Why do you always think the worst of people?*

Kneeling, Nigel carefully zipped up the flap. Kneeling, Helen lit the little camping lantern.

A small muscle in the corner of Nigel's mouth twitched. Helen pressed her lips tightly together. Then both began to laugh at the same time. Almost immediately, tears ran from Helen's eyes and trickled down her cheeks. Nigel watched but didn't touch her or offer comfort.

'You were joking,' sniffed Helen, sitting up very straight on her knees, wiping away the tears with the back of her hand. 'You weren't planning to have your evil way with me at all.'

But Nigel put his hand behind her head and drew her damp face towards his, in the same way he had done on the night they met. 'Whatever gave you that idea?' he asked softly, as he slid his sharp tongue through her Julie Christie lips and slowly slipped his free hand inside her shirt.

John and Jemma heard the laughter and smiled. 'See?' said John. 'He was stirring.'

'Well, that's a relief,' breathed Jemma. 'So now are we going to, um, what was it he said — oh yes: screw each other silly?' Sucking in her breath at the thought of it. Already excited. Fancy me wanting to, she thought. Fancy *me* feeling like this. Like melted butter. Like runny oil.

'No,' said John, lying down beside her. 'I'm going to make love to the most beautiful woman in the world.'

Helen, on her knees, said nothing, did nothing.

'You like that, don't you?' murmured Nigel, unbuttoning her shirt, pushing it open. 'Not wearing a bra again,' he said conversationally. 'I've noticed you've been trying to give them up.'

Helen remained perfectly still, watching him. He leaned forward, brushed her mouth with his and, as she parted her lips, slid his tongue so far down her throat that she began to gag. She tried to push him away but he grabbed her hands and kissed her properly, gently, a man's kiss instead of a snake's, lulling her into arousal, before biting her sharply on her bottom lip and then lowering his golden head and nipping each of her nipples, watching them harden, then nipping them again.

'Pretty,' he said. 'Much nicer than those big fat knockers that appeal to men with small brains.' Bending his head again, he sucked deeply on each of her creamy breasts, their large dark aureolas disappearing into his greedy mouth.

She knelt there, with her hair falling over her face, and

watched him. Waited for him to do more. To love her some more. To hurt her some more. Whatever.

'You like that, don't you?' he murmured again, as he undressed her like a doll, lifting her arms and legs to remove shirt, shorts and panties, neatly folding her clothes and placing them in a little pile in the corner. Licking her as he removed each garment, slipping his tongue into her ear, over her eyelids, nipping her lips, pinching her nipples between his thumb and forefinger.

Even the Helens in her head were silent now. Surprised, she thought, like her. Disappointed and disgusted that she was letting this happen to her again. But saying nothing.

'Open your mouth and close your eyes,' said Nigel, and kissed her like a snake again, striking several times with his darting tongue, drawing his head back when she tried to meet his lips with hers, teasing her.

He sat back and took off his own clothes quickly and efficiently, considering the length of his frame and the small amount of space in the tent. Helen looked at his thin golden body with interest. His genitals were pale and small. She gazed at his nakedness without comment. Nigel smiled, unembarrassed.

'We're so much alike, you and I,' he said, sitting down comfortably with his legs bent at the knees so as not to impede her view. 'Slender but perfectly formed. Yes, fair Helen, I think you and I definitely have the better side of this deal.'

He reached for her hand and drew it towards his penis, showing her how to hold it, how to move her fingers so that it swelled and grew within her grasp.

'This is Oliver,' he said pleasantly. 'My dearest friend. Shake hands.' Oliver was silky and soft, not at all what she had imagined. 'You've given Oliver a growth spurt,' said

Nigel, and Helen was pleased with herself. She had done that. *She* had made that happen. She lifted her eyes to Nigel's. He was supervising carefully, his hands hanging limply over his knees. Not sure whether to keep going or to stop, she watched Nigel carefully; Nigel, her teacher.

After a while he gave a little sigh and leaned forward, took her face in his hands and kissed her gently. She relaxed, curiosity giving way as the familiar feeling of longing stirred within her taut little frame. Tired of kneeling, she started to uncurl her legs, thinking they could lie beside each other now. But he finished the kiss and moved his hands to the back of her head, drawing it down.

'You like that, don't you?' gasped Nigel, but he was still in total control, and when she tried to jerk her head away he wouldn't let her.

'I can't believe how you make me feel,' sighed Jemma, embarrassed at how desperately she wanted him. He was kissing the smooth curve of her belly. She grasped his tufty hair. 'No, stop, you're making me feel crazy and I might scream.'

'Scream then,' murmured John.

'But I'm the captain, remember,' said Jemma, grabbing his head, 'and I told you to stop.'

'This is a mutiny,' said John, moving his face up over her body to kiss her on the lips. 'I want to have some ideas of my own.'

Jemma shuddered deliciously.

'You're going to have to marry me, you know,' she said. 'I don't sleep with anyone I'm not planning to marry.'

He hadn't even had to ask. John couldn't believe his luck.

★ ★ ★

Helen discovered she did quite like it. Soft and sweet and strangely comforting. As if she were a baby, sucking on a very large, silky thumb. But she heard Nigel's breath grow ragged and eventually he pulled her head carefully away. He finally let her lie down and he lay beside her on the sleeping bag, slinging his long leg over hers. He ran his tongue over her lips and smiled. 'I can taste me,' said Nigel. He looked into her startled eyes. He didn't seem to expect her to talk.

She liked that too.

'Why did I make you stop?' he asked conversationally, slipping his fingers between her legs. 'Well, fair Helen, even I am not such a bastard that I would destroy your first sexual experience by coming in your mouth.' She continued to stare at him, but fear flared in her eyes. She was frightened of fingers. 'You *really* like this, don't you?' he whispered. 'You had no idea how good at this I would be.' He was right, she thought. He wasn't hurting her. She began to relax. 'What was Jemma saying just the other day,' said Nigel, his busy fingers probing, 'when she felt we needed proof of her superior intellect? Oh yes. You can't judge a book by its cover.'

'Only we can't live in Siren's Rock,' Jemma said breathlessly, as their bodies undulated on the big mattress. 'I'm not going home to get married ... and have babies and be a ... a housewife. I want to do wonderful things. I want to ... oh John!'

'I love you,' groaned John, his face in her neck.

'But will you mind?' gasped Jemma, hugging him like a life raft on a choppy sea. 'Will you help me?' panted Jemma. 'I mean ... will you want to be with me ... even if I'm famous ... or travelling all over the world ... or being chased everywhere we go by reporters?'

'Jemma,' gasped John, 'I'll be there. Always. Now for God's sake stop talking.'

'This *is* your first sexual encounter, isn't it, fair Helen?' Nigel asked after a while. 'Well, that's what you've had everyone believing all this time, isn't it?

'I'm such a nasty old cynic, why do I have trouble accepting that, I wonder?' he mused. 'Perhaps because I suspect this is what you do to yourselves. Isn't it? You and Jemma, masturbating together while you discuss the requirements of Mr Right? Playing with yourselves, and maybe each other, while you imagine Prince Charming coming . . . and coming . . . and coming?'

She shook her head, but at the same time she opened her legs. Nigel pushed them closed again, with a humiliating gesture. 'No, no, darling, no need for that. Prince Oliver always travels incognito,' he whispered. 'He's going to slip in through the back.'

Helen opened her eyes.

'I don't want you to touch my bottom,' said Helen, speaking at last. 'It hurts.'

'But how would you know what hurts and what doesn't?' Nigel asked slyly. 'A sweet little virgin like you?'

Jemma couldn't breathe and said so. John rolled away, then lay on his back and pulled her over to sit astride him. He reached up to hold her lightly around the waist and moved her into his rhythm. From this angle her body was impossibly perfect. She was flushed and tousled. Any man in the world, thought John, would wish to be me right now.

He moved his hands to her shoulders and pulled her forward so he could bury his face in her wonderful breasts.

'If anybody *were* watching us,' said Jemma, 'can you imagine how *silly* we would look right now? With my huge bum in the air?'

John's voice was muffled by her flesh. 'Nobody is watching us, Jem.'

'I know, but if they were.'

'Jemma,' said John, 'stop thinking. Just *feel*.'

'I just wish I knew what they were doing,' said Jemma, rocking thoughtfully. 'I think I'll pop into my tent in a minute, to see if she's okay.'

'No.'

'Well, you go then,' said Jemma.

'No.'

'Not even for your captain?' she asked, leaning further forward and kissing him.

'No.'

'If he hurts her,' said Jemma, 'I'll kill him.'

Having caught her unawares with his question, Nigel turned her onto her stomach before she had gathered the strength to fight. Or perhaps she really was just light and cheap, like plastic, easily manipulated.

'No,' she growled from deep in her throat, from a part of her that Nigel had not reached, would never reach, no matter how many positions he tried, how many angles he attempted or instructions he gave.

She began to struggle, but he rammed one long, strong hand across the small of her back and pressed his knees into the backs of hers. He was stronger than he looked.

'Now it *will* hurt if you don't relax. You see, I like it this way,' he said, panting a little, and it was almost as if he was finally excited because he had found something she didn't enjoy. 'Honestly,' said Nigel in a sing-song voice, as he lifted her hips, 'for your very first sexual experience, I can *personally* recommend this position.'

She stopped struggling and lay still. The line of least resistance. She remembered it well.

She should never have let him come into her tent.

She should never have climbed into the back seat.

She should never have been such a bad girl.

'But for your information, fair Helen,' said Nigel, 'unlike other naughty boys we've been to bed with, I am *not* aiming for your delectable little bottom.'

Helen pushed her face into the silky lining of her sleeping bag and uttered a low, helpless little moan. Not long afterwards, she realised Nigel had known all along what he was doing. He had opened her up, wet and willing, and he wasn't hurting her at all.

He wasn't loving her either. But when had Helen ever expected that?

They remained on Lassos for another two weeks, but nobody would remember much about the place. Jemma gave up keeping her travel diary altogether and Helen didn't worry much about taking photographs, so afterwards they couldn't recall a great deal about the island or what they did there during the daylight hours when they came out of their tents. They dipped themselves into the sea from time to time, they chatted a little and drank a lot and went on a few picnics. The rest of the time they made love.

Or had sex. Nigel told Helen it was all a matter of semantics.

For the first time in years, Jemma and Helen had very little to say to each other. Helen assumed that Jemma preferred to talk to John. Jemma was afraid that anything she confided to Helen might get back to Nigel.

For several days Jemma convinced herself that nothing was going on between Helen and Nigel. The prospect of them becoming a couple was too appalling. It would be such a waste, she thought to herself, if all those years of protecting Helen from herself had come to this. To Nigel. A nasty bit of work who had no respect for women. Who wouldn't love Helen the way she deserved to be loved. Who had no idea how special Helen was. The possibility of their intimacy was the only shadow over each new, golden day.

And yet she had to know. It wasn't in Jemma's nature to pretend problems didn't exist.

John said he couldn't see why it was a problem. If Nigel and Helen were having even half the fun he and Jemma were having, there was no need to worry about them. He said Nigel wasn't nearly as bad or devious as Jemma thought.

Susan laughed when Jemma told her she didn't think anything was actually happening. Grezza just shrugged and scratched uncomfortably, but Jemma told John that if Grezza had not been so smitten with Susan, he would have been as concerned as she was.

Finally, in the shower block of the hotel, Jemma asked Helen with even more than her usual directness if she and Nigel were having sex.

Helen looked surprised. 'Of course we are. You know we are. Just like everybody else.'

Jemma still didn't want to believe it. 'But you don't love him,' she said.

'I might,' Helen replied. 'I think I'm starting to.'

'You don't *think* you love someone,' said Jemma, at her patronising best. 'You *know*. And he doesn't love *you*. He hardly ever even *touches* you. Ten days ago you and I were convinced he was a homosexual, for heaven's sake.'

Helen looked at Jemma with hurt eyes. 'He's not,' she said. 'They tried to make him into one at school, because he was delicate and pretty ...'

'Pretty?' shrieked Jemma. 'Nigel? *Pretty*? Whose opinion is that, Julie? His?'

'... and blond,' Helen went on, 'but he didn't let it get to him. And then John found out how good he was at running and tennis and they got to be friends and the others left him alone. He acts camp, but it's an act. It's his protection.'

'If you can't beat them join them,' said Jemma dully.

Helen looked annoyed. 'We're not like you and John yet,' she said. 'But we're getting there.'

Jemma stared at her friend in the mirror over the sinks and changed tack. 'Do you like him making love to you?' she asked softly.

Helen hesitated. 'Nigel is very inventive,' she said. 'We try lots of things. It's ... you know ... interesting.'

'Is it all you imagined it would be?'

Helen kept her eyes lowered.

'Is it?' Jemma pestered. 'Is it wonderful?'

'No,' said Helen, 'but that's because of me, not him.' She gave an odd little laugh.

Jemma gave up her attempt at sweetness and raised her voice. 'We said we would only sleep with someone if we loved them! That was the rule.'

'That was your rule,' said Helen softly. 'There was one rule for you and another rule for me.'

'No,' said Jemma, shocked at such injustice, taking a breath. 'That's not fair,' she continued more quietly. 'It was *our* rule. Yours and mine. Love before sex. I know I love John. And he loves me. So what we are doing isn't wrong.'

'So what Nigel and I are doing is wrong?'

Jemma hesitated. 'Yes,' she replied after a few seconds. 'Yes, I think it is. If you don't love him. And you couldn't. Not Nigel.'

Helen looked back at Jemma in the mirror. It reminded her of the one at St Patrick's College; past its prime, speckled and yellowing, it made both girls look sallow, despite their Mediterranean tans.

'Nigel wants me, Jemma,' Helen said in her husky voice. 'He wants *me*. He *wants* me. Just *me*, Jemma. He wants to make me laugh, and he does. He wants me to care about him, and I do. He *wants* me. Can you imagine how good that feels? No, you can't,' Helen's voice began to rise, 'because you are *used* to being wanted. You take being wanted for granted. Your mum and dad and your family, they all want you. John wants you, more than anyone in the world. People *care* about you, Jemma,' she was shouting now, 'they adore you. And so do I. But nobody has ever wanted *me* before.' Her voice sank back to a whisper: 'Not just me.'

Jemma's face had grown hotter as she stared at Helen. '*I* want you,' she said quietly. 'I wanted you for my friend from the very beginning.'

'Yes, but just because I was *there*,' said Helen. 'Just because you found me and helped me. Which was wonderful for me. And I'm really grateful to be your friend. But if you had never found me, you know, it would have been no loss to you —'

'Now that's *really* not fair,' Jemma interrupted her. She turned away from the mirror and looked into Helen's face, speaking slowly, in an attempt to stop her voice from quivering: 'You have been my best friend from the first day we met. I thought you were special then and I still do. I've never wanted any other special friend but you. Oh *Helen*!' Jemma uttered a sound of exasperation, a cross between a sob and a bark, and suddenly threw her toothbrush across the room. It clattered lightly on the concrete floor, a small plastic anti-climax.

'If I have somehow made you think you were less important than me,' said Jemma, 'I didn't mean to and I'm sorry. I thought we understood each other better than that.'

'No,' said Helen slowly. 'Not always.'

Jemma brushed away her tears. 'I'm sorry.'

'You don't have to be sorry,' said Helen. 'I have loved being your friend. But now you have John. And I don't . . .' Helen's own voice quivered now, and broke. 'I don't know what I'm supposed to . . .'

Jemma stared into Helen's face. 'What?' she cried. 'What? If I have John I can't have you? Is that it? So you are replacing me with Nigel? You didn't even wait twenty-four hours before you let Nigel take you into our tent. Nigel, who will play with you for a while and then toss you aside like a toy as soon as some other boy or girl takes his perverted little fancy? Who will drop you as sure as God made little fishes? Why?' she pleaded. 'Why can't you wait for someone better than Nigel? Someone like John?'

Helen stared back at her in silence.

'And *why* can't I be John's lover as well as your best friend?' Jemma asked desperately. 'Why can't I be *both*?'

There was silence in the washroom while Helen searched for her words and Jemma, knowing what she was doing, ground her teeth together and forced herself to wait for a reply.

'John is your best friend now, Sophia,' said Helen at last. 'There's nothing wrong with that,' she went on, speaking over Jemma when she tried to protest again. 'It's normal. It's what happens. But it's normal for me to want someone too,' she whispered. 'You know. Someone who wants me back.'

Jemma could think of nothing else to say. Or at least, nothing that wouldn't hurt Helen. All she could do, unwillingly, was let it alone and wait for Helen to realise she was making a terrible mistake.

Jemma went back out into the sunshine where she focused the full blaze of her personality on John, who was almost blinded by her light.

'You can't have everything,' Helen whispered to herself in the washroom.

With the virginity question out of the way, and their tents rocking with new night-time rhythms, there was no further need for Jemma and Helen to protect each other from men or from themselves. Their only remaining concern was to make sure they took their little white pills at the right time every night, praying that they'd work.

It was the end of The Plan.

Part Five

HAMISH

'You can do it,' his mother had said.

He stood in the sweltering church and remembered her wide white smile, and the way warmth, faith and encouragement had shot like sky rockets from her green eyes. Brilliant! Inspiring him, making his heart race, like fireworks. For a while. For a magic moment or ten, while the sparks and stars soared, anything was possible. Until reality returned.

You can do it, she always said. You can jump that high, run that fast, stop that goal. You can learn those tables, play that role, win that debate.

You can do it, she said. You can do anything you want to do. Practice Makes Perfect. Slow and Steady Wins the Race.

So he tried. He worked and trained and practised all the things his mother wanted him to do. All the things his mother had wanted to do herself, he decided as he grew older, before she had interrupted her path to fame and recognition in order to bring him up. Just him. When he had asked his parents for a brother or sister, his mother had patiently pointed out to him that bringing a child into the world was a serious and time-consuming business and, while she had done it once, to do it again wouldn't be fair on

Hamish or a new baby. Anyway, she'd said, neatly concluding her argument, why did he need a sister when he had Caitlin?

Hamish was well aware from an early age that Jemma Sullivan was an important person in Siren's Rock. But being a good wife and mother was her highest priority and took up a lot of the time she might otherwise have spent courting her own, more glorious ambitions.

The least he could do was achieve the goals she set for him. Well, no, the *least* he could do was try.

Growing up, Hamish had thought of himself as the extra-curricular kid. He had tried every sporting and cultural activity available to the children of Siren's Rock and beyond, getting up before dawn to train with the Nippers at Mermaid Cove, attending athletics carnivals, spending weekends traipsing inland to hang from cliffs in abseiling harnesses or explore caves. But nothing Hamish had tried during the anxious and action-packed years of his childhood and adolescence had excited him very much, and it was this that Jemma found most difficult to understand. And he'd feel bad about it because, after all, she only wanted what was Best for Him.

Still, it wasn't as if she nagged him; she preferred to show her disappointment with silence. Almost guiltily he recalled how peaceful it was at home when Mum wasn't speaking to him.

Hamish liked his home. He liked the big, airy rooms with their gleaming timber floors and vivid rugs; he liked their plain wooden furniture, most of it made by Dad in his workshop up the back. And he liked the lack of clutter, although when he looked at the austere arrangements on their shelves and benches through Nanna's eyes, he could understand why she thought their house was too bare. 'People don't cover every available surface with ornaments and flying ducks any more, Mum,' Jemma had told her. 'Not busy people anyway.'

Marte had sighed and nodded. 'All the same,' she'd whispered to Hamish, 'a few of those lace curtains would make it pretty.' Even aged ten, Hamish had shuddered at the thought of lace at their windows.

Most of all he liked the wide wooden verandah Dad had built around the house, with its curving iron roof that meant the three of them could sit outside on their creaking rocking chairs in every kind of weather. Dad had made them a chair each; he said you shouldn't have to wait until you were old and creaking yourself to enjoy the pleasure of watching a Siren's Rock sunset in a rocking chair. The house was on the very edge of the town and faced west, away from the coast. Many of Hamish's happiest childhood moments were the ones he spent on the verandah with his mum and dad, ice cubes tinkling in their glasses as they watched the sun sinking into the distant hills, blotting the blue sky with splashes of tangerine, staining the horizon.

His other favourite times were the nights they went to the drive-in. Mum loved the movies. She was always asking him which movie star he would most like to be, but he could never decide. She told him that when she was young she looked like Sophia Loren, but he hadn't seen enough movies with Sophia Loren in them to remember who she was.

Even though there were only three of them, theirs was a noisy house. The radio and television were always on, so that Mum would miss nothing. The phone rang constantly and the rooms echoed with her conversations. During the hours that Jemma spent at home, the washing machine whirred, the vacuum roared, the fans hummed. Visitors were expected and welcomed. The house echoed with talk. Even without visitors Mum talked almost all the time.

It was very different at Helen's. You could spend hours at Helen's without anyone speaking to you at all, without anyone expecting you to make an effort of any kind. He often went to Helen's to use her computer: it was a basic one, but modern, because of her job, and at least there he could tap away, exploring cyberspace without interruption, without having to listen to and sympathise with whatever current crisis might be enraging or exciting his mother.

Helen's house was smaller than theirs and much more messy. The computer was in the dining room, often hidden under the lumpy bundles of ironing which seemed to have been waiting for attention since Hamish was about five years old. There was always a faint perfume of crushed rose petals and the sound of ethereal flute music wafting from the aging stereo.

And besides, Caitlin was sometimes there.

Hamish leaned forward in the pew to look at Caitlin. She sat very still; only her hands moved, sliding up to her eyes from time to time to blot the tears that kept falling.

It was strange that of all of them, it was Caitlin who wept so constantly. You might have expected it of Nanna, or Pop, or even John. Certainly he expected it of himself. And Tom. But Tom was fiercely self-contained today, focusing his small bright eyes sternly on Granny Winter's back and demonstrating no sign of his normally excited, interminably questioning self. A good kid, thought Hamish. He had been glad enough, in the last few days, to have Tom's company, to have to answer Tom's questions, questions that had driven Caitlin mad but made him think, forced him to find the right words to explain a situation that had left two families confused and floundering.

Hamish's mother had wanted him to study law at Wentworth, but Dad had managed to persuade her that information technology at the University at Bridgetown would be a useful degree.

He liked IT. He liked the way there were logical rules to be followed. He enjoyed talking to people on the Internet without the embarrassment of meeting them in person and being horribly aware that his hands were too big and his lips too red and that he liked to think first about what he wanted to say.

'Anybody can play on a computer,' Jemma had said.

Except her. She had no idea. The only time Hamish felt genuinely useful to her was when his mother needed to use the computer for her various projects and schemes. She might have been able to type faster than a speeding bullet, but when it came to cutting and pasting, saving or moving files, she was useless.

'I'm not a technical person,' she'd say. But she was an everything else person, so nobody held it against her. Hamish didn't hold it against her either, he just wished she had a greater appreciation of the fact that he *was* a technical person and that without him she would have needed professional help to do all the things she wanted to do.

Of course, Dad could have helped her. But Dad had a lot on his plate. Being Jemma Sullivan's husband took a lot of effort, even Hamish could see that. A lot of patient listening. A lot of driving, discussion, encouragement. A lot of child minding, after work.

Dad would come into the house, his shirt and forehead creased with fatigue, and Mum would tell him all about her day. Dad never talked much about his own job, but it was important. It kept the roof over their heads, said Jemma. Most adults spoke about their 'careers' or 'professions', whereas Dad just called what he did his job. As if it didn't deserve a name. As if Keeping the Roof Over Their Heads didn't count for much.

Dad had started out as an engineer and for many years he had been the engineering manager at 2SR, the Siren's Rock radio station. (His friends joked that 2SR was the only Rock radio station in the country that never played Rock.) Dad was responsible for the maintenance of all the equipment that was necessary to run a radio station, for links with the national broadcasters, for anything and everything technical. Surely such responsibility was worthy of being called a career?

His father had seen 2SR grow from a small community-focused station to the region's most successful, and he'd played no small part in that growth. Eight years ago, when the station manager had retired, Dad had taken over his position, and had quickly accelerated the expansion of the station. Because he was fair and sensible and smart, John Sullivan was a success and was well respected in the town and beyond, thought Hamish. Only, apart from the air of quiet authority he always exuded, and the fact that he and Mum had to go to a lot of dinners and functions to suck up to the region's business people who advertised with the station, you would never have known. You would certainly never have thought of his father's *job* as being more important than his mother's *work*.

If Hamish had been the extra-curricular kid, John was the extra-curricular father. Treasurer for the primary school Parents' and Citizens' Association. Football coach. Scout leader. Lighting designer for the school plays. Sound-system collaborator and scenery-builder for the Sirens, the town's amateur theatrical society. And secretary of the Siren's Rock Combined Playgroups Association. (Mum was founder and president — there had been no such thing as a playgroup in Siren's Rock until Jemma Sullivan had a baby. Now there were eight!) A good bloke, that was Dad.

A tireless community worker, actress and writer, that was Mum.

A wonderful couple, said the people of Siren's Rock.

Mum had stayed at home to look after Hamish, and Caitlin too, during what she knew from her intensive research were the all-important formative years of their lives, the first five. When they started school she was always home by three, busy at her bench top, cutting fresh sandwiches and fruit for their afternoon tea (how Hamish longed for shop-bought cake and chocolate biscuits), and getting started on the dinners which the family enjoyed together at the table if she was staying home, or which he and Dad ate on their laps if she was off to a meeting or rehearsal.

For years his mother had appeared in the plays that the Sirens put on in the town. She rarely accepted the heroine's role, gracefully giving way to star-struck local girls with slender figures and pretty faces, although there were occasional exceptions — nobody would forget her magnificent Lysistrata. Whatever role she chose, whether she was roaring, raging, rampaging or clowning, nobody looked at anyone else once Jemma Sullivan was on stage.

As well as acting, Jemma produced and directed plays, while Helen and Nanna made the costumes. After she turned forty, declaring that she was now too old to strut the stage, she rediscovered her passion for writing, turning out plays and revues specially written for the appreciative audiences of Siren's Rock.

Hamish helped with the music for the revues, finding lyrics via the Internet, linking his computer with his stereo system to create interesting arrangements.

Jemma never seemed to grow older, like some mothers, whose chins and shoulders and bellies sagged further with each successive child. Even streaked liberally with grey, her coppery hair swung and shone. Her eyes danced. Her skin was soft and firm, and early in the mornings, before she applied soap and shampoo and perfume, she had a warm, comforting smell which Hamish breathed in deeply when she hugged him. She hugged him often, him and Dad. Big, reassuring hugs, brief but energetic, before she got back to whatever business was in hand. Churlishly, Hamish sometimes thought she had hugging written down on her copious lists of things to do each day.

Wednesday, June 4 — Hug my boys.

Unlike a lot of theatrical people, Mum didn't hug anyone much, so really he and Dad were fortunate that she made an exception for them. Her boys, she called them, throwing her arms around them and burrowing her head first into John's big shoulder and then into Hamish's skinny one.

Hamish didn't like men liking the way his mother looked, but neither did she, so that was all right. She didn't dress like a teenager, the way some of his friends' mothers did. But she had a way of striding into a room or along a footpath that made people notice her and sometimes, especially when she was on the stage, she attracted the eyes of men to her in a way that made Hamish feel angry and uncomfortable.

But then she would come on for her curtain call at the end, tall and beautiful, her cheeks reddening with delight as waves of cheering crashed around the tiny theatre; as often as not she would sweep off her hat or her helmet or her bear's head and shake loose her mane of copper hair, and like a queen she would acknowledge the applause. She never bowed. That was her trademark. Not bowing. Standing with her head up, watching the audience with glittering eyes.

Making the Most of It, she'd say.

And then Hamish would want to shout loudly, his own eyes bright with pride: 'That's my mum. She belongs to me.'

Helen hugged him much more often than Jemma did, but then Helen hugged everyone. Or she held his hand, or stroked his neck. 'Relax, Hamish,' she would say in her soft husky voice. 'You're all tight. Breathe. In. Slowly. Out.' Helen always smelled wonderful. Hamish wasn't sure if it was her perfume or her hair or the lotion she massaged into her hands, but whatever it was, she was nice to be around.

Well, *he* thought so. Caitlin didn't agree of course. Caitlin and Helen didn't get on. Nobody really understood how anyone could have trouble getting on with Helen, least of all her own daughter, but nevertheless Caitlin didn't. He had asked his mother about it, but she had sighed and said it was too hard to explain and it wasn't really their business. This surprised him. He thought Helen and Caitlin and Tom *were* their business.

He had also asked Caitlin. She had disembowelled him with one of her steeliest stares, tossed her plait and told him to go away and fuck himself.

He was tempted to ask Helen, but Helen didn't talk much about herself. She was a listener. She was such a good listener that she had ended up making a career of it. You could talk to her about anything and she would always concentrate carefully on what you said, waiting while you found the right words. Helen never kept lists. But she remembered the important things.

I'll go over to Helen's when this is over, thought Hamish, out of habit.

Helen will make me feel better.

The memory of Helen, her soft, kind face, her sweet smell, her sad eyes, stroked his mind with a light, familiar touch. He breathed in.

Reality struck like a slap across the face.

Helen would not be there.

He couldn't breathe out. A lump like a golf ball blocked the air in his throat. His eyes stung. He looked in mute appeal at Caitlin, but she was still staring at her feet, shredding tissues onto the carpet between the pews.

The minister was nodding at him. It was time. He stood up, still trying to breathe properly. The others made way for him. Dad touched his shoulder. It seemed to take hours for him to walk up the three broad steps to the pulpit.

'You can do it,' his mother had said. 'You can read this.'

'No,' he'd said. 'I can't. You know me. I might —'

'It won't matter if you do.' She never let him finish a sentence. 'But you won't. Not this time.'

'Get Dad to. Or Pop.'

Lids drooping down over her feverish green eyes. 'They'll be . . . too sad.' A quiver in her voice. Finally.

'I can't,' he'd said. 'Don't make me.'

She wasn't here but his mother was in his heart. Refusing to let it break.

'You're stronger than you think, Hamish. You can do it. I know you can.'

'*Death is nothing at all* . . .' Hamish read, then looked up. Saw the sea of sweat-sheened faces in the modern church, some with lowered heads, most looking at him. How Mum would have liked to be the one standing there.

'*I have only slipped away into the next room,*' Hamish continued, in his soft, clear voice.

'*I am I and you are you . . . whatever we were to each other, that we are still*

Call me by my old familiar name, speak to me in the easy way which you always used

Put no difference into your tone, wear no forced air of solemnity or sorrow

Laugh as we always laughed at the little jokes we enjoyed together

Play, smile, think of me, pray for me. Let my name be ever the household word it always was

Let it be spoken without effort, without the ghost of a shadow on it

Life means all that it ever meant. It is the same as it ever was; there is absolutely unbroken continuity.

What is this death but a negligible accident?

Why should I be out of mind because I am out of sight?

I am but waiting for you, for an interval, somewhere very near, just around the corner. All is well . . .'

Hamish returned to his seat. As his mother knew, he was stronger than he thought.

NAPPIES

'Everything's fine,' Jemma said to Helen, hooking the telephone receiver under her jaw so she didn't have to stop stirring. 'I'm making the cheese sauce for her lunch and she's really looking forward to it, aren't you, Caitlin?' She glanced down at the miniature human being standing like a doorstop beside her leg.

'Yuck,' said Caitlin.

'She said "yum",' said Jemma brightly. 'And they've had a pretty busy morning ...' she looked at the scene of devastation around her, 'so I'm going to put them both down for their sleep as soon as ... hang on a sec ...'

She put the phone down on the stove and crossed the kitchen and adjoining family room in several strides, lifting her feet high like someone from the Ministry of Silly Walks in an attempt not to tread on or trip over any of the paraphernalia spilling from the bright blue and yellow toy crates on the floor. She reached Hamish, whose intense and anxious search for the final piece of his jigsaw puzzle had involved him getting his head stuck in the puzzle bin. She dropped to her knees and tried to release his head without leaving his ears behind, an almost impossible feat. When she finally succeeded, she gathered him into his arms and tried to quieten his sobs. The odour of his nappy took her breath away.

She suddenly remembered the phone, plonked Hamish down and raced back across the room to the kitchen, where Caitlin, a blob in a padded track suit, had managed to pull the telephone receiver off the stove so that she could suck on it. Nor did she wish to stop when Jemma attempted to retrieve it.

'Say hello to Mummy!' she bellowed over Caitlin's furious screams, finally wrenching the receiver back and trying to manoeuvre the entire phone as far away from the roaring child as she could. It wasn't far enough.

'Stop worrying, Julie,' Jemma shouted. 'Everything's normal!'

She hung up and put the phone on a higher shelf. The house needed more protection from Caitlin Connor, baby dynamo.

She looked over at Hamish, now sitting quietly, carefully taking his puzzle apart so that he could do it all over again. It was two and a half years since her first incredible sight of him, but even now she sometimes found herself forced to stop absolutely still, just to stare at the miracle of him. A child. Another human being, created by her, by them.

'I suppose you two think you're bloody clever,' George had said at the hospital, his bloodhound eyes shining with a happiness she had never seen in them before. 'Bloody brilliant, that's us,' John had agreed, grinning widely enough to crack his face in two.

Now Hamish stood up to reach for a puzzle piece, his little black quiff of hair vertical on his rosy head. He beamed at her. She beamed back as he sat down with a plop to resume his task. She heard the squelch of his nappy from across the room and the smile sank from her face.

The sauce had turned into a mixture lumpier than a fat man's cardigan. She madly started stirring again, to no avail. 'Yuck,' said Caitlin, shaking her halo of russet curls.

'Yum,' said Jemma.

'Yuck,' said Caitlin.

'Well may you say yuck, Caitlin,' said Jemma briskly, 'because unlike most incoherent one year olds, you have somehow communicated to your mother your passion for corn in cheese sauce. Despite the fact that your vocabulary is limited to three one-syllable words, you have convinced your mother that nothing so boring, simple and easy as mashed vegetables will do for Caitlin Connor. Oh no.'

'Yuck,' said Caitlin.

'Your mummy says you must have corn in cheese sauce,' said Jemma to the blob, 'even though your mummy doesn't have to *prepare* said cheese sauce, as she is sitting in a nice quiet office where there is no noise and no mess and no cheese.'

The phone rang again. It was Diane Bevan, who was working with Jemma on her plan to start a playgroup in Siren's Rock. 'Feeding the animals,' said Jemma. 'Have to ring you back.'

'Sorry,' said Diane, 'but the council is considering our application to use the hall today. All I need to know is how many members are we expecting? And do we need access to the toilet facilities?'

'Well, of *course* we need access to the toilet facilities,' said Jemma. 'These are mothers of young children we're talking about. Their pelvic floors are a distant memory. Those who still have them are nurturing new foetuses in their wombs even as we speak. And I don't know how many members we can cope with until I know whether we are allowed to have the hall!'

'There's no need to yell,' sniffed Diane.

'Well, I'm sorry, but there is,' said Jemma, 'because I can hardly hear myself speak. Caitlin Connor is bashing her plate up and down on the high-chair tray wanting her corn in cheese sauce and Hamish has just started to howl because he has poohed himself!'

'How about if I just tell them ten members to start off with ...'

'If we tell them ten they won't let us have the hall, they'll probably just give us the annexe and then we won't have room for a craft table or anywhere for them to ride their little bikes ... oh *shit*! I've got to go, Diane, Hamish's nappy is leaking brown murk over the blocks and Caitlin Connor's unbreakable bunny plate has just smashed into a thousand pieces on my floor! Tell them twenty at least and say the list is still growing.'

Every second day Jemma, Hamish and Caitlin went out, the babies strapped into a huge double stroller that was almost as big as Jemma's car and much harder to drive. In the park, at the shops, just walking from the baby clinic to the butcher, Jemma almost always ran into other women with young children and, once they had exchanged essential information relating to sleep and bowels, she never lost an opportunity to bring up her ideas for starting a playgroup. Or she produced one of her petitions to the Siren's Rock Council — to upgrade the equipment at the local park, put a pedestrian crossing opposite the hall, or install a mothers' room with baby-changing facilities in the shopping centre.

The result of these often prolonged conversations, punctuated with the howls of impatient children, would be a late arrival back at the house, and meal and sleeps delayed. And potential disaster lay in the possibility that after missing their nap, one or both children might fall asleep during their dinner — a terrible prospect which would cancel out any chance of getting them to bed early at night and snatching a few hours for her real work. Jemma's life revolved around her lists — the endless domestic chores she could do while the children were awake, such as washing dishes, hanging out clothes, preparing casseroles and changing beds, and, more appealingly, the creative and organisational things she could do when they were asleep, such as research, play-writing, letter-writing and planning.

There were other lists as well. Ideas for books and stories. Cute things Hamish had said. Lists of phone numbers and contacts — people who might be able to help her with her projects to improve the lives of mothers in the town. Nothing gave Jemma greater satisfaction than crossing an item off a list of things to do. Sometimes, when she had done something without actually writing it down, she wrote it down anyway, just so she could put a line through it. In the back of her mind was the possibility that when the last of the lists had finally been ticked off, her own life, her real life, might finally begin again.

Nobody seemed to care about mothers. All this talk about women's liberation and equality in the workplace was fine for the women who *were* in the workplace, thought Jemma, but what about the others? In 1980, the majority of mothers with young children were at home, trying to feed a family on a single income in an increasingly expensive world, trying to nurture their babies so they'd develop into healthy, intelligent, sharing, caring people.

'We're doing the most important job in the nation,' Jemma told her mother, 'but who gives us credit? We're well educated and well trained but it's as if we've all had to put our career aspirations on the burners at the back of our stoves, for them to simmer for … how long? Ten years? Fifteen? Twenty?'

'What credit?' Marte would say. 'You make a happy family. That's your credit. That's your reward.'

In twenty years I'll be fifty, thought Jemma. I'll be an old woman, fat and wrinkled, and nobody will care who I am or what I've done ... She shuddered as she spooned yellow slop into Caitlin's mouth and watched Hamish making patterns with his Vegemite triangles. Doing everything except eat them.

Sometimes, when the prospect of all that she had to do — and all that she would not be able to do — overwhelmed her, Jemma just wanted to lie down and howl, the way Caitlin did when she didn't get what she wanted. Sometimes when Caitlin woke and bellowed for her — and especially if she had been woken many times the previous night by Hamish — Jemma would actually sink to the floor and pretend not to hear. Hamish would patter over and stand in front of her, his face contorted with anxiety, pointing towards the bedroom and the demanding roars.

Jemma would sigh and reach for him and hug him until he squeaked, overwhelmed with all sorts of fears. Why was he such an anxious child? Would he ever be happy? How would he survive at school — would he be picked on? Would he be clever? What if there was a war? What if he was killed? Or a car accident? How would she survive her loss of him? How would he survive if she wasn't around?

Would he ever be toilet trained?

Of course it wasn't always difficult. When Helen arrived early in the morning, with Caitlin on her hip and the enormous baby bag over her shoulder, her curly perm still damp, her smart clothes already wrinkled and her make-up not thick enough to cover the fatigue below her eyes, Jemma was usually still in her dressing gown. She would take delivery of the bag and the blob, temporarily immobilised by her padded parka, and wave goodbye as Helen raced back to her car and headed to work, her breath white puffs in the cold morning air. And all Jemma had to do was go back into her warm house and put the kettle on and sing along with the television while the little ones watched their favourite shows.

It was constant rather than hard. That was the essence of motherhood. There were no breaks. Weekends and holidays offered no reprieve. You were needed all the time and sometimes the responsibility seemed unendurable.

And at the end of every day, after another exhausting struggle with her priorities, Jemma would hurl herself into her big bed with a sigh of relief rather than satisfaction. But if John reached for her, she sometimes gave in to a rush of rage. Everyone wanted her, she would say, pushing his big hands away. Everyone wanted a piece of her all day long and now, in the peace of bedtime, he wanted her as well.

Reeling from regular rejection in the early months, John had learned not to reach for her very often. He waited patiently, understanding her fatigue as his own increased, making do with his memories.

Occasionally, when she was satisfied with her achievements, or had actually finished writing something, he was rewarded. His wife would snuggle up against his back, reaching her arms around his big torso and pressing her heavy breasts — lower now and traced with silver — against him. And he would lie there, suffused with happiness but sometimes too tired himself to do anything but close his eyes and bathe in her embrace.

Motherhood is a role you can't imagine until you've played it, thought Jemma, as she tickled Caitlin's stomach in an inept attempt to stop her howling while she laid her out on the change table, quietly chanting her creed: *I am doing the most important job in the universe. Without children, civilisation would not exist. Creating the people of tomorrow is the most fulfilling thing I have ever done. My reward is in my happy family.*

But no one had told her how time-consuming the most important job in the universe would be, and nobody had provided her with any training in how to create the people of tomorrow. Not even Marte. She didn't feel altogether convinced.

THE GOLDEN YEARS

Jemma's brilliant career had begun, as she had anticipated, within weeks of her return from Europe. She applied for a job in the promotions and public relations department at a Sydney television station and got it without the slightest difficulty.

She had discarded her cheesecloth blouses, embroidered jeans and baggy shorts and bought two tailored trouser suits, one navy and one red. Not many women were wearing trouser suits to work in Australia in the early seventies, but Jemma had loved the look of them on working women in London. She looked, said Helen, the way women who worked in television should look but so rarely did. Unless they were in front of the cameras.

Jemma suspected she would be in front of the cameras before long.

She loved working at Channel Three, loved the way the sun glinted on the glass windows as she strode up the broad concrete stairs in her high platform shoes, loved the way people waiting in hope in the glossy foyer whipped their heads around to watch her walk through the sliding doors that led down increasingly less shiny corridors until she reached the tiny office that was hers. She would flip back her hair, remove a chunky earring, jam the telephone receiver to her ear and deal with the constant requests for promotion and coverage. Smiling warmly, charming every caller, even when she was knocking most of them back. She liked threading thick cream sheets of paper into her typewriter and rattling off proposals and estimates, costings and reports, fingers flying over the keys, before snapping out the paper and striding to her boss's office to show him what she had done.

Joe Berriman was big and soft and bald, with a taste for David Frost striped shirts with white collars, although they were always wrinkled under the braces he used to keep his trousers up. She liked the way he looked up at her, exuding gentle yearning, shyly reminding her that he would leave his wife whenever she was ready to have him. He said she was the best thing that had ever happened to the Channel Three publicity department and he knew he would lose her soon.

Meanwhile, Helen had slipped back into shirts, skirts and secretarial skills. She worked for a law firm where the staff were busy, quiet and mostly over forty, but she didn't mind. Every night she came home to the flat the girls had found on the edge of Sydney Harbour — a canvas of glimmering water, displaying a myriad of lights, boats, ferries, the brand new Opera House with its controversial sails and, of course, the Harbour Bridge. They took it in turns to cook dinner — steaks the size of shoe soles, slabs of baked pumpkin and crispy potatoes, salads with tomatoes as big as breasts. Fruit that was firm, fat and sweet. Good Australian food. Food they had missed on a shoestring budget in Europe.

They ate out with John and Nigel at curry or steak houses. They visited smart new wine bars with crazy names like The Grapes of Sloth or Plonk Stop. Other nights they would all curl up on the girls' fat twin sofas, striped white and blue, and watch television together. It was hard to get used to black and white screens again after the luxury of colour in Europe. John said Jemma and colour television would hit Sydney at about the same time — she'd look wonderful in colour.

'Surely everyone looks better in colour,' drawled Nigel.

'No,' said Helen. 'I wouldn't.'

'Little Helen,' smiled Nigel indulgently. 'A small drop of modesty, swimming bravely through an ocean of ego.'

Every night at about ten, John would turn to Jemma beside him on the couch and wrap his arms around her. By some unspoken pre-arrangement (at least, Helen hoped it was unspoken) Nigel would stand up, place his long cold fingers on Helen's neck and guide her silently into the bedroom she shared with Jemma. Where he would do interesting things to her. Or not, as the mood took him. Some nights they just read their books. Or Nigel would talk to her about the desperately inferior and grossly uncivilised people who crossed his path during the course of his day. Whatever they did, after an hour or two Nigel would get up and glide away, leaving her curled up in her bed, sometimes still fully dressed and absorbed in her novel, sometimes naked or in her knickers, almost too exhausted by their sexual exertions to pull the sheet over her slender body.

Eventually John would leave too. Helen was pretty sure that Jemma had introduced some new code relating to sexual conduct on weeknights. Certainly she and John were very quiet, whatever they were doing. She assumed John and Jemma were able to make love to each other properly at weekends, when she and Nigel left them alone. She didn't know. She didn't ask and Jemma never said. It was strange how the girls rarely referred to their sex lives at all any more.

Once you were going all the way, Helen supposed, there was no point in talking about the journey. Or what happened when you arrived.

Nigel often took Helen to the movies, obscure foreign language films that nobody else had heard of, and sometimes they went to concerts. Chamber music mostly, and some jazz. Helen liked Nigel best when they went to hear music with which she was unfamiliar, because he took pains to explain it to her and she listened closely and quietly, her eyes never leaving his face. On these occasions, more than at any other time, she wondered if he loved her.

Nigel was living in his parents' apartment at Darling Point. Sometimes he took Helen there. The view showed the harbour from a different angle, sailing boats rather than ferries — rich men's toys. The apartment was lovely: bare, full of glass and gleaming tiles and exquisite figurines in cabinets. Helen never felt comfortable there and was frightened when Nigel made love to her on the big, hard satin-covered bed in the master bedroom. If making love could ever describe what Nigel did to her.

John went back to his aunt's house but soon revolted against the confines of family life and found a small flat near Sydney University. The new job, which he had postponed while he had his European holiday, was working out well. He was saving more money than the rest of them and with good reason. As soon as he saved enough to put a deposit on a house, he announced in front of everyone, he and Jemma would get married.

'And as soon as you manage to have an orgasm,' said Nigel to Helen, 'we can get married too.' Everyone looked embarrassed, even Polly and Tim, the newlyweds from the flat downstairs.

'How do you stand him?' Jemma asked Helen that night, as they brushed their teeth together in their small bathroom. 'I mean, I know he's funny and everything, but you're not seriously thinking of marrying him, are you?'

Helen spat out and shook her head. Her hair was shoulder length again, and fat, thanks to daily blow drying. 'I don't know what we're going to do,' she said. 'We like the same books. I'm learning to like his sort of films. And music. He's teaching me to cook.'

'That's not love,' said Jemma.

Helen frowned. 'Sometimes I feel really sorry for him. He has had a pretty lonely life. His parents really *don't* like him, you know. He's not just saying it for effect. And I know how *that* feels.'

After a while, looking at Jemma in the mirror, Helen had a stab at breaking the new rule. 'Sex is interesting, isn't it?' she said tentatively. 'Better than I thought it would be.'

Jemma looked cross. 'Sex has always turned you on. That doesn't mean Nigel does. Any more than anyone else would.'

Helen looked ashamed. She swallowed hard a few times and her eyes danced over the bathroom tiles. Finally she said: 'Yes. But at least he wants to do it with me and nobody else.'

Jemma made a snort of incomprehension.

'Look,' said Helen, 'I mean, sometimes he makes me miserable. Sometimes he makes me laugh. He makes us all laugh, you know that. Anyway, it's up and down. I suppose that's love.'

'No,' said Jemma. 'It's not. John never makes me miserable. And he wouldn't dream of talking about my orgasms in front of people.'

Helen chewed her lip. 'He's worried about it. He's determined to make me have one.'

Jemma snorted again. 'Nigel's quest,' she said nastily. 'And *have* you ever had one?' she asked.

'I'm not sure. I don't know.'

'You'd know,' said Jemma.

'Well,' said Helen resignedly. 'Anyway, we're grown-up now. We've both got our blokes. Isn't that what we wanted?'

'You're my friend,' said Jemma. 'I want you to be happy with Nigel but I'm not sure you are. Making you laugh isn't the same as making you happy.'

'I'm happy,' said Helen. And she often was. Their dream trip was over but these were still their golden years. Shiny with promise. Glowing with hope. The future was theirs. Anything could happen.

THE WHOLE
CATASTROPHE

Grezza went back to his home town in western Australia and almost immediately wrote to tell them that he was planning to marry a local girl who had patiently waited for him during his three years away.

'I never heard of any local girl,' said Jemma incredulously. 'That dark horse. Pretending all that time that he wanted to go to bed with me!'

Judy is the best girl, he enthused. *I'd forgotten how beautiful she is. And she doesn't talk all the time like Jemma. Fact is, she's nearly as quiet as Helen. You'll love her. Her dad's going to give me a job with his firm. Tractor maintenance and technical backup. Says I'm a natural. The wedding's in June. Can any of you get over?*

PS: Jude's making me wait till we're married. Mum's the word about you-know-who, okay?

'Mum's the word,' nodded Jemma. 'Wouldn't want to get the little sweetie in trouble with his new missus.'

'I think someone should write to Susan,' mused Helen. '*She* might like to come over for the wedding.'

'I know,' said Jemma. 'We should write to Grezza, *telling* him we've written to Susan.'

'And we should tell him Susan is so thrilled for his happiness that she's booked her ticket to Perth already,' said Helen.

'And that she has bought a special dress that she won't be wearing for the occasion,' gurgled Jemma.

'It would be kind of us,' said Helen, as they folded up with laughter.

'Tarts with hearts of gold, that's us,' Jemma declared.

'Hey,' said Jemma, wiping her eyes. 'Remember that letter you made me write to John? When he was in boarding school? Did you know he kept it? Used to sleep with it under his pillow? He thought it meant I loved him.'

'Well,' said Helen. 'You did.'

'Not then.'

As it turned out, they couldn't afford to go to Perth, and they didn't meet up with Grezza again until Jemma's wedding the following year.

John and Jemma were married in the imposing grey stone Catholic church at Siren's Rock, on a warm autumn day in April. The sun, almost as carried away with the happiness of the occasion as Marte, lightly kissed everything and everyone it touched.

Grezza's Judith was a pretty brunette, a Roman Catholic like John and, as Jemma pointed out, one of the few people in the church who knew when to sit, when to stand up and when to kneel down. 'You have to have good knees to be a Catholic,' said Marte, but she was overjoyed even so.

Shortly after his return to Australia, John had reverted to his mother's faith. Helen thought this was somewhat ironic but didn't say so, and Jemma didn't question it at all. By the time they were married, she was used to it. 'John is a very good man, so credit where credit is due,' she said to Marte, who nodded. 'Anyway, it doesn't bother me which church we go to, as long as I can still talk to God at the beach.'

They had the works. The Whole Catastrophe, said Jemma. The bride wore a long veil and a sculpted white satin dress. There were flowers and bridesmaids and the 'Wedding March', as well as 'Ave Maria' and 'Here Comes the Bride'. There were tears at the church and belly laughs at the reception in the town hall function room. Marte, in jade brocade, was in her element as she supervised servings of prawn cocktails and Chicken Maryland, followed by Peach Melba. 'Everything on the menu has a double-barrelled name,' Jemma said to Helen. 'You'd think we were the Basingstoke-Browns.' The happy couple were toasted with bubbly Cold Duck and cheered off to the honeymoon suite at the Berry Beach Motel, where they arrived deafened by the sound of a clattering chorus of beer cans. Jemma had refused to stop and remove the cans or the cream coating their car. 'It's our day,' she said to John. 'I want everyone to know about it.'

'The best man was a bit of all right,' Cindy-Lou Smith, nee Basingstoke-Brown told her mother, as the reception wound down. 'Really witty, his speech was, lovely voice, like a radio announcer. Good looking in a skinny, elegant sort of way. And really tall. How you'd imagine Oscar Wilde.'

'So Helen Winter's done all right for herself then,' said Cindy-Lou's mother disconsolately. 'Babs will be pleased.'

Babs and Douglas Winter were unable to hide their surprise at Helen being lucky enough to snag someone as desirable as Nigel Connor. 'A wealthy family with a big property in the country and an apartment in the best part of Sydney,' said Babs to her friends, trying to keep the wonder out of her voice. 'And he seems to find our Helen quite attractive.'

She didn't mention Nigel's glassy gaze when Helen had introduced him earlier in the evening, or the fact that while he had been impeccably polite and repeated the required phrases, he had stared over their heads in a supercilious fashion. Joy had giggled breathlessly at him when he said: 'Don't tell me — this must be little Joy. Very little Joy.'

'I don't think Nigel is as nice as he seems,' Joy confided to her mother later. 'We'll see,' said Babs, not quite able to put her finger on it either. 'At least the family has money.'

'So will we be hearing more wedding bells?' asked Edna Egan eagerly.

Babs patted her hair and made a moue with her scarlet lips. 'I think they are just feeling their way at present,' she said coyly.

Nigel turned Helen around to face the wall, hoisted up the bell-shaped skirt of her taffeta bridesmaid's dress and plunged his fingers down into her powder-blue panties.

With an effort she ducked away from him, yanking her skirt down again.

'No,' said Helen, sitting down on the bed.

The Sea Breeze Motel was a short walk from the reception place, but spending the night there with Nigel was the last thing Helen had considered doing after John and Jemma's wedding. She had gazed pathetically at the sight of her parents' car departing with Joy sitting prettily in the back seat, forced a small, embarrassed smile for the benefit of other departing guests.

'Show me the way to go home, sweetness,' Nigel had murmured in her ear. 'I've had a little drink about an hour ago and it's gone right to my head.'

Knowing that her reputation would be ruined forever in this town if she spent the night with her boyfriend, Helen had nervously tottered along beside Nigel in her blue bridesmaid shoes.

It was just one of those silly details that was overlooked in the business of putting on a big wedding, said Saint Helen.

They didn't even ask you if you wanted to go home with them. Didn't spare you a single thought, said Helen the cynic.

Nigel, looking attractive in a tailored tuxedo, was drunk and more than a little disorderly as he'd jiggled his room key, singing softly to himself. 'I'mmm … going to screw the bridesmaid, the bridesmaid, the bridesmaid,' he'd warbled. 'Hey Siren's Crack, Dougy Winter's little girl is going to crack it tonight,' he'd said, sotto voce, trying to get his key in the lock.

Helen had shushed him, half laughing. A tear dropped on her turquoise taffeta.

Now she sat on the bed and looked at him defiantly.

'Good lord!' said Nigel in highest camp mode. 'Rejection, is it? I thought the day would never come!'

Helen said nothing.

'Come to think of it,' said Nigel, 'I thought the *bridesmaid* would never come! Oh, that's right. She hasn't!' He sat down in the standard motel chair and began to giggle.

'Helen, my dear,' he said finally, 'your usual silence is inappropriate in this particular circumstance. If you're not going to let me have a little ride, you will have to tell me what you *do* want to do. But it does seem rather a shame to destroy your reputation by being in this ghastly room without making it worth your while.'

Helen chewed her bottom lip and folded her hands in her lap. 'Nigel,' she said softly, 'I do want you to make love to me.'

He smiled at her. 'Of course you do. When did fair Helen ever *not* want to be screwed? Now take off that hideous

262

dress, there's a good girl. No, better still, leave it on and let me get underneath.' He leapt out of his chair and dropped down on all fours.

Helen stayed on the bed. 'No,' she said. 'I want you to make love to me, Nigel, but in the normal way. In the conventional way.'

'What?' Nigel raised his head to look at her. 'Missionary position? You on the bottom, me on the top?'

'Yes.'

'In out in out in out and then bang?'

'Yes,' said Helen. 'For once.'

'What?' Nigel blinked. 'We've never done the missionary thing?'

'Never,' said Helen.

He got to his feet and swayed. She looked at him nervously. 'Give us a cuddle then,' he said. 'If you're lucky I might go all the way.'

She stood up and put her arms around him. He gazed over her head, humming softly.

'Nigel?'

'Hmmm?'

'It was such a romantic wedding.' She looked up at him with a little smile. 'They're going to live happily ever after.'

'Of course they're not,' said Nigel. 'Nobody does.'

He held her very formally. There was no clinging or clutching, no passionate embrace. There never was. After a while Helen reached up and pulled his head down towards hers.

'I love you, Nigel,' she whispered, her lips very close to his. She thought she felt his mouth tremble for a moment, and then he laughed a little and nipped her on the bottom lip.

'No,' said Helen.

'No *again*?'

'No biting.' She kissed him again. 'And I don't want you to touch my bottom.'

'All these instructions,' sighed Nigel, lying down beside her on the bed. 'I hope I remember everything in the right order.'

Nigel and Helen finally made love on a double bed at the Sea Breeze Motel, in the traditional way but without the joy, the fulfilment, the enthusiasm or the noise ('At last I can scream!' Jemma was saying to John) with which their best friends were consummating their marriage a few miles away on the coast.

'God,' said Nigel, rolling off Helen's small frame about twenty minutes later.

'Yes, my son?' whispered Helen, stealing one of his favourite jokes. Her eyes were wide open in the darkness. 'Was it worth the sin?'

'On the contrary, your grace,' said Nigel. 'That was just about the most boring thing I've ever done.'

SAY IT WITH FLOWERS

Jemma was finally in front of the cameras. It was only a temporary job but she was there, her cheekbones deepened with several tones of brown powder, her lips warm and gleaming red, her hair shimmering in the light. She was to host the Channel Three Women's Hour.

She had been seen in the corridors, had smiled at the right people, asked the right questions, flirted with the right executives and finally, stuck without an anchor woman, someone had thought of her. The regular Women's Hour hostess was in hospital with suspected appendicitis and the show's regular reporter was stuck somewhere on a plane. There was a line-up of guests too important to let down. They were actually grateful to Jemma for being willing to step in at such short notice.

Sitting with her legs elegantly crossed in a blue velvet chair on a silver pivot, Jemma was poised to seize the chance of a lifetime.

Four hours later John found her at home, a mountain of limbs and tissues on their king-sized raft of a bed. They had bought the bed the week after they had returned from their honeymoon, having realised that connubial bliss would be under threat until they found one big enough for both of them. It was much too big for John's tiny flat, but it would be fine when they found a house. Meanwhile there was no room for any other furniture in the bedroom and the only option for John was to stand beside it, like a supplicant, or to climb on board and attempt to steer his sobbing wife through a froth of tissues and a heaving sea of saltwater tears.

'What?' he said, over and over again. 'What? Has someone died? Has something happened to your mum?'

'No,' she wailed. 'No, no, no, no, no!'

She had failed. She had failed her first attempt at fame.

The production team had been nice enough about it. 'It's as much our fault as yours,' the producer's assistant said afterwards. 'You weren't properly briefed. And let's face it, you're no journalist.'

That really hurt. Jemma thought she really *was* a journalist. Jemma had never doubted that she could be anything she wanted to be.

She had asked too many questions. She hadn't waited for the answers. She had gone off on tangents, interrupted, confused everyone, talked too much. The eminent novelist couldn't get a word in because Jemma started talking about her own unpublished travel memoir. The biomedical scientist had been rendered speechless by Jemma's description of her own inept experiments with a Bunsen burner. The woman who wanted more women to come to her rape crisis centre was incensed by Jemma's questions about what victims were wearing when they were attacked. 'Nothing as revealing as the suit you're wearing right now,' the woman had said icily. 'You'd better watch your back.'

'But it was your first time,' said John. 'All you need is more practice. More experience.'

'You don't understand,' sobbed Jemma. 'I saw the videotape. I was awful. All you could hear was me, going on and on, and all you could see was them, looking disgusted. And worst of all,' she threw her head between her knees, 'worst of all I looked so *fat*! I'm *huge*. I looked like I had two rhinos dancing down the front of my jacket!'

'Well, of course you're not fat,' said John. 'The camera puts on ten pounds, doesn't it, or more for some people? Look, that suit sometimes makes you look bigger than you really are. Next time you can wear a dress.'

But that definitely wasn't the right thing to say.

Helen couldn't afford to keep the harbourside flat on her own. Twice she advertised and interviewed potential flatmates, but she found the whole process humiliating and difficult, embarrassed that even the most straightforward questions made her feel patronising, while queries from the girls who came reduced her to a mumbling mess.

'It's ridiculous, isn't it?' said Jemma. 'Now that you and Nigel could have the flat to yourselves, he's not around to enjoy it.'

'Thank goodness,' said Helen, and Jemma smiled approvingly.

He couldn't believe it at first. When she had dressed and left the Sea Breeze Motel without another word to him. He couldn't believe that he had finally gone too far. Not by what he did to her — though he was original in bed and possibly depraved, he had never hurt her — but in the cruelty of what he had said. He had wounded her with his words, struck at her with his needlessly vicious attitude. Helen had given Nigel her body with a declaration of love and he had responded by pushing her into a pool of humiliation in which she could no longer stay afloat.

So she left him. Without regret. Without a lift.

She had walked home. All the way to Grand View Crescent, wearing her turquoise bridesmaid's dress and carrying her shoes. But then, for years now, thanks to Jemma, Helen's feet had been good and hard.

Nigel had neither begged nor pleaded, but when she had been back in Sydney for two weeks, he rang. He rang her at work and told her not to be silly. That he missed her and that they needed each other now, with John and Jemma gone.

She hung up.

He rang every day for a week and then he stopped. After that he left her alone.

When the honeymooners returned they visited her flat often, but John and Jemma were consumed by the second big blaze of their love affair and always went home early.

Helen was lonely but she had been lonely before. She put up with it.

After two months she came home from work one Friday afternoon to find Nigel sitting like a grasshopper on the floor outside her apartment, holding a huge bunch of daffodils between his knees. He stood up and looked at her sadly over the yellow blooms. Helen looked at the floor, clutching her keys, and said nothing.

'Of all the camping joints in all the world, why did you have to walk into mine?' he murmured.

She didn't reply. He didn't seem to expect her to. He waited a minute or two and then began to sing. Rather well, she thought. He could carry a tune. His voice was thin, like him, but quite melodic.

'*You must remember this,*' he sang, '*a kiss is just a kiss . . .*'

He kept singing while she unlocked the door and went inside. He stood in the hall and kept singing until he had finished the song, even humming the piano bits at the end.

Helen made an effort not to laugh and went to stare out of the window at the ferries. She felt as if she hadn't laughed for a long time. She wanted to, but not with him.

'Can I come in?' he called from the doorway.

She shrugged and kept looking out of the window, heard him come in and close the door.

'I miss Jemma,' said Helen, without turning around. 'I don't miss you.'

'No, well, that's not surprising,' said Nigel softly. 'I was cruel to you. I said horrible things. I was drunk. I'm a bad drunk. I'm sorry.'

'You said I was boring.'

'I didn't say you were boring,' said Nigel. She wondered how drunk he had really been. 'I said what we did was boring. It was a stupid thing to say. I suppose I was just feeling inadequate because I have never been able to make you feel . . . as happy as I'd like to.'

Helen turned around and looked at him. 'Is that why you're here, Nigel? I don't remember my happiness being high on your list of priorities before.'

She stopped. She was impressed with herself. Nigel looked impressed too. But of course, she'd had plenty of time to practise.

'Or,' she continued, her eloquence giving her confidence, 'are you here because you're lonely? Because you miss John and nobody else will put up with you?'

Surprising her again, he said: 'Both reasons.'

Helen nodded, took a deep breath and put her hands in the pockets of her new black trouser suit.

'So don't tell me, let me guess,' she said. 'You would now like me to whip you up a nice omelette, with real butter and a pinch of fresh herbs, just the way you taught me to do it. And after we've washed that down with a superior little white ... um ... what will happen next? Oh yes. You will require me to take my clothes off so you can fuck me stupid from every angle. Oh, as long as we don't use the missionary position. In out in out bang.'

He slipped his hand into his jacket pocket and pulled out two tickets. 'Actually, I thought we might buy a choc top and go to a movie.'

She did laugh then. She laughed until the tears trickled down her cheeks and Nigel kissed them away. He held her gently by the shoulders and told her he was sorry again, called himself stupid and said he hadn't realised what he had until he lost her. Then he kissed her properly on the lips, gently, no biting, and in the end it was Helen, wanting to be touched, who sought his tongue and slipped her hands up under his shirt to feel his skin. And eventually they did everything she had known they would do as soon as she saw him in the hall with his arms full of daffodils.

Hours later, lying in the dark, watching the harbour lights merge with the stars, Nigel said: 'Did you mean it when you said you loved me? I think I'll marry you, fair Helen. Mainly because this is a bloody nice flat but also because I think I may love you too.'

The movie tickets were for the following night. Nigel was many things, but he wasn't stupid.

GOING HOME

Jemma was appalled when they told her they were getting married. She was even more appalled by the speed with which the arrangements were made and by the cold and godless service at which Helen and Nigel tied their proverbial knot. She and John were the only witnesses and the registry office ceremony, if you could call it that, was as bad if not worse than anything she had seen on television.

'I don't get it,' she said sadly to John as they drove home from the restaurant where they'd celebrated, Jemma having eaten and drunk far too much in order to camouflage her outraged emotions. 'It's not as if they have to get married to have sex. Not in this day and age. And she's not pregnant.'

'I think he really loves her,' said John.

'Don't be silly,' snapped Jemma. 'The only human being Nigel loves, apart from himself, is you.'

'Give me a break.'

'You know it's true,' said Jemma. 'Helen and I worked it out ages ago. Everyone picked on him and hated him, and at the lowest time of his life you saved him from all that. You're his hero.'

'I'm nobody's hero,' muttered John. 'Anyway we're not talking about me.'

'Well, Helen doesn't love Nigel,' said Jemma. 'She just thinks he needs her.'

'He does,' said John. 'And maybe, in her own way, she needs him.'

Still, Helen and Nigel seemed happy enough in the harbourside flat, apparently suffering no ill effects from their sterile wedding service or the Arctic silence that followed Helen's phone call to her parents to tell them she was a married woman.

Marte and George were bitterly disappointed. 'You could have been the matron of honour,' Marte wailed over the phone to Jemma. 'She didn't have her special day. Every bride deserves her special day.'

'I know,' said Jemma. 'I told her. But you know Helen. She has a mind of her own. And Nigel is just as bad.'

Three years later they were all still working in the city, saving hard for some vague and undefined future. The four of them ate out together frequently, or held ambitious dinner parties in their flats, with Jemma and Nigel competing for the culinary honours and John and Helen doing a lot of washing up.

Jemma tried hard to like Nigel, for Helen's sake, but she noticed his spiteful tongue was growing sharper. Too often, his jokes were at Helen's expense.

'He scares me sometimes,' Helen admitted to Jemma. 'He's moody. And he's awful when he drinks.' She didn't add that he became much worse when he smoked dope — suspicious, paranoid, sometimes hysterical — and she didn't tell Jemma about the terrible row they'd had when he put them both at risk by planting his own marijuana in a window box on the balcony of their flat.

'The trouble is,' said Jemma, 'now that you're married, you can't just *leave* him. You promised to stay with him forever. That's why I was worried about you doing it in the first place. It's too late now.'

'I feel sorry for him,' said Helen. 'He's so clever, but he rubs people up the wrong way.'

'Even John is getting sick of him,' said Jemma. 'Mainly because he is so awful to you.'

'I know,' said Helen. 'But I'm all he has. He knows it, and he doesn't like it.'

Despite her admission to Jemma, Helen pulled down the blind, tried to convince herself that no relationship was perfect, not even Jemma and John's.

The Sullivans had recently moved into a larger unit while their search for the house of their dreams continued. Everything Jemma liked was out of their price range. Sometimes she thought they would still be renting a flat when they retired.

'No,' said John, 'we'll have to be in our own home before we start a family.' Jemma had frowned and changed the subject. Starting a family was still a long way off. Stardom had to come first.

But Helen knew that John would steer them through this looming threat to their happiness. He was too deeply in love with Jemma.

Jemma was now assistant publicity manager at Channel Three, but every Saturday she scanned the classifieds for work that would place her in the public eye. Since her spectacular disaster in front of the cameras, her job had never held the same promise of better things to come. True, Joe Berriman still looked at her with beseeching desire and the visitors in the foyer still gazed at her enviously each day as she hurried in and out of the inner sanctum. But no matter how high she held her head, she knew they gossiped about her — she had tried and been found wanting.

Jemma's next opportunity to improve her situation occurred when Joe Berriman called her into his office to run through her plans for the promotion of the channel's new hour-long news program. When they had finished, he pushed away the pile of papers and looked at her quizzically over the top of his glasses. 'I'm moving on, Jemma,' he said. 'Would you like my job?'

She laughed. 'You're not serious.'

'Couldn't be more so,' said Joe, hanging on to his ugly braces. 'You'll do a better job than me. You're smart, organised, efficient. You can get people to do anything you want. You understand the industry. You know what's wanted. I'd like to recommend you. It's a lot more money.'

'Joe,' said Jemma slowly.

'I know what you're going to say,' Joe cut in.

'It's just not what I had in mind,' Jemma spoke over him. 'A career making other people famous.'

Joe chose his next words carefully. 'Did you ever think,' he said, 'that it's not the on-camera personalities and the so-called stars who hold the power in these places?' He smiled. 'It's the suits upstairs. With what you've got in your suit, and a sharpish brain as well, you could rise very high in a place like this.'

But the suit comment was a mistake.

'It's not what I had in mind,' she repeated sullenly.

'Okay,' said Joe. 'If you're sure.'

'I'm sure,' said Jemma.

'So you'd better go down and see the news producer,' said Joe.

Jemma looked at him, startled out of her sulk.

'There's an opening for a presenter on the new program,' said Joe. 'I've already told them upstairs that you could do it. I just wanted to make you my own offer first.'

Jemma closed her eyes and thrust her hand inside her jacket to massage her heart back to normal. Joe's own heart lurched as a consequence. He would miss seeing that magnificent bosom heave.

It had taken Joe Berriman a long time to work out why his assistant looked so much sexier in her trouser suits than other women who wore them, but he had finally realised the difference. Jemma never wore shirts. Just the trousers and the jacket, buttoned up below her cleavage. No wonder they'd jumped at the chance to have her as their weather girl.

Jemma was back at home, taking refuge in bed, worn out with crying, when John telephoned her to say he would be late home. 'What's the matter?' he asked, alarmed. She sounded as if she was speaking from inside a submarine.

'They offered me a job,' she sniffed. 'As their weather girl! *Weather girl!*' She screamed the words. '*Weather girl!*'

'Weather girl,' John repeated carefully. Then, tentatively: 'You're not a *weather girl!*'

'I know,' she sobbed. 'But that's all they think I'm good for. Prancing around in a bikini — or a tiny little raincoat with a pointing stick. Just because I've got big boobs. And I'm ta-all . . .' She began to sob again.

'Listen to me,' said John. 'You're a beautiful intelligent woman. You're going to be famous one day. You're going to be a writer or an actress or maybe a politician. But you're never going to be a weather girl!'

'I'm leaving that place. I can't stand it there any more. They already stare at me and talk about me behind my back and now it will be worse.'

When he finally came home she was peeling potatoes in their small kitchen. She asked him belatedly why he had taken so long. His eyes were too bright. He didn't look at her.

'What?' she asked him. 'What's happened?'

'There's a job I'd like to go for,' he said slowly. 'I don't know if this is a good time to talk to you about it. But as you're thinking of leaving the channel anyway ...'

'Leaving the channel?' said Jemma. 'Do you mean if you get this job, I would have to leave mine?'

'We'd have to move,' said John. 'We'd have to move out of Sydney.'

'And go where?'

John sighed and gave her a look so desperate for understanding that her own distress dissolved. She put down her potato peeler, crossed the room, put her arms around him.

'It's okay,' she said softly. 'I'll follow you to the ends of the earth, you know that. If this is what you want to do.'

He held on to her tightly, as if he was afraid that when he spoke she might disappear.

'I know you'd follow me to the ends of earth,' he said slowly. 'But would you follow me back to Siren's Rock?'

For about thirty seconds there was no sound in their tiny flat but the splat from the tap as it dripped onto the potato peelings in the sink.

'They need an engineering manager at the radio station,' John continued, 'and that is exactly what I want to do.'

He held his breath. He held Jemma as well.

'We could afford a nice house at Siren's Rock,' she said slowly.

'Much nicer than in Sydney, that's for sure,' said John. 'We could *build* a house. The house of our dreams.'

'And with my city experience I could probably get a job at the television station at Bridgetown.'

'That's a great idea.' John smiled, letting out his breath. 'I hadn't even thought of that.'

'And if we went home,' Jemma smiled back at him, 'maybe we could have a baby.'

MARRY IN HASTE

Most nights, John came home to a mess. Arsenic hour, Jemma called this time, and he had learned not to comment on the obstacle course which made his path from the front door to the family room so precarious. She would have cleaned up, except that this or that drama had happened or someone had rung at the wrong time. 'Such are the trials of an everyday housewife,' she would say, tongue in cheek, because they both knew Jemma was no such thing.

Tonight Helen was still there when John arrived; she had stayed to help Jemma clean up. 'However would any of us survive without you, Jemma?' she said. 'Another day of domestic chaos and yet here they are — clean, happy and safe, all because of you. You're doing the most important job in the world.'

'Oh I know, I *know*,' said Jemma, clutching her heart, but smiling.

'Has it ever occurred to you,' asked Helen, 'that you are a true feminist?'

'No,' chuckled Jemma. 'That's you. You're the single parent

competing with men in the workplace. I'm the little woman looking after the kids at home.'

'But you're also doing things that get women a better deal — what with lobbying for the playgroup, and more facilities for women and children,' said Helen. 'And caring for kids is surely one of the main ideals of feminism?'

'Helen's right,' said John. 'You're probably the first true feminist in Siren's Rock.'

Nigel had not stayed around for the birth of his daughter. He hadn't even lasted as long as Helen's morning sickness.

He lost his job shortly after John and Jemma moved back to Siren's Rock and Helen briefly entertained the hope that they might return to live there too. 'What? So we can frolic in all the places you used to play with yourselves and have Sunday lunch with Mummy and Daddy Winter?' Nigel asked scathingly, and Helen flinched and hunched her shoulders, wondering, as she often did, how much about her history he had guessed.

Nigel also lost interest in sex. Sometimes he stayed out so late that she went to bed alone and frequently found herself alone again next morning. For a while she didn't mind, then one day, without even thinking about it, without knowing when the possibility had first entered her mind, she said: 'Are you seeing some other woman?'

He looked at her slyly. 'Another woman, another man ... Why would you care, fair Helen? You've been resisting my irresistible charms with distressing frequency.'

'That's not fair,' said Helen. 'It's you who's acting bored with me.'

Nigel lifted his eyebrow. '*Acting*? I don't have to *act* bored. You never talk. You never laugh. You never venture an opinion. You never want to go out. Jemma goes back to

Siren's Crack so you become a one-dimensional frigid bitch.'

Helen thought about this. 'I'm sorry,' she said at last. 'I do miss her but I didn't think it was so obvious. Shall we go out now?'

But it turned out that he didn't want to go out at all. They stayed in while he did things to her that he hadn't done for months. Helen pressed her face into the pillow and thought of joining John and Jemma in Siren's Rock.

They went back to visit when Hamish was born and for a while things improved. Nigel was extraordinarily funny, saying outrageous things about the baby, which neither Jemma nor John seemed to mind. They drove up to Siren's Rock every two or three months after that, and Helen and Jemma walked on the beach at Mermaid Cove while the men stayed home and doted on the baby.

'I thought I couldn't love John any more but I do,' said Jemma. 'He's so gentle and wonderful with Hamish and he's not jealous or anything. In fact, he loves to watch me feed him, now that the milk has settled down. You know, after all I've been through, I'm thinking of writing a manual for nursing mothers.'

'That's a great idea,' said Helen, 'the sort of thing you could do until you've got time to write your play. And he's sleeping well now?'

'I found his thumb for him and put it in his mouth. I kept doing it until he got the idea. It was the smartest thing I've ever done. You don't have to sterilise thumbs.'

Helen became pregnant because she had forgotten to renew her pill prescription and didn't think it mattered — Nigel was leaving her alone again. But he surprised her by coming home late one night and slipping into her bed and into her body so quickly and gently that she was hardly aware it was happening, until his undulations woke her to full consciousness and filled her with an intense desire which surprised both of them.

'Nigel,' she murmured, winding her arms around his neck, 'it's happening, I'm ...'

'You're awake,' he said, and sounded disappointed, although he continued the intercourse, sliding his hands under her and clamping them around her bottom. She smelled some strange, exotic scent on his body and her desire dwindled away. This would be another of his little perversions — to have sex with his sleeping wife while he was still wet from another woman. Or man.

I'm even more perverse than him, Helen thought, when, despite her suspicion that Nigel was being unfaithful, she realised she might be pregnant and almost choked with excitement.

On the phone, Jemma was delighted but anxious. 'What will Nigel say?'

'I think he'll be thrilled,' said Helen. 'I really do. This might be just what he needs.' Not adding that she hoped this would bring him back.

'I'll keep my fingers crossed,' said Jemma dubiously.

Helen had trouble telling Nigel her news because he didn't come home before three am for nearly a week. On the seventh day she woke up awash with nausea. It was just after dawn and she was still alone in bed. She hurled herself off a rising wave of sickness, raced into the bathroom and dropped to her knees in front of the toilet bowl, where she threw up and retched long after there was nothing left to come.

When she looked up, Nigel was leaning against the bathroom doorframe. His coppery hair was a mess and his shirt was undone. His red tie matched his eyes and hung limply in two strands from his collar. He looked pale and as dissipated and as ill as Helen felt. It was six in the morning but he was obviously drunk. Or drugged. Or both.

He looked at her, on her knees beside the toilet, her fine blonde hair sticking to her grey cheeks.

'You are the most disgusting sight I've ever seen,' said Nigel.

Alone in the city, she worked throughout her pregnancy and was still at her desk when her waters broke. Jemma drove all night to arrive just in time for the birth. Caitlin Connor shot into the world swiftly and without complications, a situation she would spend her childhood and adolescence seeking to rectify. The two friends hung over her hospital crib, adoring her together. For the second time in her life, Helen fell in love. But once again, there was no suggestion that it might be a reciprocal arrangement.

DAYCARE

'I can do it,' Jemma said. 'I'd love to do it. I mean, I have to look after Hamish anyway. It's not as if it involves any huge sacrifice on my part.'

'But what about your career? Your writing? Your acting? Everything you want to do with your life?' Helen sat hugging herself on one of the striped sofas they had originally bought for the harbour-view apartment. They had taken one each. Jemma's was in the spare bedroom in her house at Siren's Rock. Helen's was here, in the small inner-city flat she had moved into when Nigel had lost his job.

'I miss you,' said Jemma. 'I want us to be together again. Like it was before Nigel came on the scene.'

And John? What about what happened when John came on the scene?

'I wouldn't dream of asking you,' Helen said, her husky voice almost inaudible. 'It's more than anyone should ask a friend.'

'You didn't ask,' said Jemma briskly, busy brewing cups of tea in the tiny kitchenette. 'I offered. And I am determined to do it, so you could save us both a lot of stress by just agreeing.'

'I can't.'

'John is really keen for us to do this,' said Jemma. 'He wants to help. He feels so bad about Nigel walking out on you. He thinks it's all his fault because he brought you together.'

Helen sighed and hugged herself more tightly. 'It had nothing to do with John,' she said.

'So what *are* you going to do then?' asked Jemma. Her voice always sounded so loud when she was having one of these conversations with Helen. She looked over at the basket in which baby Caitlin lay sleeping, her tiny fist clenched into a ball no bigger than a large marble. 'Is there any chance Nigel will come back?'

'No. Disappeared without a trace. The telephone at his parents' unit has been disconnected. I think he's gone overseas.'

'You never met his parents, did you?' asked Jemma curiously.

'No, and I don't want to.'

'I don't think Nigel *has* parents,' said Jemma. 'I think he just erupted out of a boil somewhere. Anyway, you stuck by him, no matter how horrible he was, so *you* did the right thing and *he* didn't. You have nothing to feel guilty about.'

'I know,' said Helen.

'So,' said Jemma, bringing over the steaming cups and plonking them on the coffee table. 'You must have thought about it. What *are* you going to do?'

Helen reached for her cup and warmed her cold hands around it. She'd had her hair permed and it suited her, framing her small face with a mass of fashionably straggling curls. But she lowered her frothy head in shame. Because she hadn't thought about it. Had made a point of *not* thinking about it. Had pulled a blind down on the questions, the terrifying questions, that had to be asked about her future, and Caitlin's as well.

She sighed and didn't look up. 'I've got three months' leave from work — one month on pay and two months unpaid. They said they'd like me back, as long as I didn't let having a baby interfere with my work. It would save them training someone else or something.' She sighed again. Jemma nodded, listening. 'Anyway,' Helen continued, 'I suppose I'll have to pay someone to look after Caitlin. Another mother with a baby, maybe. Or I might find one of those centres where they look after little children. There's a few of them about.'

'You'll be lonely,' said Jemma.

'I've been lonely for nine months,' said Helen. 'Longer.' She felt she would never have survived her pregnancy without her weekend phone calls to Jemma and Marte.

'Paid maternity leave,' said Jemma, kicking off her shoes and curling up beside Helen on the couch. 'And professional child care for women who want to work. That's what we need. Why should women have to give up their professions just because they have children?'

'Because their husbands are meant to keep them,' said Helen. 'Because most women are smart enough to keep their husbands.'

'Helen, give me a break,' said Jemma. 'You don't for a moment think you're the only woman whose husband has run out on her when she's pregnant?'

'No,' said Helen. 'Of course not.'

'Life doesn't always work out the way we plan it,' said Jemma. 'Look at me. Where's my fame? Where's my fortune? I'm living in my old home town, spending every hour of every day looking after a baby. Did either of us imagine that would ever happen to me?'

'You'll still be famous,' said Helen. 'You have plenty of time. But in the meantime, the last thing you need is another baby to look after.'

'It's *exactly* what I need,' said Jemma. 'I can't seem to justify my life at the moment. I'm flat out all day and I'm up half the night, but all I'm doing is bringing up one little boy. I feel as if I'm marking time. If I was looking after Caitlin as well as Hamish, I would feel as if I was doing a job that was really worthwhile. Besides,' added Jemma, 'I hate not having money of my own. I hate being dependent on John for every penny.'

Helen looked at her. 'You'd let me pay you?' she asked.

'Of course,' said Jemma. 'What I'm suggesting is that you find somewhere to live, preferably really close to us, and you get a job and earn good money and pay me to look after Caitlin for you.' She flicked aside her hair. 'You didn't think I was offering to do this for love, did you?'

For the first time, Helen smiled. 'Yes,' she said.

When Helen returned to Siren's Rock with her baby, Babs asked her to come for afternoon tea so that she and Douglas could meet their new granddaughter. But Helen left Caitlin with Jemma and went to Grand View Crescent alone.

She was surprised when her mother served tea in the lounge room, from her best bone china.

'You chose not to involve us in your marriage,' said Babs, putting down her teacup and dabbing at her lips with a white linen napkin, 'so we are not in a position to comment on what went wrong.'

'No,' said Helen. 'You're not.'

Her mother looked at her coldly. 'Let's just say that marriage takes a lot of work and a great deal of patience and you have never displayed either of those qualities.'

'So it's my fault, of course,' said Helen.

'Marriage is a two-way street,' said her mother. 'I'm sure Nigel had his faults. You have never been a very good judge of character.'

Helen knotted her hands in her lap. *Why does nothing she says ever surprise me?*

'I can't say your father and I are surprised at this turn of events.'

'Of course you're not,' said Helen.

'Men have, um, needs,' continued Babs. 'Whether we enjoy it or not, we must accommodate them. And no man wants a wife who doesn't look after herself,' she added, speaking very quickly, glancing at Helen's face and letting her gaze trail down to her feet.

'Actually,' said Helen, 'Nigel screwed me senseless every night of the week and I enjoyed every minute of it.' She smiled as she watched her mother's lips disappear. 'But you're probably right about the other thing. I think he left me because my handbags *never* match my shoes.'

'You're being facetious,' said Babs, taunted into deviating from her script.

'Am I, Mummy?' said Helen pleasantly.

With what was obviously an enormous effort, Babs Winter took a deep breath through her thin nostrils and placed her ringed fingers on her knees. 'I have always been pleased to notice,' she said slowly, 'that whatever may have been happening behind closed doors, your handbags have *always* matched your shoes.'

('She didn't!' Jemma screamed afterwards, grabbing her crotch to stop herself peeing with mirth. Their laughter rocked the house and woke both babies.)

A small dimple appeared at the corner of Helen's mouth. She looked down at the rose-patterned carpet. 'I'm glad I've done something to make you happy, Mummy,' she said.

'Now,' Babs continued, 'you'll need help with ... the child. You can't bring her up properly and earn a decent living. If you pay for your board and lodging — Daddy is working that out — and contribute your share of household expenses, we could probably manage to have you and ... the child living with us.' They both heard the front door open and the heavy step in the hall, but Babs kept speaking. 'I have no intention of getting up at night to a crying baby,' said Babs, 'so you would have full responsibility for her. But at least ... the child ... would be brought up in a respectable home.'

'Her name is Caitlin,' said Helen.

'I know one or two young women, *full-time* mothers, *very good* mothers, who would consider taking the child during the day, while you go to work,' Babs went on.

Helen looked past her mother at the light glinting on her father's glasses. The sliding doors into the hall were open and he stood just outside, his shoulders thrown back and his stomach thrust forward, a study in belligerence. She couldn't read the expression on his face.

'I wouldn't bring my little girl into this house,' Helen said softly, 'if *you* paid *me*. And I think you both know why.'

'Get out and go to hell then,' her father roared, striding in and standing over her. 'You little slut!'

But Babs rose quickly and laid her hand on his arm. 'Don't get excited,' she said, pursing her lips. 'You know what the doctor said.' She looked at Helen. 'You'd better leave then,' she said, with some dignity, 'if that's the way you feel.'

Helen picked up her handbag, soft black leather exactly matching her shoes. 'I'm renting a place on the west side,' she said to her mother. 'You're welcome to visit your granddaughter as long as I'm home when you come.'

'Don't come crawling back,' shouted her father, as she ran down the front steps.

Helen drove fast up the winding black road out of Grand View Crescent, but as she reached the intersection with the main route out of town she stomped suddenly on the brakes, sending stones flying. For a few minutes she let the car idle there, tempted to turn left, to head for the highway, to leave it all behind, to stay away forever.

She wouldn't look back. She would drive away on the road she'd learned to walk on without shoes.

She was an adult now, in charge of her own life. She could go back to the city and get a job, ask Jemma to bring Caitlin when she was established. Jemma would do that. Jemma would do anything she asked.

Jemma, her friend.

Jemma, whose best advice she had ignored. Jemma, the queen of cliches, who had never once said, 'I told you so.'

Jemma, who had offered to raise her child. Jemma, who had saved her the first time and so many times since. By loving her. By arming her with courage and hope.

Courage and hope were badly needed now. And Jemma was waiting for her.

Helen turned her car right, headed down the hill and into the heart of the town. Past the older houses on stilts and the new brick bungalows on their concrete slabs, spurning stilts for air-conditioned comfort. She drove through the shopping centre, past Vale's department store and the Chinese restaurant and the Working Men's Club in Turner Street, and out through the tacky side of town, where people lived in fibro cottages with cheap tin roofs, untidy shrubs and broken bikes scattered through their yards. On the outskirts of Siren's Rock, where the road snaked up to Rocky Mountain and Bob Snell Memorial Park, she turned west.

She drove with an aching heart, with raw, sore eyes, a hurting head and a feeling of sickness in her stomach.

Her father was right of course. She was a slut. Had been a slut all her life, even as a child. She had let men do things to her for as long as she could remember. Starting with him, she had let men touch her and grope her and press themselves against and into her small, insignificant body in whatever way they liked. Her father, the boy at Mermaid Cove, drunken clods in pubs, boozed blokes in campsites, Nigel, who really loved John, John, who had always loved Jemma.

What a slut.

None of them had loved her and she had loved none of them, she thought, and courage and hope slipped further away.

On the western slopes that rimmed the town, facing the mountains instead of the sea, stood the Sullivans' brand new timber home. John and Jemma's house of dreams.

Helen pulled up outside the house with its stained timber walls, its wide wood-framed windows and the gleaming corrugated iron roof.

John ran down the driveway to meet her. He was wearing jeans and a paint-spattered T-shirt — he had been measuring up the verandah he was planning to wrap around the house. He looks so strong, thought Helen. Stronger than us all. Even on the day of their very first meeting. A small and skinny boy, but strong even then. Strong in spirit.

John smiled at her. His big, handsome, familiar smile, the smile that always left her breathless, no matter how many times she saw it.

As she drove through the gate and he saw her face, his smile faded. A watery sun glinted on her hair as she climbed slowly out of the car.

'Hello, gorgeous,' he said, and he put his arms around her and hugged her so tightly that she squeaked like a child. He surprised her by resting his cheek on top of her curly head. 'You shouldn't have gone,' he said softly. 'I should have stopped you. I knew what they'd do.'

'I saw the two of you out there,' Jemma told him that night, as they floated towards sleep. 'I thought it was good that she had a strong man to lean on for once. Just for a little while.'

'She looked so small and hurt,' he said. 'The way she used to look when we were kids — after her dad had been giving her a rough time.'

Helen knew she should have pulled away quickly, as she always did from an embrace with John, but today she had stayed there, resting in the protective circle of his arms, feeling courage and hope return. *Just for a minute*, said Saint Helen. *Just for a little while.*

'Are you all right?' he'd asked. Concerned eyes roving over her small face. 'Seriously, did they hurt you?'

She had looked up at him and managed a smile.

'Hey,' she'd said in her husky voice, 'I was never there.'

Part Six

BABS

What on earth were they playing now, wondered Babs, as the bearers shouldered the coffin for the second time. She turned around to look up at the organ but it was silent. The music was coming from some sound system which had no place in a house of worship.

Her eyes met those of Tom, her grandson, standing behind her in his white shirt and tie. For an instant she thought he was grinning but he quickly poked his mouth down into a straight line and met her suspicious eyes with his own. A fine way to behave at a funeral, thought Babs in disgust. As she turned her gaze away from him she noticed a hairy black grub on the pew. She flicked it to the ground. Disgusting. Even churches weren't clean any more.

The congregation rose. Babs stood up, straightened her face and her coat, cleared her throat and brushed a little powder from her lapel. Both her trousers and her coat were lined with synthetic silk and horribly hot but she didn't regret wearing her best ensemble. She was carrying her age well and she looked all the better for wearing a pastel shade. Look at Marte, for instance, all in brown and leaning on her husband like some kind of cripple. Old before her time. And that terrible dye job, the grey re-growth showing in the parting. Surely she could have visited her hairdresser before coming to something as public as this? Where so many people were bound to be looking at both of them.

Strange words for a funeral song. Something about roses. A bed of them.

A tiny sneer flickered across the old woman's prim red mouth.

There was no doubt she was the smartest of the older women in the church. The new colour in her hair suited her. It was subtle, just a hint of strawberry blonde blending nicely with the silver. Silver threads among the gold, the airman might have said, had he been at her side now, small, dapper, distinguished. That's how she imagined him these days.

Back then he had looked so smart in his uniform. The creases pressed sharp as knives. The shiny buttons. The smart khaki cap that sat just right on his oiled and gleaming curls. And the boots! Gleaming too. Like mirrors.

As well as looking smart, his family had money, which Mother said was the main thing, when all was said and done. Mother was very keen for Babs to marry into money, as being widowed for so long had made her life difficult. Well, more than difficult. Life for Mother and Babs and her three big bull-necked brothers had been terrible since her father went off and died. That was how Mother put it, pressing a hanky tightly against her nose — 'he went off and died' — and Babs, who was only eight at the time, imagined him putting on his hat and coat and walking purposefully from the hospital to the cemetery, with his battered briefcase in his hand.

Babs boasted shamelessly about her airman to the women at work. She wrote to him every day — increasingly passionate letters which at first he answered with equal enthusiasm. Then the letters slowed down and finally the last one came. Other girls had begun receiving terrible letters too. Their sweethearts and husbands had been injured or were missing believed dead.

Babs' airman hadn't even had the decency to get himself killed.

Dear Babs, he had written. *I am sorry to have to write this letter. I have met another woman . . .*

'Babs isn't well enough to come out,' Mother had said, when her friends came around. 'She's been let down.'

Mother was careful not to say Babs had been 'taken advantage of'. That would have set their tongues wagging. 'Let down' was a better way of putting it.

Mother was furious. The girls at work laughed behind their hands when they saw her, so she stopped going anywhere except to church. Which is where she met Douglas Winter, a big, pious, serious young man, with gimlet eyes behind black-framed glasses, and black hair, already thin on top. Douglas had been exempted from active service because he had a weak heart.

Douglas Winter comforted her, and held her hand, and told her she was the prettiest little thing he had ever seen. He said if he ever met the man who had broken her heart he would smash him to pulp, weak heart or no weak heart. Babs rather liked the image of the smart airman pulped to pieces and bleeding. Making a mess of the Mess, she thought, with a brief, bitter smile. This undercurrent of violence in Douglas's nature added an element of excitement to their friendship which was otherwise missing.

Six weeks after they met, Babs and Douglas announced their engagement. Douglas had been prepared to wait longer than that, but Babs wanted to be able to hold her head up again in public, to look her 'friends' in the eye and to both refer and defer to her fiance. *So you thought I'd been jilted? That I couldn't get a man? So what about this big fellow then? This respectable, reliable man who worships the ground I walk on.*

They had to put off the wedding for six months when two of her brothers were killed in action. During that time Babs learned that Douglas was an orphan who had spent most of his childhood in children's homes. 'The little girls would cry their eyes out,' said Douglas. 'Us bigger kids, we'd — you know — cheer them up.' But Babs didn't know. Her big, square-headed, bull-necked brothers had never cheered her up, even when she had been beaten with Mother's wooden spoon. They were just glad it was her and not them.

'Douglas has made something of himself,' Mother told Babs. 'If you're lucky, he might be able to make something of you.'

When Babs confided to her mother that Douglas had not yet aroused any passionate feelings in her wounded heart, Mother had snorted in disgust.

'Passion only happens on the wedding night,' Mother said. 'The sex act is ugly and painful for the woman, although the pain generally lessens with time. But passion doesn't come into it and one man is much the same as another.'

So Barbara Prang married Douglas Winter on a chilly June day in the local church. It was the church where he had seen her first, huddled in the back pew like a lost little girl, weeping into her handkerchief over the loss of the airman.

And when they consummated their marriage that night, and on the nights that followed, Babs found out that Mother had been absolutely right. But she wished her mother had told her more.

Helen was a difficult baby. Giving birth was horrendous, painful and messy, leaving Babs exhausted and whimpering. Then, when she brought Helen home from the hospital, her own weeping was drowned out by the baby's howls. Babs walked the floor with her at night, then pushed her around in her pram half the day, while she tried to do her housework. Douglas went to work earlier and earlier and came home later.

Babs was too tired to put her face on, almost too tired to comb her hair. She knew she looked old and worn out, knew she was losing her looks — and didn't care. She stopped caring about anything much at all.

'I can't go on like this,' Babs wailed one night, and Douglas turned his back on her in disgust. She followed him in fury, beating her small fists on his broad back. He swung around to face her, his eyes black and angry and his lips protruding. He raised his arm and struck Babs across the face.

She screeched and staggered, staring at him as she clasped her cheek with both hands. Douglas was breathing heavily, but he spoke calmly enough.

'That's enough,' he snarled. 'I've had enough. You're a woman. You have a child. Look after it. Do your duty. Leave me alone to do mine. And *never* . . .' he paused and stared at her, but the light reflected off his glasses and she couldn't see his eyes, '*never*,' he repeated, 'raise your hand to me again.'

He left the flat and Babs curled up on their bed, holding her throbbing face. She cried louder and longer than Helen.

When Douglas arrived home from work the following night, he was carrying a bunch of roses, which he deposited in a vase without comment. Babs had put her face on, with extra powder to cover her swollen cheek. She had cooked a leg of pork and made sherry trifle for dessert. Miraculously,

Helen lay quietly in her pram while they ate. This didn't last, of course, but when she forked into the foetal position and started her paean of pain that night, Babs took her into the back bedroom so that Douglas would not be disturbed. The events of the previous evening were never discussed again.

Things improved after Helen's first birthday, when the colic attacks diminished and she started sleeping through most nights. But Helen was growing into a sulky, sullen child. She was a fussy eater and nervous; she flinched whenever she heard a loud noise or when strangers came too close. When she wouldn't eat her dinner, Douglas took her into the bedroom and smacked her. As she grew older and her eating habits and personality failed to improve, he regularly gave her a good hiding. Douglas said they'd all had hidings at the children's home; it had been good for them. Babs wasn't sure about that. She remembered Mother's wooden spoon, and didn't think it had contributed anything to the way she had turned out.

People were standing and waiting silently in the pews as the bereaved families moved out and shuffled — shuffled was the only word for it — up the aisle. Babs refused to shuffle. She walked carefully, with her head up.

Marte and George were ahead of her. Marte and George Johnson, who had given their daughter ideas well and truly above her station, when all was said and done. It was Marte and George who were responsible for spoiling Jemma, always trying to convince her she could do anything she wanted. To think they believed that! Marte the cleaner and George Johnson, that lumbering grey turtle from the fish and chip shop!

Marte, being from an immigrant family, probably knew no better. She wanted a good life for her daughter. You couldn't blame her for that. But under the current circumstances, what a waste of all her efforts!

Babs held herself straight and took small, lady-like steps as she walked up the aisle. People were standing back as she passed, giving her space, showing respect, but even so, it was slow going. People moved so slowly at funerals.

This was only the second funeral Babs Winter had attended in her seventy years. Ladies do not attend funerals, Mother had said. Only lower-class women who know no better, and foreigners who weep and keen and carry on in an unseemly way. There would certainly be no unseemly behaviour from Babs Winter at this funeral — nothing for people to stare at and gossip about afterwards. When it came to sorrow, Babs Winter knew better than most that there was a time and a place!

As she reached the wide glass doors of the church, the silly words of yet another inappropriate song filtered through her thoughts.

Something about an angel. In the morning.

Babs walked out of the church alone and, as she reached the portals, the heat flowed in to confront her. The first person she met outside was Marte, who turned to her with stricken eyes and a face worn with weeping.

'One thing is certain, Marte,' said Babs Winter, greeting Jemma's mother dry-eyed. 'Our girls were no angels.'

Babs turned away and, shielding her powdered face from the unforgiving sun with her service sheet, scanned the people milling about in the few precious patches of shade, talking in murmurs, kissing, hugging, their faces damp from tears and perspiration.

'What was that dreadful music they were playing at the end?' she asked, flapping at a fly, as Joy and Warren approached. Joy looked shifty and gazed nervously at Warren. It annoyed Babs the way Joy never seemed able to speak for herself.

'It was a compilation,' said Warren gently, blinking through his thick glasses. 'You know. Parts of all her favourite songs strung together. Apparently Hamish did it on his computer.'

'May God forgive him,' sighed Babs. 'And when you think of all the lovely hymns there are to choose from.'

George Johnson loomed in front of her. He looked like a groper, she thought. Every part of his face was drooping downwards. Sweat oozed from his forehead, from his top lip. A fly clung to a grey crease under his eye. He had been staring at her all through the service. What was wrong with him? Apart from the obvious, of course.

'Babs,' he said slowly, holding out his hand. 'We are so sorry about Helen.'

'Well,' said Babs, watching him take her small claw in his big hand, watching him close his other paw over it. 'She never had any luck with cars,' she muttered, but then she heard Joy, talking over the top of her and putting a firm hand — far *too* firm, as it happened — on her other arm.

'We're sorry too, George. For you and Marte.'

Babs squeezed her flaking red lips together and looked at her shoes. They were copper-coloured, a shade that teamed well with her suit. A good choice, she thought.

'It's a sad day for us all,' said George Johnson.

Babs often wondered how things might have turned out for the Winter family if they had never moved to Siren's Rock. Or if Douglas had finally got his promotion, enabling them to move back to the city. But year after year they'd waited and the promotion never came. Douglas stayed in the same job, a devoted family man of course, but a disappointed man all the same.

In the early years he had punished Helen for his disappointment. She knew that. She even knew that it wasn't fair, and yet she understood, even sympathised with Douglas. She knew how Helen could arouse feelings of intense fury, even hatred, in any normal person. With her silence. Her sulking. Her tense, tight little face. Her flinching. Her curled-up, cold little body. And as she grew up, her smart remarks. Her sarcasm. Her ingratitude. The way she spoke to both of them, as if she was superior to them. As if they were ignorant! She and Douglas! Ignorant!

Of course Douglas punished Helen. Who could blame him?

But not Joy. When Joy was born nothing was as expected. The doctor suggested a Caesarean section, and by the time Babs regained consciousness, the mess and pain were over. *What a clean and tidy way to give birth,* she wrote to Mother in Sydney. *I expect the day will come when doctors arrange for everyone to do it this way.* She spent more than a week in hospital being pampered by the nurses and when she eventually took the baby home, Joy slept for hours, waking up at exactly the right time for her bottle, smiling and dribbling at everyone she saw, and then falling back to sleep again with barely a squeak.

Douglas had smacked Joy once, very hard, when she was two. Babs was not going to let this happen to sweet Joy.

'If you touch my little girl again,' she had said nervously, looking down on him lying on the bed, 'I will leave you and I will never come back.'

Douglas's eyes were on the ceiling. 'What sort of idiotic rubbish are you spouting now?' he asked nastily.

'I will go and live with Mother,' Babs had continued bravely, 'and I will take Joy with me. And you will be disgraced.'

She had meant to walk straight out of the room after saying her piece. Quickly and quietly, with dignity. But when she reached the door her throat had thickened with something more than tears. There was bile in there, and years of anguish, years of being hurt by men. First her father, who had gone off and got himself killed without looking after her the way a father should. Then her big bullying brothers. Then the airman. And finally, Douglas, this big man who had hit her dear little girl.

She turned around. 'You're a coward, Douglas,' she said. And then, as he turned his head towards her in surprise, she added: 'Why don't you pick on someone your own size?'

He hadn't answered her or followed her. That incident, like all the others, was never mentioned again.

But he never hit Joy again either.

Yes, Babs thought, I learned how to handle myself in marriage. So, it seemed, had Joy. But not Helen. Babs hadn't experienced a moment of surprise when Nigel had grown tired of Helen so quickly. It would have been too much to hope for — that Helen would do the right thing by them, that she would settle down into respectable married life with a smart, clean and wealthy young man.

Still, when Helen came back to Siren's Rock, a deserted wife with a child to support, they had done the right thing. They had offered to take her in, Helen and her baby. Even when she had thrown their kindness in their faces, Douglas had tried to help her find Nigel. Helen did nothing about it, absolutely nothing, said she was glad to see the back of him. But Douglas had reported Nigel to the social services for not paying Helen maintenance. Douglas said the time would certainly come when Helen would ask them for money.

They never found Nigel. But his father, when Douglas finally made contact with him, threatened Douglas with some sort of court order to keep him away. As if *Douglas* was the criminal. His chest pains started soon after that. When Douglas died, Babs made no secret of the fact that the stress of sorting out Helen's problems had contributed to his heart attack.

Douglas was right about Helen coming begging in the end, because she changed her tune when he was gone. She was short of money, behind with her rent, had huge problems with her car and no money for Caitlin's Christmas. With her father in his grave, she had swallowed her pride and asked Babs for help. Babs, being a good mother, had agreed.

By then Babs had moved from Grand View Crescent into a nice little valley villa, blonde brick, part of a smart new development on the eastern road that linked Siren's Rock to Mermaid Cove. Caitlin was four, toilet trained, past the bleating stage and almost as quiet as Helen had been at that age, although much more attractive. Except for that dreadful red hair.

Helen and Caitlin had lived with Babs for seven years. You would never hear Babs Winter use the word sponging, but other people might. Babs had made it possible for Helen to give Caitlin a much nicer home and a more respectable family life than she had any right to expect.

The arrangement had suited Babs well. Neither of them were there much during the day. Helen worked long hours at the dreary accounting office and Caitlin went to Jemma's after school until Helen picked her up and brought her home. When Caitlin was nine or ten, she had started coming straight home to the villa and spending hours in her tiny bedroom, listening to her dreadful music or watching soap operas on television with Babs.

'You love the soaps, don't you, Granny?' she would say, wandering out of her room and curling her long legs beneath her on the couch.

Helen would often become angry when she came home from work and found Babs and Caitlin watching television together. 'Have you done your homework?' she would snap. 'Have you done anything about dinner?' Of course, Caitlin had never done any such thing and Babs wasn't about to tell her to. Cooking was Helen's job. She was the mother. Babs had to smile to herself. Now it was Helen's turn to find out what it was like to have a silent, selfish daughter.

Helen paid Babs for board and lodging for the two of them. She also cleaned the villa and did all the washing and ironing, although not very well. 'You're so careless,' Babs would tell her. 'You never do anything *properly*.' Babs always ended up finishing off everything Helen touched, tidying and flicking and fiddling until all her bits and pieces were neatly in place and the villa was exactly as she liked it again, and ready for the eyes of her friends.

Helen never argued with her mother. They didn't fight. Fighting would have involved words, conversation, emotion.

At weekends, after Helen had cleaned and done the household shopping, she and Caitlin would usually disappear to Jemma's, where, Babs was sure, there were probably enough words and emotion to last them the rest of the week.

When Helen told her mother that she had lost her job, that she could no longer afford the rent Babs charged her for the villa and that she and Caitlin were going to stay with John and Jemma for a few months, Babs was angrier than she had been for years. Here it was again. The ingratitude. The lack of appreciation. The irresponsibility. And Jemma again. Always Jemma. Jemma beckoned and Helen ran.

It took Babs months to find a good cleaner. And then there was that ghastly day when Edna Egan rang and asked her how long Helen had been pregnant! Babs had to pretend she already knew. The shock had nearly killed her.

Babs was very glad then that she had kept that strange letter, the one addressed to someone called Julie, the declaration of undying love from someone who had found Helen's library card. It had all fallen into place then. Babs had given a copy of the letter to Jemma. She was still waiting to see what would come of that. In the meantime she had the original safely hidden away.

The lining of her coat was sticking to her arms. Sweat trickled down her back. She looked up from her shoes and the sun sent long shafts of light straight into her eyes, blinding her to the dark, sorry faces around her. She held the service sheet over her forehead again, wishing Joy would steer her towards some shade. 'Can we leave now?' she asked Joy. Or was it Warren? 'Is it time to go to the graveyard?'

'It's a cremation, Mum,' murmured Joy. 'We're not going to the cemetery. Nobody is.'

'Good,' said Babs crisply. 'Then let's get away from this farce and go home.'

'Mum!' said Joy. Babs heard the tearful shock in her daughter's voice and changed the tone of her own.

'I'm not used to funerals,' Babs whined. 'It's not my fault.'

It wasn't her fault. Nobody could blame her for what had happened.

People were still standing about, some talking quietly in groups, some weeping, holding each other in a way that wouldn't be considered natural at anything other than a funeral. Men and women kept coming up to her telling her they were sorry. Sorry sorry sorry. I'm sorry. Sorry about Helen. Sorry to hear, sorry to say, sorry today. What a sorry lot they were.

Saying sorry doesn't help, thought Babs. Sorrow is an empty, useless emotion, like a shell, pretty on the outside but empty within.

The airman had said he was sorry, but that had not brought him back to her.

COME ON

The twenty-four hours that changed Helen's life forever began outside the airport terminal, when she wrapped her arms around Grezza's neck and hugged him. Grezza, hugging her back, held her too tightly and for too long. Held on to her and put his sweaty forehead against hers.

'Would it have worked for us, Julie?' he said softly. 'If I'd taken my eyes off Jemma long enough to take a gander at you? Before that stupid bastard Nigel stole you away?'

Helen smiled and tried to push him off in a nice way. Not an easy thing to do.

'Maybe we could still give it a go,' he said, tightening his arms. 'I'm getting a lot of business on the east coast. I'll be back soon.'

'Grezza,' said Helen, 'you're just feeling neglected. Go home to your wife.'

He tried to kiss her on the mouth but she ducked her head. He let go of her then and gave her a dirty look. He was still blond and had grown more handsome since Judy had persuaded him to have his teeth fixed, but he hadn't shaved and he had a pot belly growing under his belt.

'It's still John, isn't it?' he said. 'You've never been able to hide anything from me, Julie. I've been here for a week and I've seen the way you look at him. It's always been John and now the lucky bastard has you both.'

He picked up his bag and slung it over his shoulder while Helen stared at him, speechless. 'Seeya,' he growled, as the doors slid open and sucked him into the terminal.

Helen climbed back into her car, stuck her foot on the accelerator and shot out from the kerb.

Where did that come from, she thought, winding down her window and letting the breeze lift her fair hair off her neck. All the way to Bridgetown airport at this ungodly hour of the morning, just to see him off, and not even a thank you. Just a bloody insulting load of crap!

She screamed around a bend in the hot road, scaring a cyclist who gave her the finger. Helen fingered him back. 'If he had just taken a *gander*,' she muttered aloud. 'What? I might have got lucky? I might have got *Grezza*?

'What? And I still could? Even now? Because Judy has turned into a wife, while I, of course, am available as always? Goes without saying,' she hissed. 'Obviously the only reason I turned him down is because I've got the hots for my best friend's husband.

'*Shit!*' screamed Helen as she hit another curve too fast and veered out into the path of an oncoming lorry, which responded with the full ferocity of its horn.

'*Get stuffed!*' she shrieked over the blare, but she slowed down, took some deep breaths and turned off the highway onto the road that would take her back to Siren's Rock. Another car came towards her, and tooted. So did the next one. She put her finger down and realised the grinding noise that had been ringing in her ears since she left the airport was not the sound of her own teeth. It was the rim of her wheel.

The jack wouldn't work and, as no one stopped to help her, she was obliged to walk all the way back to the highway to thumb a lift. Her hat was back in the car but she trudged on, the heat creating little rivulets of sweat on her forehead, under her arms, down her back. 'Sorry about that,' she chanted to herself. 'Sorry about the hat.'

Four more frustrating hours passed before she arrived at work, hot and harassed, with dust sticking to her damp patches and clothes that looked as if she had changed the tyre herself.

She walked through the glass doors, anticipating a sheet of cool air, and was enveloped instead by a warm and suffocating blanket.

'It's broken again,' said Gordon, the junior clerk.

The second person she met on her arrival was Clarence Bredow, the new broom who had been appointed to sweep the office clean of dead wood — twigs really — and increase the profits of Hobson, Hobson and Handle. Clarence Bredow, whose forehead was so high it met the back of his neck, had informed her on his first day at the office that single parenthood was no excuse for slack performance.

'In what way has my performance been slack?' Helen had asked, aware that everyone in the office was listening intently from the other side of their partitions.

'I have not yet had the time to gauge individual performance,' Mr Bredow had replied, unfazed. 'But I know what the excuse will be when anything goes wrong. So let's just get the record straight, right from the start, shall we?'

'This is not the start for me,' Helen had said pleasantly. 'I have been here for five years and I have never received a complaint about my work in that time.'

'I think you know what I mean,' he'd concluded the exchange, raising an eyebrow.

'My lateness today has nothing to do with my being a single parent,' Helen now said, on meeting Clarence Bredow as she emerged from the ladies room. 'I had a flat tyre on the way from the airport.'

He glanced at her skirt, grubby, with pulled threads. 'Indeed, Mrs Connor. You came to work at Siren's Rock via Bridgetown?'

'I was seeing off a friend. I left hours before I had to get to work.' Her heart was beating furiously with the effort of remaining civil. I am forty-one years old. I am a mature woman. I am good at my job. He has no right. *He has no right.*

'How fortunate for your *friend* that your predicament occurred *after* you had delivered her to her plane,' said Clarence Bredow. He looked at her for a long moment. She looked back.

'Yes,' said Helen finally. 'He was on the early flight.'

'He?'

'Yes, Mr Bredow,' said Helen firmly. 'He.'

Clarence Bredow smiled. 'And yet you say your lateness had nothing to do with you being a single person.'

Helen blushed with fury. 'I said single parent. And it didn't. It had nothing to do with —'

'I suggest you get back to your desk, Mrs Connor. The work has been piling up in your not inconsiderable absence.'

The work had more than piled up. There was a skyscraper of paper on her desk.

'I'm sorry,' whispered Zelma Frank, who was dabbing at her neck in the next cubicle. 'He just kept telling me to pass them on to you. He hates you, Helen. What have you done to him?'

'It's what she hasn't done to him,' whispered Gordon, on the other side. He rolled his chair back and leered at them both. 'Ten bucks says it's his way of coming on to single older blonde chicks.'

Helen's mouth twisted as she plopped into her chair. 'You could have left out the "older".'

Gordon grinned, tapped his nose and looked straight at her legs. He was a twenty-five-year-old clerk, conceived by clerks, destined to live forever in a world of clerks. He even looked like a clerk, thought Helen. 'I can assure you,' she said coldly, 'that the last thing on Mr Bredow's mind . . .' She hesitated.

'Want to bet?' whispered Gordon.

'You're on,' said Helen. 'One bottle of good red.' She stood up and walked over to Clarence Bredow's open door.

'Mr Bredow, I will have to work back tonight to catch up,' said Helen. 'If you are working late too, I should probably order some dinner to be sent in for the two of us. The thing is, we have to let Jack's know early.'

He stared at her. 'Mrs Connor, unlike you I *have* a spouse, who keeps my dinner warm for me no matter how late I am.'

'Well,' said Helen. 'Okay then.'

'Put that in your pipe and smoke it,' she said to Gordon, choosing one of Jemma's favourites.

'That proves nothing,' hissed Gordon. 'Wait till we've gone.'

'Shut up, Gordon,' Helen sighed. 'Now that we have dealt with the crucial issue of me being the office slut, we can all get back to work.'

'You should be ashamed of yourself, Gordon,' said Zelma. 'Helen is a very nice lady. And she is practically old enough to be your mother.'

Helen looked at her. 'Thank you, Zelma,' she said.

She worked through her lunch hour, but the phone kept ringing with queries and she had barely dented the first report by one o'clock when Jemma called.

'It was nice of you to take Grezza all the way to the airport,' said Jemma. 'I was so tired after entertaining him all week and trying to do my work after he went to bed — I haven't had more than four hours' sleep any night for a month. I'm obsessed with writing my play.'

'Great,' said Helen.

'Anyway, speaking of plays, is there any chance you can take a couple of hours off and come with me to watch Hamish do his thing at the concert this arvo?'

'Oh Jemma, I'd love to but I was late for work and I've got to work back. I was going to ask you if you could keep Caitlin.'

'Sure. Why don't you let her stay for tea? John and I will take them out to celebrate afterwards. Caitlin's done a great job.'

'Of what?'

'The scenery. She painted all the scenery. Didn't she tell you?'

'Caitlin never tells me anything. You know that,' said Helen crossly. 'If I had known, I could have taken a flexi-day. Damn. I could have taken Grezza to the airport and then spent the day with you. I bet it's cool at your place.'

'Yeah, the fans are all working overtime,' said Jemma. 'Look, don't worry about it. Mum and Dad are coming anyway. I'd better get cracking.'

'Tell Hamish good luck from me,' said Helen.

The afternoon crept slowly past. Helen tried not to think about the heat, tried not to think about what Grezza had said, tried not to think about the huge pile of ironing that was waiting at the villa, while her mother sat beside it, watching television, tried not to think about Caitlin, whose latest method of punishing her for being her mother was to withhold information.

Everyone else packed up and left at five-thirty. Helen worked doggedly on. She could feel sweat in the creases of her eyelids, pressing them down. At least the phone had stopped ringing. Then it rang. She swore and picked it up. 'Bredow here,' said her new boss. 'Just step into my office for a moment, would you?'

He was sitting on the edge of his desk with his legs apart when she walked in. He smiled. It was not a pretty sight.

'Mrs Connor,' said Clarence Bredow, 'I was forced to be a little harsh with you today, in order to avoid showing favouritism.'

A nasty worm of unease uncurled itself in Helen's stomach. 'Oh, you certainly didn't do that, Mr Bredow,' she said.

'Had I allowed you to get away with arriving at work so late, it would have set a very bad example to the other staff.'

'That's true,' said Helen bleakly. His hands were dangling in his lap. His legs were dangling off the desk. He had loosened his tie. His forehead-neck was shiny. For the first time, Helen realised how much he looked like her father. She felt sick. She waited for it.

'Your suggestion that we share a meal was not as unwise as you might have concluded, given my intentionally negative reaction,' he said. 'Again, I was thinking of the impression on others. In fact, the idea is a good one and fortunately,' he smiled, 'Mrs Bredow is a very understanding woman.'

And there it was.

Helen turned around and walked back to her cubicle. She turned off her computer screen and picked up her bag. She walked past his door without looking in. She said nothing. The right words never came unless she practised first.

Sorry I can't stay, Clarence, thought Helen, too late. I've just realised I have to ... what? Find a new job? Not cry?

Pick up a man with a clearly discernible division between his forehead and his neck and bonk his brains out?

Helen no longer needed The Plan. All things considered, as she said to Jemma — especially all the things Nigel had persuaded her to consider — she hadn't enjoyed sex as much as she thought she would. Life was simpler without it. Besides, she thought, although she didn't share this particular conclusion with Jemma, she was no good at it. It was probably something to do with her father. Or Nigel. Who knew? Who cared? All she wanted when she came home from work, after putting on a load of washing, cooking dinner, hearing her mother's complaint of the day and going a few rounds with Caitlin, was a good book, clean sheets and either her electric blanket or her ceiling fan, depending on the season.

If she drove fast she might just make it to the kids' celebration.

But of course it wasn't that sort of day.

'You missed them,' said Jemma as Helen came into her kitchen. She poured tall clinking glasses of her special iced tea. 'John's taken the kids to Maccas. I decided to grab another hour of writing time and they're bringing ice-cream back for us all. They should be back soon.'

They sat in the rocking chairs on the verandah, with its view of the valley. Helen sat up straight, alternately sipping and pressing her cold glass against her cheek, while Jemma slumped in her shirt and baggy shorts, stretching out her long brown legs as she told Helen what she'd missed.

'How did the scenery go?'

'Brilliant. Caitlin had this backdrop painted with all these beds, only each row diminished in size so it looked three-dimensional. She's very talented. The scenery painters got a special clap.'

'Great,' said Helen, sipping.

Jemma reached behind her head and twisted her heavy curtain of hair up into a ponytail, which she held in place with one fist while she searched the pocket of her shorts for some elastic. 'What's up?' she said. 'Bad day at Hobble, Hobble and Along?'

'Bad day,' said Helen. 'Bad hot day. Got a flat tyre coming back from the airport. No air conditioning at the office. Too much work.' She contemplated telling Jemma about Clarence Bredow and decided she didn't have the energy to face the fury of her friend's reaction, the inevitable debate about sexual harassment and the possibility that she wouldn't have a job to go to on Monday morning. Instead she said: 'And Grezza propositioned me.'

Jemma stared at her. 'Not sexual, you don't mean?'

'Yes. Sexual. Sort of.'

Jemma shouted with laughter. Helen smiled faintly. Jemma looked so beautiful when she laughed. Her waist had thickened and she hid her copious curves beneath oversized clothes, but her face still had the power to snatch breath away. 'The dirty little dog,' said Jemma. 'I saw him holding your hand the other night after dinner. I thought it was a bit odd that you let him, actually.'

Helen looked cross. 'We're not schoolgirls any more, Jem. If an old friend wants to hold your hand, you have to *let* them. What else can you do? Anyway, you had your arm around him for ages last night.'

'That's different. I'm married. I'm safe.'

'And I'm not?'

'Maybe you still put out a few vibes. The ones we used to worry about.'

'Oh, for heaven's *sake*,' said Helen angrily.

Jemma sighed and sipped. 'It doesn't matter anyway. What did you say to old Grezza?'

'I told him to go home to his wife,' said Helen. 'And then he got snotty and ...' She paused and looked at the brown shadows falling across the valley view.

'What?' asked Jemma, leaning forward in her chair. '*What*?'

'He said John has us both.'

Jemma laughed so much her ponytail fell down. 'Now there's a turn up for the books,' she giggled. She began to laugh again. 'What a good idea,' she gurgled.

Helen said nothing.

'Seriously,' said Jemma, gasping, 'I don't think I'd mind all that much. John is very fond of you. Why should I have all the pleasure? Truthfully?'

'I read that people who say *seriously* or *truthfully* all the time usually aren't,' said Helen flatly.

Jemma finally stopped laughing and arranged her face sensibly. 'You know what, Julie? You're lucky we're *not* sharing John. He's hardly got enough energy for *me*.

'The trouble with sex,' Jemma ruminated, 'is that it takes up so much time. I mean we're a bit past putting on *Bolero* while I whip him with my plaits. More than half the time I lie there thinking about all the other things I could be doing, and he falls asleep.'

'Jemma, that's awful,' said Helen.

'No, it's not,' said Jemma, 'it's normal.'

'You shouldn't neglect him,' said Helen. 'You don't want him feeling the way Grezza does.'

'I can't imagine John offering himself to any passing woman just because we're both a bit too tired for sex,' said Jemma.

Any passing woman?

'D'you know what your trouble might be, Julie?' asked Jemma, as they picked up their glasses and went back into the kitchen, 'you think sex is the be-all and end-all of a relationship because you don't have any. A discreet little affair might do you the world of good.'

Helen sighed. 'Sophia, I'm not yearning for sex, not even a little bit. I don't think I ever was. Besides,' and she smiled obediently, 'who do you suggest I could have a discreet little affair with in Siren's Rock? Apart from my new boss. He let me know tonight that he was available.'

Jemma stopped pulling out the ice-cream bowls and stared at her. 'No! The dreadful Clarence?' Her green eyes widened and her eyebrows shot up. 'My God, two offers in one day? Julie, for a girl who isn't interested, you're doing pretty well!'

Helen gathered spoons. 'The femme fatale of Siren's Crack, that's me.'

Jemma smiled as she took out fistfuls of paper serviettes. 'Anyway, I think it would do you good. But don't worry about us. John is very happy.'

'How do you know?' asked Helen.

'He told me,' said Jemma, just a little defensively. 'He tells me all the time.'

'What do I tell you all the time?' asked John, coming in with three containers of ice-cream.

'What flavours you were getting,' said Jemma quickly as he kissed her.

'Strawberry, chocolate and caramel,' said John. 'Hello gorgeous, you look warm.' He air-kissed the top of Helen's head as she was returning Hamish's hug and whispering: 'Congratulations, Mr Big Star.' When she let him go, Caitlin had moved out of reach.

'Dad nearly got booked for speeding,' said Hamish. 'He said it was because the ice-cream was melting, so they let him off!'

318

'Big John Sullivan,' murmured Jemma, winking at Helen. '*Everybody's* friend.'

Helen put a hand on Caitlin's shoulder. Caitlin, ten years old and already as tall as her mother, flicked her plait, managing to shake Helen's hand off in the same movement. 'Jemma tells me your scenery was brilliant,' Helen said softly.

'It's lucky she told you,' said Caitlin huffily. ''Cause you certainly weren't there to see it.'

The worm in Helen's gut turned into a knife. 'I wish I had been,' she said, speaking very quietly while Hamish chattered and Jemma dished up great globs of pink and brown ice-cream. 'If I had known about it in time I could have been there. Will I get to have a look at it another time?'

'No,' said Caitlin. 'Surprise, surprise. They actually don't open the school at weekends.' She picked up her bowl of ice-cream and went out onto the verandah. Jemma raised her eyebrows at Helen and gave a sympathetic shrug.

Helen's stomach continued to hurt. She went to the toilet and stayed there for a long time. Sitting on the loo, staring at the calendar on the back of the door, she realised she was still angry. She wasn't sure with whom.

She got up and decided a shower might wash away the sweat and stink of her bad day. The water felt good. She scrubbed her body and washed her hair. Everything she needed was available in fat clean bottles in Jemma's black and white Federation-style bathroom. Except a towel. She dried herself on John's. She knew it was his because she smelled him there, a damp clean male smell that was absent from any of the towels in her mother's villa.

In Jemma's bedroom, hanging on the back of a chair, she found the short white linen shift that she had spilled wine on the night before. It was already washed and crisply ironed, even though Jemma had been writing her play today, and been to two meetings and the school concert. Helen's library card was in the pocket of her shift. It had been taken out and neatly returned post-wash, rather than being mutilated in the machine and regurgitated all over the rest of the load — a frequent occurrence at Helen's house. She shook her head.

When she came out everyone was on the verandah. Eating their ice-cream. Second helpings. Laughing. Caitlin was laughing too. Her dark eyes danced as they all teased Hamish about getting an Academy Award. Helen's daughter was too tall and too thin, but graceful, never gawky. A light smattering of freckles smudged her luminous skin. Often, just looking at her daughter, Helen ached with pride and wonder. We did that, she would think. If nothing else, Nigel and I created this beautiful child.

Tonight she felt the wonder but the anger was still there. Why? Why does she despise me? After all I've done to make her happy? She flinched, hearing echoes of her own mother.

'We thought you'd fallen in,' said Jemma. 'Hey, you look nice. Which is great, because we've just been saying you should go out.'

John smiled at her. 'You look sixteen years old,' he said.

'More like sixty,' said Caitlin, her mouth full of ice-cream. 'It's Friday,' she added. 'Jemma said I could sleep over.'

'Julie, we've just decided you should go out somewhere tonight and have some fun,' said Jemma. 'You've spent every night this week with us. Seven nights of boring family stuff. No, eight!'

'*Eight days a week*,' sang John. '*I lo-o-ove you . . .*'

'*Eight days a week*,' shouted the others while Helen stood on the verandah, watching them. '*Is not enough to show I care . . .*' It was one of their favourites. Jemma boasted that her family knew the words to every Beatles song ever written.

'Go on, Helen!' said Jemma. 'See a movie. Grab one of your mates from work and go out for a drink and a really nice meal! Forget your bad day and let your hair down a bit.'

Helen still stood there, looking at them in the rocking chairs John had built. It was getting dark. They were all relaxed, full of ice-cream. A happy little nuclear family.

Sending her away.

'We've had our dinner, you see,' said Hamish anxiously. Helen smiled at him.

'Go out and enjoy yourself,' said John. 'Caitlin will be fine with us.'

'I'm always fine with them,' said Caitlin. 'You can leave me here all weekend if you like, Mum.'

You can leave me here forever, she means.

Helen took a deep breath. 'Okay,' she said. 'I'll go and kick up my heels. Maybe I'll hire a video and watch it with Granny Babs.'

'That's Mum's idea of a good night out,' said Caitlin to Hamish. 'Now you know.'

THE TRAVELLER

She had nowhere to go.

The four people she loved most in the world were sitting on their verandah, singing Beatles songs in the dusk. Not needing her.

Helen drove through Siren's Rock with a small sharp pain in her stomach. She was bleeding internally, bleeding self-pity. Forcing herself to concentrate only on the motions of steering and changing gears, driving too fast through the thick heat of the night, she was afraid that if she allowed herself to think at all, she would howl like an animal.

She hurled the little car through the streets of the town, getting a perverse pleasure out of the speed and noise she was making. She'd started doing this only since this morning — driving fast and loudly, using her car like a weapon against the world.

If I get nicked for speeding I'll say my ice-cream is melting and they'll let me off.

Like hell they will. She could always count on Helen the cynic to keep her in touch with reality.

She was heading out of town on the eastern road and accelerated past the turn-off to her mother's villa. She always thought of it as her mother's villa, never her home.

A little later she saw the rear reflector of a bicycle ahead and swerved out to give the rider a wide berth, but just at that moment another car came around a curve in the road towards her. Helen jammed her foot on the brake and yanked the wheel to get back into her own lane, skimming so close to the cyclist that she sent him hurtling into the shoulder of the road. She heard a clatter and a shout, but she drove on. Stuff you, stupid bastard. Glared into her rear-vision mirror, furious. Who is stupid enough to ride along a dark country road without lights?

She travelled several hundred metres before she stomped on the brake and swung her car around. What if she had killed him? Wouldn't that be the perfect end to a dazzlingly dreadful day?

The rider was sitting in the grass at the edge of the road. Sturdy legs and a ponytail. It was too dark to see properly. Helen did another U turn and parked. Before she turned off the headlights, she saw that the cyclist was a male. A hippie, in denim. Conscious, thankfully. She got out of the car and walked over to him.

'I'm sorry,' she said. 'I was trying not to hit you and then I nearly did. Are you hurt?'

'I'm sorry too,' he said. He had a soft, light voice and an accent. Canadian? Irish? 'Stupid of me to be riding along a strange road with no lights. You didn't hit me. You just sort of scared me into this reasonably soft grass. It was nice of you to stop.'

'Are you hurt?' repeated Helen. She had been prepared for insult and invective. His apology soothed her, took the edge off the pain in her gut.

'I do believe I'm fit as a fiddle,' he said. There was a flash of a smile. 'But my bike is as dead as a doornail. So there are two cliches for you in one sentence, to be going along with. Or are they similes? Can a cliche *be* a simile, in fact?'

She wondered if he was concussed. 'Can I give you a lift somewhere?'

'Now that would be most appreciated,' said the rider. 'I only arrived in this part of the world yesterday and somewhere happens to be exactly where I was heading.'

'What about your bike?'

He looked over at the mangled metal. 'The bike is dead. It's passed on. It's a late bike. It's gone to the great big bike shed in the sky.'

In the dark she saw the flash of a smile. 'I bought it yesterday,' he said, 'from a man whose eyes and nose pointed in three different directions, for the princely sum of twenty dollars. I had a nasty feeling it wasn't a long-term investment.'

He went to stand up and groaned. Helen leaned over to help him. 'Oh no,' she said, grasping his bony forearm. 'You *are* hurt. I am so, so sorry. I was driving far too fast.'

But he stood up very quickly and she took her hand away. 'Honestly, I'm fine,' he said. 'I always groan when I get up. It's the only way I can get any attention.'

Helen laughed. He took a step and yelped. Helen grabbed his arm again.

'See,' he gasped. 'Works every time.'

She laughed again. He retrieved a small backpack from the remains of his bike and they walked back to her car. She opened the passenger door for him and he folded himself in. He was of average height, lean and angular. She went around to the driver's side and opened her door. As the light flashed on and she climbed in beside him they looked at each other properly.

Helen saw a man of indeterminate age, dressed in a denim shirt and jeans, with deep-set blue eyes, gaunt cheekbones and a dented chin. Hair as thick and rusty as her daughter's was yanked back from a high forehead and tied into a ropy tail.

The red-headed stranger saw a small blonde woman in a short white shift, with sad brown eyes, and a heart-shaped face framed by a halo of pale hair. She had the figure of a young girl and small, slender fingers which she curled nervously around her steering wheel.

'Wow,' he said softly. 'Julie Christie, I presume?'

Helen laughed. 'You can call me Julie.'

'Really? Your name is Julie? You probably don't even remember who Julie Christie is. But you look as if you've come straight off the set of *Shampoo*. Or *Dr Zhivago*.'

'I know,' said Helen.

'You know?'

'Yes,' said Helen. 'But you don't look anything like Omar Sharif.'

He grinned. He had wonderful teeth, white and even, and a generous mouth. Helen gazed at his lovely smile and registered that the pain in her gut had reduced to a gentle throbbing.

'Maybe just a bit like Warren Beatty, though?' he asked hopefully.

'Nope,' said Helen. They continued to smile at each other. Helen reached to pull her door shut and the light went out. Still they looked at the shadows of each other's faces.

'How do you do, Julie,' said the red-headed stranger softly. He put out his hand. 'My name is Oliver,' he said, but the moment was destroyed because Helen burst out laughing.

'What?' he asked, grinning.

'That was the name of my ex-husband's penis,' said Helen pleasantly, putting both hands back on the wheel.

'Why did I say that?' she asked him later. 'It was such an entirely inappropriate thing to say to a total stranger. Not like me at all.'

He laughed and laughed. Hit his knees, kept looking at her. Drummed the palms of his hands on her dashboard and grinned at her again.

'Well, thank you, God,' he said when he could finally speak. And then he wound down the window and stuck his head outside and yelled: 'She's the answer to all my prayers! She's the miracle I've yearned for all my life. You've sent me an honest woman!' Then he pulled his head back inside and looked at her solemnly. 'Don't try to spare my feelings or anything, Julie,' he said, 'but I think for both our sakes, you had better call me by my middle name, which is Tom.'

'God didn't send me,' said Helen. 'I came all by myself. I am having a night off from family duties, so God probably wouldn't approve at all.'

'Family,' said the stranger. 'Damn.'

'Anyway ... Oliver,' Helen said, trying not to giggle, and failing.

'Tom. Please.'

'Okay, Tom. Where do you want me to take you?'

He put his head back and wriggled his bony frame around in the seat, getting comfortable. 'Everywhere but home,' he said softly, and closed his eyes.

Helen sat at the wheel and wondered for a little while what to do. Eventually, as he made no other suggestion, she turned on the ignition, pulled back onto the eastern road and headed towards the coast.

'I've always loved sitting in a car at night,' said Tom, 'heading into darkness, not knowing what's ahead.'

'That's a shame,' said Helen. 'Because we're nearly there.'

'Nearly where?'

'Mermaid Cove. It's a little seaside place. There's a pizza place there, if you're as hungry as me. There's also a backpackers' hostel.'

He sighed. 'I know. My gear is already safely stowed there. And although I am hungry, I am not hungry enough for the Mermaid Cove pizzeria. I ate there last night.'

'Oh,' said Helen. 'So you were just visiting Siren's Rock. And you're based at the Cove?'

'I'm just visiting, period. I'm not based anywhere. Two nights in one place is about all I can manage,' said Tom. 'And I prefer one. I'm seeing the world, Julie,' the man continued in his musical lilt, 'and you don't have to tell me I'm the luckiest man alive to be able to do that, because I know, and if my knees weren't giving me hell I would go down on them daily and thank the good Lord for allowing it. But listen, I want to make two suggestions to you. If you hate them both, you can drop me at the backpackers' hostel and I will always remember your kindness. If you like them, the possibilities for tonight are unlimited.'

Helen's headlights swept over a sign. *Mermaid Cove: 5 kilometres.*

'I'm listening,' she said.

'Suggestion one,' Tom began. 'Let's just keep driving. Obviously we rather like the look of each other. So let's stay together for a while and enjoy each other's company. Does that idea appeal at all?'

'What makes you think I like the look of you?' asked Helen.

'Ah well, d'you see,' said Tom, 'that question leads me straight into suggestion two. Now the way I see it, we haven't got long to be friends. I'm moving on tomorrow. You, no doubt, will soon be back on family duty. So let's not play any of those little man–woman games that waste so much time and insult the intelligence. Let's play the honesty game instead.'

'What's the honesty game?' asked Helen. But she already knew, really.

'Hell, Julie,' he said. 'I think you know it already.'

He smiled at her. He was incredibly handsome. Only you didn't realise, because of the hair. 'For one night,' he said, 'for this night only, we tell the truth at all times. We tell each other exactly what we are thinking. We don't protect ourselves or each other from our thoughts, our doubts, our fears, our prejudices. We tell it like it is.'

Helen drove past the turn-off to Mermaid Cove. 'Fine,' she said.

'Are we agreed? Absolute truth? No matter what?'

'What if we hurt each other?' asked Helen.

'Well, we've only just met. We can't hurt each other very much. And we're parting in the morning. So we'll get over it fast. On the other hand,' he glanced over at her and smiled, 'we might help each other. We might make each other happy.'

'Ah,' said Helen. 'You mean we might have sex?'

He threw back his head and roared with laughter again. He stuck his head out of the window and shouted at the sky again: 'She's doing it, God! She's already in the lead!'

'I wish you'd leave God out of this,' said Helen. 'I'm sure He has better things to do than referee any game we might choose to play.'

'I'm sorry,' said Tom. 'It annoys a lot of people. If I have to do it again, I'll call Him Charlie. It's less confronting.'

'So,' Helen smiled back at him, 'can I go first?'

'But you already have,' said Tom. 'And I must answer truthfully. But being absolutely truthful doesn't mean knowing all the answers. So to answer your sex question, I really don't know. It's not at all necessary. It probably depends on how we end up feeling about each other.'

'I thought you would at least *offer* to have sex with me,' said Helen, 'because that would make it three offers in one day, which could be a record.'

Tom shouted with laughter. 'Thank you, Charlie!' he whooped from his window. He pulled his head inside. 'Some people take years to decide,' said Tom, suddenly serious. 'We haven't got that long.'

'Because you're moving on tomorrow?'

'Because I am moving on tomorrow, yes,' said Tom.

'Okay,' said Helen. 'What I really wanted to say is that I'm starving. I had breakfast at five am and I haven't eaten since. Not even an ice-cream,' she added unnecessarily.

'Now that is a problem,' said Tom. 'You share my priorities. Food is much more important to a relationship, even a fleeting one, than sex.'

'We can go all the way up the coast to Berry Beach,' said Helen. 'But there are no food places on the way.'

Tom reached into his backpack and scrabbled around, eventually producing two apples and a large and chunky chocolate bar. 'Problem solved,' he said. Helen's eyes shone with delight. 'Chocolate,' she sighed, 'is absolutely my favourite fruit.'

PSYCHOLOGY

He was born in Northern Ireland, in County Down.

'My family lived on the coast, in a little place called Maighdean,' said Tom, and Helen felt as if he was reading to her from a storybook. 'I was very happy as a kid. Ten Liffey Street was a normal, happy home.'

In his teenage years his family had moved to England when his father took up a teaching position in Suffolk. Tom loved books and writing, so he became an English teacher — but he later studied psychology in Dublin and became a student counsellor which he enjoyed too much.

'Too much?' asked Helen.

'Some of the students who came to talk to me fancied they were in love with me,' said Tom. 'It's a hazard of the profession.'

'Especially looking the way you do,' said Helen.

He smiled at her quickly, but went on. 'Some of them made me weep. Trouble is, kids get upset when their counsellor cries. One of them told her parents I had taken advantage.'

'Did you?'

'No. But someone had. Her brother. The result was that

she was desperate for affection. She used to touch me, try to get close to me. Strange, isn't it? You'd think that sort of abuse would have put her off.'

'Not necessarily,' said Helen.

Tom paused, looked at her, then broke off another piece of chocolate.

'She was only a little girl,' he said. 'Little girls need to blossom and flower. Some of them get nipped while they are still in bud. After that they never blossom as brilliantly, as beautifully, as they might have done.'

They drove for a long time in silence before Helen asked if the little girl had got him into trouble.

'Yes, there was a court case. I was acquitted but after that nobody came to talk to me any more. It hurt my parents more than me. I went back up to the North and found a job running a shelter for troubled kids. Soccer instead of bombs, that sort of thing.'

'Were you mixed up in the Troubles?' asked Helen.

'The kids I was trying to work with were,' said Tom. 'One day somebody let off a bomb in the street where some of them lived. Two of them died. Their fathers, too. A third will never walk again. It was too much.'

'More weeping?'

'More weeping. I decided I needed to go some place beautiful. To get back in touch with ordinary people. People who didn't spend their lives hurting kids. So I decided to take a trip.'

'Is this it?' asked Helen.

'I'm still on it.'

'But I should think you'd have trouble finding any country where nobody is hurting kids.'

'I don't know about that,' he said easily. 'I'm never anywhere long enough to find out.'

'How long have you been on the road?' asked Helen. 'How do you afford it?'

'Five years. Since I was thirty. My mother died shortly after I went north and my father decided to emigrate to Canada to live with my sister. He gave me a small property that my mother had inherited, a cottage right in the heart of Dublin. Tourists love it; it's cheaper than staying in a hotel. Mainly I live on the rent.'

'And wherever you go, you never stay more than two nights in any place?'

'Unless I'm working. Sometimes that's necessary, to top up the funds.'

'So you're a traveller of the world because being on the move is better than stopping long enough to get too close to anyone.'

After a while Tom said: 'You worked all that out just by watching the way I break up chocolate? Have you studied psychology at all?'

'Nope. I've read a few books on the subject, but I never went to university. Psychology is just common sense,' said Helen. 'And listening well.'

'Very well,' said Tom.

'And I suppose there have been a few lovers along the way? Men or women?'

'Julie,' said Tom, smiling. 'For a small-town girl, you display a remarkably broad view of the world and its ways.'

'Well?'

'Women. And I'm a vegetarian.'

'Of course you are. No meat to contaminate your system. On the other hand, you probably wouldn't be averse to a few chemical substances?'

'Not any more. I want to be awake for it all,' he said, and then paused. 'I know it's your turn, but I'm tired now, Julie. I think I need a break before we do any more personal stuff. Especially if it ends up being mine.'

'I'm sorry,' said Helen.

'That's not the truth at all,' said Tom. 'You're not one bit sorry. You know more about me than I do about you and you feel good about it.'

'You're right,' said Helen. 'I hadn't thought . . .'

'We spend our whole lives lying to each other,' said Tom. 'Or covering up. That's the root of every problem in the world. Imagine what would happen if all the world leaders told each other the truth about their countries, about how their people felt, about their worries, about their God, their families, their lovers, their bodies, their tax systems — how they felt about leading their nations into the new millennium.'

'They'd probably all blow each other up,' said Helen.

'No,' said Tom softly. 'They would empathise. The way women do. They would look at each other with fresh understanding. They would become friends.'

'Jesus Christ,' Helen said, then muttered, 'Sorry. I just meant that's who you sound like.'

For the first time, Tom looked profoundly uncomfortable, so Helen changed the subject and they swapped travel tales, then discovered they shared many favourite authors. Helen slid her favourite Simon and Garfunkel tape into the stereo. They talked all through 'The Sounds of Silence'. At ten pm the lights of Berry Beach twinkled into view. Now what, thought Helen.

BERRY BEACH

The food tasted so good, Helen wondered if it was just the fact that she hadn't had a proper meal all day or whether the Dolphin Brasserie at the Berry Beach resort was the best restaurant she'd eaten in for years.

They sat out on a verandah overlooking the sea, but the moon was too high to illuminate the waves and they heard rather than saw the ocean. 'Wonderful place,' said Tom.

'We need something like it in Siren's Rock,' said Helen. 'Everything except the pubs still closes before ten. Even on a Friday night.'

'That'll change, you know,' said Tom. 'Give it ten years. Supermarkets will open until midnight, like they do in America. You'll have all-night restaurants. And with your delightful climate, people will sit outside to eat. On the footpaths. Like they do in France. They will.'

'Not in Siren's Rock, I don't think,' said Helen, 'but it would be wonderful.'

'Of course,' said Tom, 'you'll still need someone to eat *with*. On your nights off from family duties.'

She looked at him. 'You're not playing the game. You're not saying what you mean.'

'Let's walk,' he said, pushing back his chair. 'It's your turn.'

Tom paid. When Helen offered to share the cost, he put his hand on her cheek. 'You can pay tomorrow,' he said.

'But we won't be together tomorrow,' said Helen. 'You're moving on.'

'Shush,' he said, walking a little ahead of her, towards the path that led to the beach. 'Let's not think about tomorrow. It's your turn,' he repeated.

As they walked along the sand, cool now and soft beneath their bare feet, he listened without comment while she described her neat, tidy childhood. And the difference moving to Siren's Rock and meeting her best friend Jemma had made to her life. They walked in silence for a while.

'I was thinking about that little girl,' said Helen. 'The one who accused you of taking advantage of her. The one with the brother.'

'Bernie,' he said.

'Bernie,' said Helen. 'You probably don't have to worry about her as much as you obviously do. She'll probably be okay, you know. You get over those things.'

'Do you?' he said, glancing at her.

Helen raised her eyes to look at the moon and took a breath. 'My father fiddled with me a bit,' said Helen.

She heard herself say it, heard the matter-of-fact tone in her voice, tested her reaction to her own words, found she felt quite calm and went on: 'Quite a lot in fact. He used to hit me with a cane and then he would ... interfere with me.' She paused and thought about the picture her words would draw. 'Not the whole performance,' said Helen. 'Just his fingers. Anyway, it didn't put me off men.'

He was watching her in the dark. 'You became a nymphomaniac?'

'No,' said Helen, and laughed. It was a natural, normal laugh. There were no tears. No strangled sobs were trapped in her throat. It had been so easy. After all these years of keeping it behind the blind, telling no one. Not even Jemma. Not Nigel, however much he had guessed. Never saying the words. Now she had said them. To a red-headed stranger who was willing to care about her for one night. Tomorrow she would be a story, an experience to add to his reasons for moving on, along with the little girl who thought she loved him and the boy who would never walk again.

'No,' she repeated. 'But I liked being touched. Weird, isn't it? You'd think I would have hated it. But when I was a kid, a teenager, I was always wanting to be cuddled. Held. Any bloke at all would do.'

'Did your mother cuddle you when you were a little girl?' His was the voice that sounded slightly strangled.

'No,' said Helen. 'But she spent a lot of time trying to make me look pretty.'

'And your father? Did he cuddle you? I don't mean when he was ... interfering ...' Tom stopped talking. His voice ran down, the music whining out of it as if his batteries were flat.

'No,' said Helen.

Now they walked for a long time in silence until Tom eventually spoke again. 'Did anyone? Hold you? Hug you? When you were young?'

'No,' said Helen. A cliff loomed up in the dark ahead of them. They had almost reached the end of Berry Beach.

'So you liked being touched. By women as well as men?'

'Well ...' she paused.

'The truth, remember,' said Tom. He cleared his throat. He *had* been shedding a few tears, thought Helen. A soft man in a hard body. 'You said any bloke at all would do,' said Tom. 'What about any woman?'

Helen thought about it. 'Anyone really,' she admitted with surprise. She glanced at him. 'I suppose I just craved affection generally.'

'So do you enjoy sex?' asked Tom, as they reached the cliff.

Helen sighed and sat down on a rock. It was cold against her bare thighs. She tried to pull her shift down underneath her but it was too short. 'I'm not very good at it.'

'Who told you that? Your husband?' Tom didn't sit down.

'No. I worked it out for myself. Nigel tried to make sex good for me. He did everything he could think of to arouse me. He and Oliver.' She chuckled. To her relief, Tom chuckled too. 'It just never happened,' said Helen matter-of-factly. 'It wasn't their fault.'

'Oliver knew where to go? What to do?'

'Believe me,' said Helen, nodding vigorously, 'Oliver knew his way around. He went everywhere.'

'Must be something about Olivers,' said Tom. They were both giggling now.

'D'you want to go for a swim?' Helen asked suddenly. She had been arrested by the idea of a soft heart in a hard body. She imagined Tom naked, plunging under a wave in the moonlight. She looked up at him and smiled.

He shook his head. 'I think it's time we went back,' he said.

'What are you thinking?' he asked as they wandered back, more slowly than they had set out. 'Do you wish you hadn't told me about your father?'

'No,' said Helen thinly. 'That was a relief. I've never told anyone before. Not even Jemma and I've told her everything else. Well, almost everything.'

'There's something else you haven't told Jemma?'

'Yes.'

'Tell me.'

'No,' said Helen.

'You're breaking the rules of the game.'

'There are exceptions,' said Helen, 'to every rule.'

'I know,' said Tom. 'There is someone you love more than Jemma. More than Caitlin. Your one true love. And you've never told anybody who he is.'

Helen was silent.

'Okay,' said Tom. 'Technically I should disqualify you. But I'll give you a second chance if you tell me exactly what you are thinking right now.'

'I'm feeling embarrassed because I asked you to go for a swim and you turned me down and you probably thought I meant we should swim nude and I did, so actually you were turning down more than a swim.'

Tom roared with laughter again and hit his thighs with delight. 'Excellent. Excellent truth telling. You wonderful woman, I'll forgive you everything. You are no longer in danger of disqualification from the game of truth. And here is the best example of how much it helps. I turned you down for one reason only.'

'Sure,' said Helen, kicking up sand. 'You don't fancy me. I'm too small. I'm a good listener, but when it comes to sex, I'm the kind you feel you should throw back. Unlike Jemma. I wish you could meet Jemma,' said Helen. 'She would love you. You would love her. You would definitely not have turned Jemma down.' *On the other hand,* said Helen the cynic, *Jemma would not have made him the offer.*

'I would have turned Jemma down,' said Tom. 'Even Jemma can't be big enough to fight off sharks.'

'Sharks?'

'I read all about Australia on the way here. Sharks feed at night. I'm scared of sharks. So you see, you don't have to feel rejected. You don't have to feel bad about yourself at all.'

'I don't feel bad about myself,' said Helen.

He stopped walking. 'Really, Julie?' Ahead of them the blue neon of the Berry Beach resort twinkled brighter than the stars. Tom took Helen's face between his hands. 'Are you telling me the truth, Julie?'

She brushed his hands away and strode off through the cool sand.

'Okay,' said Helen, walking faster. 'If you *want* to spoil the night. *Yes*, I do feel bad about myself, almost all the time. My mother thought I was an ugly little nuisance as a child and now I am only useful to her as a housekeeper. My father, for reasons I don't even *want* to understand, physically and sexually abused me until my teens. I let strange boys touch me and I would have let them do a lot more if Jemma hadn't saved me.'

The wind whipped her words out of her mouth and flung them at the waves that rushed growling at their feet.

'My husband treated me like some kind of sex toy,' Helen continued, 'and left me when I got pregnant. I've never enjoyed sex much, I've never even had an orgasm and, to be quite honest, I've stopped caring. The daughter Nigel planted in me before he left hates me,' said Helen, walking faster, 'because I abandoned her at birth in order to go off to my dreary job, which by the way I probably don't have any more. I'm not organised or interesting or good at anything. I've never done anything worthwhile in my entire life, except give birth to Caitlin. I love her desperately but Jemma, who doesn't love her at all, is a better mother to her than I will ever be. *Gee*, this is a fun game,' she turned to face him, 'I don't know about you, Oliver, but I'm just loving it.'

Tears were running down her face.

'And now,' she said, 'I'll tell you the bad stuff.'

He put his arms around her and held her while she cried, an agonised series of howls. She buried her head in his denim shirt front and soaked it with her tears, her anger, her hurt, her fury and her pain. The red-headed stranger held Helen firmly in his bony, furry arms, and stared over her head at the sea.

When she finally stopped, he held her head in his hands and told her what she needed to hear. How she was wise and good. How Caitlin was the luckiest girl alive to have Helen for a mother. How she had worked hard, all on her own, to provide a good life in a good town. How Caitlin would realise that in time, even if it wasn't until she had daughters of her own. How Jemma was lucky to have her for a friend and obviously loved her very much and wasn't it a wonderful thing that her husband wasn't jealous of the closeness between the two women, as many husbands are. In fact, John obviously loved Helen too ...

'*No*,' said Helen, jerking her head up and staring fiercely into his eyes. 'No, not John. John doesn't love me, I don't even *want* John to love me ...' She spoke in broken jerky sobs. 'I don't want you to talk about John,' she said.

'Okay,' said Tom. He kissed her then, but she barely noticed, because she was trying to talk, trying to argue that the good things he was saying couldn't possibly be true. So he kissed her again and told her she was sweet and beautiful, every man's dream and especially his. And finally Helen heard him and slipped into his kiss, realised it was the nicest kiss she had ever known. After a while she drew away and, with a small sigh of regret, walked on towards the lights.

A LITTLE MAGIC

The Berry Beach resort nightclub was still open when they got back, its neon dolphin flashing, dance music thudding from inside. Helen went into the toilets, washed her face and her feet, vigorously brushed her hair and swallowed two aspirin tablets with a flair that would have made Babs proud.

It was a shame about all the tears, she thought, and, with hindsight, the kissing had probably not been a good idea. On the other hand, sooner or later her unhappiness was bound to come pouring out like that and who better to soak it up than a stranger she would never see again?

And you stopped! said Saint Helen proudly. *It was you who walked away.*

When she emerged, Tom was standing in the corridor, holding out his hand. 'Let's dance,' he said. 'I feel like dancing.'

They danced in the Dolphin Room, with blue lights winking at the window and around their feet. There were only three other couples shuffling together on the tiny parquet square. The band had gone home but music was coming from somewhere. '*You made me love you ...*' Tom crooned along with the song. He couldn't sing very well but he knew all the words. He also danced amazingly well and he was the right height for her, taller but not too tall. She told him this and he laughed. His mother had taught him to dance, he said. He had adored his mother.

Driving home in the early hours of the morning, they played silly car games to keep Helen awake. And they sang. Tom taught her the choruses to some bawdy Irish ditties, all of them with an eye-rolling number of verses. He had a good memory all right, thought Helen. Where had he learned them all? His father's brothers, he said. They had their own band, sang in a pub.

They ate their apples and had a competition to see who could chew more loudly. They dribbled juice and laughed a great deal and said a lot of things that made no sense. Tom offered to drive but Helen said he wasn't insured. Besides, she wanted to hold on to the wheel. She felt it was very important to keep her hands on something other than Tom. She was afraid that if she put her hands on him again, she would not walk away a second time.

This was a brief encounter. She knew it was important not to spoil the end, not to think about tomorrow.

'What are you thinking?' he said.

'I'm happy,' said Helen. 'I don't want tomorrow to come.'

He looked out of the window. 'Me neither,' he murmured, 'but it's here.'

Dawn the colour of spilt milk was seeping through the sky. They pulled up outside the backpackers' hostel at Mermaid Cove. The pain in Helen's gut was beginning to return. She put her hand on her stomach and squeezed the flesh, as if she needed to hold it together.

There was so much more she wanted to say to him.

She remembered Jemma, on Lassos, telling her how she

and John would need a lifetime to say all they wanted to say to each other.

It was still pretty dark and the street lights were on as Tom climbed out of her car. He walked around to her window and she wound it down and looked up at him. She pulled her lips into a determined smile.

'Thank you for a wonderful night,' she said. She said it well. She'd been practising in her head.

'Thank *you*,' he said, smiling. He had magnificent cheekbones, she thought, and a truly beautiful mouth. It was a good thing that Jemma would never meet him. She didn't want to share this one.

'Goodbye, Tom,' she said. But she didn't take her eyes from his face and he seemed unable to stop looking at her.

'Julie,' he said softly. He hesitated. Helen kept her eyes on his face.

'Wait here a minute,' he said.

Surprised, Helen waited in the car. She wondered what was coming. A memento of the night, perhaps? Something small to remember him by? A few minutes later he was back, slapping the boot. She pulled the small lever that snapped it open and he heaved something large and unwieldy inside.

'It's not tomorrow until the sun comes up,' he said. 'Let's go down to the beach.'

Mermaid Cove was deserted. A faint flush of gold lined the horizon where the sun would eventually appear. Helen pulled into the deserted car park and Tom jumped out and unloaded an enormous swag, army green, the biggest she had ever seen. 'My only home for the past five years,' said Tom, lugging it down the steps on his back.

The heat had finally worked its way out of the night and now, in the dawn light, there was a faint chill in the air. Tom staggered over the sand ahead of Helen, lurching along until he reached the dunes. Helen followed slowly, gently massaging her abdomen. He disappeared among the slopes of sand. She found him a minute later, surveying a smooth stretch of sand ringed by tufty grass, out of sight of any early-rising fishermen.

'I will now drop my bundle,' Tom said gasping, and did so, immediately going down on his knees and efficiently releasing buttons and zips. The swag obediently unrolled itself and turned into a bed.

Tom turned back the top flap and crawled inside. 'I'm still telling you the truth, Julie. I need to sleep. You need to sleep. Let's sleep together until the sun comes up,' said Tom. 'I can't think of another soul on this earth with whom I would rather share my first glimpse of sunrise over the Pacific Ocean.'

Helen knelt beside him. Slipped into the swag. 'It's like a giant envelope,' she said, snuggling down, relishing the warmth. Posted, she thought. I wonder where I'm going?

When she peered over the edge of the flap, she could see the sky beginning to glimmer with gold. When she turned her head to tell Tom, he was asleep.

They slept for half an hour and then, woken by some inexplicable magic, some silent siren's song, they opened their eyes and propped themselves up on their elbows in time to see the orange rim of the sun slide up over the horizon and keep climbing until it hung there, a golden globe of heat and light, suspended above the sea.

They turned to each other then, shed their clothes, began their second dance. Deep in the envelope of the swag, their bodies flowed together in the rhythms and movements that lovers have performed since the beginning of time.

'Sun's up,' Tom whispered, leaning over her, kissing her neck, her forehead, her nose, her cheeks and finally her mouth, running his long fingers over her arms, stroking the white curve of her belly, gazing at the creamy globes of her dark-tipped breasts, caressing them.

'What are you thinking?' murmured Helen, watching his eyes, enjoying the pleasure reflected there as he looked at her body, feeling his fingers rove over her singing skin, music almost forgotten for a dance she had never truly learned.

'It's time to pretend,' Tom whispered against her mouth.

'I knew we'd have to lie to each other sooner or later,' sighed Helen, walking her fingers across his collar bone. 'Do you want me to say you can sing as well as you dance?' she asked, smiling, kissing him as his fingers slid over the silky flesh of her inner thighs.

'Pretend I'm the man of your dreams,' said Tom, 'the man you've always wanted.'

He rolled onto his back, gently lifting her as he moved beneath her, kissing her breasts as they brushed his face, lying her body over his, easing her onto his chest so that she was looking down into his face through her cobweb of hair. She was silent now.

He pulled her head down to his, kissing her warm lips, her cheeks, her eyes still swollen from all the weeping in the dark, hooking his lean legs through hers, leading her slowly through the stages of the dance, seducing her with his lips, his fingers, his toes. As he had seduced her all through the night with his stories, his truths, his tears. He made her swoop and sway until her breath came in sobs. He led and she followed, Tom the choreographer, Tom, who knew the moves, knew the rhythms, Tom, who knew that in this dance, and with this woman, timing was precious. And envied the man Helen loved, the man who would give her all the time in the world.

Slowly the sky turned pink and the sun spread a crimson sheet over the sea.

'Pretend I'm your one true love,' whispered Tom, as she began to shudder above him, his lips moving on hers as he reached her deepest place. And reached it again and again as their hips rose and fell, as he finally heard her gasp, as their bodies blended, as the frenzy of the dance carried her to a place she had never been.

Part Seven

MARTE

'Watch yourself, Marte!' the men used to say, just before they opened the gate.

It always seemed to her that there was one Marte enveloped in dust and sweat, gripping the leather reins and clenching her knees against the horse's heaving flanks, while another Marte stood watching, wondering whether she would stay the distance.

Now there were two Martes in Jemma's kitchen, surrounded by funeral food.

The first Marte Johnson surveyed the laden benches with tired but practical eyes; ran her index finger down the stacks of waiting crockery — the bread and butter plates from her own best floral-patterned china and Jemma's two plain dinner sets — and did a final count before taking the teatowel off the basket of forks.

Best wishes from Dubbo, the teatowel said. It bore a brown picture of a homestead.

The other Marte watched the teatowel being folded up and put aside, wondered where it had come from.

Marte knew none of the family had been to Dubbo,

because Jemma used to say quite often that they should all go one long weekend, to visit the zoo.

Now they never would.

The watching Marte, the anguished woman who had been at the funeral, thinking and grieving, was useless in the kitchen. She existed on another plane, silent, stunned with sadness, sheltering in her own cave of grief, haunted by a litany of now-they-never-woulds.

But the first Marte Johnson knew life had to go on, as it always did. Knew what Jemma and Helen would have asked her to do if either had been here.

John would have taken it all upon his own broad shoulders, but John had been in Ireland. By the time he arrived back in Siren's Rock, Marte had bravely stepped outside the cave and organised the funeral food. And more.

She had purposely avoided the Greek pastries that her mother-in-law would have recommended and, apart from her special apple cake, there was no German food on the menu either. She had prepared traditional, comforting sandwiches, white bread triangles encasing chicken, slippery strips of ham, mushy egg and salad; she had made iced slices and three kinds of cake. She had borrowed three hot-water urns, one each from the Catholics, the Baptists and the Anglicans, and had made filtered coffee for the young people.

They had decided John and Jemma's house was the best place for the wake. It was spacious, cool and clean, with room on the wide verandah for the visitors to spill out for some fresh air or a smoke. The Sullivans didn't have air conditioning, but the big ceiling fans whirred away and Marte and George had opened all the windows and doors in the hope of capturing any breeze.

It was pleasant in the kitchen, quiet, cooler than the church. The sun's light had dimmed. But despite all the windows and doors, this was a dark house — dark stained timber, wooden floors, blackwood cupboards, big black beams. Marte would have preferred to work in a kitchen with gaily coloured vinyl floors and shiny laminated bench tops. Clean, pretty, light, bright, that's what she liked in a house.

George lumbered into the kitchen, opened the fridge and took out more jugs of fruit cordial, clinking with ice. On his way out he paused and looked at her. His face broke her heart.

'You staying in here?' he asked, and she nodded. She was comfortable in the kitchen. She could concentrate on the food, and she could sit on a good straight-backed chair if her bad leg played up on her. She wouldn't have to talk to anybody she didn't want to. She was no good at talking today. 'There's clouds,' observed George as he shuffled out. 'Maybe rain.'

John was still at the church. A television crew had turned up, as well as a few newspaper reporters — one had even come from Sydney. John, quietly furious, was dealing with them. Trying to send them away — unsuccessfully, no doubt. This death was news.

It was a shame John was so angry, thought Marte. Hadn't it occurred to him that Jemma would have been delighted? Thrilled to pieces, she would have been.

The house was crowded with people. They had come from everywhere. There were lots of locals but there were folk from Sydney too, even Brisbane and Melbourne.

Marte saw the television crew arrive in the yard from her vantage point at the kitchen window. They must have struck some kind of deal with John, she thought. She saw Tom edge up to look at the camera on the shoulder of a shaven-headed man. A journalist immediately pounced on him, no doubt knowing he was Helen Connor's son. Hamish was beside him in a flash, leading him away. Poor darling Helen, Marte sighed, hers was the *real* news story. Front page.

'The food looks beautiful, Mrs Johnson,' said a cushion-shaped matron in the doorway. 'You're a wonderful cook. I don't know how you manage it.' The first Marte Johnson smiled. The other Marte Johnson wondered how she had managed it. The food. And the smile.

Fame, thought Marte. That was all Jemma had ever wanted. And although she and George would have given their souls to make her happy, fame they couldn't provide. However hard they had laboured.

Was it my fault, Marte wondered, removing plastic wrap from the last of the large white plates of sandwiches, that my daughter longed so passionately to be noticed, that she was driven all her life by her desire for recognition? Was it those early stories about the Louisville Lady Rider that had sown the seed? Or was it the dancing classes, the speech lessons, the drama coaching — all those opportunities Marte had worked so hard to provide for her daughter because she herself had never had any opportunities at all?

What *was* the catalyst that had sparked Jemma's craving for fame?

If only she could see what she has, Marte used to think. If only she could stop thinking about being noticed long enough to notice herself. To watch herself, to look at her life.

'You are loved, you have a safe home, a happy family,' Marte had frequently said to her daughter. 'That is our gift to you. That is what you need to give your own children.'

Jemma had taken their gift and made a copy of it for her own family, and even for Helen's family. But she hadn't wanted it for herself.

Marte doubted that Jemma had ever been truly content. Brilliant, ambitious and passionate, yes, cheerful and hard-working too. But never content. Never still. Never satisfied with what she had achieved. And she had achieved so much.

Jemma had had so many happy experiences, of course — her wedding, Hamish's birth, her triumphs on the local stage, her community work, her writing successes, all sorts of recognition. She'd even had a television program made on all her achievements. But, ultimately, none of those things had given her lasting fulfilment.

Marte shook her shoulders, shrugging off the sad thoughts that threatened to knock her down. Sometimes in the last few days, she had been afraid that would happen; that her burden of grief would send her crashing to the ground; that she would never get up again. It was the good memories that helped her stay standing.

At least there had been years of good memories, thought Marte. After the war, George bringing her to Siren's Rock. Such a nice town for a young family. Sure, the reception from old Maria hadn't been the greatest show of affection on earth, but what woman never had a problem with her husband's mama? Could she honestly say she herself thought that city girl Janelle was the perfect wife for her Nick?

She had stopped worrying about Maria with Jemma's incredible arrival into the world. It was as if Jemma's little beating heart had set her own life on track. All that had happened to her before Jemma's birth ceased to matter. And there had been so many happy times since. Christmases. Birthdays. Anniversaries. Picnics. Family traditions that gave life meaning; memories that made even days like this one bearable.

As the wake moved into its second stage, the young people came into the kitchen to collect the silver salvers of cakes and slices, and the trays of tea and coffee. It's getting darker, they reported. The clouds were thick and grey. The sky was turning green. There's going to be a storm, they said, but nobody really believed it would finally happen.

Marte noticed that even after days of talk and tears, none of them was saying what was really on their minds or in their hearts. Even Caitlin's red-rimmed eyes were finally dry.

Everyone was speaking sadly but well of the departed. And being together with friends and relatives they hadn't seen for a while, they were starting to talk about other things as well — the economy, taxes, exam results, house renovations, holidays, divorces, births, illness, other deaths, even marriages. And the weather. Some people were even laughing a little, or occasionally a lot.

She saw George, John, Hamish, Caitlin and Tom moving quietly among their guests, their hearts still freshly breaking, their wounds pink and seeping bitterly, and she wondered at the ability of others to be talking and behaving normally, chewing, drinking, laughing, chatting, acting almost as if nothing had happened.

There was no doubt now that clouds were gathering. The sun had lost its searing strength and turned from blinding gold to a deep dense orange. The humidity had increased and, even with Jemma's fans going flat out, bubbles of perspiration were appearing on lips and brows. Blots of moisture oozed into the underarms of shirts and dresses.

If it rains, thought Marte, that's the first thing the people will remember when they wake up tomorrow. They'll be relieved. Then today will hit them. The memory of what has happened.

They will sigh, thought Marte. They will press their lips together and shake their heads. They will adjust their hearts and minds to their sorrow. But their lives will go on. They will get out of bed and wash and dress themselves, crunch their cereal, slide margarine over their toast, clean their teeth and go on with their work, their school, their days. Small steps, thought Marte. We will all take small, ordinary steps and that will help us cope with the unbelievable.

It had all gone off very well. Marte was standing at the sink, washing all the awkward things that wouldn't go in the dishwasher. A crutch was propped beneath her left armpit. Caitlin had offered to wipe up but Marte had waved her away. Not for the first time, Marte thought it was a tragedy that Caitlin behaved so normally, so *nicely*, when her mother wasn't around to see it.

Jemma herself could not have organised the funeral better, thought Marte, tears starting, making their way down her seamed cheeks and falling into the sudsy sink. Marte had done it all. The notices in the paper, the choice of clergymen, the cremation, the order of service, the coffin, the food of course — and, with help from Caitlin and Hamish, the music and the flowers.

It was the other Marte Johnson, the one nobody knew, the useless one who watched herself and worried too much, who had contacted the press. Ah yes, the media. Without telling a soul at home, Marte had sent faxes and made calls to let the television, radio and newspaper people know about the funeral and the wake. Even George didn't know she'd done that and hopefully John would never know.

She hadn't done it for John.

This funeral would be in the news all over the state tonight. Marte had made sure of that. Marte Johnson, the cleaning woman with the peculiar accent, the uneducated wife of the fish and chip shop man, the Louisville Lady Rider. Marte Johnson, mother of the town's first feminist — Marte Johnson had seen to it that this would be the most famous funeral ever held in Siren's Rock.

And at last, the rain came.

LATE ARRIVAL

'God Almighty,' said Jemma, who so rarely blasphemed. 'How the hell did this happen?'

Helen lay on her friend's maize-coloured couch. Her face was the same colour. Her skin was clammy. She had just vomited in Jemma's Federation-style bathroom.

'I don't know,' croaked Helen pathetically. 'Please don't rouse on me. I can't bear it.'

Jemma stood over her, wrapping her arms around herself, exuding a volatile mixture of surprise, anger, indignation and distress.

'You're forty-one years old, Helen. You're single. You're pregnant. You must know how it happened. How can you say you don't *know*?'

'Stop yelling at me, Jemma,' moaned Helen. 'I didn't do it on purpose.'

Jemma threw her hands up in the air and began striding up and down her family room.

'I repeat. You're forty-one years old. You're *single*. You're *pregnant*. Nobody would be *stupid* enough to think you did it on *purpose*! But why did you do it at *all*? And who with? *Who is the father*?'

'Jemma, will you stop talking in italics,' said Helen, reaching for the damp wash cloth that Jemma was waving about. She clamped it on her forehead and closed her eyes.

'I'm not telling you who it was,' said Helen. 'He was a stranger. And he's gone. The last time I saw him he was sound asleep in the biggest sleeping bag I've ever seen. He couldn't contact me even if he wanted to . . .' She stopped as her voice threatened to turn into a sob. She took a breath. 'And I never expected him to. He doesn't even know my name.'

Helen followed Jemma with her eyes. Even that hurt. 'We both agreed that we only wanted one night together. But it was wonderful, Jemma. It was *wonderful*. He made me feel . . .' She stopped. 'Wonderful,' she said feebly.

'A stranger. A one-night stand. And no condom,' said Jemma.

'You told me to go out and have a good time,' Helen said weakly. 'I did. I had the best time. You even told me a discreet affair might do me good . . .'

'A discreet affair!' yelled Jemma. 'A *discreet* affair, Helen! Not a bonk in the sand with some randy bastard and now a baby at forty-one! You've always been slightly crazy, Helen, crazy in a quiet sort of way, but I think you've completely cracked up! A stranger, a one-night stand and no condom! You might have caught AIDS, did you think of that? Or some other ghastly disease. Good Lord, if I'd known this was going to happen I would have made you stay and listen to John singing Beatles songs all bloody night long. It probably wouldn't have been as exciting as what you were doing but at least you wouldn't be pregnant again!'

'Why do you keep saying pregnant *again*, as if I do this all the time? This is only the second time after all.'

'Yes, but you didn't mean it to happen the first time either,' said Jemma. 'You get pregnant at the drop of a hat.

I've only ever managed it once and here's you having a baby the minute anyone looks at you sideways!' Her eyes filled with tears.

'But Jemma,' said Helen, carefully sitting up. 'What on earth do you mean? You said you didn't want any more children after Hamish.'

'John would have liked more,' said Jemma, throwing herself into a chair. 'Ten more, probably. If I *had* got pregnant again, it wouldn't have been the end of the world. But I didn't.'

'Oh Jem,' said Helen weakly, 'I'm sorry.'

'Hamish was such a lovely baby,' said Jemma. 'And if we'd had a huge family it might have made up for not being a star!'

'Oh Jemma,' sighed Helen, slightly surprised at how quickly they'd returned to Jemma's perennial problem, 'you've achieved so much already, and you'll continue to. You *are* going to be famous. The ABC is going to love your play. They'll love it! They'll probably ring you any day now and they'll . . .'

'They've rung,' said Jemma. 'They don't want it. Try again, they said. Shows promise, they said. Doesn't quite work for them. Rework it, they said. Again. Again and again and again. All that time, wasted.' She looked at Helen. 'Anyway, it's *you* we're talking about, not me. And you're pregnant! Now I won't get any more time to write at all,' said Jemma. And she put her head on her arms and cried as if her heart would break.

Helen crawled off the couch and hobbled over to Jemma, put her arms awkwardly around her friend's heaving shoulders.

'Not you,' she whispered. *Me. It's me. It's mine* . . . But words failed her as usual and tears began seeping from her own eyes.

Jemma's family room, usually a thriving hub of activity, was shocked into silence. No phone rang. No music played. No orders were given. There was just the sound of two women sobbing.

Jemma stopped first, blowing her nose noisily, sighing, sitting up, reaching out to touch Helen's cheek. 'I'm sorry, Julie,' she snuffled. 'That was terribly weak of me. You just caught me unawares, that's all. It's much more awful for you, of course. But don't worry. We'll get through it. I'll organise something.'

'Jemma,' said Helen.

Jemma wiped her hands over her face. 'Of course your mother will be useless and will only make trouble, so you'll have to get out of the villa.'

'Jemma?' said Helen.

'Wouldn't it be wonderful if you had a little boy this time?' said Jemma.

'*Jemma!*' said Helen.

'What?'

Helen looked at her desperately. It's not your problem, she wanted to say. It's not your life. It's not your baby. It's mine. All mine. I can look after myself.

But the words wouldn't come.

'From calling me a stupid cow to offering to take us in,' said Helen, when Jemma had made them both a cup of tea, 'in less than thirty minutes. You're extraordinary.'

'I never said you were a stupid cow,' said Jemma.

'No,' said Helen. 'That must have been what I was thinking about myself. I suppose you're wondering if I've thought about an abortion ...'

'No,' said Jemma. 'I wasn't wondering that at all. I know you wouldn't. You know I wouldn't. It's just the way we are.'

Helen's eyes filled with tears again.

'It's all the wrong way around for us, isn't it?' said Helen. 'You should be the one out having a career. Doing something brilliant. And I should be at home, looking after the children. I'd love to be doing that.'

'I know,' said Jemma.

'Yet here you are,' said Helen, 'offering to start all over again. And if I let you, you would do it brilliantly. Because you do everything so well, Jemma. Everything.'

Jemma stood up and walked slowly to the window. 'No, I don't,' she said, with her back to Helen. 'If that was true my life wouldn't have turned out to be so . . . *ordinary*!'

'But Jemma,' said Helen, loudly for her. 'What *is* so terrible about that? What's wrong with ordinary if you're *happy*?' she asked. 'Ordinary is *good*. God, I'd give anything to be ordinary.'

Jemma turned around and looked at Helen. 'I know,' she said. 'That's because you're not.'

FATHERS

Caitlin decided that her father must have come back. Who else, she reasoned, would be crazy enough to sleep with someone as old and unsociable as her mother? This story that Jemma had conjured up about some 'very dear friend' turning up out of their past, planting a baby in her mother and then conveniently taking himself off again, was too ridiculous to be true. Unless the very old friend was Nigel Connor. Caitlin knew it was. She'd seen enough television soaps to know how the story went.

Helen wouldn't admit it because she was ashamed and embarrassed, as well she might be, having made it quite clear to Caitlin that even if Nigel turned up out of the blue and wanted them both back, she wouldn't have anything to do with him. 'He wasn't a good husband and he wasn't capable of being a good father,' Helen had said many times. 'He was clever and interesting and entertaining and you have inherited all that from him. But Nigel and I should never have married.'

Caitlin didn't believe her father would come all the way back from England, or whatever glamorous foreign country he lived in, without attempting to see her. The only explanation was that her mother had talked him out of it. She'd probably lied, told him Caitlin was away or something.

'That's not true, Caitlin,' said Jemma. 'I know why you wish it was your dad but it wasn't. Your dad did not come back. If he had, of course he'd have wanted to see you. He would love you,' said Jemma. 'He would be so proud to discover that he had such a gorgeous, clever daughter. But he is not the father of this baby. It was someone else, someone your mother . . .' she paused, 'loved.'

But Caitlin couldn't let it go. When they moved in with the Sullivans ('just until the baby is born,' Helen assured Jemma and John), she brought it up often. 'That night when my dad came back . . .' she would say, watching Helen carefully for her reaction. 'My mum had sex with my dad,' she said casually to her friends, to Hamish, to Jemma, to Marte. It reached a point where most of the time they didn't argue.

'If it makes her happy . . .' said Helen.

'It doesn't make her happy,' said Jemma. 'It's tearing her apart.'

Finding Caitlin in tears on the couch after school one day, Jemma sat down beside her, imprisoned her unwilling hand in hers and took it upon herself to tell her that fathers weren't all they were cracked up to be.

'I've been lucky,' said Jemma. 'John hasn't. His father used to beat him. It was worse for your mother. Her father was very cruel to her. When she was the same age as you, and for years before that, he made her life more miserable than you could ever imagine.'

Caitlin stared at Jemma, her mouth damp and quivering.

'Now listen to me, and listen carefully,' said Jemma sternly. 'John may not be your father but he loves you like a daughter. You're the only daughter he will ever have and you are very special to him. The same with Poppy George,' she went on. 'He loves you like a granddaughter. It is very important to have men in your life, Caitlin,' said Jemma, 'but they don't have to be related to you to love you and care about you.'

A tiny dribble ran from Caitlin's nose and clung to her top lip. She stared at Jemma with moist, red-rimmed eyes. 'What did Grandad do to my mother?'

'What the hell did you tell her?' screamed Helen. Screamed, yes. Barged into Jemma's big airy bedroom, with its view of the mountains, banged the door against the pristine white wall and screamed her question at the top of her voice. '*What have you been saying to my daughter about me?*'

Jemma was red-faced, ashamed, embarrassed, frightened. She couldn't find the right words. Nor would Helen let her.

'How dare you?' Helen shouted. 'How *dare* you speak to my eleven-year-old child about what happened to me!' She was shouting, taking small, sobbing breaths, gasping for air. 'How *dare* you tell her things that are my business only. Do you hear that, Jemma? *My* business! *Not yours!* You can't star in this particular drama, Jemma, and do you know why? *You weren't there.* This had nothing to do with you at all. It is *mine*, Jemma, *it happened to me.*'

'I'm sorry,' said Jemma, inadequate, feeble, blown back on the bed by Helen's rage. 'Please calm down. I was only trying to help. I was trying to be kind . . .'

'There is nothing *kind* about telling an eleven-year-old child about perversion and abuse. And you don't *really* know about it. I never told you. Did Nigel tell you? I never told him. He would have been guessing. *You're* guessing. How *could* you, Jemma?'

'Of course you told me,' said Jemma, frowning, feeling ill. 'He hit you. He said horrible things to you and he caned you when you weren't even bad …' Her voice faded away. She sat on the edge of her bed, lumps of the quilt clutched in her hands. She looked at the agonised, distorted face of her friend and bile rose in her throat.

'Oh God, Helen. What else did the bastard do to you?'

'I can't believe you didn't guess,' said Marte.

Jemma was incredulous for the second time that day. 'You mean *you* knew, Mum? You knew and didn't tell me?'

'What could you do?' asked Marte. 'What could any of us do?' She rested her head in her hands.

'Listen, Jemma,' said Marte. 'Now is not the time to open that can of worms again. Caitlin's been told her grandfather used to beat her mother. That's enough. That's all she knows. Helen will forgive you,' said Marte. 'It was a misunderstanding, you just didn't know. It was nobody's fault. You are her best friend, you made her happy at a time when she was a very sad little girl. Now you are looking after her again. Plenty of love, that's what she needs,' said Marte, 'that's what they both need. And you and John, you're the best two people in the world to give it to them.'

'We'll have to talk about it, though,' said Jemma. 'Talking helps.'

'Not this time, I don't think,' said Marte.

'I'm so desperately, desperately sorry,' said Jemma. With the silence broken, the same subject kept resurfacing.

Helen's eyes were still welling with tears. 'I know,' she said. 'But it's Caitlin I'm worried about. I'm worried this will damage her. This whole mess I've made.'

'She'll be okay,' said Jemma.

'Do you think she'll be messed up?' asked Helen, as if Jemma hadn't spoken. 'Is her life ruined forever?' she asked

Marte, who had just come into the living room with an armful of ironing. Marte had always done Jemma's ironing.

'She'll be fine,' said Jemma. 'We'll spoil her rotten and she'll forget all about it.'

But Marte put the ironing down on the couch and sighed. 'It will become a part of her,' she said. 'What's past makes us all who we are.'

'You mean what doesn't kill us makes us strong?' said Jemma.

'No,' said Marte. 'That's not what I meant. Caitlin is still a child. That saying isn't right for children.'

Helen went over to Marte and put her arms around her.

Marte smiled at Helen, flashing her xylophone teeth. 'Look at us,' she said. 'Look at what we have.'

Helen sniffed loudly and smiled back. 'We're okay,' said Marte to Helen, not taking her eyes off the younger woman's face. 'We're a happy family. We all have each other. That's what makes us strong. And it's our revenge on the wicked people.'

Clarence Bredow had accepted without comment Helen's return to work after her memorable weekend, but as soon as her pregnancy began to show she knew it would be impossible to remain there. And Helen simply couldn't face the prospect of telling Babs about her condition.

While Jemma was now devoting herself to Helen and Caitlin with renewed zeal, the new living arrangement wasn't without its advantages. With Helen cooking delectable meals at night, revelling in time she had never had to experiment with recipes, as well as washing for the five of them and answering the phone, Jemma was able to get through a lot more of what she called her 'real' work. Of course Jemma still cleaned — Helen had never been much good at that — but with Helen also available to type clean and beautiful pages of copy, Jemma actually finished the fourth and final version of her television play in record time.

She worked at it for most of the day and even at night, while John and Helen sat in the family room and read or chatted. Helen had developed a taste for historical and political biographies and would often discuss the books she read with John. She also enjoyed hearing John talk about the radio station. 'When you're ready to go back to work,' John said, 'we ought to think about getting you a job at 2SR.'

Both of them read Jemma's play as critically as they could and said they thought it was her best effort yet. When it was ready for submission, Helen persuaded Jemma to write an accompanying biographical note. 'They'll want to know why you wrote about life in a country town,' said Helen. 'It will help them decide if your script has universal appeal.' So Jemma wrote about the Sirens and her work in the community and permitted Helen to edit it down from ten pages to two. John suggested that, as the manager of a radio station, a supporting letter from him might not go astray. Jemma laughed. 'Don't you think they might work out you're my husband?'

Just before Easter, a woman from the ABC contacted Jemma.

'They've rung, they've rung and said, they've said, they've rung to say . . .' Jemma was incoherent with excitement.

Helen, much larger now, heaved herself up from the couch to hug Jemma. 'They like your play!' she said. 'They like it and they want to produce it!'

'No!' Jemma shrieked, grabbing Helen's shoulders and shaking her a little dangerously. 'They want me to go down to Sydney to talk to them. You know that program they do where they feature people who've done interesting things for their community? Like in the arts or special fundraising projects or huge acts of bravery or something . . .?'

'Hang on,' said Helen. 'Are we talking about your play? Or something else?'

'Both, I think,' said Jemma. 'I couldn't quite work it out. They said they like it and they can use it, but in conjunction with this other thing. The bigger picture, they said. They were really interested in the biography. They said I was a "grassroots feminist". They want to talk about all the plays I've put on here in Siren's Rock, but they also want to cover the other stuff I've done, the playgroups and fundraisers and everything. So they're interested in doing something on . . .' She closed her eyes and slumped down onto the couch. Helen sat down beside her and squeezed Jemma's shoulders hard.

Helen began to smile. 'No!' she said, 'It's finally happened, hasn't it? They want to do a program about *you*!'

'They want me to star in "One Australian",' said Jemma and burst into tears.

FAME

It was better than sex.

It was better than Florence, better than Greece; it was better than having a baby or getting the Siren's Rock citizenship award, or standing centre stage in front of a cheering throng of friends and neighbours. It was even better than saving Helen. It was better than anything Jemma had ever done.

It was better because it was hard work with a purpose, an achievable, visible goal. It was better because the meetings took place in Sydney, where Jemma was treated like the intelligent, creative, generous woman that she was, and not like John Sullivan's wife or Hamish's mother, or the daughter of George and Marte Johnson, the girl who had done quite well for herself despite her humble background.

It was better because it was a professional production and everyone knew what they were doing, including Jemma herself. She threw herself into the project with enthusiasm, studied all the previous one-hour episodes of 'One Australian' and knew what they wanted, knew what she had to do, knew how she had to be. She had worked in television. She could talk the talk. She fitted in.

It was better because it was going to make her famous.

Jemma was dropping weight like a hot air balloon on the rise; fame was more satisfying than food, and with no effort at all she was casting off ballast in order to fly. By the time the Sydney meetings were over, the scripts prepared and the research done, Jemma was back into her size-fourteen jeans and had discarded her vibrant overshirts in favour of tailored jackets. When the production crew came to Siren's Rock, they loved her. The camera rested lovingly on her luscious curves as it followed her down Malley Street, as she dropped into Vale's department store, strode to the Council chambers and chatted with the leading lights of the town. They filmed her trying on hats for the play, laughing into the lens as they finally focused on her lovely smile. Her green eyes danced with excitement as she talked about her work. Her projects. Her wonderful, wonderful town.

They interviewed Marte, who had promised faithfully not to mention the horse show. They interviewed John, stern and succinct, Hamish, who tried too hard, and Caitlin, who didn't. They interviewed the mayor, the Council's tightly permed manager of community and youth services, the freckle-faced playgroup director who only realised when it was over that she had baby vomit on the shoulder of her best blouse, and a theatre critic from Melbourne who regularly holidayed at Mermaid Cove and said Jemma's previous productions would stand on their own in any capital city. They didn't interview Helen. A pregnant, single woman taking refuge in Jemma's house was an irresistible angle in a story on rural feminism, but Jemma made it clear that they must resist.

Mostly they interviewed Jemma. Jemma's voice, punctuated with her big laugh, would be the main feature of the sound track. Frequently she said too much and went on too long, but it didn't matter. The director said too much was better than not enough.

The ABC weren't producing the new play. Once again, the Sirens were doing it. But this time the television crew were filming the production in rehearsal, following its development from Jemma's script, written at home in the hours snatched from her other community work, to its eventual opening night. The camera went in close to convey the sweat and tears, the effort and dedication that went into community theatre. Because the team couldn't wait until the play opened, they set up shots of wildly applauding local audiences. Most of Siren's Rock was thrilled to bits to help out. Miss Mirabelle's fashion boutique and Vale's department store recorded rocketing sales as the town frocked up for the ten–second take.

Jemma entered a period of unparalleled popularity. The ABC crew were under her spell and the locals decided they loved her too. Jemma Sullivan had finally brought fame and recognition to Siren's Rock.

'You can say what you like about her,' said Cindy-Lou Smith to her sisters, 'but thanks to Jemma, nobody will ever again say they've never heard of Siren's Rock.'

'Violet Crumble came to watch today,' said Jemma to Helen, whose pregnancy was keeping her at home. 'I think I saw Peach-Melba and Fish-'n'-Chips in the crowd as well. They're all the size of houses,' she added, unable to suppress the delight of a woman still savouring the recent rediscovery of her own hips.

'Don't,' giggled Helen, 'I'll wet myself or go into labour.'

'My God, that would be the perfect climax,' said John, walking in on them. His tie was loose and there was a new and lively light in his brown eyes, which probably had a lot to do with Jemma's rejuvenated libido. John was suddenly finding time to get home from work at any time of the day. 'They could film the whole thing,' he said. 'The tireless community worker delivers her best friend's baby on her own family room floor.'

And then it was over. The crew checked out of their motel and took their cameras and their cords and their sound equipment back to Sydney. Jemma plunged back into rehearsals so that her new play could open as soon as possible after her episode was shown. Record crowds were guaranteed. Who knew? If the program struck a real chord, people might come from further afield.

A date was set for Jemma and John to fly to Sydney to see the final cut. They wanted Jemma to top and tail the piece in the Sydney studios. She couldn't wait. The show was to be called: *Jemma Sullivan: A Feminist in the Wings*.

Early on a golden winter morning, a week after Marte and George had left for the Great Barrier Reef for their first holiday away together in twenty years, and the day Jemma and John were due to fly down to Sydney, Helen went into labour.

'I can't believe it,' she winced, too appalled to meet Jemma's stricken gaze. 'It's too early. It's not due for weeks.'

'Ten days,' whispered Jemma, standing awkwardly beside her bed. 'It's not as if we don't know the exact date of conception.'

'Ten days, two weeks, what the hell,' groaned Helen, as another contraction seized and lifted her. 'Go,' she gasped, as the pain released her and she flopped back on her pillow. 'Just go. I'll be fine. I've done this before, remember. I'm good at this.' She tried to smile and failed.

Another contraction grabbed her. She arched and panted. John knelt down beside the bed and put a hand on her forehead. 'Breathe,' he said. 'In out. In out. Remember?' Helen breathed. John looked up at Jemma. 'Go and get ready,' he said. 'You should still go.'

'I can't,' said Jemma hoarsely. 'Not now. I won't leave her on her own.'

'She won't be on her own,' said John.

Compared with Caitlin's birth, Tom's arrival in the world was agonising, drawn out and complicated beyond Helen's worst imaginings.

She had never known such pain.

'Get it out!' she screamed at the nurses, hours after they'd told her it would all be over soon. 'Rub my back!' she roared at John, who sat beside the high metal bed, holding her hand through all the sweat and pain, as contraction after contraction clamped her belly, back and legs, and threw her into a paroxysm of agony.

John, his face contorted with distress, tried to talk, to soothe, to instruct, to breathe. Rubbed her back, held her hand, pressed ice against her lips, held cool cloths on her forehead. Nothing worked. The contractions went on and on, intense, tightening around Helen's lower body like a steel trap, tearing her apart.

They said it was too late for an epidural. They thought it would be quick, like the last one, after a text-book pregnancy. They said the doctor was coming, but he didn't. They said the baby was coming, but it didn't.

Somewhere in the dimmest regions of her conscious mind, Helen knew she was behaving very badly, knew she should make an effort, concentrate on controlling the pain. But there was no time, no time. Every time she made an effort to regain control, to breathe properly, she felt the pain starting up again and she panicked.

'Make it *stop*!' she sobbed, her throat raw from yelling.

John sat surrounded by steel tables and trays, leaping to his feet when Helen screamed, moving aside to let the nurses examine her. He was beside himself with worry. The midwife said she thought the baby was a 'brow'. He was coming the right way, but the broadest circumference of his head was jammed into the cervix at the wrong angle. 'When the doctor gets here he might decide on a caesarean. But we'll give it a bit more time. Sometimes they move their heads into the right position.'

'Stop the pain!' Helen implored John, sobbing. 'Tom!' she suddenly screamed, ropes standing out on her taut throat. 'Tom!' she bellowed. 'You bastard, where are you? Where did you go? I want him,' she whimpered to John, and the tears leaked from her eyes and trickled into the lines of pain around her mouth. Her nose ran. 'I don't want to raise another baby on my own,' said Helen pathetically. 'It's too hard.'

'You won't be on your own, Helen,' John reassured her. 'We'll be with you. We've always been with you.' But that didn't seem to be the right thing to say. There was no right thing to say.

Helplessness, compassion and guilt writhed together in John's gut almost as violently as the baby's struggles to be born. Never before could he remember feeling so bad, so useless, so frustrated. He desperately wanted to help this woman who had been his friend for a lifetime, but he had no idea what to do or say.

Foolishly, and knowing it was foolish, he tried to distract her with conversation.

'Tom?' he said. 'That's a nice name. Is that what we're going to call the baby?'

She slumped on the bed and stared at him, gripping his hand. 'Don't patronise me, John,' she said, in a perfectly normal voice. Then the pain came back and she began to pant again, short, panic-stricken breaths.

'It could have been yours, you know,' spat Helen, sweat gluing her hair to her face, the silly hospital nightie riding up over the heaving hump that was her belly.

John held her hand tightly. 'No, Helen, it couldn't. This baby is yours. Yours and . . . the father's.'

'But it *could* have been,' gabbled Helen, refusing to be distracted, panting angrily, talking fast. 'If this was a movie you would have made me pregnant that time at the drive-in, and now you'd be devastated by guilt because you love Jemma most but you fathered my, fathered my . . .' She screamed again as she was swept into another wave of pain.

John was distraught. 'Helen,' he said softly, glancing at the two nurses who were busy with the bottles and tubes that hung beside the bed, hoping desperately that their professional ethics would prove reliable. Doubting it. 'Helen, that must have been twenty years ago. We were kids. And I made sure, I mean you couldn't . . .'

'So you *do* remember,' said Helen. She pulled her hand out of his and gritted her teeth, preparing herself for the next contraction.

'No!' Helen protested, as the nurse moved to take the baby. 'Not yet. Please.' The nurse nodded and moved discreetly away.

Helen turned her head slowly and looked at the man who sat beside her. One of her hands lay lightly on her baby's tiny, slimy head. Her face was grey and worn.

Deep brown eyes met deep brown eyes. Tom mewled faintly. Helen said nothing. Not thank you. Not sorry. There was too much to say. To unsay. So, as usual, she said nothing at all.

John reached out a hand and laid the back of it against her cheek.

'I'll look after him for the rest of his life,' he said softly. 'We both will.'

'Oh no,' whispered Helen though cracked lips. 'I'm not giving this one to Jemma.'

Helen, Caitlin and Tom moved out of the Sullivan house when the new baby was six weeks old. Apart from a rather wobbly neck, which the doctor said would tighten up in time, Tom was none the worse for his difficult exit from his mother's womb. 'It was so lovely putting him in there,' said Helen, 'but so hard getting him out.'

'Listen to you,' said Jemma, 'getting all coarse and common in your old age.'

'Common as muck, that's me,' said Helen happily. 'Made poor John blush to his roots with my language in the labour ward.'

John smiled sadly. He was always looking sad lately, Jemma noticed. She put it down to the return, for all of them, to normal, boring old life.

Helen had found a house to rent on the west side, within walking distance of Jemma's. It was an old place and shabby, but it had a sunny porch and a new kitchen and Helen said she felt comfortable there. She loved the big, untidy garden.

'You're looking at years of work,' said Jemma, but Helen said she didn't care. There was an option to buy the place when she'd had a chance to think about it. 'What with?' asked Jemma.

'I'll save up,' said Helen. 'And apparently there's some money from one of my uncles. Joy's had her share for a while but my mother conveniently forgot about mine until the family's solicitor wrote to me directly. It will help me with the deposit.'

When Tom was three months old, and doing everything he was supposed to be doing, Helen started looking for a job. It was a month after 'One Australian' had been screened nationwide and had received rave notices, on the far north coast at least. Documentaries on the government channel rarely attracted huge national ratings, but every television set in Siren's Rock and all the surrounding towns was tuned to *A Feminist in the Wings* on that particular Friday night. Jemma's play had been a triumph as well. She could go nowhere in the town without people stopping to tell her they'd seen her either on television or on the stage. Teenagers asked for her autograph. She had been elevated to celebrity status and she was loving it. She had never been so happy.

Even the people who had once seen her as a pushy do-gooder — a woman, as Babs Winter remarked to her friend Edna Egan, who would stop at nothing to draw attention to herself — agreed that 'One Australian' had been good for their town.

Only Marte was dubious about her daughter's success. 'Mum can never admit she's wrong,' Jemma told Helen when she came over to get Jemma's help with composing job applications.

Their efforts became redundant when John joined them at the Sullivans' solid kitchen table and told Helen he wanted her to come and work with him at 2SR.

'In the accounts office?' asked Helen dubiously. 'Wouldn't Edith be furiously jealous if another woman moved in on her territory?'

John looked at her admiringly. 'See, now that's what I mean,' he said. 'You always know who's who. You always know how people feel.' Helen was looking pretty again, he thought. Her cheeks were pink, her fair hair was fluffed out around her face. She looked plumper than usual, mainly because her breasts were swollen with milk. She smiled at him. He smiled back, slightly embarrassed that she had seen him looking at her boobs. Quickly he looked at Jemma, who was waiting for him to go on.

'Not accounts,' said John. 'Kevin Rort, my morning announcer, is leaving. He's heading for the big smoke to do a midnight-to-dawn shift with one of the new FM stations.' He turned back to Helen. 'I'd like to try a woman on mornings and I think you're the one.'

Jemma and Helen both stared at him. Then Jemma threw back her head and laughed loudly.

'Helen?' said Jemma. 'On air? Talking on air?'

Helen laughed too. 'Are you crazy? I can't sling three words together under pressure.'

'She can't, you know,' said Jemma eagerly.

'That's a myth,' said John, speaking slowly, being careful, Jemma saw, about slinging his own words together.

He thinks I'll mind, she thought with surprise. As if I would.

'What I know,' said John, 'is that both of you built these images of yourselves years ago, and you've never realised how much you've changed. You girls,' said John, 'are still stuck in the sixties.

'Jemma, the sexy Sophia Loren of Siren's Rock, is actually a brilliant, hard-working playwright, producer and stage actress.'

'Don't forget tireless community worker,' interrupted Jemma. 'A worthy woman but definitely not a sexpot.'

'You've never wanted to be a sexpot,' said John. 'You're sexy to me of course, but that's different.'

'I don't think I'm even sexy to you these days, John,' said Jemma.

Helen shifted uncomfortably in her chair. 'What about me?' she asked. 'So I'm not Julie any more?'

'It's always been a myth that you're the quiet type,' said John, 'the timid little blonde. You've always had your own views on just about everything and you've never been backward about telling people who know you how you feel. You're better informed on politics and books and everything that's going on in this state, in this country, probably in this world, than anyone else I know.'

Helen blinked.

'I know you get nervous when you're caught on the spot and you're expected to say something,' said John. 'But when you have time to think about what you want to say, you talk well. I've noticed. You're older and wiser now. What's more important for radio, you don't rave on. You say exactly what needs to be said and then you shut up.'

'Thanks,' said Helen, adopting the same sardonic tone Jemma had used a few moments earlier. She wanted to hide the feeling of breathlessness, to disguise her excitement. She wondered what he would say next.

Jemma laughed suddenly. 'I was just thinking,' she said. 'The most talking you ever did was the night you saved me from that priest at St Patrick's. You talked like a threshing machine then. All you were thinking about was me and how I was feeling.'

'You're a thinker, Helen,' said John, 'but you're also a good listener. You always ask the right questions. See, radio people don't have to be good talkers. All the commercials and traffic reports are written out for you. You've got a wonderful voice for reading. But it's more important that you get other people to talk.'

'What about Tom?' asked Jemma. She was listening carefully. He had put a lot of thought into this, she could tell.

'He's three months old,' said John. 'Helen needs to spend as much time as she can with Tom, but she also needs to make a living.' He smiled at both of them. 'The morning shift would involve three hours on air but you'd be out of the studio by two. The afternoons, evenings and weekends would be entirely yours to spend with Tom and Caitlin. And I'm offering better money than you'll earn in any accounts office,' he finished.

'I'd be *terrible*,' said Helen. But her eyes were bright. She was excited.

She wants to do it, thought Jemma incredulously. She's going to say yes.

'You'll be brilliant,' said John.

And she was.

THE PICNIC

It was weird, Jemma thought, that even when she became a grown woman, Marte seemed unable to understand her. Couldn't connect. Lovingly but stubbornly refused to join Jemma on her wavelength. 'She's my *mother*, for heaven's sake!' she would say to John. 'And she still doesn't understand me at *all*.'

The windy picnic celebrating Tom's third birthday at Mermaid Cove was a case in point. Marte loved every minute of it. For Jemma the day was a disaster.

The day was sunny, but the wind was cold and, for various reasons, none of them was really in the mood. They all went for Tom's sake, and because Marte had planned the event with such pleasure.

There was doubt and tension in the chilly winter air — the adults had been too busy, the kids were growing up too fast — but Marte had insisted, and so they had packed up all the party food, the paper plates and serviettes patterned with clown faces, the bags of lollies, the bats and balls and rugs, and taken them to the Cove. John and Jemma were there with Hamish, Helen with Tom and Caitlin, Marte and George with the birthday cake and their green folding table and chairs.

Marte had stayed up until midnight, icing the cake — a huge rectangle with a chocolate rim framing a sticky green football field. The goal posts were made from pink musk sticks. The sidelines were jelly snakes. A solid bar of milk chocolate provided the grandstand; the roof was tiled in rainbow smarties. In bright orange icing across the playing field, Marte had written: *Happy Third Birthday Tom. August 1993.*

'Hansel and Gretel, eat your hearts out,' John had said.

Reverently Marte laid the massive cake on the table while they all admired her creation. John lifted Tom so he could see it properly. He was a small child, light as a feather with sprouty red hair. His eyes were round with delight and excitement. 'For me!' he squealed.

'Unless you feel like sharing it with us,' Hamish said seriously.

'Put it down on the rug, so he can see it,' said Jemma. 'We'll all keep an eye on it.'

With some trepidation, Marte and George carefully lowered the cake onto one of the tartan rugs that had been spread on the grass. Tom sat down cross-legged beside it and beamed. Marte looked round at them all, the circle of faces reflecting the little boy's delight.

Considering Hamish and Caitlin were in their prickly teenage years, Marte thought fondly, it was so nice that they were still close. Almost like sister and brother, but without the constant fighting and rivalry that had marred Jemma and Nick's relationship.

'So have you done it yet?' asked Caitlin, as they set off to explore the rocks, glancing back quickly to make sure they were well out of hearing range.

Hamish walked with his head hanging forward, staring at his feet.

'Have you done it?' she persisted. 'I mean with someone else, not yourself. I don't just mean jacking off.'

'Shut up,' he growled. 'Your mind is always in the gutter.'

She laughed. He hated her when she laughed at him. She had such perfect teeth, pure white, and her skin was white too. He thought she was glorious.

'You're a bit slow, Hame,' said Caitlin. He hated it when she called him Hame. 'There can't be another guy in Siren's Rock who's fifteen and hasn't done it with *someone*. Even if you've only had a bit of head! Come on, Hame,' she cooed, wheedling, needling. 'You can tell me. You know what Nanna says. I'm like your *sister*, Hame.' She looked at him sidelong as the wind blew strands of copper hair across her face. 'Except the good news is that I'm *not* your sister so, technically, you're allowed to fuck me ...' Hamish flinched. It was the worst word. Nobody at home used that word.

Suddenly she put out her hand and grabbed his long blotchy fingers in hers. He held on. 'Tell me what you've done with girls, Hamish,' she said, baring her small perfect teeth. 'At least tell me what you'd *like* to do.'

When they reached the rocks she dropped his hand and started climbing. He followed, looking at her slender white ankles, letting his gaze travel up her legs in the ragged cut-off jeans, resting his eyes on her bum, tightly encased in denim, as she bent over to steady herself with her hands. She looked at him through her legs, upside-down triangle face, sharp blue eyes meeting his soft brown ones. Catching him.

'Get your eyes off my butt, Hame,' she said. 'If you like butts, try a guy. Maybe that's your problem, Hame. Maybe guys are your thing.' She leapt down into a shaft-like space created by bundles of smooth brown rocks on every side. It was a long jump in a tight space. Hamish hesitated.

'Coming down?' she said softly. And he jumped.

John took Jemma's hand and they strolled down the sand towards the water. Jemma stopped to remove her shoes. It's an obscenity, she always said, to wear shoes on the beach. You had to feel the sand between your toes or you may as well not be there. 'Aren't you going to take yours off too?' she asked, squinting up at him.

'No,' said John.

Jemma stood up and looked at him. 'What's the matter with you?' she asked. But he looked past her, out to sea. 'And don't say nothing,' said Jemma, 'because you've been sulking for days.'

They wandered closer to the water. Jemma ran towards the tiny waves that rippled around the shore, her hair lifting and flowing like a sheet, her red sweater billowing in the wind. John watched her and started to smile.

'Come on,' said Jemma, 'take your shoes off and paddle with me.'

John sighed, sat down and removed his shoes. 'I'm not sulking,' he said. 'I'm tired. I can't sleep. We've lost some big advertisers with Dawson's closing down and the tyre people relocating to Bridgetown.'

Jemma took his hand and pulled him towards the water. 'Can I help?' she asked.

John tightened his grip on her hand. 'You could love me a little,' he said awkwardly.

Jemma turned around to face him and wrapped her arms around his big, firm body. 'John!' she said, surprised. 'I do love you. I love you a lot!'

'I meant you could show me.'

She laughed and hugged him more tightly, growling with the effort, like a bear.

'No,' said John, and Jemma immediately dropped her arms and moved away.

'No?' she said, instantly terse.

'Not words,' said John. 'Not hugs. We haven't made love for two months.'

Jemma contemplated the waves. After a while she said: 'Let me get this straight. Is it sex or sleep you need?'

'Both,' said John, grinning. 'One generally leads to the other.'

'Okay,' said Jemma finally. 'Maybe you should ask me on a date. How long is it since we went out to dinner? Just us. It's not all up to me, you know, John. You have to make an effort too.'

'Jemma, I try more than you know,' he said. 'You miss the signals. You're always so busy. I would just like a bit of your attention. We don't even have to have sex, if it comes to that . . .'

'So actually you *don't* want sex,' said Jemma. 'You just want my *time*. You're jealous of the time I spend with other people.'

'What are you trying to do?' he said, looking at her steadily. He was wearing a blue jacket and the collar was standing up around his brown face. Age had heightened John's forehead but had not thinned his hair. It was still thick and tufty, streaked with grey. The stiff salty breeze blew it into small clumps.

'I'm just trying to work out what you want,' said Jemma. 'I'm a bit confused.'

'I want to be with you more,' said John.

'Oh great,' said Jemma. 'Fine. That's fine, coming from a man who only makes it home for dinner four times a week. Helen sees more of you than I do these days. Tom sees more of you than Hamish does.'

'Hamish is fifteen,' said John. 'He goes to school, he goes out with his friends. Tom is *three*. The only man in his life is me. And anyway,' he smiled suddenly, the way everyone smiled when they thought of Tom, 'he likes me dropping in.'

Jemma was silent.

'Helen *works* with me,' said John. 'It's not the same thing and you know it.'

'That would be because you and Helen are doing *important* work, whereas I am just the little woman at home, cooking and cleaning and raising the kids.'

'Hardly the *little* woman,' said John, and immediately wished he hadn't.

'Terrific, isn't it,' said Jemma to the waves, 'that you spend more than half your life with Helen and Tom and then you come home and complain that your fat wife is not providing you with enough sex.'

They both looked at the ocean. Jemma waited for him to escape from the disaster he had created. She waited for him to apologise, to sigh in his resigned way and explain what he really meant, because obviously he had not meant to say what he did. She waited for him to repair the damage and save the day.

John looked back towards their picnic spot, where Tom had finally lost interest in his cake and was waiting wistfully for someone to kick his soccer ball with him.

Without offering any other words at all, he left her and walked back up the beach.

They stood facing each other in the narrow space, their feet on the soft dry sand, their backs against the rocks, their bodies only a few centimetres apart. Caitlin ran a hand over one of the stones and closed her eyes.

'Do you think about touching me, Hamish?' she asked softly. There was a small, sly smile on her mouth. 'I think about being touched. I think about it all the time.'

Hamish felt dizzy. He wanted to touch her all right. Yearned to touch that gleaming white skin. They had lived in the same house, shared the same bath water, frequently slept in the same room, camped in the same tents and even tangled their bodies together in the same family football games, but years had now passed since he had touched anything but her hand. He couldn't imagine doing more than touching her. Just touching her would be enough.

Still, he hesitated. Paralysed with uncertainty.

There was her age. Caitlin moved like a woman and spoke like a slut, at least to him and to her mother, but she was still only a kid. There was the mantra, repeated so often that it made both of them want to throw up, that she was virtually his sister. There was the fact that he knew she would do almost anything to punish her mother.

Perhaps he didn't want to be the tool she used to do that. Perhaps he liked Helen too much to risk doing something that would hurt her.

'Do you remember,' he began, but his voice disappeared and he had to cough and start again. 'Do you remember when we were little? What we played in the bath?'

Caitlin opened her eyes very slightly and looked at him, slits of blue through red lashes on white skin. 'Let's pretend we're getting ready to have a bath,' she said softly. She took the zipper of her tight knitted top in her fingers. Slowly she unzipped it, right down to the waist.

Testosterone cured his paralysis. Hamish groaned aloud and wrapped his arms around himself. Caitlin smiled at him above the smooth V of her porcelain chest. She wasn't wearing a bra. She ran her small tongue over her top lip and slowly pulled back one side of her cardigan to reveal a perfect, pink-tipped breast. Hamish had never seen anything so beautiful in his life.

Nor had he ever felt so helpless. What was he supposed to

do? Touch it? Kiss it? But what would she do if he did? He hadn't even kissed her lips.

She was so brave, thought Hamish. Brazen but brave.

It was his last coherent thought before he heard his mother and for a moment assumed that it was simply her voice, as usual, in his head. But only for a moment.

'Put it away please, Caitlin,' called Jemma from above. 'You might get bitten.'

Marte and George were playing soccer against John and Tom and Tom's team was winning. 'Let's walk,' Jemma said to Helen when she came striding back from the rocks. 'It'll make us hungry for lunch.'

They set off at a rapid pace along the shore, Helen doing a little running step now and then to keep up with Jemma's angry stride. The wind was getting worse. 'I hope it doesn't wreck the cake,' said Jemma.

'It's a lovely cake,' laughed Helen. 'Tom is ecstatic. I love it when he's happy.'

'Tom's always happy, isn't he?' asked Jemma, thinking of Hamish, as anxious at three as he now was at fifteen, salivating over Caitlin's silly little tit. Wishing her son and Helen's daughter would surprise her, instead of constantly conforming to type.

'He's certainly a pretty happy little guy,' said Helen. 'I've been very lucky with this one so far.'

'Yes,' said Jemma, deciding not to say anything about Helen's other one. Instead she said harshly: 'I've decided that the worst thing about being a forty-four-year-old mother of teenagers is always being right.'

Hamish and Caitlin watched their mothers marching along the distant shore. Caitlin scowled. 'She couldn't wait to

387

provide a blow by blow report,' she muttered. But Hamish shook his head. 'She won't tell your mum,' he mumbled without looking at her. 'She'll probably lecture *my* ear off, but she won't want to worry Helen with it.'

'What would you know?' hissed Caitlin. 'You're such a dork, Hamish. I bet you've never seen a boob before in your life.'

I know more than you think, thought Hamish, but he didn't say so, because she was right about the boob thing and he didn't want to hear anything more on *that* subject.

'I can't believe it's been three years,' said Helen. 'Remember how horrified you were when you found out? How scared I was? But it's turned out so well, thanks to you and John. And I've never regretted it.'

They walked in silence for a while until Jemma said suddenly: 'Are you ever going to tell me how it happened? I mean, it's the only secret you've ever kept from me. I can't believe Tom's father was really someone you only knew for one night. Had you already met him when you were on your own in Sydney, after Nigel shot through? I could understand that now, Julie, truly I could.'

'No,' said Helen. 'He was a total stranger.'

Jemma shook her head and grunted. 'So. Just a conman who sweet-talked his way into your pants. Got you pregnant and ran for his life.'

'No.' Helen frowned. 'It wasn't like that with him. He was a good person. If he had known about Tom, I think he would have come back. But he set me free, Sophia. How could I turn around and tie *him* down?

'I spent so many years wanting to be loved,' she went on after a while. 'Wishing I had what you and John have always had. And then I met this man and I knew. I knew almost straight away that with him it would be wonderful. And it was.'

Jemma glanced at her friend's rapturous face. She felt a small knot of envy in her breast. Fancy being envious of Helen, she thought.

Envy is the cancer of the soul. Where had she read that?

Her earlier conversation with John pushed itself back into her mind. She pushed it out again but it was immediately replaced with an image of Hamish, mute with lust as Caitlin flashed her tiny boob.

'Sex sex sex,' said Jemma. 'Good lord, can't people think of anything else? Anyway, you and Nigel had already had plenty of decent sex long before the stranger came along.'

'No.' Helen shook her head. 'Sex with Nigel was anything but decent. And he always talked all through it.'

'With me it's the talking that sometimes puts me in the mood,' said Jemma.

'I never had an orgasm with Nigel,' said Helen.

'Oh, that's magazine talk,' said Jemma, kicking at shells. 'Sex can be lovely, even if you never reach a climax.'

'Perhaps,' said Helen. 'If you're making love to the right person. If you've loved each other for a lifetime, like you and John.'

'You know,' said Jemma, 'that's not really true. About John and me being lifelong sweethearts. He was just a kid I played with. Until Florence.'

'You two were always meant to be together,' said Helen.

'No,' said Jemma. 'I was meant to be famous. You know that. Marrying John and settling down, that put a stop to the fame idea. Marriage has always been very much a consolation prize for me.'

'Oh Sophia, how can you say that?' exclaimed Helen, pushing her fair hair back in exasperation. 'When you two fell in love in Italy, when you finally got together in Greece —

you said the sex was sensational! He lit you up like a candle! Like a volcano!'

Jemma shoved her hands in her pockets and quickened her stride. Helen skipped, panting a little. 'Yes, but I was so uptight,' said Jemma. 'So bloody *frustrated*. *Anyone* could have lit me up.'

'Jemma Maria Johnson!' said Helen, coming to a halt. 'I mean Sullivan. That is simply *not* true. You had plenty of offers but you never took them. You wanted to wait for the right man, and you did. And it *was* right, for both of you.'

Jemma walked on angrily and Helen didn't catch up with her until they both reached the headland. Jemma sucked deeply on the salt air, turned around and began marching straight back the way they had come. 'John and I ...' She frowned. 'We're never on the same wavelength any more. I never know what he's thinking. We've been married all this time but sometimes I think we got together for totally different reasons.'

'What do you *mean*?' Helen sounded like a little girl who has just been told there is no Santa Claus.

'I don't understand him,' replied Jemma. 'I don't even know if I want to.'

Helen's concerned, anxious gaze faded. 'I understand him,' she said. 'I know that all John has ever wanted is to make you happy.'

'Nobody can make another person happy,' said Jemma. 'It has to come from the person herself.'

'He wants to,' said Helen. 'That's what counts.'

Women's magazine words. She must think she's on the air, thought Jemma. 'I'm not saying he's not a wonderful husband,' she said.

'Good.'

'He does everything I ask him to. And he's a gentle lover.

Considerate. John takes his time. He'd take all night if you let him.'

'That's the best kind of lover,' said Helen.

'Well, you'd know,' said Jemma nastily.

For a fleeting second Helen looked stricken. Jemma was ashamed. 'Well, you said Tom's father made you feel . . . you know.'

The fear left Helen's face and she smiled.

'Is that funny?' said Jemma.

'Well, actually, yes,' said Helen. 'You always make it sound as if I go through life seducing every man in sight.' She chuckled. 'Sophia, the last time I had sex was nearly four years ago. And I was celibate for eleven years before that. I can't help thinking that you and John are well ahead of me in sexual experience.'

Jemma couldn't understand the simmering resentment which was threatening to boil over them both. She took deep breaths. Adjusted the heat. Attempted to reduce her anger.

'I wish you had a man of your own to love,' said Jemma. Finding it too hard to smile. 'I wish I could find you a devoted husband who would give you a cup of tea every morning and an orgasm every night. And fat smiling babies.' She made her voice warm. 'And a sensible retirement plan.'

'Oh well,' said Helen, still smiling. 'There seems to be only one man as perfect as that. Actually, he's married to my best friend.'

Jemma laughed unpleasantly.

'Well, *actually*,' said Jemma, 'at least he took time out from being married to *me* to make *you* famous. Which *some* people might appreciate! Although obviously not you, because we all know you are above such shallow ambition. *Actually!*'

Helen finally stopped smiling. Jemma turned away, flushed with shame, and ran as fast as she could back along the beach.

Which was a mistake, because running made her breasts hurt like hell, and now her chest was sore both inside and out.

The wind was positively howling by the time everyone gathered for lunch. Marte and George had used their folding chairs and the eskies as wind breaks and had spread the party food on the rugs to stop them blowing away, and put rocks on the paper plates. George was cross because he wanted to go home and have the party in his nice warm lounge room. Marte wouldn't hear of it. They would rise to the challenge. She had arranged a family picnic and a picnic they would have.

'I hope this wind doesn't wreck the cake,' George muttered to Jemma, who rolled her eyes. 'Yes,' she muttered back bitterly. 'War, famine, fire, flood, rebellion, a cure for cancer — none of those events can compare with the production of Tom's cake.'

Marte clapped her hands and grinned broadly at them all.

Nobody grinned back. Everyone looked strained and bleak. Everyone but Marte and Tom.

'It's okay,' she said. 'We're not gonna let this wind spoil Tom's special day. Now for Tom there's a big birthday bottle of cherry cheer. And for the rest of us ... George! Open the champagne!' And right on cue the cork shot out of the bottle with a bang and Tom nearly jumped out of his skin.

'To our happy families!' boomed Marte, raising her glass.

'What a lovely day we're having!' Tom squealed, heading towards the bottle of pink drink.

He walked straight through the cake.

He flattened the football players and left one fat footprint in the green icing.

For an instant, a blink, an eyelash of time, all of them froze in horrified disbelief.

And then they started to laugh.

A PHONE CALL

On the following day, Jemma drove her shiny red car along the straight black road from Bridgetown to Siren's Rock — straighter and wider as the Council improved the inland link with every passing year — and listened to Helen on the radio.

'You keep saying "you know" but in fact I don't and neither do my listeners.' Helen's throaty tones made Jemma smile. 'Perhaps you could explain exactly what the government is planning to do about this problem.'

'Well now, Helen, you know you can't just write a blank cheque to cover all children's health services,' said the politician.

'No, you can't,' said Helen. 'Not when the cheque book draws on the taxpayers' dollars.'

'Exactly,' said the polly. 'So in the course of time the government will make some very important decisions about how these services can be funded. And when the ACS and the DGP . . .'

'When?' asked Helen.

'Pardon?' said the politician.

'When will the decisions be made?' asked Helen. 'How long is "the course of time"?'

'Well . . .' the man fumbled.

'As long as a piece of string, perhaps?'

Jemma chuckled, put her foot down more firmly, and shot through the green hills towards home.

The laughter at the picnic had been cathartic and for once Jemma had slept soundly all night, instead of waking intermittently with lists prattling in her head. Her period had come and John had apologised before breakfast. He loved the way she looked. He always had.

She felt better. Now she would apologise to Helen and they could all move on.

John had said Helen would be brilliant on radio but even he had no idea how concise and fair her interviews would be. Or how much people would enjoy her taste in music, books, movies and shows, or how interesting it would be to hear her put a local angle on the news of the day. And who would have guessed that mothers would cleave to the radio to hear this woman, this single mother of two, confide her own sense of frustration and inadequacy when it came to bringing up children in the nineties?

'Young children need time to dream,' said Helen to parents struggling with toilet training, interrupted sleep, colds, rashes, ADHD, extra-curricular activities, school projects, parent–teacher interviews, nightmare fetes and sheer disobedience. 'Have you ever lain on your back in your yard, with your child beside you, and spent an afternoon looking at the shapes made by clouds?' asked Helen, and while some of her listeners sneered despairingly, some of them followed her advice and felt better for it.

'Teenagers are growing up in an increasingly fluid society,' said Helen to parents struggling with drugs, binge drinking, eating disorders, nose rings, tattoos, brand name clothing, orthodontists' bills, MA ratings and suspicious sleepovers. 'We know we're supposed to set boundaries for our children, but what happens when they knock the boundaries down? They make it so hard to love them, and we feel like giving up on them and letting them go. But we are still the grown-ups here,' said Helen. 'Whether our kids believe it or not, we are older and wiser than them. It's up to us to forgive them and start guiding them again. Every time.'

For the past three years, while Helen had been building up a loyal following at 2SR, Jemma had been working at FNC, Channel Five, the television station in Bridgetown.

She had been persuaded back into public relations. Initially she had been offered the position of public affairs manager but she didn't want to work full time. Instead she whirled in for half the week, overwhelmed Gail Turner, the official head of the department ('thin arms, no make-up, flat shoes, you know the type,' she said to Helen), and achieved in three days what it took the rest of the staff weeks to do, before whirling out again, hair swinging, jacket flapping, to attend to her community work at Siren's Rock. As the child-care centres were well established now, she had turned her attention to adolescents and the lack of recreation facilities in the town, which sent too many of them down to the beach.

'It wouldn't matter if they were going there to surf,' she told John, 'but most of them never put a foot in the water. They go there to smoke dope or drink themselves senseless and they end up dumb and depressed.'

'Sure,' said Hamish, exchanging an eye roll with Caitlin.

Being the station manager's wife made it tricky for Jemma to be interviewed on 2SR, although Helen had once persuaded her to come on the show to talk about the need for a local youth centre. Helen had introduced Jemma as Siren's Rock's first feminist, alluding to the achievements that had been chronicled on 'One Australian'. But a caller had rung to say it was easy to be a feminist if you had a husband who could keep you in fine style and, after that, Jemma had refused to go on air again.

'Are you aware, sir,' Helen was saying to the politician, 'that adolescents are the only group in the country whose health has actually deteriorated over the past thirty years?'

'Well, it's easy to skew statistics, Helen, as you would know, and we would like to provide equality of health care for all groups in the community . . .'

'When?' said Helen again.

'I don't think this line of questioning is getting us anywhere,' expostulated the government's man.

'Let's forget statistics and time frames then,' said Helen, 'and take a philosophical view. Most people would agree that the way a society cares for its weak and vulnerable is a measure of how civilised it is. Would you agree with that?'

'Of course, but . . .'

'Does your government support the view that a society that fails to cherish its youth fails?'

'Yes, Helen, we do.'

'So when are we going to start?' asked Helen.

'Brilliant,' murmured Jemma, pulling up outside 2SR.

'You made mincemeat of him,' she said to Helen, when she came out of the station's new steel and glass studio, pulling on her jacket.

Helen shook her head. 'I was so hoping he'd tell me they were doing something. That they had actually talked about it and come up with a plan. But they hadn't. "In the course of time"! I mean, honestly!

'How are you?' she said. 'I've been desperate to talk to you. Do you still hate me?'

Jemma laughed. 'I've come to say I'm sorry and to take you to lunch. I behaved stupidly yesterday. I'm a jealous, stupid cow. I'd been having a row with John, as if that's any excuse. Anyway, we've made up so now you have to forgive me as well. And *what* did you think of Mum's face when Tom walked through that *cake*?'

They went out through the automatic glass doors together, whooping with laughter, Jemma tall and tailored, her broadening hips and heavy breasts encased in a smart green suit, her burnished red hair glinting in the winter sun; Helen, slender in her black coat, silver blonde hair floating in a cloud around her face.

Friends again. With the difficult spectre of fame pushed firmly out of the picture.

The trouble with spectres is that they can reappear at any time. Controversy returned to haunt them nearly eighteen months later, just after New Year, when most of Siren's Rock was steeped in the annual lethargy that follows late nights, too much rich food, and the excessive consumption of alcohol in humidity thick enough to carve.

On a warm January morning, an unidentified caller rang Helen on air and told her, between muffled sobs, that her father had raped her.

Everyone who heard the broadcast that day remembered it for years. The anguish of the caller, who was obviously a child. The long, agonised silence on air, interspersed only with the small, whimpering sobs of the girl. The tension sliding like tentacles around the bones and bloodstreams of all those listeners waiting for Helen to reply.

'Or for the panel guy to cut to a commercial, which would have been the sensible thing to do and would have put an end to the whole catastrophe before it began,' said Jemma crossly when she and John — like the rest of the town and, within hours, like the rest of the country — were talking about what had happened.

Garry was the freckled panel operator's name. He was looking at Helen through the window that divided the control room from the studio, waiting for her to let him know what she wanted him to do. 'She was just sitting there,' he told his mates afterwards, 'just sitting there, slumped over, with her hands clutching her earphones and her forehead on the desk. I didn't know if she was crying or what,' said Garry, 'and then finally she sat up, and she started to talk to the kid. There was a commercial break coming up but she didn't stop. She just carried on with it.

'Then the boss came in,' said Garry, 'and he just signalled me to wait. Just waves his hand at me like this, and says wait. So I waited.'

'How old are you, sweetheart?' asked Helen softly.

'Ten,' said the child.

'And do you know what rape is?' asked Helen.

'Yes.' Sniffing.

'How do you know?'

'My sister told me.'

'Is your sister there?' asked Helen.

'She ran away,' said the child. 'She's turning sixteen. She went on the bus. But I can't run away,' she took a shuddering breath, 'because I can't leave Mummy.'

'Is your mummy home?' asked Helen.

'She's at work.'

'Is your daddy home?'

'He went out.' She sniffed again. 'I hurt,' she said.

'I'm going to give you a number to ring,' said Helen. 'So someone can help you.'

'No!' said the child with a little scream. 'No,' she whimpered. 'They'll say lies.'

'I won't tell you any lies,' said Helen. 'You know that, don't you?'

'Mummy says you're the lady with the chocolate voice. She says you help people.'

'Does your mummy know what your daddy did to you?' asked Helen.

'He said if I tell Mummy he'll go away and leave us, like my real daddy did. And then we'll have no money and no one to look after us again.'

Helen looked up at last. In the control room, John was pointing to her monitor. She read her screen. The call was being traced. She swallowed and nodded.

'Listen to me,' said Helen. 'Listen very carefully. I want to tell you a story. Will you listen while I tell it to you?'

'Yes.' Sniffing.

'It's a true story,' said Helen. 'Are you ready?'

'I like stories,' whispered the little girl.

Drivers in their cars on the sizzling streets of Siren's Rock clenched their steering wheels and gritted their teeth. Women bathing babies in their homes lifted wet hands to brush away tears. Workers stood like statues with lumps like melons in their throats. All over the town, the people of Siren's Rock waited for Helen's story.

'Once upon a time,' said Helen's husky voice, 'there was a little girl called, um, we'll say her name was Jane. Okay?'

There was a long silence. Finally the child said: 'You said it was a true story. You must know her real name.'

'Okay,' said Helen after a short pause. 'We're not supposed to use children's real names on the radio. I can't tell you hers and you can't tell me yours. But the rest of the story is true, I promise.

'Jane lived in a lovely house with big woolly carpets and fat comfy chairs and pretty flowers in the garden. Jane had a

399

mummy and a daddy and a sister and they all loved each other very much. And they all loved their fat cat.'

There was a sound on the line and Helen stopped. 'What did you say, sweetheart?'

'Whiskers,' said the girl. 'The cat can be Whiskers.'

'That's right,' said Helen. 'Their fat cat was called Whiskers. Only one day the daddy went on a trip and when he got back he had changed. He started being horrible to Whiskers. Then he started being horrible to Jane.

'Jane's daddy was under a spell,' said Helen. 'When he was away on his travels, something evil entered his soul. He turned from a good man into a wicked one. He still looked like a good man, but that was just his disguise, so people wouldn't guess what had happened to him. But when he was alone in the house with Jane, he did bad things to her.'

'Did he hurt Jane's sister too?' asked the child.

A tear began to run down Helen's cheek. 'No,' she said. 'In this story, the sister wasn't hurt. And she didn't run away.'

'She was lucky,' said the girl.

'Very lucky,' said Helen. 'When Jane was old enough, she left that house and she travelled to many faraway countries. She had lots of adventures and she made many good friends.'

'Did she get under a bad spell too?' asked the girl.

'Oh no, Jane was not bad at all,' said Helen. 'But that is a very good question. Because Jane couldn't forget the things her daddy had done to her while he was under the spell. Do you know what she thought?'

'That she was . . . bad,' whispered the child.

'Yes,' said Helen, 'Jane thought she was a bad person too. She was ashamed because she thought he had put his wickedness into her.'

'Yes,' said the child. She gave a long, shuddering sob.

'But then something wonderful happened,' said Helen, as

John made a thumbs-up sign through the studio window. 'When Jane came back to her own country, she met a *good* wizard. He was a very powerful wizard who could see right inside people. This good wizard asked Jane why she felt so sad. And she told him. She told him her secret. And then she asked him if he could use his magic powers to put a spell on her, to take away the evil.

'And the good wizard said: "I don't have to put a spell on you, Jane. I can see that there is nothing bad in you at all. In fact, there never was."

'And because she had told the good wizard her secret, Jane felt better. She knew she was a good person. Nobody could do anything to her that would make her bad. She was special, like you. And she stayed special for the rest of her days.'

There was a long silence.

'And that's a true story?' said the girl.

'That's the truth,' said Helen. 'Do you believe me?'

'No,' said the girl. She began to cry. 'I hurt,' she sobbed.

Helen closed her eyes and rubbed her hand across her mouth. She licked her lips and took a deep breath. John came into the studio and put a hand on her shoulder. She pressed his fingers. 'It's okay,' he whispered. 'The police are on their way there with a social worker. They're getting in touch with her mother.'

'Please believe me, sweetheart,' said Helen urgently into the microphone. 'You *are* special and good, like Jane. Nothing your daddy did to you will change that. I know.'

'You don't know,' said the girl.

'I do know,' said Helen. 'I know because Jane wasn't the girl's real name. Her real name was Helen. The girl in the story is me.'

★ ★ ★

The repercussions rattled the walls of homes across the country. The media again descended upon Siren's Rock and this time they came for Helen.

Politicians, state and federal, were bailed up on their office doorsteps and quizzed about child protection laws. Community health officers, social services staff, police, teachers, behavioural scientists, psychologists, psychiatrists, social workers, lawyers and, of course, a horde of passionate parents, all had their say.

Every politician Helen had ever interviewed about improvements to children's health services ran for cover.

'January has always been a bad month for news,' said John to Jemma as he fielded wave after wave of telephone enquiries, faxes and messages from newspapers, radio and every television news team within a thousand-kilometre radius. 'What we need now is a train crash or a cyclone.'

Helen held up well. She was both attacked and congratulated. She was torn to shreds in some newspapers and all but deified in others. She was accused of exploiting her caller to grab ratings, and hailed as a heroine by abused and damaged young people in every state. With John frequently at her side, she continued to demand money and resources from the government for children's and adolescents' health services, pointing out that 'the Jane call', as it came to be known, provided all the painful proof that any government needed to be convinced that communities everywhere were crying out for more people to listen and to care.

But she refused to discuss her family or her personal life with anyone, friends and colleagues included. She divulged that, yes, she had met her caller and that the young girl was now out of danger and receiving the appropriate counselling, but she was adamant that the child should not be identified. The media, wary of the legal implications, respected this condition but were less co-operative when it came to Helen's own children. When she arrived home from work one day to find them camped outside her front fence, she sent Caitlin to John's sisters in Sydney for the rest of the school holidays.

When asked by a short shrewish female journalist, who pounced on her in a car park, whether she felt guilty about the effect of her revelations upon her own mother, she said: 'My mother didn't know,' and refused to comment further. When asked the identity of the magic wizard in her story, she said, 'Every doctor and counsellor in the country. Every loving partner. Every genuine friend.' And when a younger, more personable male reporter, who made a proper appointment, asked her whether her own wizard had been a counsellor, a partner or a friend, she had replied, 'It doesn't matter. Anyone who truly cares can make the miracle work.'

'So you've recovered from being abused as a child?' the reporter persevered. 'You've never been depressed or suicidal? Recovery is possible?'

'Yes,' said Helen. 'If you share your problems with people who care about you. If you learn to like and respect yourself. That's how you show the evil ones that they didn't succeed. That they didn't destroy you.'

'The evil ones? With respect, Helen,' said the reporter, and she sighed, because she knew that meant he had none and she'd been wrong about him, 'isn't that a bit melodramatic?'

'By evil people I mean men and women who hurt children,' said Helen. 'And I include the men and women who know about it and don't act. That's not too dramatic, is it? It's not hard to understand. It's hard to protect our children from evil, but we have to try. Write that down,' said Helen, and she smiled into his frank blue eyes.

Then a jumbo jet crashed with hundreds of people on board and a bomb went off in Northern Ireland. The media went back to the city and peace slowly returned to Siren's Rock.

'Trust Helen Connor to bring a nasty taste into the town and disgrace her mother's reputation,' said Edna Egan to Beryl Basingstoke-Brown. 'Not like that nice program Jemma Sullivan made.'

'I always liked Jemma,' said Beryl. 'I don't know how many times I tried to tell Babs that her Helen couldn't be trusted.'

But many people respected Helen even more after the Jane call. She was invited to appear on talk shows in Sydney and Melbourne; she was asked to write guest columns in magazines. Wherever she thought she might do some good, she agreed.

A week before Tom's fifth birthday, Helen rang Jemma at work.

'They want me to write a book,' she said.

'Of course they do,' said Jemma.

FALLOUT

What none of them had realised at first, because people rarely notice change until afterwards, was that from the moment she shared her shaming secret with the red-headed stranger on Berry Beach, Helen had begun to heal.

'I told him the truth about myself,' she said to John, late in the evening of the extraordinary day when she had revealed her secret on air. It was after eleven pm. The airwaves had finally — albeit temporarily — stopped rattling with the immediate impact of the rock Helen had hurled into the solid wall of complacency behind which respectable society prefers to hide. At that stage, Helen hadn't even begun to realise how far the fractures would spread and how many people were likely to be affected.

She was much more worried about going home.

She had already spoken briefly to Caitlin on the phone. 'So that's the excuse,' Caitlin had said sullenly. 'That's why we are all supposed to forgive you every time you go off with men and get pregnant and everything.'

Helen and John sat together at the broad desk in the deserted studio, yellow lamplight draining their strained faces.

'I raised the blind,' said Helen. 'You know how Jemma always said I have this habit of pulling down a blind on anything I don't want to think about? So I pulled it up and I looked through the window at myself. I thought I was showing *him*, Tom's father, but I had a good look too. I saw myself when I was little and I remembered how bad my parents made me feel. Almost all the time. But when I thought about it I realised I wasn't a bad child.'

'Of course you weren't,' said John. 'None of us were. But how did Tom's father talk you into it?' Quickly he added: 'I mean, facing the truth.'

'He said little girls need to blossom and flower,' Helen said to the ceiling. 'He said if they get nipped while they are still in bud, they never blossom as beautifully as they were meant to do.'

John sat wordlessly beside her. After a while she leaned forward and laid her cheek on the desk. Without speaking, John picked up one of her slender, dangling hands and held it gently in both of his own.

In the beginning it had been Jemma who saved her. But when Helen finally began to climb up into a world where she could learn to like herself, it was John and not Jemma who was there to provide a banister for her to grip whenever there was a risk of her slipping back.

Their stronger connection began with Tom. Hard as John had always tried to treat Caitlin as a daughter, he had never felt for her the same overwhelming love that Helen's small, sprouty-haired son aroused in his big heart.

It might have been because he had been so closely and painfully involved in Tom's birth. But he was also aware that his role in the little boy's life was crucial; that he was the closest substitute for a father that Tom was ever likely to have.

Inevitably, John and Helen became even closer when Helen went to work at 2SR. They talked; the same ideas excited them. They listened, to others and to each other. The same frustrations made them swear.

Everyone liked working with Helen and John. They were a good team, said the people at the station. Very professional. But the staff all knew Jemma too, and liked her. For a group of people who enjoyed a good gossip, they were surprisingly reluctant to speculate about the nature of John and Helen's relationship.

John wasn't sure when *he* started thinking about it.

'I have sinned in my thoughts and in my words,' he chanted at Mass most Sundays. Thinking about committing a sin was as bad as doing it, the priests had told them at school. John had considered this dictum a great deal and didn't agree. That view removed the element of self-discipline, of that same self-control which the Brothers urged the boys to develop. How could you make a conscious effort to stop yourself, thought John, if you hadn't thought about what it was you were not allowing yourself to do?

John did not fantasise about committing a sin. He fantasised about a sin he had already committed years before.

In truth, he could barely remember what had actually taken place on that night long ago when he had gone looking for Jemma and found Helen instead. But ever since Helen had taunted him about it while giving birth to Tom, a picture more than twenty years old sometimes flashed like a video clip onto the screen of his mind. To his dismay it was an erotic image rather than a shameful one.

Meanwhile, between Jemma and John, a rift barely discernible to anyone but themselves was widening. They still slept together in their big bed, but a small amount of rot had begun eating into the sturdy frame of their marriage.

Jemma said John had handed Helen fame on a plate. A big silver plate that glittered in a spotlight that John had turned on.

She laughed when she said it, and George, who had dropped in with the ironing, laughed too. But when George told Marte what Jemma had said, Marte frowned and went off to find something large to clean.

Jemma had been grateful for John's support throughout her quest for recognition. He had helped her with Hamish and the house, so that she could do all that she needed to do to achieve the success she craved. Apart from bringing her back to Siren's Rock, a move she had been happy about at the time, he had never allowed his own career hopes to take precedence over hers.

But it had been her battle, thought Jemma, not his. He had sat on the sidelines, cheering her on, watching to see if she would succeed.

And then he had taken Helen's unwilling hand, peeled open her fingers and offered her the winner's trophy.

She didn't blame Helen. Helen needed all the help she could get.

It was John she couldn't forgive.

She could not forgive him for loving her, marrying her, building her a beautiful home, giving her a child and making her happy.

She couldn't forgive him for making the wrong dreams come true.

'Helen's book will be a bestseller,' Jemma said. 'As sure as God made little fishes.'

John said nothing. There was nothing safe to say.

They were on their way home from the high school variety concert, the last they would attend as this was Hamish's final year of school. They had dressed up for it, but their efforts were wasted on Hamish, who hadn't even bothered to come and see them during the interval. He was operating the lights. Hamish had given up acting. 'Not before time,' John had remarked.

'Don't be cruel,' Jemma had said. 'It's that sort of comment that put him off.'

'No,' John had replied, 'it was lack of talent that put him off.'

'I wish he had tried out for *something* on stage,' Jemma said. 'Nobody notices who does the lighting.'

'He's a tech head, not a performer,' said John. 'He doesn't care if nobody notices him.'

'How would you know what he really feels?' asked Jemma.

'Because he's my son,' said John testily. 'Because he's just like me.'

They drove in silence until they reached the house. 'I had a mammogram today,' said Jemma as they pulled into the driveway.

John stopped the car halfway to the garage and looked at her. 'Why didn't you say so earlier? Were you right? Was it a lump?'

'Just a harmless little cyst,' said Jemma briskly. 'Nothing to worry about.'

They had told her at the new medical centre in Bridgetown that the ones to worry about were harder. Craggy. Like small chunks of smashed concrete. What an image! They said she was okay. She didn't feel okay. The fright was still there, tainting the relief.

'Thank God,' said John, moving the car forward again. 'But you should start having regular mammograms.'

'No, thanks,' said Jemma. 'They hurt.'

'Jemma,' said John, exasperated. 'Don't be silly.'

'There was a poem on the wall at the X-ray place,' said Jemma. She pulled a piece of paper out of her handbag and turned on the interior light.

'*This machine was designed by man,*' she read.

'*Of this I have no doubt*
I'd like to stick his balls in there
And see how they come out!'

Jemma chortled. John looked uncomfortable.

'It takes a lot to make you laugh these days,' said Jemma.

'Breast cancer is not something you generally laugh about,' said John.

'Everything's funny sooner or later,' said Jemma. 'It's easier to deal with life if you can laugh about it.'

'Not everything,' said John. 'Ask Helen.'

'Oh, for heaven's sake!' said Jemma loudly. 'I wasn't talking about Helen. Could we have *one* conversation without you bringing Helen into it, do you think?'

She got out, slamming the car door, and went up the steps onto the big verandah while John put the car away. She heard him pottering around in the garage. So he doesn't have to talk to me, she thought. She stood at the verandah rail for a little while, looking out at the black hills, taking in the wide sky and the stars.

She wanted to whinge. But to whom? Certainly not John. Not her mother, who was off colour. Again. The obvious person was Helen. But Helen wasn't as accessible as she used to be. At night she stayed home with Tom. And, of course, during the day she was busy being a celebrity. It was Helen, nowadays, who had trouble finding a free day for lunch.

Sometimes, snatching an hour for a walk along the shore at Mermaid Cove, Jemma made do with imagining that

Helen was with her. But she had realised in recent weeks that it wasn't Helen she was talking to . . .

So listen. I know I'm not at the Cove right now, but if you're listening . . . thank you. Thank you for giving me a good result on the dreaded lump. I suppose that was your doing. I've been really worried. That little bunch of peas was making me paranoid. They said to keep an eye on it, to come back in a month. Hell, not again. You could spend your whole life keeping an eye on your body, worrying yourself sick. I've already imagined the worst. Having a breast off and how weird I would look. Talk about lop-sided. And losing my hair and all that business. Anyway, I knew I wasn't the type. I'm too busy. Helen would say I'm too lucky. Helen thinks I have everything in life that a woman could want. What she means is that I have everything in life that she wants.

I should feel really happy and relieved. I wonder why I don't.

Okay, so what IS wrong with me?

Let's look at the list.

Hamish. He hates me. He didn't even come and talk after the show. John said he had a party on but I know he was just trying to embarrass us. Me. Okay, I shouldn't have accused him of panting after Caitlin. I shouldn't have said panting. But why does he follow her around like a big floppy dog? Why is he always over at Helen's? His finals are only weeks away. He should be buried in his books. Or getting drunk with mates. Not mooning about.

I bet Caitlin's at the party. Of all the girls . . . why Caitlin? She has spent her whole life teasing him. She just likes making him miserable.

John. He doesn't enjoy being with me any more. Is it me? Or is it him? Why is he always going to see Tom? And when he does come home, all he does is read the paper or watch television. Why doesn't he ever DO anything? Why does it always have to be me?

Mum. What's wrong with her? She always used to pride herself on her good health. She says she's tired but she never stops. I do everything

I can to stop her working so hard but she still finds more to do. Why can't she accept help? Dad would be happy for me to do everything. Even wash his car. But then why should I wash his car? I'm trying to hold down a job, run my own house, and help Mum with all those bloody shrubs, not to mention mopping all her floors if I get there early enough, but wash their car? Who does he think he's kidding?

The Sirens. They've got themselves into such a pickle with money and now they expect me to sort it out for them and I can't. I don't even want to. I'm the producer, the writer, the director — you'd think they could find someone else to worry about the dollars. Surely I don't have to do everything?

My job. Surely I don't have to do everything?

My life. Surely I don't have to do everything?

The worst thing about Jemma's list was that there was nothing to cross off. Nothing at all.

John came up the steps. 'Not going in?' he said.

She looked at him. 'What's wrong?' she asked. 'Why aren't we happy any more?'

He looked back. At least he's not going to pretend he doesn't know what I mean, thought Jemma. He's good like that. No games. There were never any games. Maybe that's the problem.

'I hate it when you sound jealous of Helen,' he said. 'It's not worthy of you.'

Jemma's face became sullen; clouds over the sun. 'Don't be so stupid,' she hissed.

In the living room she pulled off her shoes and sank down onto the couch. John went to put the kettle on, then he came and sat down beside her. He picked up her hand but she pulled it away.

'I think you *are* envious of Helen,' he said gently, 'and I can understand why. But Helen would give up everything she has for what you have . . .'

'For what?' snapped Jemma angrily. 'What have I got that Helen's so keen to have? An ungrateful son who has wasted every opportunity he's been given? A lovely house? You know I never cared about material things! Parents who never let me forget that I wouldn't know hard work if I fell into it? A husband who's never home, and never listens when he is . . .?'

'That's not fair,' said John, stung. 'I've listened to you for years. I've done nothing *but* listen . . .'

'. . . who spends more time with my friend's son than his own, who gave my best friend the chance of a lifetime . . .'

'I *knew* that was what this is all about,' interrupted John. 'Jemma, I just offered Helen a job. The rest she did herself.'

'Oh and of course *I* have never made any effort at all. I'm just a fat lazy housewife,' shouted Jemma. 'And the little matter of me giving up any prospects *I* had for a distinguished career in order to raise our child and Helen's as well,' she sneered, 'that's hardly worth considering.'

'Nobody has ever called you a fat housewife, Jemma, and you know you're not!' John realised he was shouting and he stopped and took a breath. More quietly, he said: 'Just for the record, Helen is very much aware that you virtually raised Caitlin for her. I'm trying to help her with Tom so that you won't feel obliged to do it all again.'

'Well, lucky old me,' said Jemma.

'Yes,' said John, and she realised belatedly that he was angry too. Not defensive, as he usually sounded when she was upset with him, but coldly, furiously angry. '*Lucky* you,' said John. 'And if you want to take over and rewrite her book for her, I'm sure she'll be eternally grateful to you. That's if it's possible for her to be any more grateful than she already is. I'll say it again. You have everything Helen ever wanted but never for a moment of her life has she begrudged *you* any of it.'

'Including you,' said Caitlin.

Jemma's head whipped around. Caitlin was lounging in the doorway in a T-shirt and jeans. Caitlin had not considered it necessary to dress up for variety night. Even the way the end of her plait pointed at her small nipple, clearly discernible under the thin cotton, suggested insolence.

'Where did you come from?' snapped Jemma, getting to her feet. 'What were you doing in Hamish's room?'

'Giving him a blow job,' said Caitlin. 'You can't get pregnant that way.' She walked past them both to the front door and opened it. 'It's a shame my mother didn't know about blow jobs, isn't it, John?' And with a sense of timing that Jemma might have admired at another time, she went out into the night.

Jemma found herself hanging tightly on to the back of the couch. 'Oh God,' she said faintly.

John went into Hamish's bedroom and quickly returned. 'He's not there,' he said. 'It was just Cait being Cait.' He looked at Jemma's stricken face. 'Jemma,' he said quietly, 'she was stirring. She stirs all the time. You know that.'

'Is it true?' asked Jemma in a thin voice.

'You heard me,' said John. 'Hamish isn't even home ...'

'I mean about Helen.'

John stared at her. 'Is what true about Helen? That she'd love what you have, yes ...'

'That she loves you?'

'Jemma,' said John. 'Helen loves *you*. And I love you. Think about it.'

'Are you Tom's father?' said Jemma.

John's face and neck flushed a dark, mottled red. Without a reply, he picked up his car keys and strode out through the open door.

Jemma stood still for a few minutes, her eyes wide and her hands clutching the back of the couch. When she heard the car engine she raced out onto the verandah.

'Come back!' she yelled. 'For once in your life come back and *fight*!' she screamed.

The front door slammed behind her.

A chill colder than winter had slipped into the house.

TEMPTATION

John drove all the way up Rocky Mountain and parked at Bob Snell Memorial Lookout, where he stared straight ahead at the lights of the town in order to keep his gaze from the exertions of the couples in the other parked cars. He soon gave up, noticing to his discomfort that they were making him feel randy, and drove aimlessly around the streets of Siren's Rock for more than an hour. But in the end, of course, he drove to Helen's.

She made them both strong cups of coffee and removed a pile of ironing from her best armchair so he could sit down and stretch his legs. Helen sat opposite, perched on the edge of a straight-backed chair.

'Jemma's having a rough time at the moment,' said Helen. 'Haven't you noticed? And you know, when you're unhappy you always take it out on the one you love most.'

'We're all having a rough time,' said John. 'That doesn't give any of us the right to accuse people of things they've never done ...' He faltered. He hadn't told her what Jemma had said. How could he? All she knew was that they'd had a huge row.

'John,' said Helen gently, 'I know you're always inundated with work worries, but I don't think any of us realise how much Jemma has on her plate. Marte isn't well and George can't cope,' said Helen. 'Did you know he keeps asking Jemma to go down there?'

'No,' said John slowly. 'I didn't know that.'

'And Hamish is giving her a hard time, you *do* know that. And she's been worried about her breast for ages, longer than she let on to us, I think, although at least that's one thing off her mind now. And the Sirens are in dire financial straits. She needs more time, but she doesn't want to leave her job. I think she sees FNC as her last chance, her last link with show business.'

John took off his tie and opened his collar. 'I don't know how to make her happy,' he sighed. 'I never have.'

'You've made her happy all her life,' said Helen softly.

'She doesn't need me,' he said. 'She's fine on her own. She'd probably be happier.'

Helen frowned and sipped her coffee. She looked at him across the cluttered room. There were cushions everywhere, piles of magazines and books on every surface. Empty chocolate boxes. Bowls of pot pourri and vases of flowers in various stages of vitality. A soft red glow from two small lamps lit the room. It was warm and comfortable and slightly scruffy. Faintly, from somewhere, soft flute music was sweetening the air.

'I think she needs you now more than either of you realise,' said Helen.

'She's got a bloody funny way of showing it.'

'Jemma's tired,' said Helen. 'All her life she's been the one who gets things done. All her life she's helped me, she's helped you, she's helped everyone who needed her. Maybe she would like to be looked after for a change.

'Why don't you take over? Why don't you tell her you want her to give up her job and all her projects and do something she really wants to do? Tell her to stop *talking* about writing a book and to actually start writing one. A book or another play. Tell her a writer writes.'

'She'd pulverise me,' said John.

'You're bigger than she is,' smiled Helen. She looked at him over the edge of her cup. *He's so huge.* Her eyes rested on his big brown face and tufty hair, on the tanned brown skin of his neck inside the pale-blue shirt collar. A small pulse began to beat deep inside her body.

John glanced up and caught her looking at him. 'Where's Caitlin?' he asked suddenly. 'Did she come home?'

'She's in bed.' said Helen. She heard the huskiness in her voice and tried to clear her throat. 'Asleep, I hope. Tom too.'

Carefully John put his coffee cup on a small, crowded table, his eyes on Helen's face.

'Helen, I like being with you. You and Tom. It's ...' He hesitated. 'It's so peaceful,' he said.

'Peaceful!' said Helen brightly, looking with intense interest at her knees. 'Well, that's the last word I'd choose to describe 2SR *or* my house, with Caitlin and Tom doing their best to destroy it and each other.'

John tried again. He looked at her bent head, the fair hair tinged with pink in the lamplight. 'What you said in the hospital when you were having Tom ...' said John.

'I was in agony,' said Helen. 'Give me a break.'

'Didn't you wonder why I never came back?' John persisted softly. 'Why I never tried to find her again? Why I didn't ring the number you wrote on the envelope?'

Helen kept her head down. 'I suppose because of ... I suppose you felt too guilty.'

'Yes,' said John. 'But then we all ended up in Florence, so ...'

'Everything turned out fine,' said Helen quickly.

John watched her. 'After Jemma and I were married, I told her about keeping the letter. And she said it was really from you. That it was your idea. That as far as she could remember, you dictated it and she did the writing. She laughed,' said John. 'She thought it was funny that I'd kept it. Kept it and not answered. Not *done* something. Typical of me, she said.' He paused, waiting for Helen to respond, but she didn't.

'I should have realised it was you,' said John. 'It was brief and to the point. Not like anything Jemma would have written.'

Still Helen said nothing.

'Julie,' said John softly. 'I sometimes think about what might have been.'

Helen looked up.

'Do *you*?' asked John, more softly still. 'Do you ever think about me? About what might have been possible between the two of us?'

Brown eyes met brown eyes. Helen had to remind herself to breathe. As each breath escaped from her lips it fluttered between the two of them, caught on a memory. Somewhere, louder than the flute music, a clock was ticking.

Helen sat very straight and looked at the man she had loved all her life. She looked at his broad shoulders, his tanned throat, his stern, straight comic-book hero's mouth. She looked into his dark, sad, questioning eyes.

Less than two metres separated them.

What if she went to him, Helen wondered. What if she took his face in her hands and, for the first time in their lives, kissed him on the lips? What if she pressed his handsome head to her breast, pretending just for a moment that he was hers to comfort and to love?

How long would it take her to cross that space, thought Helen. A second? A lifetime?

What would it take to keep them apart?

Nearly forty years of friendship. One small act of kindness.

'No,' said Helen. 'Actually, I don't.'

After Helen had sent John home to Jemma, Caitlin came out of her room. She stood behind Helen while her mother rinsed the coffee cups. Helen had taken her shoes off. She felt as wrung out as a rag, twisted tight as rope.

'I was listening to you and John,' said Caitlin.

Helen's shoulders jerked. She sounded strained: 'You're up late. I thought you were asleep.'

'I was at Jemma's earlier on. I heard her and John as well,' said Caitlin.

'You've had a busy night,' said Helen dryly. She put the back of her damp hand to her cheek. Her face was still burning. Both her heart and her vagina were throbbing. She felt most peculiar.

'I owe you an apology,' said Caitlin.

The coffee cup slipped from Helen's hand and smashed into blue and yellow pieces in the sink. She turned to stare at her daughter.

'Well, this is a first,' said Helen.

'I thought you and John were having an affair,' said Caitlin, tossing her plait off her shoulder. 'I thought John was Tom's father.'

'*What*?'

'Well, it made sense. If the mystery man was this old and dear friend you talked about. Only I didn't know how you'd managed to deceive Jemma,' said Caitlin, 'because Jemma's a pretty smart woman.'

Helen tottered to a kitchen stool in her stockinged feet.

'Anyway, it turns out that Jemma is dead jealous of you but not over John, it's because you're famous and she's not. And after what you said to John tonight,' said Caitlin, 'I figured out you two went out while Jemma was at uni, but naturally he preferred her in the end. And when you sent him off like that ... well, I know you wouldn't have done that if he really *was* Tom's father. It was pretty gross anyway, the thought of old guys like you having sex. Anyway, he only likes you because you make him feel *peaceful*. God, how pathetic! Anyway ...' Caitlin concluded shakily, 'so I'm sorry, okay?'

Helen looked at her daughter and slowly, hopefully, opened her arms. Caitlin hesitated, then walked over to her and dropped to her knees on the floor. Even kneeling, she was almost as tall as her seated mother, but she wrapped her arms around Helen's waist and put her face into her shoulder. Helen held her carefully and quietly, not daring to speak. After a while, she felt hot tears on her neck.

'Don't cry, Caitlin,' Helen whispered, her own mouth quivering with the effort not to sob with relief. 'You'll always have me, you know, sweetheart. I promise. Even if you don't think I'm much use.'

Caitlin snuffled. 'It's just ...' Her voice was muffled. 'When I worked out it was John, I started thinking ... you know ...' Her body quivered.

'That it might have been quite nice,' said Helen.

'Just that I wouldn't have minded all that much,' Caitlin said into Helen's shoulder.

Seconds became minutes. Helen held her daughter gently in her arms, wishing with all her heart that the minutes would last forever.

At least it was a start.

Part Eight

JOHN

When it finally rained, late on the day of the funeral, it didn't stop for three weeks. Everyone agreed it was an unusually heavy wet season, even for the far north coast. But nothing had been usual or normal at that time. Everyone agreed about that as well.

John remembered how the rain began falling as the wake wound up. Steadily, heavily, constantly. As if heaven would never again put an end to its tears and wipe the sky dry.

John had wanted to stay at home to comfort the kids, especially Tom, but he'd had to go straight back to work. Radio 2SR had been on air twenty-four hours a day, broadcasting flood warnings and calling for volunteers to help the police and local emergency services sandbag the riverbanks. Anyone willing to help shop owners stack stock and perishable goods out of the way of the rising flood waters was asked to do their bit. A convoy of rescue vehicles snaked along the soggy road from Siren's Rock to Bridgetown, where the crisis had become extreme.

Schools, which had only just reopened after the holidays, were closed. Girls and boys rowed boats down the main street of Bridgetown, making rafts out of what they could find. In Siren's Rock the children were disappointed. The Tiddley River was too far from the town centre to do any damage, even when it swelled to three times its normal size. The kids had to make do with trips into Bridgetown to see the devastation, to grab a share of the excitement.

Fifteen months later, the Easter rain reminded him of it all again. Well, not *reminded* exactly — because that suggested that at some stage he had stopped thinking about it. The funeral. The flood. The family. Jemma. And Helen. Whereas, in fact, the memories had become a part of him, living daily in his mind, accompanying him when he worked and when he slept. Which is all he seemed to do these days.

Now, on the long journey to Sydney, it was raining again.

Ruffles of water billowed out from the wheels of John's four-wheel drive. The going was slow on the long and twisting rural roads, but eventually he reached the highway, where steadily, reluctantly, the gleaming road gave up the miles.

He drove in silence, not sure whether music would wake Tom, who was propped against pillows in the back seat.

He drove through the night, with water pattering against the windscreen and the wipers sweeping back and forth, back and forth, in time with his memories.

When he reached Kempsey and Tom hadn't stirred, he finally slipped a tape into the deck. It was a present Caitlin had given him last Christmas. *Autumn Leaves.*

He thought of Jemma as a child, laughing, kicking up leaves with her plump brown legs, sweeping them out of their newly raked piles so that they rose in clouds and fell in showers onto her mother's neatly mown lawn. Shouting at him to have a go.

She'd been bigger than him then.

He thought of her in winter, building cubbies in the bush. Lying on warm rocks, telling stories to the Wildcats.

Jemma herself, the leader of the pack, would always have the biggest horse, the whitest unicorn, the fastest carpet.

Helen had come in the spring. He remembered how together they had tried to save her. How, after that, Helen had almost always been there.

He thought of Jemma in the summer time, racing ahead of them through the paddocks, brown legs crashing through the crackling grass, the rest of them following, never catching up.

He remembered being sent away to school and, for a long time, losing her.

He saw her again on that bright, cold winter's day, when she stood silently beside Marte while his mother's coffin was lowered into the ground. How Jemma's bent head had gleamed in the watery sunshine. How strange it had been to see Jemma like that, quiet, with her head down. How odd it had felt to be taller than her.

He remembered receiving her letter and reading it so many times that the paper had become weak and torn; he had pasted it onto a fresh white sheet to keep it strong. He still had it, filed away in the cardboard box Jemma had given him to store what she called Significant Memories. She had written *John — SMs* in black texta pen on the side of the carton.

He hadn't liked seeing her as Bottom in *A Midsummer Night's Dream*. When she strutted the stage, ugly and loud, his mates had laughed in a derisory way and cracked his ribs with their elbows. At fifteen, he hadn't wanted to see Jemma like that.

There had been many girls at university, girls with soft bodies and sweet smiles, but compared with the captain of the Wildcats, they had been like candlelight against the sun.

He thought of her in Florence, more beautiful than he had even imagined. It was a miracle, Jemma turning up like that in Italy, the answer to every prayer he had ever prayed. And then the second miracle, when almost immediately she had begun to love him.

He had never questioned God again. It was why, when he brought her back to Australia, he had returned to his mother's church.

A promise is a promise.

He thought of her in the tent on Lassos, her magnificent body as ripe and sweet as a bowl of fuzzy golden peaches; his incredulity that she was giving this fruit to him; their delight as they discovered each other. His wonder. Her passion. Their joy.

Show her, Helen had said.

He pushed the thought away. He was not yet ready to think about Helen.

He remembered Jemma his bride, tall in her white gown, standing at the altar, her smile flashing. A lovely lighthouse above a sea of happy faces.

In the beginning they had agreed on almost everything.

As the years rocketed on, he realised that agreeing with her did not necessarily mean understanding her.

As he grew older he had wondered about this a good deal. Did men ever understand women? Were men destined always to be the physical lovers of women, while the women fell in love with each other's minds, understanding and nurturing female feelings as faithfully as they understood and nurtured their children, revelling — even wallowing — in their sensitivities and emotions? Certainly Jemma and Helen enjoyed a marriage of minds with which he couldn't hope to compete.

Jemma had a theory. Men and women were meant to live apart, she would say, with the women raising children and crops while the men were off hunting and gathering and building corporations. Once a month, when the women were ovulating, they would welcome their husbands home to make love to them. Then the men could go off again, making money, having adventures and leaving the women in peace to feed and teach the next generation. That way everyone would be happy.

'But who would be the writers and the artists?' Helen asked.

'Who would provide the role models for the boy children?' John wanted to know.

Jemma had laughed at them. 'Details, details,' she'd sighed. 'John always gets bogged down in details. Worrying about details stops you actually *doing* anything.'

Jemma always knew exactly when her egg dropped. Every few weeks she would roll over to his side of the bed and embrace him with such enthusiasm that she often literally knocked the breath out of him.

In the car, a faint smile turned up the corners of his mouth.

He remembered Hamish's birth, Jemma's pure joy in creating this tiny human life. And the busy, messy, frantic years that followed. He remembered Jemma the mother, Jemma the playgroup co-ordinator, Jemma the producer, Jemma the writer, bashing away at her keyboard long into the night but up before all of them the next day, to clean up and cook dinner before racing off to a meeting, a rehearsal, a show.

He thought of Jemma the star. Standing in the spotlight, shaking back her curtain of hair, lighting the stage with her smile as the audience cheered. He thought of Jemma, finally famous for fifty minutes, winning hearts all over the country when 'One Australian' went to air.

He thought of Jemma the station manager's wife, how she had loved it at first, schmoozing with the advertisers and their wives; how she deferred to him in front of his staff and clients, gazing up at him with solemn attention, making him look better than he was.

How she never deferred to him at home, except in bed. And as the years rolled on, and the eggs dropped at increasingly inconvenient times, not even there.

They had always made their plans together and shared the same goals. But it was Jemma who remained the captain, while he was the loyal adviser and deputy, happy to let Jemma take the lead.

'Well, I have to,' she said once, when she overheard George teasing him about it. 'Otherwise John would make a million plans but we would never actually get anything *done*.'

She left money matters to him. And she had always respected his return to Catholicism, although she called his church the Chapel of Special Occasions, because that was when she went with him. 'God knows I love Him,' she would say. 'We chat all the time. I don't have to be in church to do it.'

Very occasionally, when facing difficult decisions, particularly those involving the children, she had been willing to compromise with John. 'Okay,' she would say. 'I suppose I'll have to grin and bear it.' But for the most part, John and Helen went along with what she wanted.

John and Helen. Vice captains. First mates.

He pushed the thought away.

It came back.

He missed her most of all in autumn. Then in June, lying cold and alone on his empty raft, he realised that he missed her more in winter. And the same in the spring. And he had missed her unbearably in the summer time, when he sometimes opened their louvred cupboard doors and buried his face in the bright silky shirts that hung there. Remembering the sight and sound and smell of her. The way she filled his arms. The way she had filled his life.

It was autumn now. And raining again.

Dawn was breaking in a barely discernible way when Tom stirred in the back seat.

'Are we nearly there?'

'No,' said John.

'Can I come in the front?' Tom's voice was woolly with sleep. John slowed down while the little boy climbed over and made himself comfortable beside him. 'Put your seat belt on,' said John. 'Snuggle up under the rug.'

Tom wriggled further into the tartan blanket and peered through the window. 'I love long car trips,' he said. 'Especially at night.'

'Your mother used to feel that way too,' said John.

'Did she?' asked Tom. 'How do you know?'

'She told me. Several times. And Jemma told me too.'

'You know a lot about my mummy, don't you, John?'

'Well,' said John, 'I met her when we were both ten. That's only two years older than you are now,' said John.

'Yeah,' said Tom. 'You've known me since I was born. It's in my poem.'

'I'm in a poem?' asked John. 'Do I know this poem?'

'I don't think I've said it to you,' said Tom. 'It was sort of meant for just Mummy and me.'

'Oh,' said John. 'Okay.'

There was a pause. 'Maybe I'll say it just very softly,' said Tom. 'You might be able to hear a little bit.' He looked over at John. 'It doesn't rhyme,' he said apologetically. Then in a sing-song voice, he began.

> '*My real father was a red-headed man*
> *Who travelled the world doing good deeds for people*
> *Which is why Mummy loved him very much.*
> *My real father made Mummy happy*
> *And planted the seed that would grow into me*
> *But that was the easy part.*
> *John helped me come into the world*
> *Which was much harder.*
> *John and Jemma are our very best friends*
> *And they've been looking after me and Mummy*
> *And Caitlin too*
> *Ever since.*'

John kept his eyes on the road. He supposed it was necessary to provide this sort of explanation to an illegitimate child who had apparently come into the world via a single night of passion with a stranger. He didn't understand why.

'Sometimes I think about a different ending for my poem,' said Tom. 'Sometimes I wonder what it would be like if my real father had stayed to look after me, instead of you.'

'I can see why you would wonder that,' said John.

'My real father's hair was the same colour as mine,' said Tom.

'Well,' said John, 'that makes sense.'

'I wonder if I'll be taller than him,' said Tom. 'He wasn't *really* tall, you know. Not like you. Or Caitlin's father. Mummy said my real father wasn't too big and he wasn't too small. He was *just* right.'

'Look at the horizon,' said John. 'It's getting lighter.'

'You used to be very good at looking after people, didn't you, John?' said Tom.

'Sort of,' said John. He wondered about the use of the past tense.

'Until you went to Ireland, of course,' said Tom. 'That's when you stopped.'

John slowly spread his fingers, keeping his palms on the wheel, then gripped it again. He leaned forward and switched off the tape.

'Well, Tom, you know what happened while I was in Ireland,' he said quietly. 'It was hard for me to know what to do. Who to look after.'

'Oh, it's okay,' said Tom brightly. 'I'm sure you did the right thing. Mummy once told me you always do.'

'What a wise woman,' said John.

'Actually Jemma said it as well,' said Tom. 'So that means it's true, because Caitlin said Jemma always was a pretty smart cookie. Well, *actually* Caitlin said Jemma was a pretty smart *woman*, but I put in "cookie" because I read it in a book. A smart *cookie*,' he repeated with satisfaction.

'When you talked to her on the phone,' said Tom after a short silence, 'did she say she was excited?'

'She told me to tell you she was busting,' said John.

After they had stopped for petrol and had breakfast in the 'almost-still-dark', as he described it, Tom went back to sleep.

'Busting,' he whispered to himself, before drifting off again.

The rain began to clear as they reached the heart of the city. John drove down towards the harbour. In the distance, Anzac Bridge hung from the sky above the wide silver water.

'I love that bridge. It's as if God's invisible fingers are holding the strings,' Helen had said, the last time they were in Sydney; the three of them had made a weekend trip to see the latest David Williamson play, just before their last Christmas together.

Crossing the Harbour Bridge, John saw the sun coming up. A damp haze blurred the rooftops clustered around the harbour coves. Small boats were already busy on the grey water. The sails of the Opera House were pink.

A plane flew across the rosy sky.

Tom stirred beside him and opened his eyes.

'Nearly there now,' John said.

It was crowded at the international terminal. Tom, refreshed after a long night's sleep, raced up and down, occasionally disappearing, while John, tense and tired, strode behind him.

When they were finally standing still, scanning the arrivals board, Tom hopped up and down on one foot and then the other. John's nerves were twanging like a synthesiser. He bit softly on his tongue to stop himself telling Tom to stand still.

'I keep thinking it will be the two of them,' said Tom suddenly, shoving his hands in his pockets and tipping back his sprouty red head to look up at John. 'Like always.'

'Me too,' said John.

CHRISTMAS

On the night Helen sent John back to Jemma, he talked to himself all the way home. Muttered under his breath, practised different versions of what he should say to his wife. He had steeled himself to cope with a metallic silence, or to deflect sarcasm, but when he walked into the living room he needed neither of them.

Hamish, home at last from the first school variety night he had actually enjoyed, looked up anxiously from the couch, where he was ineffectually patting his mother's back. Jemma lay face down, rocking with tears.

'Nanna's had a stroke,' said Hamish in a frightened, disbelieving voice. He had never seen his mother in this state. He had rarely seen his mother cry, except over movies. And not like this.

John strode across the room as Jemma raised her face from the couch. 'Dad said she can't move at all on her left side, and she can't talk,' she sobbed. 'She might never walk again. Or talk. My mum, John. My mum!'

Her face was blotched and soaked with tears. There were loops of soft mauve skin beneath her eyes and her hair lay in lank ropes around her face. She looked fat and old.

'They said she could have another one any minute,' she cried, flinging her arms around his neck as he wrapped his around her. 'She might die.'

John looked over her head at Hamish, whose own eyes were wet and worried. 'I offered to drive Mum to the hospital straight away,' Hamish said. 'She wanted to wait for you.'

'I can't do this any more,' sobbed Jemma. 'I can't do this on my own.'

'You don't have to,' said John, rubbing her back. And wondered what she meant. Jemma had never been on her own. She had always had her devoted parents, her devoted Helen. She had always had him. Disappointing her, but devoted nevertheless.

Ashamed of such unworthy thoughts, he gently helped her up. Then he did what he had always done.

He took care of them all.

'You could have phoned me,' John said on the way to the hospital. 'I was at Helen's.'

Jemma looked at him with an unfathomable expression in her swollen green eyes. 'Of course you were,' she said.

'Jemma,' said John desperately, 'just for the record, Helen loves you a lot more than she loves me.'

'I know,' said Jemma wearily. 'I'm sorry. I was having a bad day.'

They drove the rest of the way in silence, without alluding to the fact that the day had just become much worse.

Christmas that year was difficult. They were all rudderless without Marte to steer them through the turbulent sea of compulsory goodwill. Marte had always been the captain of the Christmas ship, with Jemma her capable first mate. Jemma had always shopped and wrapped but Marte would cook enough food for a long ocean voyage, create costumes for their traditional Christmas Day family concerts, help the children trim the trees and load every wall, window sill and ceiling with decorations, swinging from ladders and clambering from chair to table top. She had done this for years and years, happily managing them all with her huge crazy smile and an infectious excitement which annually created an epidemic of frenzied anticipation in all three households.

With Marte still in hospital, defying death, laboriously learning to walk and talk again, Jemma took on Christmas with a dogged determination to make it as good as ever. Helen helped. But the fun and joy were missing until the day itself, when everyone made an admirable effort.

Throughout the following year, Jemma raced between her parents' house and her own, organising domestic help for George and Marte on the days she couldn't get there, but basically running two houses and nursing her mother back to health with a resolution that was both passionate and practical. Throwing herself into this new challenge with all the energy and enthusiasm she had once devoted to the other consuming passions of her life.

She seemed happy again, thought John. Jemma had always thrived on hard work with a purpose; as her mother took the small uncertain steps that would lead her back into normal life, Jemma once again had an achievable, visible goal.

Tom had started school, and was driving his fluffy little teacher mad with his constant questions. Helen had more time to concentrate on her book. Like Helen herself, it was short, succinct and effective, with a few select case histories, skilfully told. While *Goodnight, Princess* was never destined to be a bestseller, it won favourable reviews in all states and became an essential reference for research into paedophilia and child abuse. Helen began receiving lucrative offers from radio stations eager to lure her to the city, none of which she ever considered.

Hamish was accepted into the new university at Bridgetown, and elected, after three months, to share a house there rather than commute daily from home. 'You've got enough to do without looking after me any more,' he said to his mother. Not mentioning how much he enjoyed his independence.

'Hamish is talking to me again,' Jemma told Helen. 'Absence makes the heart grow fonder.'

Caitlin started her last year of school and surprised everyone by studying hard.

'I want to do well in the finals,' she said to Jemma and John, pyjama-clad and dozy, when they found her in Hamish's bedroom at three am, riffling through his old notes.

'A brilliant pass is the best way of getting out of this hole,' said Caitlin. 'I'm not going to Bridgetown. I'm heading for Sydney. I'm going to do something that will make me rich and independent. Maybe medicine. Or dentistry.'

'A girl after my own heart,' smiled Jemma, as John shuddered at the thought of Caitlin in control of a dental drill. 'You sound just like me at eighteen.'

'Not really,' said Caitlin dryly. 'I'm interested in money. Not fame.'

'Oh, *fame*,' said Jemma, with surprising good humour considering the disgusting hour and the fact that she had just noticed a packet of condoms on Hamish's desk. 'Been there, done that.'

'Money isn't everything, Cait,' said John. 'You can't buy happiness.'

'Oh *please*,' said Caitlin. 'Why are you guys always obsessing about *happiness*?'

'Hamish ran away to Helen's to study,' croaked Jemma as they padded back to bed. 'Caitlin comes to us. Wonderful!'

★ ★ ★

The second Christmas after Marte's stroke was brilliant in comparison with the one preceding it. Jemma had finally left her job at the beginning of December and had devoted the following weeks to making it the best Christmas ever.

Marte had made a good recovery and, despite a bad leg and a slightly lop-sided smile, she declared herself to be as good as new. 'She's not really,' said Jemma to Helen. 'She has shrunk. I'm taller than her now. And she gets tired really easily. But of course she'll never admit it.'

Helen and her children arrived at the Sullivans' early on Christmas Eve and stayed until late on Boxing Day. John slipped off to Mass by himself on Christmas Eve, but after the presents had been opened the next morning he accompanied the rest of them to the Christmas Day service at the modern Uniting Church, which Marte and George regarded as their own. When they got back, champagne corks bounced off the beamed ceiling and vast amounts of salmon, prawns, pork, turkey, ham and crunchy salads were consumed, followed by pineapples, watermelon, mangoes and strawberries and Marte's famously thick, sweet ice-cream. Wine, conversation and laughter flowed. Even the weather was exceptionally pleasant for a Siren's Rock December. It was more like spring than summer; the air was soft and warm, with no sign of the stickiness and heat or the flooding deluge that was still to come.

Jemma glowed through it all, glamorous in a flowing crimson trouser suit, the grey tinted out of her hair which was back to its burnished red-brown. She had lost a lot of weight. In the cool of that summer evening, under swathes of green leaves and scarlet balls, their faces speckled with reflections from the peripatetic lights of the giant Christmas tree, they sang every verse of every carol they knew.

JUST GOOD FRIENDS

That was the year when Hamish finally accepted that he was never going to have sex with Caitlin.

True to form, she managed to ruin the last few hours of Christmas Day by having a row with her mother. Helen had told Caitlin she was *not* going on from the Sullivans' to an all-night party with her friends down at Mermaid Cove.

'You've had very little sleep and a lot to drink,' said Helen. 'I don't want you going anywhere else tonight.' Caitlin had argued — something about studying her arse off for her finals and Helen never being satisfied no matter how hard she tried. Meeting a union of unsympathetic grins, she had sworn, shrieked and refused to walk home with Helen and Tom. Nobody was sober enough to drive.

After seeing them off, Hamish found Caitlin in his room and lay down beside her, squashing up close to her on his single bed. Knowing this was bound to annoy her. As he anticipated, Caitlin immediately rolled off and marched to his door, but she surprised him by closing it, locking it and returning to the bed.

'What are you up to?' asked Hamish lazily. He had drunk more wine than he was used to, even after a year of university life. Beer had been the preferred fluid for getting wasted.

'Let's have sex,' said Caitlin.

Hamish sighed and stared at the ceiling. 'Sure,' he said. 'That'll really show both our mothers what a mature and rational girl you are.'

'No,' Caitlin snapped. 'That's not why this time.'

'Sex as Revenge against Mothers,' said Hamish, failing in his attempt to sound light-hearted. 'Anyway, you always change your mind.'

'This time I won't,' said Caitlin, lying beside him. 'I'm sick of being a virgin, Hamish. I'm sick of boys wanting to do it to me and having to fight them off because they're not worth it. I'm sick of not being allowed to go to parties because somebody might jump on me while I'm drunk. I'd just like to get it over with and it might as well be you.'

'Gee, thanks,' said Hamish.

'No, I don't mean it like that.' She hitched herself up on one elbow and looked down into his face. 'Face it, Hamish,' she said matter-of-factly, 'we've loved each other all our lives.'

Hamish looked at her white oval face and laughed. A derisive bark.

'I'm serious,' said Caitlin crossly. 'Come on, you know you want to fuck me. You've wanted to ever since you were about twelve.'

Hamish lay with his arms folded behind his head and watched her face. 'Prove it,' he said. 'Prove you mean it.'

Caitlin hesitated, sighed, and then, in a business-like way, slipped her hand down his jeans, found the top of his underpants, kept going and finally closed her fingers around his balls.

Hamish caught his breath and she gave his prick a gentle squeeze.

With a sterling effort, Hamish managed not to howl with delight. He gripped his arms more tightly behind his head. 'Now kiss me,' he said, trying to keep his voice normal.

Caitlin, propped on her skinny elbow with his gear stick held as firmly as if she was preparing for a racing start, stared down at him. She looked at his black hair, his dark eyes, his beautiful lips.

'You've got a girl's mouth,' she said, with a slight but unmistakable grimace.

Hamish sighed again. And for the first time in their eighteen-year relationship took control of the situation.

The year Hamish had spent living in a house with a group of blokes had been far from wasted. A lot of beer had been drunk and a lot of mess had been made. Drunk and sober, happy and sometimes sad, a lot of talking had been done as well. And talking to young men with the same pressures and prospects as his own had proved a lot more edifying than talking to his mother.

They had also tampered with a reasonable number of girls at the uni bar, awakening Hamish to the realisation that, despite what his mother had told him, some girls didn't take sexual intercourse any more seriously than a good meal.

He gently pulled Caitlin's hand from out of his pants. Noticed she looked relieved. Sat up and put his hands on her shoulders, turning her around so that her back was to him. Carefully took the black elastic from the bottom of her plait. Began pulling the auburn strands free from the thick rope that she always made with her hair.

'What are you doing?' asked Caitlin, intrigued.

'Remember that story Mum used to read to us?' Hamish whispered. 'Rapunzel, let down your hair.'

But Caitlin's hair was thick, curly and coarse. When Hamish had freed the strands from the plait, she looked as

442

mad as Medusa. He turned her around to face him again, pushed his fingers into her hair, loosening and untangling it until it stood out like a wild jungle bush around her pale oval face. He wound his fingers back through the strands and pulled her face towards his.

With his perfect white teeth, he nipped lightly at the tip of her tongue, the source of a lifetime's jibes, insults and obscenities.

Then he kissed her so violently that for fifty long, horrified seconds she didn't know what had hit her. His red girl's mouth swallowed hers. Teeth smashed teeth and his tongue filled her throat, choking her. When he finally released her face from his, she stared at him. Her lips were swollen and redder now than his. Slowly he disentangled his fingers from her wild hair. Caitlin put a hand to her mouth, as if to check if it was still there.

'Why did you do *that*?' she asked in a shocked and tiny voice. Her lips hurt. Her eyes stung. She felt sick.

Hamish was breathing heavily. 'Because I've wanted to ever since I was about twelve,' he said. 'Because I've thought about it more than is healthy.' He took a deep breath, stretched out a finger and laid it on her cheek. She jerked away.

'Because I wanted to do it just once,' said Hamish softly, 'before I never do it again.'

A tear overflowed and dribbled down Caitlin's cheek.

'That's right,' she said. 'You won't. You're a terrible kisser. You're never going to get a girlfriend, that's for sure.'

'I've had several girlfriends,' said Hamish coolly. That was a bit of an exaggeration. 'I don't kiss them like that.'

She stared at him. 'You hurt me,' she said. Another tear made its way down her face.

'I know,' said Hamish. 'Just like you've been hurting me for years. Trying to make me feel as bad as you do.'

'I don't feel bad,' said Caitlin.

'Yes, you do, Cait. You don't even *try* not to. You *wallow* in feeling bad. You want us *all* to feel bad. Your mum. Me. All of us.'

'I hate you, Hamish,' said Caitlin.

'Aren't you getting a bit old for that?' asked Hamish. 'When are you going to give up trying to hurt the rest of us and just take responsibility for yourself?'

'Shit on you!' screamed Caitlin, finally finding her voice. 'Us! What's all this *us* business. You're one of *them*, are you, Hamish? Another neurotic woman! You sound just like your mother! Or worse still, mine!'

Hamish stood up, walked over to the door and unlocked it.

'We're never going to have sex, Cait,' he said.

'Oh, that's for sure,' said Caitlin, getting up, grabbing hunks of her hair and twisting them up behind her head as she strode towards him and the door. 'You got *that* one right.'

'One day you will understand why it just wouldn't be right, and ...' he sighed, 'you'll forgive me for turning you down.' He smiled at her and turned the door handle. 'After all,' said Hamish sweetly, 'we're family.'

In bed that night Jemma and John discussed what Hamish and Caitlin had been up to. They'd heard Caitlin shouting obscenities, but that wasn't unusual. She had looked pretty wild, in more ways than one, when she emerged. 'She's jealous,' said Jemma. 'Always has been.'

John looked surprised. 'Surely not. Queen Caitlin jealous of Hamish?'

'The son and heir,' said Jemma. 'The boy with a mother and father and everything that's normal. Whereas she's the little girl we minded. It doesn't matter how many times we tell her she's the daughter we never had, she doesn't believe us. She likes being with us, so she's reasonably nice to you and me. But she takes out her anger and spite on Hamish. And Helen too, of course.

'Remember when Caitlin used to bite Hamish? Before she could even talk? And how she pinched him? And later on she would dob him in for anything she could find. And ever since she hit puberty, she's been using sex to make him miserable. I told you about that day on the beach.'

John never ceased to be amazed at how clever Jemma and Helen were at working people out. Years of practice, he supposed. Years of dealing with people rather than events or machines or cold hard facts. 'Well, whether she's biting him or flashing him,' he said, 'I hope she does get into a Sydney university. They're better off apart. And I think Helen would benefit from the distance too.'

Jemma rolled over in bed and cuddled up to her husband. Caitlin's tantrum had not deflected the glory from her wonderful day. The success was hers. She'd worked hard, staying up so late to get everything done that on most nights during December she had felt sick with exhaustion. But when Christmas arrived, the adrenaline she'd been counting on had kicked in. She looked good and felt marvellous. She had made them all laugh and sing. She had made everyone happy. She curled her arms around John's neck.

'I wish Helen had a good man,' she said. 'Good loving is all she needs. Don't you think?'

John, about to put his arm around his wife, lay still and was silent. He no longer knew how Jemma expected him to respond when she talked about Helen.

John wished that when he was in bed with his wife, Jemma would talk less and do more. But for Jemma, talking often proved to be an aphrodisiac. Unfortunately, the talking often went on for so long that by the time Jemma was in the mood to make love, John would be too close to sleep to raise any enthusiasm.

'It's a cruel world,' said Jemma, as if she'd glanced into his mind.

Of course, John and Helen had never discussed sex. It would have been like playing football blindfolded at the edge of a cliff. But Jemma and Helen discussed aspects of their own sexuality quite regularly and Jemma had apprised John of more than he needed to know about Helen's physical requirements.

'She doesn't really want sex at all, you know,' Jemma went on. 'She just wants love. Security. Someone to hold her and protect her and make her feel safe. Now that I know how horrible it was for her as a child, I can understand that, can't you? She never got that with Nigel. From what I can gather, she just did everything he told her to do, no matter how weird it was. She just obeyed him. She seems to behave as if every man is her father and she's frightened not to do what they want.

'I think, deep down, Helen actually hates men,' said Jemma, as John lay beside her, staring at the ceiling, wondering how to shut her up without sending her into a sulk. 'Have I ever told you that she never even had an orgasm until she met Tom's father? Of course she didn't hate *him*. She says she loved him, but if that's true, it's hard to believe she only knew him for one night. Real love takes years to grow.'

Jumping on her wouldn't work, thought John. He'd tried and failed too many times. Even kissing her passionately no longer had any effect. She usually just kept talking.

'He must have said something or done something to make her fall in love with him awfully quickly,' said Jemma, 'something no man had ever done to her before . . .'

John didn't want to think about Tom's father doing something to Helen that no man had done before. He toyed briefly with the idea of sliding down in the bed and trying something no man had ever done to Jemma. He sighed. Anything other than conventional lovemaking was strictly against her rules. He was likely to get his head crushed between her thighs.

'...anyway, she finally had an orgasm,' Jemma was saying, but things were looking up. She was casually unbuttoning her pyjama jacket. 'Just the one, though. Imagine that,' said Jemma, with a faraway look in her eye as she absent-mindedly reached for John. 'One orgasm in a lifetime.'

John turned towards her and obediently cupped his hand around her beautiful breast. 'Well,' said John. Jemma finally looked at him. He was smiling. She grinned back and he relaxed in the warmth of it. Long before he had become acquainted with Jemma's body, it was her smile, her wide white smile, which he had loved most.

Busting, thought John. That was how he'd felt getting ready for his trip to Ireland. Busting to get away from it all. From work, from committees and meetings, from disaffected small-town advertisers whose egos needed to be constantly stroked. From home, from the mowing and pruning and crumbling grouting, from the timber that always needed another coat of stain, from the windows that always stuck. Who had managed to convince him that a timber house would be as easy to maintain as brick? Yes, truthfully, he had even wanted to get away from his marriage, just for a little while. From the constant maintenance that had been required since secrecy and guilt had set in and weakened it more than either of them would ever admit.

He had wanted to go to Ireland ever since he was a child. He remembered the strange black fantasy tales his mother had told them at bedtime in her soft sing-song voice, stories of banshees and leprechauns, of brave deeds and terrifying creatures, of spells and enchantments, reading to them from old books with crackling pages that her own mother had passed on to her. In fact, it had been John's extensive knowledge of warrior knights and magic creatures which had equipped him for rapid promotion through the ranks of the Wildcats.

For years he had longed to see the country where his father and mother had been born, to visit his grandparents' graves, to see the emerald green vistas, to eat black pudding and potato cake, to drink Guinness in pubs full of music. To play soccer on a field of satin grass. To ride a horse along a beach. To go back to where the story of his life had really begun.

He had intended going on his Irish adventure in 1971. But then he had met Jemma and everything had changed.

Largely because of John's interest in all things Irish, for the past ten years 2SR had enjoyed a relationship with a sister station near Dublin, in the coastal suburb of Strangle. Two years earlier, the manager of Radio Strangle had been to visit Siren's Rock, taking back with him a briefcase full of Australiana and a fat list of ideas for Irish–Australian radio promotions. The highlight of Callum Clancy's visit had been the nights he spent with John, Jemma and Helen, eating Helen's best recipes, drinking John's best wines and giving them all lessons in Irish dancing — for which he had been rewarded on his last night with Jemma's boisterous demonstration of all he had taught her.

Callum was now keen to return the hospitality and John was in a position to take him up on it. As the post-Christmas period was the quietest time of the 2SR year, John decided to make the most of the opportunity. First, he'd visit a few English stations, to take a good look at the BBC's regional programming. Then Jemma would join him in Ireland, where they'd embark on a three-week driving tour, spending two days at Radio Strangle when they reached Dublin.

'Don't be silly,' Helen said to Jemma after Callum Clancy had called to extend his invitation to include 2SR's top-rating personality. What he'd actually said to John was: 'Bring that gorgeous, sexy wife of yours. And bring the little blonde honey for me.'

'It's a brilliant idea,' said Jemma. 'If you won't come, I'm not going.'

'What a gooseberry I'd be!' said Helen.

'Don't be silly,' said Jemma. 'You two will get much more out of it than I will. John's always wanted to see Ireland and so have you since you had Tom. And you can do interviews with the Dublin people, and run them on your show when you get back.'

'John can do that,' said Helen. 'I really don't think ...'

'You're going,' said Jemma.

THREE WISHES

On the first of January, like a reluctant housekeeper catapulted into action by the new year, summer finally gathered up her energy, sighed in resignation and started. Slapping her hot, wet sponge over the town, damping down the air and the people, sending moisture to seep into clean washing and sugar pots and the pages of books. Setting up shrill choruses of birds, toads and multi-legged creatures. Sweeping out any remaining crumbs of human vitality and replacing them with inertia.

But there was plenty of human activity at the Sullivan house. Jemma was throwing John a leaving party. And what a party. Everyone who could be spared from the radio station was there, and so were all the friends John had made during the years when Hamish was the extra-curricular kid. Jemma's playgroup girls came with their children, and her friends from FNC Channel Five. The local councillors courted Helen, while two local politicians avoided her. The Sirens came, postponing auditions for *The Importance of Being Earnest* but taking the opportunity to plead with Jemma to return to the stage to play Lady Bracknell. Hamish's house-mates came and so, to their delight, did Caitlin's remote, snake-hipped girlfriends in their tiny tank tops and tight pants. John's favourite sisters flew up from Sydney.

Grezza made it over from Perth with his new young wife, all red lipstick, big breasts, thin legs and teeth that were a magnificent tribute to her orthodontist. 'Renee's just told me she's pregnant,' he grumbled to John as he helped him distribute beers. The skinny boy he used to be was lost in layers of padding; his blue eyes were bloodshot. 'Jeez mate, I've already done this once and me kids are nearly grown-up and Judy's doing very nicely, thank you very much, Grezza — and now Renee wants to start all bloody over again.'

Even Babs came over from Bridgetown with Joy, Warren and the children. Joy, her golden hair coiffed, her make-up faultless, her clothes pressed to perfection, looked more like a young version of her mother every time Helen saw her. She had a social smile now, which she clicked on and off like an electric light; in this thin, self-satisfied, immaculately groomed woman, Helen saw no sign of her plump and giggly little sister. It made her shiver.

Babs moaned to Marte that Siren's Rock had never been the same for her since Helen had been working in radio. 'I couldn't live in a place where people point and whisper about me,' she said, flicking crumbs from her rose chiffon blouse.

'People have always pointed and whispered in this town, Mrs Winter,' said Marte. 'It happens to us all, sooner or later.'

'You know what I'm referring to, Marte,' said Babs. She glanced around. 'Is *anyone* going to offer me a cup of tea, I wonder?'

'Helen said you knew nothing about *that* business, Mrs Winter,' said Marte coldly. She was resting in a chair and couldn't decently get away. 'That's what all the papers said. She never blamed you to nobody.'

'Helen's a liar,' spat Babs. And then flushed in confusion beneath her powder.

Jemma held the party in her mountain-facing front yard and hired a huge spit roast. Hamish and his friends hacked off hunks of meat for the guests, sandwiching the lamb into cones of fresh pitta bread and ladling Helen's homemade onion gravy over the lot.

'Souvlakia!' said George, licking his grey chops and directing people to the salads gleaming with olives and fetta cheese.

'I always think foreign food is so difficult to digest,' Babs murmured to Marte.

Wine and beer flowed. There was good music, a great deal of talk and laughter, and several people proposed toasts to John and Jemma, generous hosts, pillars of the community, a charming and genuine couple who had put Siren's Rock on the map.

It was a great party. It cost them a fortune. But, as Jemma said to John afterwards, it was a great excuse to get everyone together, and they all had a whale of a time.

Two days later, on the eve of John's departure, the house was clean and tidy and back to normal.

'It's time for a talk,' Jemma told him, as she brought two glasses of cold white wine out to the verandah and they sat down in their rockers.

'That sounds ominous,' smiled John. 'We'll only be apart for a couple of weeks.'

She smiled. 'I want to ask you something important before you go.'

'I love you,' said John obediently.

Jemma smiled at him and sipped her wine. 'I know,' she said. 'But have I made you happy?'

'Yes,' said John. 'And with a bit of luck you're about to make me even happier.'

'I'm serious,' said Jemma.

'So am I. I've got an early start. Let's drink up and go to bed.'

'John, please,' she said. 'Not tonight.'

Jemma stood up and went to lean on the verandah rail. The sun had set, leaving streaks of pink over the distant purpling mountains. The sky behind her was still a pale, pretty blue. She turned around and looked at him steadily. 'What I want to know is, are you happy because of me?'

John sighed. 'Jemma, you've been making me happy all my life. My only regret,' he added slowly, 'is that I haven't been able to do the same for you.'

Jemma looked miserable. 'I knew you thought that,' she said. She turned her back on him and gazed at the last traces of sunset.

'Well, it's true,' said John. 'We can't pretend otherwise.'

Jemma leaned back against the rail, cradling her wine glass in both hands. 'You've made me happy on this verandah,' she said. 'Right here, when we've just been sitting and talking and being together, this is where I've had some of my happiest times. Because of you. And on holidays. In Florence and on Lassos of course. And all those weekends at Berry Beach and the picnics at the Cove. Diving under waves. Reading on the beach. You and me together. The others too, but mainly you and me.'

John began to wonder where the conversation was leading. Tiny feathers of anxiety fluttered in his chest. 'What's wrong?' said John. 'What are you trying to tell me?'

'Only that nobody is happy all the time. But *my* happiest times, my most fulfilled and peaceful times, have been because of you.'

She was speaking with a backing group, a chorus of cicadas. John waited. He felt there was more.

'About my wanting to be famous,' said Jemma.

And there it was.

'I know what you're thinking,' she said.

He laughed without humour and began the required response: 'You've done so much for this town. You've helped so many people, probably saved hundreds of young mothers from chucking their babies off their patios . . .'

'I know,' said Jemma. 'You don't have to say it all again.'

'You've given Siren's Rock a standard of theatre we had no right to expect,' said John, ignoring her. He was sincere but it was hard not to give the impression that he knew the words by rote. 'You've created, you know, a culture in this place which would never have existed without you. And most of all,' said John, 'you've looked after us all.'

'And you've done the same for me,' said Jemma. 'I have been so blessed.'

For a minute or two John was so surprised he could think of nothing to say. He stood up. 'I wish,' he said, looking past her at the mountains, 'that being blessed was enough.'

'It is,' said Jemma softly.

'No, it's not,' said John. 'The truth is,' he said quietly, 'that your dream came true for Helen. And you got hers. I wanted you to have it all, but . . .'

'I *have* had it all,' said Jemma. There were tears in her voice.

He came close, put out a finger and touched a teardrop that stood on her cheek. He put his finger in his mouth and tasted the salt. He didn't know what to say.

'I'm sorry,' said Jemma. She put her empty wine glass down and slipped her arms loosely around John's neck. 'I'm sorry I have spent so much of my life trying to be some

454

kind of star, when all that really meant was being recognised and admired by people I don't know or care about. You're the only people who count, you and Hamish, Mum and Dad, Tom and Caitlin. And Helen.'

He put his arms around her and she leaned lightly against him, gazing over his broad shoulder into the house they had built together.

'I have three wishes,' said Jemma, sliding her arms away from his neck and putting them around him. 'If you happen to come across a leprechaun in Ireland.'

'What are they?' asked John, no longer sure of what she might say.

'My first wish would be to make Hamish like himself.'

'Hamish is going to be okay,' said John. 'Just give him time.'

'And my second wish would be to make you as happy as you've made me,' said Jemma.

He kissed her. 'This leprechaun will get off lightly,' he said, 'because being married to you has always made me happier than I had any right to be.'

She smiled. 'You have every right to be happy,' she said. 'So that leaves us with my third wish.'

'Which is?'

'To give Helen what I've always had. What I've always taken for granted.'

'Well,' said John. 'That might be harder.'

'Helen's not happy,' said Jemma. 'I wanted to make her happy, but in the end I couldn't manage it.'

John tightened his arms around her. 'We're not talking about Helen,' he said, almost impatiently. 'We're talking about us.'

'Helen is part of us, John. She always has been. You know that.'

He didn't answer.

Jemma smiled. 'At the risk of enraging any feminist fairies who might be lurking in the shrubbery, all Helen has ever really needed is a lovely man. It's just that lovely men are a bit thin on the ground, especially when you get to our age.'

John sighed.

'Maybe she'll meet one in Ireland,' said Jemma.

John put his head into the curve between Jemma's neck and shoulder. 'Let's go to bed,' he said.

He made love to her after all. Gently, taking his time. She didn't seem to mind. For a change, she wasn't in a hurry. For a change, she didn't seem inclined to talk. He noticed her body was almost as perfect again as it had been when she was twenty-one. 'You're more beautiful than you've ever been,' he whispered as he stroked her flat belly. 'Without even trying,' murmured Jemma vaguely but he was too absorbed in her to wonder what she meant.

Afterwards, when Jemma rolled away to her own side of the bed and pulled the sheet up to her chin, John stretched and smiled.

'Have we done it?' he whispered. 'Is this us finally living happily ever after?'

JUST THE TWO OF US

He had almost literally crushed her in his arms at Belfast airport. She had emerged from the arrivals gate smiling, her cheeks unusually pink, a long cream wool coat wrapped around her slender figure and tied tightly at the waist. The coat was soft but her hair was softer, a cloud of silvery gold. He held her for far too long, inhaling her heavenly smell, keeping her close, and instinctively she seemed to curl up inside the protective circle of his arms. For a moment neither of them spoke.

It wasn't until they were walking together towards the exit doors, John pushing her luggage on a trolley and Helen exclaiming in delight at the vast map of Ireland etched into the carpet under their feet, that he said, 'So she's really not coming then? Do you know where she is? What it is she's doing?'

'No,' said Helen. 'None of us is allowed to know. She says she wants to see if she can do something all on her own.'

John snorted. 'How's Tom?' he asked as he lugged the bags into the back of the hire car. 'And Caitlin?'

Then he turned to her and smiled. 'I've decided not to mind,' he said. 'We're going to have a marvellous time anyway.'

'That's what she wants,' said Helen, exhaling relief as John started the engine.

A week after John's arrival in the UK, Jemma had rung him to tell him she wasn't coming. 'I'm sorry. I don't want to disappoint you, but something's come up.'

'What?' John realised he wasn't as surprised as he should have been. He had called her twice before, and she had been unusually evasive about herself, wanting to talk only about what he was doing.

'Well now, here's the thing,' Jemma had said. 'You're going to have to trust my judgement on this. It's been a big decision, obviously, and I'll tell you about it when you get back. But for the time being, I want to keep it secret. All I can tell you is that it's huge. And I have to do it by myself.'

'Well, is it a show?' John had asked. 'Have they talked you into doing Lady Bracknell?'

She had laughed. 'No, I'm not doing Lady B again. Don't guess. Just have a good time with Helen and tell me all about it when you get back.'

'So Helen's still coming?'

'Of course. And she can't wait. You know how much she's been wanting to see Ireland. And how much I haven't, if it comes to that.'

'So have you found yourself a new job? Is it something in television?'

'John,' she had said, beginning to sound annoyed, 'I said don't guess. It's something hugely important that I've never done before. Please let me do it and don't make a fuss.'

'You were never coming, were you?' John was furious. 'You had this . . . this *idea*,' he'd spat the word, 'long before I left, didn't you? I've only been gone a week. Nothing that *huge* would have come up that fast.'

'Okay,' Jemma had replied. 'Yes. A little while before.'

'So what you said, about feeling fulfilled by our life together ... that was all bullshit.'

'No,' Jemma's voice had echoed on the other side of the world. 'I meant every word. I still do. John, please trust me.'

'All that talk the night before I left,' he'd said, beginning to think about it. 'You said you wished you'd enjoyed our life together more. Why? Are you leaving me? Is there another man involved?'

He'd heard her take a deep breath. 'John, don't do this. You know you are the only man I have ever loved. You always will be.'

'Then come to Ireland.'

'No. I want to do this and I have to do it now. It can't wait. John, please don't make this any more difficult than it already is.'

'It doesn't sound as if it's very difficult at all,' he'd said tersely.

'Well, actually, it is. There's a lot of organisation involved. But for once I want to do it all by myself, without you having to help me. I want to pull this off *alone*.'

'And who is going to look after the kids while you're off *alone*?'

'John, I was going to be away anyway. Hamish is still on holidays, so he'll be at home. Caitlin is perfectly capable of looking after herself and Mum and Dad have Tom. Anyway, I'm not going far,' she'd added quickly. 'I'll still be available if they need me.'

He was silent. She had waited for him to speak. Amazingly she had waited for quite a long time. Finally she said: 'This is costing a fortune. Maybe you could call me back when you've calmed down.'

John had taken a deep breath. 'No need,' he said. 'Good luck then, Jemma. Hope it goes well. See you in a few weeks. Give the kids my love. Tell Helen I'll meet her at Belfast airport on the fourteenth. As arranged.'

And then he had hung up.

They drove from Belfast to the harbourside town of Larne, where they lunched on scampi and chips and glasses of beer, and Helen told John what Tom and Caitlin and Hamish had been up to in the previous fortnight, carefully not mentioning much about Jemma.

The day was cold and bleak but it was cosy in the car. As they drove alongside the green Glens of Antrim, John talked about all that he'd seen and done in England. They passed through Ballygalley, Glenarm and Cushendall, with the slate-coloured sea brooding silently beside them. When they reached the Giant's Causeway, they stopped and ambled down the sweep of hilly land which led to the extraordinary layers of hexagonal columns. John was fascinated by it all, racing from one vantage point to another, climbing the green hills and running down again, finally grabbing Helen's hand and tugging her along with him as they picked their way over the columns, the icy breeze making their eyes water and their noses run. 'I'm not dressed for this,' said Helen. 'I'll be more sensible tomorrow.'

She was exhausted by the time darkness fell. They found a cottage offering bed and breakfast not far from the Causeway and booked two bedrooms for the night before finding some dinner. But a grey veil of fatigue drifted across Helen's face before she had even finished her salmon and the delicious meal was wasted. She kissed John's cheek at the door of her room and thanked him for a beautiful day.

They met at the breakfast table, where their hostess, a large woman with loose lips and a stiff perm, plonked huge helpings of eggs, bacon and sausages in front of them. Helen drank three cups of strong, sweet tea, while John ate everything in front of him and thought how Jemma would have panicked loud and long at the prospect of starting the day with so much food — before demolishing the lot.

He then produced his guide books and showed Helen the route he had mapped out for their tour. His plan was to drive right around the island, beginning and ending in the North, but allowing plenty of time to explore the South.

They drove through Derry and Donegal to Bundoran, where John fulfilled his dream of riding a horse along the beautiful ocean beach. Then down the west coast, past great glooming tablelands and the frowning Cliffs of Moher. '*Ryan's Daughter*,' sighed Helen. 'One of our all-time favourites.' They toured the Ring of Kerry and, turning east, made their way to Cork by way of Killarney and Macroom, then on to Waterford. Everywhere they went there were sheep, stone walls, green grass and misty rain. But despite the short distances they travelled, the landforms varied enormously, from the shimmering lakes of Killarney to postcard meadows, mauve mountains and rocky hills.

They passed through villages of pastel-terraced houses and stopped at a variety of pubs to eat crispy pasties and ploughman's lunches, washed down with Guinness, dark and foaming in the glass. They clambered up into the hills, walked along flat country roads past farms and flocks of sheep, and wandered through the cobbled streets of tiny towns. Often they drove in silence, listening to the music from flutes and haunting pipes that John was collecting at the tourist shops along the way. It was restful, thought John, being silent with Helen. There was no pressure to speak. There was no one calling him on the phone, or briefing him for a meeting, or shoving piles of paper under his nose and asking him to make a decision. There was nobody shouting or showing off or telling him what he had to do.

There was just Helen, speaking softly from time to time, or laughing with delight in her husky way, or sitting silently, peacefully beside him.

Each afternoon when it grew dark, they would look for a house offering bed and breakfast. They stayed in cottages, farmhouses and a few modern bungalows, all of them offering thick floral quilts, corner cupboards full of ornaments and family photos, and feeble, frustrating showers. 'There must be a rule book,' said Helen, 'with a list of B&B essentials: fat quilt, doilies, picture of Uncle Seamus on the mantel, statue of girl with ringlets, frilly curtains, dodgy shower.'

'Bacon and eggs,' said John.

'Potato bread and tea,' added Helen.

Some of the places in their directory had closed for the winter, but there was no shortage of houses with a bedroom for each of them. And if the friendly couples running these cosy establishments wondered at the obviously close relationship between the two, they kept their thoughts to themselves.

Sometimes they talked about Siren's Rock. It was impossible not to draw comparisons with the small towns they were visiting. Often they talked about their children. And laughed, and wondered, and shook their heads. Gradually, inevitably, they began talking about Jemma. As the days passed, John's resentment dwindled. It was difficult to maintain the anger, when this was the best holiday he'd had since Italy and Greece, more than twenty-five years ago.

He and Jemma were both doing something they had always wanted to do. Where was the rule that said they had to spend all their good times together?

In any case, how could they not speak about Jemma? She had been involved in everything they had ever done. By the fifth day, it was possible for John to say: 'Jemma would love those mountains. Those are her sort of hills.' By the sixth night, in a small candlelit tavern, waiting for the musicians to decide on a song, Helen could comfortably raise her glass of wine and say: 'To our absent friend. Let her be having as good a time as us.'

John raised his glass too, and smiled. 'To Jemma,' he said. 'Captain of the Wildcats. Mistress of her own destiny.'

They drank. He looked at Helen over the rim of his glass, drank again, then put the wine down.

'So are you really having a good time?' he asked.

She beamed and answered but the musicians struck up a song at that moment and her words were drowned out. He leaned forward so she could put her lips close to his ear: 'I never imagined it would be so ...'

He turned his head. Her lips brushed his. She jerked her head away and sat back quickly, feeling the heat rush into her face. John, too, looked embarrassed.

'I'm sorry,' he shouted. He had to shout. The musicians were now in full voice right beside them. 'I didn't mean to ...'

She was shaking her head. Couldn't hear. She waved her hands in front of her face, indicating that he shouldn't worry. Dropped her hands and smiled at him, then looked away and became absorbed in the music.

ORDINARY OLD LOVE

'Come to the beach,' Jemma had said to Helen, a week after John had flown off to England. 'There's something I want to tell you.'

Jemma collected Helen from work and drove her straight to Mermaid Cove. A breeze blew off the water, offering a welcome respite from the blanket of humidity that was stifling Siren's Rock. The day was hazy, the sun hanging behind a deceptive screen of pale clouds. Jemma was wearing shorts and a green T-shirt that hugged her curves.

'You've got so *slim*,' said Helen, happy for her, noticing also that Jemma was wearing a lot of make-up for the beach. She must have been out somewhere flash, Helen thought. It was twenty years since Helen herself had worn the heavy pancake make-up and kohl of her youth. Her skin was good now, soft and fair, and she coloured her face only with lipstick and a little mascara. She was still wearing her work skirt and a sleeveless white top. She took off her good shoes and left them in the car. Jemma threw her sandals into the back seat. 'Let's walk,' she said.

'Not long now,' said Jemma as they set out along the sand,

heading away from the summer visitors who were bobbing about between the flags.

'I can't wait,' said Helen. 'I'm as excited as Tom was the night before Christmas.'

She turned to her friend and impulsively grabbed her hand. 'This is so lovely of you, Jemma. I wish you knew how much it means to me to have this holiday.'

Jemma glanced at their clasped fingers and Helen went to pull her hand away. But Jemma tightened her grip and laughed. 'It's okay,' she said. 'You can hold on to me as much as you like.'

They walked a little further, hand in hand, before Helen said: 'Is something wrong? Are you missing him already?'

'No,' said Jemma. 'I don't miss him at all. That's what I want to talk to you about.'

'Don't be silly,' said Helen. 'Of course you miss him. *I* miss him. Tom misses him. We all miss him.'

'I know,' said Jemma. 'That's what I want to talk to you about,' she repeated.

'*What* do you want to talk to me about?' asked Helen.

Jemma squeezed Helen's hand. 'I'm not coming to Ireland with you,' she said. 'Something really important has come up and I'm going away somewhere else.'

It was the first secret she'd kept from Helen.

Months had passed and she had managed not to say a word.

At first it was because words would have made it real. Least said, soonest mended, she told herself. Another mountain out of a mole hill. I'm not going through all that business again, she thought. It will go away. Then, when it didn't, in order to maintain the equanimity she had worked so hard to achieve, silence on the subject was a resolution.

Long before summer finally swamped Siren's Rock, Jemma's secret had become her obsession.

One day, buying magazines for her mother, she saw an article about a drug that was proving to be extremely effective as a non-invasive treatment for breast cancer. She bought an extra copy, cut the article out and put it in her wallet. She would look into that, she thought. Soon.

In her bathroom that night Jemma realised she had known all along. Had known her own body better than any doctors.

There was a fragment of smashed concrete in her left breast.

Still she did nothing. She tried not to think about it. She knew it was foolish, but she did nothing.

She told herself there was too much to do. She was so busy. So many people needed her. Doctors' appointments and tests took up so much time, especially living in a place like Siren's Rock where you had to travel so far to see anyone who knew what they were talking about. She would do something soon, she thought. Soon.

Later, lying on her pillows with her mother's rough dry hand holding hers, she would say to Marte: 'That wasn't like me at all. Pulling a blind down. That's what Helen used to do.' But Marte shook her head. 'It's not the same thing. You always ignored what you didn't want to believe.'

Jemma had given John's plane one last huge wave and driven straight from the airport to Bridgetown Hospital. She had been referred to Dr Charles Casey, who had flash rooms in the new wing, with lots of glass and modern prints in frames of pale grey wood.

Dr Casey was a specialist. She liked him as soon as he took her warm hand in both of his and drew her into his office. He had crinkly white hair, a young tanned face and incredibly blue eyes. Wore cream slacks and a pale blue shirt. Said it was an enormous pleasure to meet her and sounded as if he meant it.

'I saw you on television,' he said as she sat down and crossed her long legs. 'You have done so much for this district, Mrs Sullivan. It was a marvellous documentary on your life.'

Jemma looked at him steadily. 'The question is, is that life going to continue?'

He looked back, just as steadily. 'That's a very big question and one that is difficult for me to answer at this stage. None of us knows how long we are going to live. You might walk out of here and get hit by a bus. So might I.'

'Dr Casey,' said Jemma, 'we both know why I'm here. You don't have to flatter me — my self-esteem is fine. I also know it is possible that a crazy bus driver could knock us down on our way home this afternoon, although it strikes me that the odds of that happening to us both are pretty long. In the meantime, you have a letter from my GP on your desk which contains information about my life which I ...' Her voice suddenly ran out. She clasped her hands tightly in her lap.

He stirred. 'Mrs Sullivan ...'

Jemma unclasped her hands and reached for her bag. 'I've been reading about this drug,' she began.

He shook his head.

'Dr Rajaratnan didn't want to talk about it either,' said Jemma miserably.

'Mrs Sullivan,' he said gently. 'Early detection is terribly important with any type of cancer.'

Jemma began to knead her hands. 'I had a funny sort of lump a year ago,' she said. 'It should be on my records, there. They sent me away. They said it was nothing. As it happens, they were wrong, because it came back. Anyway, there's no point crying over spilt milk.' She choked a little on the words. 'I was too busy to worry about it.'

'But you felt something was wrong?'

'I decided to try mind over matter,' said Jemma.

'And you didn't want to know,' said Dr Casey.

'No,' said Jemma, her voice soft. 'Which is not like me at all. What worried me most was how it would affect my family if I wasn't there. They all need me, you see. My husband, my best friend, her kids, our son, my parents ...' Despite her efforts a small sound, a cross between a croak and a sob, escaped among the words. 'Usually when I'm worried about something I talk about it. This time I didn't.'

'I don't know how you've kept going,' said Dr Casey. 'You look well. But looks can be deceiving.'

'I'm not really feeling well at all,' said Jemma, suddenly sounding defeated, slowly dragging her hands down her face, distorting her eyes. 'I'm just a really good actress. I feel like shit. I've never been the type to get headaches, you know? But now I do. I worry about everything my body does, even when it's probably quite normal. Like, there's this little cloudy spot in my eye ...'

'I'd like to examine you,' said Dr Casey, 'to see if I concur with Dr Rajaratnam's diagnosis.'

On the narrow bed she closed her eyes while his hands moved professionally over her body, pressing and prodding. When she was dressed and facing him again she looked searchingly at his face.

'Please, don't beat around the bush,' she said. She made a huge effort to speak normally, although there was now a knot in her throat, and her eyes had begun to sting.

'I'll need to arrange a few more tests,' said Dr Casey, 'because of the problems you've been having with headaches and vision. Then we can decide together what treatment is best for you.'

'So it's bad? It *has* spread?'

'Yes,' said Dr Casey.

'Will I have to have a mastectomy?' asked Jemma.

'It's a possibility,' he said. 'Or even a lumpectomy, which is a partial ...'

'I know what it is,' said Jemma. 'Will I have to have chemotherapy? Radiotherapy?'

'Let's get these other tests done first,' said Dr Casey.

He was concerned when she told him she did not want her husband to be involved at this stage, and why.

'John's been looking forward to this trip for so long,' she said. 'He's finally *doing* something, and better still, he's doing it for *himself*. That's terribly important,' said Jemma earnestly.

Dr Casey began to argue. 'Your condition is very serious, Mrs Sullivan. Positive thinking is vital, but so is the support of your husband ...'

'Look,' said Jemma. 'I've thought it all through. It's not just this trip. He watched his mother die from cancer. How cruel would it be to put him through that again? Waiting and watching ...'

'How cruel would it be to shut him out?' asked the doctor.

'I'm not shutting him out,' said Jemma. 'I'm just saving him an extra few weeks of misery. I'll tell him what's going on when he gets back, but I don't want him racing home to be at my bedside. And that means keeping this from the rest of my family as well.'

'Jemma,' he said, 'I can't tell you how important it is for you to have someone to support you through this. I don't know your husband but I'm sure he would want ...'

'What *I* want is the most important thing now. *I* want John and Helen to have one more good memory,' she said.

'Helen?'

'My best friend Helen is going to join my husband in Ireland.'

He looked quizzically at her.

Jemma smiled, a lovely smile, the end of the argument. 'Look, I don't expect you to understand,' she said. 'But it's important for us all.'

Helen argued with Jemma all the way to the rocks at the far end of the cove. She was frantic, pleading for some sort of explanation. Jemma was sullenly determined to keep her secret. She had no intention of changing her mind. Of course Helen then said she wouldn't go either. Jemma said she had to. They couldn't both let John down.

At the rocks Helen sat down in the sand, disregarding her good skirt.

'This is awful,' she said. 'This will spoil everything.'

'It won't if you still go,' said Jemma, looking down at her. 'You two will have a lovely time. I know you will.'

Helen looked at her angrily. 'No, you don't, Jemma. You don't know that at all. You can't *make* us have a good time just so you will feel better about disappointing us both so horribly.'

Jemma sat down and drew up her knees. 'I know you will enjoy Ireland, Julie, because I know something you don't,' she said.

'What?' asked Helen bitterly.

Jemma drew pictures with her finger in the sand. 'You love him,' she said.

Helen sat very still.

After a while she said: 'Of course I love him. We all love him. He's a lovable man. And you love him most of all. And he loves you.'

'Maybe,' said Jemma. 'In our own way. But we're not *in* love with each other any more. We rub along well and we're good friends, but the thrill has been gone for a long time. Whereas I think you are actually *in* love . . .'

'*No!*' Helen shouted. 'No, Jemma,' she said more quietly. 'No, I'm not. I've never . . .'

'It's okay,' said Jemma. 'It's okay, Julie. I know you've never done anything behind my back.' She smiled.

Helen did not smile back.

'I know you have probably never even admitted it to yourself,' said Jemma, 'and of course *he* has no idea. But I've been doing an awful lot of thinking in the last few months. Since I left work, I've been coming down here a lot, and thinking by myself. And I've realised a lot of things. About myself and John and you. And do you know what? It should have been you and John all along.

'I mean,' said Jemma, raising her voice over Helen's protest, 'you're so compatible. You think the same way, you're interested in the same things, you're comfortable being quiet together . . . He should have married you in the first place, and then the two of you could have lived quietly and happily ever after while you watched me bucketing around the world being outrageous and famous and fabulous and wild. The way I wanted to be.'

Helen raised her eyes from the sand and stared at her.

'John had a crush on me when we were kids,' Jemma continued, 'probably because I was more interesting than his dreary little sisters. So when we met in Florence, at a time when he was pumping testosterone like nothing on earth and I was dying of frustration and desperate for romance, he married me. It was a good marriage because John and I have always been good friends,' she said earnestly, 'but until now neither of us got what we really wanted.'

Helen's heart was thumping so hard that she felt ill.

'If this plan of mine works out,' said Jemma, 'I *might* not come back. I might finally escape from Siren's Rock. And if that happens and you and John are together, looking after the kids together and everything, I won't feel so bad and everyone will be happy and . . .'

'Jemma,' Helen said. 'Stop.'

Jemma began to speak loudly and rapidly. 'Don't you see, Julie? We were cast in the wrong roles. Sophia Loren would never have been asked to play the respectable housewife. She would have been the vibrant single woman, taking lovers, scandalising the town, being famous all over the world, having the odd illegitimate child who, of course, would have been taken in and raised by the sweet but sultry Julie Christie character who was happily married to John Gavin . . .'

Helen scrambled to her feet. 'Stop!' she shouted hoarsely. 'Jemma, what are you saying? You're *leaving* him, is that what you're doing? You're leaving him and you want me to pick up the pieces? You're leaving *John*? You're leaving *me*? You're leaving us all and you think you can just organise for John and me to get together so that *you* won't feel so bad? Don't be so *stupid*, Jemma. You are being selfish and stupid! Stupid! Stupid!'

Jemma looked up. Her mouth drooped and her eyes were full of pain. 'It's okay,' she said softly. 'I don't mind you loving him. I *want* you to love him. I want you to take care of him for me. You said it yourself,' said Jemma, 'he's a lovable man.'

'He's your husband, Jemma,' said Helen.

'You can't tell me you don't fancy him, Julie,' said Jemma, getting to her feet. 'I'm actually *not* stupid.'

'He's your *husband*, Jemma,' repeated Helen.

'If you're referring to the Catholic thing,' said Jemma, 'I'm sure that wouldn't be a problem.'

They stood on the beach and stared at each other.

'I think you're sick,' said Helen.

Jemma was silent. For a long moment it seemed she was going to weep. But she took a fresh grip on her iron will and slowly, incomprehensibly, began to smile.

Helen looked at her warily. The smile widened and whitened. Jemma's lovely green eyes began to sparkle. She threw back her head and opened her mouth wide as a howl of laughter issued from her throat. The howl was followed by another. And another.

Helen began to laugh too. They stood on the beach and laughed until water poured from their eyes. They laughed until they could stand up no longer, and flopped back onto the sand.

'Look at us!' gasped Jemma. 'Listen to us!'

'Listen to us!' shouted Helen. 'Listen!' But they could neither listen nor say anything that made sense.

Eventually they picked themselves up and Jemma drove them back to Siren's Rock, but still, they only had to look at each other for the laughter to wash through them again. Helen swung between shaking her head at the absurdity of Jemma's words and letting laughter consume her. How long had it been since they'd laughed like that?

When they pulled up outside her house, Helen sighed and tried to speak normally, although the shouting and hysteria had reduced her voice to little more than a husky wheeze.

'I'm going to pretend I never heard any of it,' she said. 'I'm writing it off as the mad dreaming of a menopausal maniac.'

'That's wonderful, Julie,' said Jemma. 'You should write that down. Did you read it somewhere?'

They both burst out laughing again. Helen scrabbled around to find her shoes. It was hot in the car, even with the windows down. 'I'm serious now, Jemma,' she said carefully. 'If you must have this secret adventure, go and have it. I'll help you, I'll still go to Ireland and everything. But *only* if you promise me one thing. Promise me you'll come back when it's over. Promise me you'll come back to us all.'

Jemma frowned. Perspiration trickled from her forehead. 'Julie,' she said slowly, 'you know how all my life I've been terrified of being ordinary?'

'Oh, Sophia, you're not . . .'

'No, listen,' said Jemma. She paused, leaned her head back against the seat, closed her eyes. 'There are people out there full of hate. There are people killing each other, and cheating on each other and hurting each other. And beating up their children.' Helen flinched. Jemma opened her eyes and looked intently at her. 'But you know what, Helen? Maybe I'm naive, but I truly believe that there is more beauty in the world than ugliness. There is beauty in every ordinary little thing. And I believe that there is more love than hate. Not sexual love, just ordinary old love, the sort of love people stop noticing. And I think that the bad things that people do to each other are outnumbered by the good things. The small acts of kindness that we take for granted. It's not so bad,' Jemma smiled, 'being ordinary.'

'That's a lovely thought, Sophia,' said Helen softly. 'You really should write that down.'

'I have,' said Jemma.

'Well,' said Helen. 'So you promise you'll come back?'

For a moment Jemma looked confused. She glanced around as if she had lost something, and blinked several times. Finally she said: 'I want to see if I can achieve something all on my own. Before I get old.'

Jemma, old? It was unthinkable. Helen put out her hand and touched her friend's face. It was as familiar to her as her own, but it was changing. Jemma's face was thinner than it had ever been and she looked tired. There were deep lines around her eyes and small pleats above her top lip.

But Helen knew that she, too, was showing signs of wear and tear. Her forehead and neck and the soft skin beneath her eyes was covered with a faint filigree of lines. Sitting this close together, with the mid-afternoon sun beating into the car, their years were etched into their faces.

Slightly dazed by heat and emotion, Helen climbed out of the car. She leaned down and looked intently into Jemma's eyes.

'You have played many roles in your life, Jemma Sullivan,' said Helen. 'But you have never been ordinary.'

For a moment Jemma's beautiful mouth softened. Then she bequeathed upon Helen her huge white smile. 'I love you, Julie,' she said, and started the engine. Helen shut the car door. Still confused, she watched Jemma's car zip around the corner and out of sight.

Jemma glanced through the windscreen at the cotton-wool sky. 'Applaud me,' she said to the waiting angels.

THE IDEA

Until she had The Idea, waking up was the worst. It was always first thing in the morning, with John lying beside her, that she felt more alone than at any other time. She would lie in bed, keeping her eyes tightly closed, hoping that when she opened them everything would be back to normal.

That's what secrets do to people, she thought. She thought this increasingly often. They isolate you. The bigger the secret, the lonelier you become. That was what had been wrong with Helen, thought Jemma. All those years she kept that terrible secret locked up in her sad little soul. But it was easy to understand why Helen had kept her secret for so long. Jemma's reasons were much less comprehensible. For a long time she hardly understood herself.

Eventually she worked out that admitting her secret would mean admitting defeat. She would have to acknowledge that she was about to fail herself and all the people she loved. After spending a lifetime trying to smooth the way for them all, she was going to hurl a deadly chunk of concrete into their pathway to happiness.

How could she tell them that she was seriously ill? Remembering Marte's long and painful struggle to recover from her stroke, her angry dependence, Jemma couldn't bear the prospect of months, perhaps years, of being ill herself. She could imagine the pain, the helplessness and the ugliness of disease; she could imagine the suffering of all the people dearest to her as they made all the sacrifices necessary to care for her, as they tended her disintegrating body, watched her scrabbling for a hold on life.

Jemma saw her condition as an overwhelming failure, a failure she had no desire to share with anyone.

Three weeks before John was due to leave for the United Kingdom, worried about what could happen if she became ill while she was travelling overseas, Jemma had finally consulted a doctor — a dark-skinned young man with an unpronounceable name. Jemma could tell from the look in his sorrowful dark eyes that the news was going to be at least as bad as she had expected, but he said they had to wait for certain tests to be done and referred her to Charles Casey. Jemma decided to postpone the appointment with the specialist until after John's departure.

While John raced around in a frenzy of activity and excitement, Jemma's days dragged. For the first time in her life, she was without work, without deadlines, without dependent children. Even Marte no longer needed her as much. Jemma had to force herself to get out of bed long after John left for work; she would haul herself into the shower, dress, pick at breakfast, and wipe down the bench tops. Then she would go out onto the verandah and wonder what to do next.

She was overwhelmed with inertia. Her body, this body which had become light and shapely again with her loss of interest in food, now weighed her down more heavily than ever, even during her fattest years. Her mind was dull and her head often ached badly. Her heart was sore, squashed beneath the treacherous slab of sadness in her breast.

Sometimes she prayed, thanking God for granting her a wonderful life and asking for an extension. Sometimes she cried, but not as much as she had expected to. Sometimes she held on to the solid wooden railings and breathed deeply, in out, in out, to suppress a burst of terror. Usually she bleakly accepted that, short of a miracle, her days as a healthy, productive person were numbered.

Numbered days are hard to fill.

The Idea came to her at Mermaid Cove. She had started driving over there almost every day, because she felt less lonely at the beach; certainly she never felt as isolated there as she did first thing every morning before and even after she opened her eyes.

Someone was usually walking beside her at the beach. Someone with a capital S, thought Jemma. Neither angel nor lover, just Someone who'd always been around.

She was standing still, with the sand sucking at her toes, when something or Someone gave her The Idea. It would make up for her failure; it would make everything all right. It would require a great deal of organisation and direction, but she was confident she could manage it.

She would work out exactly what to do and say. She decided to write it all down first, learn the words by heart if necessary, just as she did for any fine performance. So that she wasn't tempted to go overboard — always her greatest weakness. She would have to be clever. Subtle. Lucky.

Plans began forming in her mind. Something to get my teeth into, thought Jemma, something to take my mind off things.

It was the best Idea she'd ever had.

A fresh tide of energy flowed in.

Driving home she wound down the windows to let in the wind and sang loudly along with the radio. It was good to be in control again.

On Jemma's second visit to Dr Casey, he told her that the cancer had spread from her breast up into her armpit and elsewhere in her body. It was possible that there was a small malignancy growing in her brain. A lumpectomy to remove the large growth in her breast could extend her lease on life but only by a few months. And possibly only weeks.

He was impressed by the speed with which she reined in her terror.

'I suppose I should have that,' she said. 'People would think it was strange if I didn't put up a bit of a fight.'

'Perhaps you should discuss it with your husband first?'

'No,' said Jemma.

'Would you consider talking to a counsellor . . .?'

'*No!*' shouted Jemma. She stopped and took a deep breath. 'Look, John and Helen will be back soon. And for now I want to do this on my own.'

'Jemma,' said Dr Casey, 'what if it happens faster than expected? Think how they would feel if they were on the other side of the world.'

'For heaven's sake,' said Jemma impatiently. 'They'll be back in two weeks.'

He looked at her. She refused to meet his concerned blue gaze. The hollow in her stomach began to hurt.

'So what should I do now?' she asked, finally raising her eyes. 'Revise my will? Clean out my cupboards? Write farewell letters to the people I love? Or are you going to tell me to think positive and pray for a miracle?'

Dr Casey got up, walked around his desk and put his arm around Jemma's shoulders.

'All of the above,' he said.

Jemma arrived home from her appointment with Charles Casey and changed into her old baggy shorts and a T-shirt. She turned on all the ceiling fans, in a futile effort to break up the sticky heat which had seeped through the doors and windows. She went into her bedroom and started pulling her clothes out of the cupboard. She filled a huge bag of the things she never wore but had been saving for a rainy day.

Later she had a shower and sorted out her books. She had a cup of tea and a sandwich and went into the study. She tidied up piles of photos and organised papers and files. She found her box of SMs and emptied it, transferring some of its contents into John's, and some into Hamish's. She looked at her special memories of her son, his first shoes, the creamy shawl Marte had made for his christening, his merit cards, his various awards and medals. His first drawings. Me and My Family. A huge Jemma with stick legs and a mat of scribbled hair. A huge John. And Hamish, with circles for eyes and legs coming from his chin.

Next she attacked the linen press. After she had pulled everything out, her head began to ache badly. She wrote a note and stuck it on top of a heap of sheets.

Hamish, please put these back for me, so you'll know where they go. Love, Mum.

She was too tired to do the kitchen cupboards.

She was asleep when Hamish came in. The rasp of the wire door woke her.

It was late afternoon. Jemma's bedroom, with the timber venetians closed, was dim and too warm. Distantly she heard Hamish make himself some food and then leave again, without finding her note or the mess in the hall. She got up, had another shower, and put on some music. *The Four Seasons.*

She sat down at her computer to work on her letters.

Jemma knew there were no guarantees that her Idea would work out perfectly, especially when she lost control of the situation, which at some stage, inevitably, she would. But from a practical perspective, her plans were falling nicely into place. Her script had been written, learned and delivered. Her main concern now was to explain her motives and to equip everyone to cope without her.

She wrote for hours. Darkness dropped its night-time blanket over Siren's Rock and Jemma typed on. She had taught herself to touch type when she was seventeen years old, tying a tea towel around her neck and spreading it over the typewriter so that she couldn't see the keys. Never, not even when she was writing her plays, had her skill and speed proved so valuable.

Outside the cicadas gave Vivaldi a run for his money.

Part Nine

THE WAVE

'Goodbye, Julie,' Jemma said at Bridgetown airport, surprising her by hugging her so tightly that her arms were squeezed against her sides. Helen could smell her perfume, mixed with sweat and the fruity shampoo she used to wash her hair. 'You're the best friend God ever made.'

Helen hugged her back. 'Sophia, you've got so *skinny*,' she exclaimed, feeling bones rather than Jemma's firm and healthy flesh.

'I *know*,' said Jemma, wriggling out of the embrace as she always did. 'See? All things come to her who waits.' She stepped back, grabbing both Tom's and Caitlin's hands. 'Remember that, Helen.'

'Just *go*,' said Jemma, as Helen hesitated. 'These kids want to start getting into strife, and I've got to pack.'

There was something wrong with the horizon. It should have been a gently curving line, separating the sky from the sea. Instead, in the distance, there was a small swelling on the water line.

Charles Casey came to see her before they wheeled her into the theatre. The pre-op had made her deliciously woozy ... she thought she had never felt so utterly wonderful in her entire life. There was no longer any need to think. To plan. To talk. To pretend.

'Please let me telephone John. Or your son. Or your parents. Or Helen,' the doctor growled.

'None of the above,' she had murmured.

He was sitting beside her when she opened her eyes. The bed was high and white and she was connected to various tubes and bottles. His blue gaze was on her face. He was holding her hand.

'So ...' murmured Jemma. 'Time to pray.'

'Time to pray,' said Charles Casey.

She closed her eyes again and realised what she could see on the distant edge of the world. It was a wave.

When she opened her eyes, Charles was back again. 'Am I going to get better?' she asked. 'I mean, for a little while?'

'Of course,' he answered. 'We'll make you as comfortable as we can.'

'I can't go home until I'm over this.'

'Jemma,' said Charles Casey, 'I have to ring someone. I have to ring your next of kin.'

Jemma nodded and closed her eyes. A tear trickled from her lashes. 'I thought I could do it on my own,' she said. 'But I can't.'

'Of course you can't,' said Charles. 'You don't have to.'

'I want my mum,' whispered Jemma.

By the time Marte came into her room, she and George had been told everything. Marte put her stick by the door and limped over to the high bed, where she took Jemma's head in her hands and kissed her daughter on the forehead.

'You're my brave girl,' said Marte. 'You're gonna get

better. Like me. That's what you said, remember, when I had my stroke? You can't keep the Johnson women down.'

Jemma looked at her with damp green eyes. George, his own eyes and heart overflowing, silently pushed a chair beneath Marte as she reached for Jemma's hands. Her daughter's grip was strong.

'You were right, Mum,' said Jemma. Her voice was faint and raspy from the tubes. 'You were right to leave the horse show.'

Tears began coursing down the furrows of Marte's cheeks.

'Family is better than fame,' whispered Jemma.

'That's right, my darling girl,' said Marte. 'And that's why we have to call John.'

'Not yet,' said Jemma. 'Let him have a few more days. Please.'

Marte stroked her cheek. 'Jemma, I know what you are trying to do. It won't work. Now is not the time. This is something even you can't arrange.'

'Why not?' asked Jemma, her voice rasping angrily. 'It's like the prisoner on death row asking for a cigarette. Or a baked dinner. Surely I can have this?'

'Shush shush,' said George. 'Don't say that. That's crazy talk. That's sickness talking. Just rest and get better.'

'You shush up now, George,' said Marte. 'Let her talk, if she wants to. It's what she does best.'

Jemma closed her eyes and she could see it. The small wave forming in the ocean. It was a long way off yet, but it was coming.

Two days later, when Marte and George had gone to the airport to pick up Nick, Babs Winter made an unexpected visit to the hospital.

She wore a lipstick-pink suit and her thick musky perfume suffocated the fragrance of the flowers that filled the room.

'I see you still have all your hair,' she said approvingly. 'I was afraid you'd be bald.'

'I haven't had chemotherapy,' said Jemma. 'They said there was no point.'

The significance of this remark was lost on Babs. 'A visit to your hairdresser when you get out of here,' she said, 'and you'll have that nice style back in no time.'

Jemma waited to find out why Babs had come.

'You're a good girl, Jemma,' said Babs. 'You turned out much better than your mother and I dared hope.'

'Thank you,' said Jemma faintly, capturing an escaping smile and locking her lips around it.

'You don't deserve to be humiliated,' said Babs.

'Humiliated?'

'By my daughter. You don't deserve to be lying in a hospital bed while she's running around in a foreign country with your husband. Everyone knows what's going on,' said Babs.

'What's going on?' asked Jemma.

'My daughter leads men astray,' sniffed Babs. 'Under the circumstances, it might be in your best interests to have this. It's a letter from that man she claims is Tom's father.'

Jemma pulled herself up, staring at Helen's mother. 'He wrote? Does she know?'

'I thought it in her best interests to keep this confidential,' said Babs, pursing her crimson lips. 'From what I gather he was a common tramp.'

'Why are you giving this to me?' Jemma fell back on her pillow. She felt very tired. Was exhausted just talking to this terrible little woman.

'It might take her mind off chasing after your husband.'

'Sort of like throwing a bone to a naughty dog,' said Jemma, 'to make her stop chewing on something she shouldn't have?'

'Exactly,' said Babs. 'That's what she's like. A bitch on heat.'

'Sort of like hitting her with a rolled-up newspaper, to train her,' said Jemma, gazing at the ceiling.

Babs frowned and hesitated.

'Or whacking her naked bottom with a cane,' said Jemma, transferring her gaze back to Babs. 'The hard end, of course. Or worse,' Jemma added icily, locking her eyes on the other woman's.

Babs' cheeks flared the colour of her suit and she stood up. 'I see my warning has fallen on deaf ears,' she said. 'That's what comes of trying to help.' She paused. 'You're a nasty bit of work, Jemma Johnson.'

'Takes one to know one,' said Jemma.

When Babs had left she curled her fingers around the letter, crumpling it into a ball.

He was a good person. If he had known about Tom, I think he would have come back.

But he hadn't, thought Jemma, dropping the wad of paper into the plastic bag the hospital provided for non-recyclable rubbish.

Sometimes Jemma felt so much better she thought she might be able to go home for a while. Other days she slept for so long that when she woke up Marte was wearing different clothes. Marte and George came every day. Nick's wife Janelle had offered to look after Tom so that they could spend every available minute with their daughter.

'People come good in times of trouble,' said Marte knowingly. 'I knew Janelle was all right underneath.'

Whenever she slept she saw the wave coming. It was growing bigger and greener and getting closer all the time. Lately she could hear it, humming steadily in the distance.

She realised the wave was going to be too big to catch. To shoot a wave that monstrous into shore would be far too dangerous. This one could snap your spine. She had warned Helen that if a wave had a curl on it like that, you should always dive under it. But diving under anything this big was a terrifying prospect as well. She hoped, when the time came, she would be brave enough to do it. It was the biggest wave she had ever seen and she had no idea what she would find on the other side.

One day the room was full of flowers and Hamish was there. He said Dad rang every couple of days and sent his love. He wanted to know why nobody would let him tell Dad she was in hospital. Why nobody had told *him* until now. He started to cry and George put his arm around him and took him outside. Jemma sighed and closed her eyes. Tears and questions. It was exactly what she had wanted to avoid. She had written all those letters explaining everything. They were in John's sock drawer. He could give them out when he came home.

She was getting another headache.

The next day Caitlin came too. It was one of Jemma's good days. She and Caitlin had a long talk. Caitlin rested her cool porcelain cheek on Jemma's and told her she was sorry for all the worry she had caused her. 'I just wanted to …' Caitlin pressed her lips tightly together.

Jemma placed a hand on Caitlin's russet head. 'You wanted to punish me,' said Jemma. 'For loving Hamish more than you. And I did. I do. I can't help it. He's mine, Cait.'

Caitlin sat up and clenched her teeth together to keep herself from weeping. Why had she expected Jemma to say she had nothing to be sorry for? Jemma was too honest for that.

'I love you very much, Caitlin,' said Jemma, 'and I've always understood how you must feel. But I couldn't love you the same way as your mother does. You're hers. That's the difference.'

'About Hamish,' Caitlin said. 'You should know I've only ever loved him like a brother.'

Jemma smiled. 'I do know,' she said. 'But tell *him*.'

'I did,' said Caitlin. 'We tried kissing at Christmas, but we both decided it just didn't feel right. So that was that.'

'A kiss in time saves nine,' said Jemma, giggling. To Caitlin's surprise, she heard herself giggling too.

'One of my best memories,' said Jemma later, when Hamish had joined them, 'is the day Caitlin was born. It was an easy birth, not like Tom's. You know what, Cait? I have never seen Helen so ecstatic as she was at the moment you came into the world.'

That's the truth, she thought, closing her eyes. I wasn't there that other time.

'Was she?' asked Caitlin sadly. 'Truly?'

'She was beside herself,' said Jemma. She snapped her eyes open. 'I knew you two would be rolling your eyes,' she said, suddenly sounding terrifyingly normal. 'Why do you *do* that? What did I *say*?'

Early the next morning Hamish and George found Jemma looking tired, pale and old. While George went in search of Dr Casey, Jemma spoke quietly to Hamish. She said there were things she wanted to tell him that were too hard to say out loud. They were in a letter for him at home. She gave him the reading she had chosen, to be read at her funeral. His red lips worked and twisted as he fought desperately to remain calm and in control.

'You can do it,' Jemma insisted softly.

'I'll do it if you let us tell Dad,' said Hamish. 'It's not fair on them, Mum. It's time for Dad and Helen to come home.'

She closed her eyes and saw the wave. She thought she would like to tell Helen about the wave. It was so close now, so deeply green, coming so fast ...

She opened her eyes. 'Okay,' she said.

Dr Casey told George about the small malignant tumour which had been detected in Jemma's brain. The lumpectomy had bought her a little time, but the end wasn't far away. An inter-cranial haemorrhage was likely soon. George went and sat in his car, where he wept for a long time. Then he tried to ring John on his mobile. But although it was only early evening in Ireland, John didn't answer his phone.

MAIGHDEAN

Helen and John arrived in Strangle, half an hour south of Dublin, in misty rain. Callum Clancy's ruddy face was a picture of desolation when he learned that Jemma wasn't with them, but he rallied his relentlessly high spirits to hurl them around the high spots of the town and they consumed more alcohol in two days than they'd had in the previous ten.

They were both interviewed by Radio Strangle and Helen, focusing hard to overcome her hangover, pre-recorded some longer in-depth pieces for the coming season.

In Dublin Callum took them on a tour of pubs and watering holes around Temple Bar, which made their pub crawl in Strangle look like Tom's birthday party. They drank and listened to fiddles, pipes and guitars, drank some more and watched slim girls in short black dresses clack and tap their tiny feet through traditional Irish dancing routines that left the tourists, the girls themselves, and John and Callum in particular, breathless.

Helen's memory of how they reached their hotel, a massive white edifice with palatial rooms, was dim. She had a nasty shock when she woke up fully dressed in a huge bed and realised that John was sound asleep in a bed of equal size on the other side of the room.

She was dressed in fresh clothes by the time John woke up. She gave him a cup of strong coffee while he sat on the edge of the soft white bed and groaned.

'What a night,' he said.

'I was just thinking how much Jemma would have loved it,' said Helen.

'She would have outshone us all,' said John. 'But meanwhile, Mrs Connor, I think we distinguished ourselves pretty well.'

Helen grimaced. 'That Callum,' she said. 'What did he do to us?'

John looked into his coffee, silent for a moment. 'Do you think Jemma is having an affair?' he asked suddenly. He didn't know whether it was his hangover talking or the fact he was missing her, but he felt his anger rise at the question once more.

Helen threw herself backwards onto the bed and sighed. What *was* Jemma doing? 'No, I don't,' she said. 'I can't imagine her being unfaithful to you. It's not in her character to do something so *wrong*, something that would hurt everyone so much. I think she just wants to get away from us all. Just for a while. She was just a bit dramatic in the way she went about it.' Helen smiled. 'That's Jemma, isn't it?'

'I don't know.' He looked across at Helen. 'The only thing I do know is that she had this whole thing planned. I've been thinking about the things she's said, and it seems almost as if she —'

'John, there's no point in churning yourself up about it now.'

'You're right, I know. I'll sort this out with her when we get home.' John stood up and stretched. 'Now, let's get on the road. Next stop Belfast and the final chapter: a nostalgic journey into my father's past.'

'Via Maighdean,' said Helen. 'You said if we had time . . .'

Maighdean clung to the coast, a cluster of grey roofs and spires, hanging on despite poor protection from the rains and bitter winds which blew in from the Irish Sea.

They were back in the north now and the pastel-painted houses had been replaced with tall terraces spackled beige and grey. In the town, John and Helen drove past an ancient church, dark stone on darker flagstones, no grass or trees to remind worshippers of God's gentler touch. The sky, the footpaths and the people's faces were grey and resigned.

'No sign of Irish eyes smiling here,' said John, as they drove through the rain and down to the beach.

They sat in the car and examined a small map they had picked up at the petrol station. Helen wanted to find the street where Tom's father had lived. Ten Liffey Street had stayed in her mind, like Ten Grand View Crescent. She thought she might take a photograph for her son, something to show him if he ever grew curious about his roots.

Outside the car the wind was getting stronger. Helen got out and walked towards the shore, crunching over the grey stony stuff that substituted for sand. She stopped in the middle of the beach and looked at the bleak sky and choppy water.

She wanted to think deep and meaningful thoughts, to conjure up the image of a small red-headed boy playing here, climbing the rocks, sending stones skimming into the sea. But all she could think was that it was little wonder he had wanted to leave.

She hurried back to the car and found John looking strained, listening to the radio. 'There's been a bombing at

Strathlee,' he said. 'Just outside Belfast. A suburban shopping centre. At least thirty people killed and over a hundred injured.'

She stared at him in horror. 'Thirty?'

'At least. Women and children mainly, they said.'

They sat in the car for a long time, listening to the radio while the angry sea raged in front of them.

When they drove back into the town the streets were almost empty. In the café where they had lunch, the people were solemn and sad. A woman was weeping quietly. This was a community used to tragedy and strife, which had faced the shocking and the unexpected too often for strident sorrow.

They were advised not to travel on to Belfast that day. 'Strathlee's only an hour from here,' said the café owner. 'There'll be soldiers everywhere. And louts from both sides looking for revenge, for trouble. If you don't mind me sayin', you'd best stay here tonight until they've got the situation under control.'

Like every other village in Ireland, Maighdean wasn't short of bed and breakfast places. They found a cream stone terrace, three narrow storeys high, with a snappy little fire crackling in the front room on the ground floor. They drank tea with the busty blonde landlady, a widow whose rolls of fat were stacked like quoits on a pole beneath her straining twin-set. All afternoon they watched the horrendous non-stop television coverage of the carnage.

At about six pm Mrs Mills took a telephone call and came to ask them if they could manage on their own. She was going to spend the night with her sister who lived in the next village. Her husband had not returned as expected from a trip to Belfast and she needed help with her five children. Mrs Mills' small mouth and red cheeks were designed for smiling, but now her mouth was a downward curve and her tiny eyes were popping with anxiety in her roly-poly face. Helen hugged her and sent her off with reassurances that they would lock up if she hadn't returned before they departed the next morning.

John got up from the sofa. 'Helen,' he said, 'I want to go to Mass. Will you come with me?'

They sat on hard, deeply scored wooden pews with the people of Maighdean, listening to the wind wailing around the spire while the rain rushed at the narrow windows. But this was an old and sturdy church and the windows were handcrafted leadlights, thick and strong, patterned with images of mourning martyrs. The dim interior remained cold and dry.

In front of the elaborately carved white altar, covered in a lace cloth and flanked by candles and statues of a groaning Christ and his long-suffering mother, the priest droned on about men's incomprehension of the ways of the Lord; it was not for mere mortals to question His will or to wonder why the lives at Strathlee had been sacrificed.

After the service Helen and John walked up the road to a fish and chip shop and ordered some dinner to take away. As they waited at the counter, two young men, pale, lank-haired and sullen, came into the shop. Helen's nostrils flared. The men, boys really, exuded the scent of cheap deodorant, overpowering but already stale, a cross between sickly perfume and insect spray.

They both wore grubby pale-grey parkas and chewed gum. One of them trailed an insolent inspection over Helen before staring at the price list on the blackboard with dull eyes.

By the time they had finished eating, Helen could stand the television reports no longer. She went up to her room and climbed into bed. It was cold away from the fire.

She took little notice when a phone began ringing somewhere in the house. Her mind was too full of the horror she had seen. The images on the television mingled with her memories of the red-headed stranger who had been born in this grim, grey town and had escaped, to wander from country to country, looking for a place free of murder, mayhem and hate. Who had found her and healed her and given her a son. And had disappeared again into a damaged world.

'Tom,' she whispered aloud. She wondered for the thousandth time where he was, and what he was doing with his life. And she thought of her son. She was missing him terribly, his bright, curious eyes, his questions, his quaint way of speaking. Then she worried about Caitlin for a while. I'm homesick, she thought.

She was almost asleep when the phone rang again. She didn't register that it was in the next room where John had left his mobile, and that John was downstairs, still watching the television.

It was nearly ten o'clock when John knocked on her door and woke her from a restless sleep. 'We've missed a few calls from home,' he said. 'Hamish has been trying to ring me. He's probably seen this business on the news; they'll be worrying about us. I've been trying to ring back but nobody's home.'

'What about George and Marte?' said Helen sleepily.

'They're all out. I even broke my resolution and tried Jemma on her mobile. No answer.'

'That's funny,' said Helen. 'It's early in the morning at home. Where could they be?'

John shrugged. 'I'll keep trying,' he said.

★ ★ ★

An hour later Helen woke up again with a start.

It was pitch black in her room but there was a roaring sound in her ears, like a huge wave breaking.

Tom, she thought. Something's happened to Tom. She got out of bed and pulled her cream coat around her shoulders as she went to the window and looked out. It was as black out there as it was inside, and the sound that had woken her was the roaring wind.

Her heart was beating so hard it hurt.

She padded along the hall to John's door. She knocked and went in. John was standing in the middle of the room.

'I'm sorry,' she said, 'I know I sound paranoid ...' She stopped. He was dressed in the grey track suit he slept in, clutching his mobile phone to his ear. In the dim light of the bedside lamp, his face was contorted and ugly. He didn't even look at her as she crossed the distance between them, but he put one arm out and she walked into its curve and stayed there. He kept his arm around her tightly, as if she was a lifeline. His body was stiff with tension.

'What is it?' asked Helen, her panic mounting. 'Is it Tom?'

'Cancer?' he was saying. 'But it wouldn't just ... it couldn't ... I've only been away for ... she didn't ... when? God help us. Who is this doctor? What's the prognosis?'

It was cold in the room. Helen's teeth began to chatter. *Who? Who's got cancer?* John tightened his grip on her.

'Let me talk to this Dr Casey,' he said. 'Then find him. Now. And ring me straight back on this number.'

John pressed a button on his phone. He looked at Helen. 'That was George. He says Jemma's got cancer. She's had an operation but it's too far advanced. She's known for weeks but she didn't tell anyone. She's going to die.'

A black blind came crashing down across the windows of Helen's consciousness.

John had a long conversation with the doctor. There was a lot of medical jargon and repetition of disjointed phrases that didn't make sense. Then he spoke to George again. Helen huddled on the bed, shaking. Suddenly John handed her the phone.

'George?' quavered Helen.

'Hang on, Helen, my dear girl,' said George. He seemed to be crying. Then, miraculously, Jemma's voice was speaking to her and everything was all right.

'I had to talk to you, Julie,' said Jemma. Her voice seemed soft and sleepy. 'I wish you could meet Charles. He's my doctor. He's absolutely gorgeous.'

'That's nice, Jemma,' said Helen witlessly. John had gone to the door to turn on the bright, overhead light. Now he strode back, holding out his hand for the phone.

'Anyway ...' Jemma went on, even more softly, 'I just want to make sure you remember what I told you on the beach. I meant it, Julie ...' Jemma's voice was fading. There was a long pause.

'Jemma?' said Helen. There was a rustling at the end of the line and Marte's voice came on. 'Hang on a minute, love,' said Marte. 'They've given her some drugs and they make her very ... Hang on. I'm going to hold the phone for her now, so she can talk to you again.'

John stood beside her with his hand out. Helen didn't look at him.

'Jemma?' said Helen. 'Jemma, are you there? Why didn't you tell us you were sick?'

'Love him for me, Julie,' Jemma whispered. 'Love him enough for both of us ...'

John's patience ran out. He took the phone out of her hand. 'Jemma, this is John. What are you doing?'

'This is what I didn't want,' said Jemma, plaintive, petulant.

There was a long pause. 'Our last talk, remember, John? On the verandah. Better than this.' She sounded calm, but dreamy, nothing like the Jemma he knew. Another pause. 'That was the truth,' murmured Jemma.

'Jemma!' he shouted. But Marte was talking now. 'John. She's very sick. She's been sick for a long time but she didn't tell anyone. Come home, John,' said Marte, taking a deep breath. 'Come home as soon as you can.'

John's face began to crumple and Helen reached up and gently took the phone from his hand. When she lifted it to her own ear there was no sound at all for a long time and she wasn't sure if they had hung up. John uttered a small moan. Helen took his hand while continuing to press the phone to her ear. She was rewarded with some muttering, followed again by Jemma's voice, faintly back on the line.

'Is that John or Julie?'

'It's me, Sophia,' said Helen. 'I'm here. I love you.'

'Just wanted to tell you,' said Jemma sleepily, 'about this huge wave ...'

'Jemma!' said Helen desperately. She gripped John's hand tightly. '*Jemma!*' she screamed.

George's voice came on the line. 'She's only asleep,' he said. 'She's on lots of painkillers. We'll call you back. Stay by the phone.' He paused. 'I'm so sorry to put you through this, sweetheart,' he said softly. 'She thought she had longer.'

He hung up. Helen looked at the tiny phone in the palm of her hand. She pressed the end call button. John sat on the bed, staring into space. She sat down beside him, rubbed his back vigorously. 'Get under the covers,' she said. 'You're freezing. You're probably in shock.' She pulled her coat around her and pulled the blankets over them both.

'I don't believe this,' said John. 'This isn't happening. She can't do this. This is a nightmare.'

'A nightmare,' said Helen. She sucked her tongue to stop her teeth clattering together. She shivered. 'We'll wake up in a minute.'

'So that was her big adventure,' he said. 'The one she wanted to have all alone.'

The pieces of the last puzzling weeks were slowly slotting together in Helen's mind. A picture was emerging. Jemma thinner, thoughtful, wearier, warier, colouring her face, covering her plans, giving permission for Helen to have her husband if the worst came to the worst. Organising everyone. Sending her to comfort John. Just in case.

'She's with people who love her,' said Helen. 'Marte and George. Hamish. I wonder if Caitlin's there?' A thought penetrated the welter of images whirling through her mind. 'I wonder who she's organised to take care of Tom?'

'Certainly not us,' said John. 'She organised *us* out of this.'

Helen said nothing, lost in her thoughts.

'You knew,' said John suddenly. 'You *knew*.'

'No,' shuddered Helen. 'Please, John, I didn't. I should have. I should have guessed. Oh God, why didn't I guess?'

But as Jemma would have said, God wasn't telling.

For three hours they huddled under the quilt, waiting for the phone to ring again. Asking each other questions that neither could answer. Thinking about the things she had said, comparing notes, working it out. Wondering how long she had known. Lapsing into long, anguished silence while they tried to imagine her pain. Her fear.

Why had she wanted to go through this disaster without them?

'To hurt us?' said John.

'To help us, I think,' said Helen.

'How could she?' said John, gripping Helen's shoulders,

giving her a little shake. 'How could she shunt us about as if we were figures on her own private stage?'

Suddenly Helen sat up. 'What are we doing *here*?' she said. 'Lying in bed *whingeing*? We have to get home. We have to book a flight home.'

John grabbed his phone but she stopped him. 'They might ring back,' she said. 'I'll go downstairs. I'm sure Mrs Mills won't mind.'

Standing in the icy hall beneath another dim lamp, she couldn't get through to the airline. Again and again she was put on hold. She began to cry. 'Please,' she told the recorded message. 'Please.' It finally registered with her that it was three in the morning. The booking office was closed. Slowly she put down the receiver and went back upstairs. Jemma, she thought with every step. Jemma. Her friend for a lifetime. Not dying, she thought. Not Jemma, of all people. This couldn't happen to Jemma.

At the top of the stairs she heard the faint jangle of John's phone. She held the door handle tightly and closed her eyes. 'Please, God,' she prayed. 'Stay with her.'

Jemma's head had cleared again. She asked if she could go outside into the sun. 'The real world,' she said. 'Is it still there?'

They lifted her into a wheelchair and Marte pushed her out onto the hospital balcony, George lumbering behind with the IV pole and its swinging bag of temporary solutions. The view of the distant mountains was similar to the one from Jemma's verandah at home.

'I would have preferred the ocean,' she said, 'but beggars can't be choosers.'

'You terrible girl,' said Marte. 'You are never satisfied.'

She asked to be by herself.

Whenever clarity returned, Jemma felt obliged to get her thoughts in order, to properly prepare herself for what was coming. Dutifully she closed her eyes and prayed for world peace and for everyone she loved to be blessed with happiness and good health. Then, not for the first time, she prayed for a miracle.

But as usual her thoughts became muddled with trivial details inappropriate to the moment. Who was going to tell John to throw out all the dead flowers? He and Hamish would sweep away the dropped petals and leave the naked stalks standing at attention in the vases. Who would remind John to put out the bins? After all these years, he still never remembered which was bin night. Helen wouldn't nag him the way she did.

Nothing would get done. Not properly anyway.

I can't go, thought Jemma. Her mouth trembled. 'I don't want to go,' she whispered aloud, opening her eyes.

A bubble of panic swelled in her chest. 'I don't want to die,' she said to the mountains.

The bubble expanded until it seemed to press against her ribs, hurting her. Her heart thudded. She was frightened that at any second, she would stop being able to breathe. She forced herself to take deep, slow breaths, but hot tears pooled in her eyes and she began to weep, loudly, like a lost child.

Marte was beside her, striding to the wheelchair, scorning her stick, kneeling at Jemma's side.

'My sweet girl,' said Marte, tears running down her own cheeks. 'Don't cry. Don't cry. Everything will be all right.'

'I don't want to die,' sobbed Jemma. 'I'm scared. I'm too young. I've got so much to do.'

George stood beside her kneeling mother. He too wept.

Marte was grasping Jemma's hands. 'It will be all right,' she said, squeezing hard. 'You'll see.'

'I'm so scared of that wave,' whimpered Jemma. But then she saw Hamish approaching. She took a deep, shuddering breath and folded her lips together over her sobs. Immediately she became aware that the roaring was back in her head.

Hamish looked frantic. His lips were moving but she couldn't hear what he was saying.

'Everything will be all right,' said Jemma calmly to her son. 'You'll see.'

There was an excruciating pain in Jemma's head.

The last time she closed her eyes the wave was rising above her, blotting out the sky.

She plunged, soared, flowed into the flowing heart of the ocean. She was folded into the glorious green iridescence of the wave and she wanted to tell Helen that in the end the pain and fear were washed away and that she wasn't, after all, alone.

GRIEF

'She didn't wait for us,' John said quietly.

'She sent us away so she could die without us,' he said.

He was lying on his back on the bed.

It was desperately cold. Helen silently pulled the blankets back over him and turned off the dingy lamp. She found a quilt in the cupboard and curled up in a large armchair in the darkest corner of the room, tucking her cold feet underneath her. She put her head in her arms.

'Promise me you'll come back when it's over. Promise me you'll come back to us all.'

But she had promised nothing. Jemma was too honest to make promises she knew she couldn't keep.

Helen began to cry.

She wept for a long time, quietly at first but eventually her body was convulsed with sobs. She cried until her jaw ached and her throat throbbed; until there seemed to be no more tears left in her head.

John made no move to come to her. Somewhere in the distant shadows of her mourning, she was grateful for that.

A long time after she was finally silent, she heard John say: 'I don't understand. Why didn't she want us with her?

We've been with her through everything else.' He sounded angry now.

And as a lonely car droned along the street outside, he shouted: 'How will I live without her, Helen? How did I ever think I could go on without Jemma?'

But Helen could think of nothing to say. She couldn't imagine a world that didn't have Jemma in it, and didn't want to try.

She remained wrapped in her sorrow until the angels took pity on her, and sent sleep.

Helen woke when she heard John sobbing.

At first she thought it was an animal, suffering somewhere out in the street. The sound of his grief was terrible. Huge sobs were torn from his big chest, raw and tortured.

The wind had died away and the rain which had sheeted against the window panes all through the previous day had not returned. The pre-dawn silence was broken only by the sound of John's pain.

Helen approached the bed where he was lying face down. He had thrown off all the bedclothes. She picked up the blankets and tried to cover him, but he flung up his arm and shoved them away.

She took off her cream coat and covered him with it. Then she lay down on the bed and tried to put her arms around him, but again he repelled her efforts, blindly pushing her away while keeping his head buried in the pillows. Sobs grinding.

'Don't,' he said into the pillow.

'Don't you,' said Helen querulously. 'John, don't do this on your own. Don't leave me.' A sob ripped through her throat. 'I can't bear it.'

And at last, still sobbing, he turned onto his side. Allowed her to put her arms around him. To hold him while he wept.

She rested her face against his chest and lay still in the warm cave of his body. After a while, she tilted her face and pressed her lips against his throat.

She felt him stiffen against her but she took no notice.

She opened her lips a little and tasted his skin. The skin in the hollow at the base of his broad neck. She smelled his man's flesh smell. She closed her eyes and he felt the butterfly kiss of her lashes on his jaw, the softness of her lips.

It was better than thinking. Anything was better than thinking.

Helen moved up the bed a little, so that she could reach his face with her mouth, and she kissed his damp cheeks, his chin and his forehead, avoiding his lips.

Stop as soon as he's feeling a bit better, said Helen the Saint. *Stop now so he can sleep.*

But she had wanted to kiss this dear, handsome face for so many years, so she kept kissing him, his forehead, his tanned brown cheeks, the crease in his chin, his 'bum chin' Caitlin called it, and she moved her lips down to his throat again, and dipped her tongue into the hollow there. When she lowered her head to his chest, it was John who took his arms from around her so he could unzip the top of his track suit, letting her lips travel unimpeded over the flesh and bone that held his wounded heart.

She helped him take his track suit top right off and then she kissed his chest again and his shoulders, her lips warm on his skin, but not on his lips. She stroked his chest and his furry belly with her skinny fingers, and kissed him there as well, slowly, breathing him in, taking her time because this was as far as she dared to go and she would stop soon, she would embrace him once more and leave him to mourn. She closed her eyes and rubbed her cheek on his stomach like a cat, but when she felt him pulling at

508

her nightdress she knew it would probably not be a good idea to take it off.

I'll stop soon, she thought, before we do something we'll both regret.

She knelt above him and pulled the nightdress over her head and he looked at her in the dim light of dawn, her small white body, her breasts.

'Helen . . .' His whisper was a hyphen linking pleasure and pain.

'Don't,' said Helen. She leaned over him and for a moment he thought she was going to kiss him, but she held her fingers against his lips instead. 'Don't think,' she whispered, and wound her legs around his hips and pressed her breasts, her amazing breasts, soft against his chest.

He reached for her then. Yes. Better this than thinking. Better this than dying like Jemma, like all those people in Strathlee, like Mrs Mills' sister's husband. Better this than feeling the pain. Yes. Better to bury his face in a woman's warm flesh, satin arms, fragrant hair. Better to hold someone soft against his skin, like a doll in his arms, her hair floating around his throat, smelling like heaven.

She had always smelled like heaven.

He tasted the fingers that still lay on his lips, drawing them into his mouth. He kissed her breasts, her belly. With a soft moan she rolled on to her back and wove her hands into his hair as he moved down. A film dropped over her brown eyes and she flung her arms up over her head and swayed as he kissed her there, singing a sighing song, a mermaid on the rock. Swaying and singing. His lips led her through her siren's song until her tide rushed in and swept her away from him.

Only when she was finally still, when she reached down to him and drew him up and back into her arms, did he cover her body with his and plunge into the depths of her, filling her for the second time in their lives with his confusion of love and grief.

Afterwards he slept with her arm across his chest, her body moulded to his. Warm. Protected. Saved.

Helen lay beside him, her eyes open, watching a watery sun appear at the window. The sun was rising on her first day without Jemma.

Their guilt that morning, combined with their grief, was hideous.

John arrived in the kitchen, showered, dressed, exhausted, embarrassed and angry. He found Helen showered, dressed, exhausted and embarrassed.

They had absolutely no idea what to say to each other.

He went outside without a word and Helen sat at the table and drank a cup of tea.

Please, she said to Jemma's God. Let me wake up soon. And if this is real, be kind to her. Be as good as she always thought You were.

Eventually John came back inside and sat down at the table. He cleared his throat and said he had tried the airline again and still couldn't get through.

'I'm not even sure if the airport has been affected by this Strathlee business,' he said. 'We may have to head for Belfast and take what we can get when we arrive.'

'Okay,' said Helen. Her voice sounded thin, artificial. She stood up. 'Do you want breakfast first?'

'No,' said John tersely. 'Thank you,' he added, frowning even more deeply. 'I'll go and get our bags.'

'Have you rung home again?' She was worried about Tom and Caitlin, but didn't dare say so. Surely he would realise she needed to talk to them, to see how they were coping?

'No,' he said. 'George and Marte will have their hands full. There'll be arrangements to be made …' He stopped. Arrangements I should be making, he thought. 'Anyway,' he said, staring over her head. 'What could I possibly say to them? *Now*,' he added in disgust.

Helen gripped the edge of the solid oak table. 'John,' she said, 'we were both distraught last night. Grief does strange things to people.'

He looked at her coldly. 'So that's going to be the excuse, is it?' he said. 'Grief made us do it? What movie did you think you were in this time? Aren't we a bit too old for *Summer of '42*?'

'Please,' said Helen. She choked on a sob and tried to turn it into a cough. 'We have to stay friends. I can't bear losing her. I couldn't bear to lose you as well.' Her voice gave out. She sniffed and said pathetically: 'This time yesterday' — *God, was it only that long ago?* — 'we were happy being friends.'

'No, we weren't,' said John savagely. 'You were ripe and I was randy. We were like dogs on heat.'

He went out.

Helen went into the hall and tried to place a reverse-charge call to her house. But her home phone rang out. She resisted the temptation to ring John and Jemma's place. She left cash for Mrs Mills, locked up and left the house. Outside on the small porch she looked at the world that had changed overnight. The world without Jemma.

It wasn't possible.

The sky was clear blue. The line of slate-grey roofs had been washed clean and shone in the sunlight. In the distance, at the end of the steeply sloping road, a triangle of grey-blue sea seemed to be wedged between the houses.

It was the same shape as her pain, a triangle digging into her chest. It hurt her to breathe.

I can't go back, thought Helen. I can't go back to Siren's Rock and not find her there.

'*If you and John are together, looking after the kids and everything, I won't feel so bad and everyone will be happy and . . .*'

I want to curl up and sleep forever, thought Helen. I never want to wake up again.

It was bitterly cold. Helen left the key in the flower pot at the back of the house as instructed, returned to the front and walked over to the car, pulling on her orange anorak.

John finished with the boot and came around to unlock the passenger door. For the first time that morning, he allowed his eyes to meet hers. His shoulders slumped and he shook his head in despair.

'When life gets difficult, you and I just can't resist a good fuck to cheer ourselves up, can we, Julie?' said John.

Her eyes darkened.

But Helen Connor was no longer the inarticulate teenager he had taken on the back seat of his car at the drive-in nearly thirty years before.

'I suppose,' said Helen slowly, 'that's the difference between you and me. I thought we were making love.'

John looked anguished and ashamed. He reached for her hand but she stepped back. 'Helen . . .' he said.

She opened the door of the car. 'Forget it,' she said. 'You were never there.'

A SNAPSHOT

The problem with lacerating exit lines, as Jemma was always finding out, was that in real life they have to be followed by normal conversation. As they headed out of town, John slowed down. 'Did you still want to get a picture of the house in Liffey Street?'

'Don't be stupid,' said Helen tersely, keeping her head averted, staring rigidly out of her window.

'No,' said John dully, wanting to do the right thing. As if that would erase his wounding words. 'I think it's important for Tom to know where he came from. We've come this far ...'

She said nothing, so he took out the map they had been using the day before and unfolded it beneath the steering wheel. He did a few calculations and turned right. A few minutes later they drove into Liffey Street.

'Let's see,' said John, hating himself, hating the world, hating Helen for making him hate her, for the stiff, hurt way she kept her face turned away from him, 'Number Ten. Well, there it is. Not a very prepossessing sort of place. Could do with some new curtains.'

Helen stared up at the grey stone terrace house. It was one more bland, undecorated house in a row of the same.

A large, muddy, blue station wagon stood in front of it. This was a dull and silent street. No music played, no children's laughter could be heard. The windows were closed, eyes tight shut, not so much sleeping as refusing to see.

Jemma, Helen was thinking. My dear, beautiful, wonderful, wise friend, this time you were wrong. You were wrong to send us away, she thought as her eyes began to sting with self-pity. You were wrong to push us together. Because I'm just a good fuck to cheer him up. That's all I am to him. All I've ever been to John. But I'm worth more than that, Jemma. *You* taught me that.

The tears spilled from her eyes. She turned away from John again, slowly lifting her hand to brush them away before he noticed she was weeping.

But John was still looking up at the house. A face appeared between the tatty curtains of one of the upstairs windows, and locked eyes with him for an instant before disappearing again. It was the face of one of the parka-clad boys from the fish and chip shop the night before.

'I don't like the feel of this place,' said John. 'Let's take this photo and get out of here.'

Their tour ended with a scream — the squeal of metal striking metal on a black road, beneath a clear, cold sky.

The battered station wagon seemed to come from nowhere.

From Out of The Blue, as Jemma might have said.

Pushed off the narrow country road, John fought to keep the car out of the deep ditch. The struggle was ended by an oak tree which crunched sickeningly against Helen's door, and threw the car back onto the roadway, somehow still standing on all four wheels. John, shaken but unhurt, got a glimpse of the blue station wagon disappearing around the next bend in a cloud of stones and dirt.

Bloodied and broken, Helen slid from the tangle of steel. Folded slowly onto the road. An accordion of skinny limbs, orange cloth and undulating hair.

The black road waited patiently to receive her.

It was strange, in a country that had grown despairingly accustomed to the violent death of its own, how much compassion and concern the people showed for the two strangers. The ambulance came quickly. The men tried to lead John away while they did what they could for Helen. But he wouldn't leave her.

The blood that stained her fair hair was crimson and gushed from a deep gash on the back of her head. The blood that turned her orange anorak black and soaked her woollen jumper came from the ruin of her left arm.

She had worn her black jeans that day, and a black jumper beneath her anorak. Small and pale, her face marked with fatigue and sorrow, she looked like a child who'd had an accident at school. Lying on the road with her head in his lap, like the little girl he had wanted to protect since she was ten years old.

How many times can one man's heart break in a single day?

She was taken to a tiny ten-bed hospital in Carrickmae, because it was closer than the city. After a long wait, John was told that Helen would be taken by ambulance to Belfast. The cut on her head was superficial but her arm had multiple fractures and an artery was torn. She had lost a lot of blood and needed an urgent and delicate operation. The young policeman offered to drive John to the hospital but John wanted to go with her in the ambulance. They said there was nothing he could do.

He wouldn't leave her.

The big hospital was a hive of activity. It had taken in many of the Strathlee victims and emergency operations were still in progress. Many of the doctors and nurses had not slept for twenty-four hours, but they admitted the new patient with a concern and efficiency which earned John's admiration. In the crowded and noisy emergency ward he was comforted by the usual sounds of the nurses' soft-soled shoes squeaking on the gleaming floors, the smell of antiseptic, the clank of silver dishes, the sight of bottles spewing tubes to keep Helen alive. For now.

The policeman smiled. 'They probably thought you were undercover, or part of another terrorist group,' he said. 'Either way, you're a bit of an eejit taking snapshots of people's houses in this country. Pity you didn't get the registration number — mind you, they've probably changed it by now.'

'I was a bit distracted,' scowled John. 'Anyway, I didn't know taking pictures was a hanging offence.'

The policeman sighed and closed his notebook. 'We're a bit strange here,' he said. 'Please God, one day things will be different.'

They told him the press would be after him but so far the police were keeping them at a distance. They told him the best thing he could do was go home as soon as possible.

The exhausted surgeon declared the operation a success. Helen swam slowly towards consciousness through a calm sea, and John finally stumbled into a hotel bed and slept for twelve hours.

When he went back to the hospital to see her, she turned her head away from him.

They had cut her hair short. It had never been a good look for her. Beneath her bandage she was two brown eyes and a small parcel of fair crumpled flesh stretched over tiny bones. An old woman. Sick of life. Sick of him.

'Helen ...' he pleaded.

'Go home, John,' she said. 'You're needed there.'

'I'm needed here.'

'Your place is not with me,' her husky voice rasped. 'Your wife is dead. Your son needs you. Her parents need you. My kids need you. Go away. Go home.'

'I don't want to leave you here alone,' said John.

She closed her eyes and rested her bandaged head back on the pillows. 'These are nice people. They know what they're doing. Callum's on his way. He'll look after me.'

'*I* want to look after you,' said John.

'You can't.' Helen closed her eyes.

As he opened the door to leave she said: 'Send me Tom.'

Callum Clancy insisted on getting Helen out of the troubled end of the country and bringing her back to the Republic. He found her a pretty bedsit in Herbert Street, in an old, established corner of Dublin, where grand houses and small hotels reclined in leafy gardens behind dignified hedges.

Callum startled her by producing a wife, a plump, conservative, gently smiling woman, a daily Catholic, a baker of biscuits and bread- and-butter puddings, and a devoted mother to their six children. Emma Clancy became her friend. And, in time, helped her make more. But not too many. People, Emma told Callum, were not what Helen needed right now.

Helen waited in Herbert Street for her body to mend, distraught with worry about Tom, spending a ransom on phone calls home and anxiously counting the days until her son and daughter finally arrived in Dublin. Tom was in a state of almost unendurable excitement and even Caitlin seemed pleased to see her, although she was subdued and aloof for most of the fortnight she spent with her mother.

Despite Helen's best efforts, Caitlin refused to indulge her mother in any deep and meaningful conversation. She missed Jemma, she said. Everybody missed Jemma. She liked university, she said. Everybody with any sense liked university. The freedom. The flexibility. No parents, forever nagging. She didn't miss Siren's Rock, she said. Nobody was there any more. Except Marte and George, who were old. And John, who practically lived at work.

Caitlin then went off on a bus tour of Europe, which Helen had paid for and arranged with the vague idea of creating some excitement in her daughter's cool and self-contained little life. After that Caitlin returned to Australia to resume her university course. She was studying dentistry at Sydney University and living in the inner city with some girlfriends; once she was back with them she showed no sign of missing her mother or brother at all.

Helen didn't send Tom to school in Dublin. Instead she taught him herself, in their big, pleasant bedsit, with its swishing white curtains and tall windows. Outside was a park crammed with orderly lines of trees.

'A year off school won't hurt him at this age,' she told Marte on the phone. 'He's young enough to repeat a year when he gets home, and he gets on well with Callum's kids. He plays footy with some nice local boys.'

In the summer, when she was strong again, Helen took Tom to France for a week. They went to the top of the Eiffel Tower and had two ecstatic days at Disneyland. When they got back, Callum offered her a shift at Radio Strangle, filling in while the afternoon announcer was on holidays. To her surprise, she slipped back into the routine easily, keeping the program low-key and non-controversial, playing good music and sometimes getting the giggles as she struggled with the accents of the talkback callers. Tom would grin at her and make rude signs through the studio glass. She always took him with her to work and he read and did his lessons while she was on air.

She relieved several announcers during the rest of the year, but she turned down Callum's offer of a permanent shift. It wouldn't be fair, she said, to him or to Tom. Sooner or later she would be going home.

Marte rang every two weeks and Helen wrote regularly to them all.

Marte told her she and George were worried about John. He had been horribly quiet when he returned. Then he went through a phase when he was angry with all of them.

'Of course it was really Jemma he was angry with,' said Marte, 'and you could understand it, with our girl keeping her sickness a secret from him for so long and then you getting injured. But I don't mean he was angry with *you*, Helen, of course not with *you*.' It was a long time before Marte realised she was wasting her phone time talking to Helen about John.

Now and then, when there was business to be done, such as finding tenants for her house, or sorting out problems resulting from her sudden departure from the station, or receiving royalties from her book sales, John rang Helen. The calls were short and efficient and the two of them conducted their business as politely and carefully as diplomats in a cold war. Which, in a way, they were.

'Stay in touch,' he always said, at the end of these calls. 'Give Tom my love.' And in October, when the trees outside her tall windows were a mass of orange and gold, he said: 'We're all hoping that you'll both be home for Christmas.'

But Helen couldn't bear the thought of Christmas in Siren's Rock without Jemma.

She sent Tom home in time to start school again in the new year. Hamish and Caitlin met him off the plane, then Hamish and his two mates drove Tom all the way home to Siren's Rock. It was very hot and they stopped to surf at beaches all the way up the coast — so frequently that they had to spend two nights in Hamish's new tent.

Tom told Hamish he was beside himself. 'That's what Jemma used to say,' he said to Hamish. 'It means I've got too much excitement for one person so there are two of me, only one of me is invisible. But we're both having heaps of fun.'

It seemed he had no sooner started school again than the Easter holidays rolled around and he was heading back to Sydney with John to meet his mummy's plane.

SYDNEY

They didn't see her at first because there were so many people, all hurrying past her and jostling and calling out to their waiting, waving friends and relations.

But then Tom shouted 'Mummy!' and hurled himself into the crowd. By the time John reached them, Tom was hanging off her like a shoulder bag, talking twenty words a second and she was bending towards him, caressing his neck, her face hidden behind her soft silver blonde curtain of hair.

It had grown again, and she was wearing her cream coat.

There was no crushing of bodies this time. He smiled, breathing carefully and regularly to control the surge of emotion that the sight of her had aroused. Just the sight of her. Wings, flapping in his chest. He thought of a kookaburra he had found caught in the filter of their swimming pool at home; he'd pulled it out and had been surprised how strongly the wings still flapped, how much effort it had taken to keep the bird in his control until he had pulled it free and could let it go.

He was surprised at how hard it was to see Helen again. He thought he had already judged just how hard it would be.

She smiled shyly, over Tom's sprouty red head.

'Welcome home,' he said.

There was a moment so awkward that even Tom stood back and looked up at both of them.

'Aren't you going to hug her, John?' he said.

They both laughed nervously and Helen moved stiffly into his arms. He kissed her fleetingly on the cheek and they moved apart again. But it was enough to satisfy Tom, who was talking again.

'Mummy, we drove all through the night, and it was dark as dark and we even had breakfast in the dark, well, in the almost-still-dark, and we played music and it rained all the way, and we're staying in Sydney for the whole weekend, in a posh hotel, with buttons for everything!'

John wheeled the luggage trolley ahead of them while Helen said that if Tom had travelled all night, he might need a little sleep when they got to the posh hotel. Tom said he'd had a *little* bit of a nap on the way and he didn't want to waste any time sleeping because they were going to have a ferry ride and he wanted to go up Centrepoint Tower to see the view because that way he could see *all* of Sydney all at once and John had said that would be a good way for Helen to know she was *really* home again.

In the car Tom said: 'You know how we don't live in our house in Siren's Rock any more, because other people are living there now, and so we live at John's house? Well, I've been sleeping in the spare bedroom that was your bedroom when you were waiting for me to be born, only it's not the *spare* room any more, because it's mine, but when we get back you can share it with me, and John said if you want to be in there by yourself I can sleep in Hamish's room with all his cups and ribbons! Because he only comes home sometimes from university.'

'Well,' said Helen, lost for a moment in her son's bright chatter.

'Although I was thinking,' Tom went on, 'that you should share with John, because he's got a huge bed and it's half empty now, without Jemma, so he's lonely. You've been a bit lonely lately, haven't you, John?'

John's face was the colour of a Siren's Rock sunset. He kept his eyes on the road.

'Just a bit,' said John.

'Well,' said Helen, 'it's very nice of John to let us stay with him until we get organised. And when we find a new house we can both have a room of our own.'

'Where would we find a new house?' asked Tom doubtfully.

'We can talk about that later,' said Helen. 'Right now I just want to look at this lovely city. In fact, we might even move to this lovely city.'

'Wow!' shouted Tom. 'Live in the city! Wow! Can we? Could we?' He frowned. 'But what about John? And Nanna and Poppy and all the people who love us?'

'Tom,' said John, manoeuvring the car through the lines of heavy city traffic, 'see that huge skyscraper? That's our hotel. Did you realise it was as tall as that?'

And so Tom moved on to the perplexing question of whether skyscrapers actually *scraped* the sky, rather than piercing it like a concrete *sword*, which was how it looked to him.

Life was pretty darned good, Tom told Helen, as they left the posh hotel together. She had showered and changed into a soft, creamy-coloured shirt and trousers. 'My life is pretty darned good,' Tom repeated. 'That's what John says.'

'Does he now?' said Helen.

'Yes, he does,' said Tom. 'And he says if your life is pretty darned good, you can't ask for much more than that.'

'Well,' said Helen, steering him into a hamburger place for lunch. 'And what about John's life? Is it pretty darned good, do you think?'

'Oh no,' said Tom, looking around, missing nothing, standing on his toes to see the glistening pictures of the meals on offer. 'John's life is no darned good at all.'

Helen looked down at her son. 'Why is that, Tommy?' she asked softly.

Tom flopped down on the flats of his feet. '*You* know why, Mummy,' he said. 'John's life is no darned good because Jemma's gone,' said Tom.

John slept, collapsing on the sofa bed in their hotel suite, exhausted after a night of driving and a morning of nervous tension. Helen and Tom stayed out all afternoon. They rode a ferry through the harbour waters, then Tom had a good long look at the whole city from the tower and entertained a lift full of Japanese tourists by reciting everything of interest that he'd read while circumnavigating the observation deck.

When they returned to their hotel, John was opening a bottle of champagne. He poured a thimbleful for Tom, who giggled when the bubbles went up his nose. 'You're not supposed to drink it yet,' said John. 'We're going out on the balcony to drink a welcome home toast to your mummy.'

They stood in a row at the railing and admired the loveliness of the city.

'There's the Anzac Bridge,' said Tom. 'We saw it from the tower.'

'Your mummy once said that bridge looks as if it's hanging on strings from God's fingers,' said John. 'Remember, Julie?'

'I remember,' said Helen. 'Jemma was with us.'

'Well,' said Tom. 'By now she'll have found out.'

They both looked down at him, puzzled.

'You know,' said Tom. 'If God's holding it. Or if it's just staying up there by itself.'

That evening they found an Italian restaurant and ate gourmet pizzas for dinner. All three of them discovered they were starving, so they had garlic bread as well, dripping with butter, and a huge bowl of salad. Tom had a gigantic glass of coke and they washed their own dinner down with a bottle of shiraz.

'We'll be pickled,' said Helen.

'It helps,' said John. She looked at him but he kept his eyes on the menu that he and Tom were studying, in search of a suitably decadent dessert. John looked older, thought Helen, and there were patches of grey in the hair above his ears. But such a kind face, she thought, and still so handsome. John glanced up and saw her looking at him. Dark brown eyes looked into dark brown eyes. Damaged hearts beat faster. Helen felt her face grow hot but she didn't look away. Neither did he.

And then he smiled.

After that it seemed to take an awfully long time to get Tom through his dessert and back to the hotel. He talked and they laughed and gently hurried him along the footpath.

John helped him into his pyjamas and Helen heaved him onto the queen-sized bed that he was going to share with her in the bedroom of the suite, trying not to mention yet again that he shouldn't pull on her bad arm. She read him some of *The Muddle-Headed Wombat*, which was still his favourite book. John put the kettle on for coffee. And finally they both kissed him goodnight.

John went out onto the balcony and looked at the myriad of lights glittering around the harbour. Okay, Jemma, he thought. So what do I do now?

Helen was in the sleek little kitchen alcove, making the coffee that neither of them wanted, when Tom came pattering out and said he wanted to sleep on the sofa bed, with the curtains open, so that when he woke up in the morning the first thing he would see was the water and the boats.

She didn't argue.

She tucked him in and said goodnight again, then turned out all the lights in the living room so he could go to sleep. Out on the balcony, through the wide glass doors, they could both see John's broad back as he stood there. Tom smiled at her. Then he burrowed down into the bed and closed his eyes.

BY HEART

John waited for her to speak.

'I miss her every day,' Helen said. 'Every hour.'

John let out an enormous breath, his eyes following a ferry chugging across the harbour.

'Me too,' he said. 'More than my life.'

'Yes,' said Helen.

'More than my old life, anyway,' said John. 'But that's over.'

She didn't know what he meant.

'I thought I'd lost you both,' he said. His voice quivered slightly.

She put her hand over his on the balcony rail. 'It must have been so terrible for you,' she said softly. 'And then I made it worse.'

'No,' said John. 'That's not true. I made it worse for us both.'

He turned and looked at her. 'Are you well again? Physically, I mean. I don't suppose you ever truly recover from almost being murdered.'

She continued to gaze at the water. 'Actually, on the grand scale of my tiny life, the crash wasn't the worst thing that has ever happened to me. I've been thinking about it, of course,' said Helen. 'It was violent and it was sudden. But it wasn't personal. I was just in the wrong place at the wrong time.' She paused. 'Just like those poor people in Strathlee.'

'I've given up going to church,' said John dully. 'All those innocents being destroyed by people who supposedly believe God is on their side.'

Helen sighed and pressed his hand hard. 'I'm so sorry to hear that, John. What happened to us and what happened in Strathlee had nothing to do with God. Men and power, that's what the Troubles in Northern Ireland are about. That's what all war is about.'

'And Jemma? Do you think she's haranguing God about the Futility of War?'

'Absolutely.' She smiled at him. 'Just before I left for Ireland, she tried to tell me that she was finally at peace with herself. With her life. With her God. And she said it again in the letter she left for me.'

'Of course,' said John. 'I got a letter too.' He glanced at her quickly. 'It was a lot longer than the one she sent to St Patrick's.'

Helen's smile deepened.

'She told me how she wanted me to feel,' John continued. 'Sad but not heartbroken. Grateful for the good. Et cetera et cetera. How I should reorganise my life. Start again. She was a control freak to the end.

'She always had a plan. We had our last talk on the verandah, the perfect setting for our final scene together. She said she no longer cared about fame, that her best times were because of me.'

He paused. 'She was always a very good actress. I think she wanted to believe it herself. It made for a better finale.'

'John . . .' said Helen.

'Jemma always believed that she could make things

happen,' he went on, as if Helen hadn't spoken. 'When life didn't go according to her plan, she revised it. She used to say I never did anything. The truth is, she never gave me the chance to do anything she hadn't organised.'

'That's true,' said Helen. 'Have you forgiven her for that?'

'I was angry with her for a long time,' he replied, 'for leaving me out. Twenty-five years of marriage and she didn't want me around at the end of her life. She turned her death into her own personal soap opera, but she didn't write a part for me.'

'That's not how she saw it,' said Helen sadly.

'I have forgiven her,' John sighed. 'I loved her all my life. When you love someone that much, you forgive them anything.'

They both fell silent.

'I would have made her fight,' said John after a while. 'No matter what the doctors said, I would have encouraged her to keep going. To try anything.'

'John,' said Helen, her voice calm and low, 'the cancer had spread to her brain. The blood vessels ruptured. There was nothing anybody could have done ... I feel so desperate when I think of what she must have been going through in her mind. She would have hated the thought of being weak and dependent.'

John turned his head and looked at Helen's profile. 'You are such a lovely person, Julie,' he said. 'I've been feeling sorry for myself. But, as usual, you've been thinking only of her.'

'I've been thinking about all of us,' said Helen. 'What she did to us might have been misguided or even just plain stupid, but I don't think she saw it as a soap opera or a movie. She just needed a plan. Jemma had to have her plans to keep her mind *off* the things she didn't want to think about. Her projects distracted her from the major disappointments of her life. She thought of herself as a frustrated bohemian, as a woman whose wild, impulsive nature was being held in check by her sense of responsibility — but she wasn't really like that at all.'

'No,' said John. 'She wasn't. She wasn't like you.'

'Actually, Jemma *liked* living an orderly life,' said Helen, hardly hearing him. 'That's why she never ran away to find fame and fortune. She couldn't have done that and remained in control.'

'So she controlled us instead,' said John.

'Only in a good way,' said Helen. 'I was grateful. I needed her. I don't think you minded either.'

John was silent.

'It didn't matter until . . .' Helen stopped. There were tears in her voice when she spoke again. 'I think once she knew how ill she was, she drew up this new plan. And she decided to . . .' She closed her eyes, reining in her distress.

'Push us together.' John said the words for her.

'Yes,' said Helen. 'But I wonder if she stopped planning *our* future long enough to come to terms with the thought of her own death. Without you beside her. Without me. I don't know . . . in the end, I suppose, we all die alone.'

'She was right about one thing,' he said.

'She was right about lots of things.'

'Life goes on,' John said to the harbour lights. 'You have to start over again, with what you still have.'

'Yes.'

'I'm sorry,' said John. He heard his voice shuddering and took a breath. At last he turned to look at her face. She was all silver and cream. Her pale face, her hair, her loose cream clothes. She seemed to shimmer in the pale light. But she didn't look at him. She held on to the balcony rail with her left hand, keeping her other hand over his, and continued to watch the boats and lights on the water.

'I'm sorry for disappointing you,' said John. 'I'm sorry for what I did to you at the drive-in all those years ago. I'm sorry for all the hurt I've caused you. I'm more sorry than I will ever be able to say for the cruel things I said to you on the morning after we ... after Jemma died. But the truth is, I'm not sorry I made love to you that night. I wanted you desperately. I needed you.' He paused. 'We needed each other.'

'I know,' said Helen.

'I was cruel to you because I felt so guilty,' said John, 'and I was so angry with Jemma. Only I couldn't take any of it out on her, so I used you.'

'Yes,' said Helen. 'I know.'

'Well,' said John. He uttered a short, nervous laugh. 'So how come you know so much, Julie?'

She turned her head and looked at him at last, raised her right hand and lightly touched his cheek.

'I know you off by heart,' she said.

Tears sprang into his eyes. He blinked them back. Helen took her hand away but she continued to look at his face.

'Julie,' said John, 'I once asked you whether you ever thought about what we might have had together. If things had turned out differently. You said you didn't.'

'I was lying,' said Helen.

The wings in his chest were back, flailing ...

'Jemma was the first person who offered me unconditional love,' Helen explained. 'I would never have jeopardised that. Not for you. Not for anyone.'

Their faces were too much for each other. They both looked back at the water, the dancing lights, the dark arc of the bridge.

'Helen,' said John. 'I didn't realise how much I loved you, until I thought I'd lost you too.'

Helen's fingers whitened on the balcony rail.

He loves me then, she thought. This is how it feels. This is what John and Jemma had, and what Marte and George still have, and what all those couples have, people as old as us and older, the ones you see holding hands in the street ... He loves me, thought Helen. He said so.

'Is that how it happened for you?' asked John. 'With me?'

'No,' said Helen.

Disappointment and embarrassment pitched into his gut. Still, what had he been expecting her to say? Jemma always came first for both of us, he thought. We both know that. Then I hurt her too badly in Maighdean, and I left her there.

'I loved you from the first day,' said Helen.

The wings fluttered and were still. A sense of peace settled over him. He looked up at the stars.

'When we met,' said Helen. 'When you tried to pull me away from my father. You tried to rescue me.'

'But I couldn't,' said John sadly. 'I even went to your house that night. I didn't know what to do.'

'You tried,' said Helen. 'It was the beginning.'

'And Tom's father?' he asked, a stab of jealousy surprising him. What right had he to be jealous? 'He did more, didn't he? He helped you more than I ever did.'

'He helped me look at my life in the light, to learn to love myself,' said Helen. 'I will always be grateful to him for that. But you did more. You stayed with me. You were my friend.'

'And now?' asked John. His peace was shattered. His heart was going at it again, as if he was trapped and frantic in a pool filter instead of standing quite still on a balcony washed with moonlight. 'I mean,' said John, 'are we *in* love? Or is loving friends all we can be?'

Helen turned her back on the view and smiled at him. 'What do you think?' she asked, in her husky, hungering way.

He put his arms around her and pulled her close to him. She was small and the curves of their bodies were not well aligned. Her hair brushed his chin. She smelled like heaven.

'I want to be more than your friend,' said John. 'I want to make love to you, Julie. I want to make love to you every day until the day we die.'

She tucked down her head against his chest. She had wanted him to kiss her since she was twenty years old. The moment had come. The kiss would be everything. But if he kissed her now the talking would stop. They might never find the courage to talk like this again.

His lips were warm and slightly damp on the back of her neck. His hand was sliding over the soft material of her jacket, curving around her breast. She wanted the hand *underneath*.

'There's one big problem,' said Helen, looking up but turning her head a little so that his lips couldn't quite reach her mouth. 'I'm sure you realise what it is. What I'm worried about most,' she said quickly, 'is that we're only doing this because *Jemma* wanted it. I mean,' she added desperately, 'she'll always be with us, haunting us ... No, that's not what I mean either.' She uttered a small moan of frustration as the words she had spent years learning to control escaped from her. 'I mean of *course* we'll remember her every day, that's natural, but not in the bedroom, because that ...' She gave a little sigh as his fingers slipped inside her jacket, searching for the skin she wanted him to touch '... isn't.'

Jemma had never sighed like that, thought John. He remembered how Helen had sighed and sung above him in Maighdean.

He hadn't been so excited, so precariously balanced on the edge of a miracle, since that afternoon with Jemma on the island of Lassos. He was daring to hope. He had thought he would never hope again.

John put his lips against her ear as she twisted her head away from him again. 'You know as well as I do how Jemma felt about sex,' he said. 'She could take it or leave it. She'll be hugely relieved that it's happening to Julie and not her.'

Helen laughed, a deep little chuckle, but she kept her face turned away because there was still one more thing.

He moved his hands down her back, lifted her off her feet and pressed her hips against his. Even through their clothes, it felt unbelievably good. He could do anything he liked with this small, passionate woman, he thought, and the prospect filled him with a powerful vitality.

Helen had begun to struggle; she was pushing at his chest, banging her knees against his legs. Shit! thought John.

Gutted with shame, he lowered her back onto her own feet. He let go of her and stepped back a little. His hands hung helplessly at his sides. 'I'm sorry,' he said, although he wondered what right he had to apologise for something he wanted to do again. His pain, mental and physical, was acute.

She couldn't bear a man's hands there. Jemma had told him that once. She had wept when she told him and John had felt like weeping too.

'You're probably right, Julie,' he said miserably. 'We should take this more slowly. Maybe in time . . .'

Helen's face was in shadow but when she spoke she sounded neither angry nor hurt, merely breathless. 'Now *is* the time,' she said. 'But there is one more thing I want you to understand.'

She reached up and took his face in both her hands. The face she knew so well.

'My name is Helen,' she said.

He stared at her for a moment. Just a moment. Then he put his arms around her again. 'Hello, Helen,' he said. And kissed her lips for the first and longest time.

Some little girls get nipped while they are still in bud, the stranger had said. After that they never blossom as beautifully as they might have done.

But in the late summer of Helen's life, nourished with love and care, she opened like an exquisite flower in the warmth of an unexpected sun.

EPILOGUE

Of course they had to leave Siren's Rock.

Even the best-disposed people couldn't help staring at them in the street or the supermarket, hoping to catch a glimpse of passion while they fingered the frozen peas. This was the woman who had drawn the national spotlight onto their town with her outspoken views on child abuse, had been almost killed by terrorists in Northern Ireland, and had now returned home to scandalise everyone by having an affair with her best friend's husband. And her lover's wife dead for barely a year.

One of the major women's magazines even ran a story on them. They couldn't get anything out of John and Helen, of course, so they focused their breathless story on Jemma: the beautiful wife, devoted mother, tireless community worker, nationally televised actress and playwright. Cheated of life, dying in her prime while her husband and her best friend became lovers. Her face splashed over three glossy pages.

Jemma would have loved it.

They sold the timber house that John had built for Jemma and paid an astronomical price for a low stone cottage behind a high hedge in Sydney. It was in an anonymous, established suburb, not too far from the city or the beach.

Tom started at a new school and found another teacher to dazzle. John was appointed public affairs manager for a national radio network; Helen said it was a very suitable title, considering their current circumstances.

Caitlin was predictably appalled and elected to remain in the flat she shared with her friends. A series of unholy rows blazed through the cottage where John, Helen and Tom were taking their first tentative steps into contentment. Caitlin's snide asides, exaggerated shudders of revulsion and strident dissatisfaction left them all tense and exhausted.

'It won't last,' said Caitlin to Hamish. 'Anyway, what about Jemma?'

'It's what she wanted,' said Hamish. 'She told me. Read your letter again. And they're happy. I'm glad they're happy.'

John's concern for Marte and George was alleviated when Janelle finally became pregnant, and she and Nick decided to raise their family in Siren's Rock.

Janelle asked Marte if she would teach her how to make her brilliant German apple cake.

'You see?' Marte said to George. 'Good things can still happen.'

Slowly, and with enormous satisfaction, Helen spent her time creating a home. Occasionally she drove to the beach and had long conversations with Jemma, who was much more entertaining than the Helens who used to live in her head.

And every evening John drove home through the ghastliness of the pushy city traffic, tense until he drew up outside the house behind the hedge where good food and quiet company were waiting in the small haven of peace that Helen had created for them.

At night, when eventually they slept, Helen lay curled in the burrow of John's body. Warm. Protected. Saved.

John and Helen returned to Siren's Rock late in the spring, when the tiny trumpets of jasmine were disappearing from the vines and the jacaranda trees were growing heavy with mauve blossoms. They came back to be married, mainly because Marte and George were too fragile to travel all the way to Sydney, but also because this was where Jemma had started their story.

The wedding ceremony was to take place in Marte's immaculate garden. Only the immediate family and a few close friends would be present. As Tom said, just the people who loved them best.

Tom was very excited. It was his job to lead his mother down the path to where the minister would be standing with John. Tom would put Mummy's hand in John's and then he had special permission to climb up into the jacaranda and watch the ceremony from above. It would look beautiful from up there, he said, like watching a movie. So Mummy had agreed.

The night before the wedding, they had a visitor. John had gone to a friend's house to sleep over, because Nanna said that was tradition. Caitlin had driven Nanna and Poppy to collect some last-minute delicacies for the wedding lunch. So Tom answered Marte's musical doorbell, and there on the doorstep was Granny Babs.

She was carrying her handbag. And an envelope.

'Hello, Tom,' she said, and she pulled back her flaky red lips and pretended to smile. Granny Babs hadn't paid enough attention to her teeth when she was young, he thought. Mummy said people didn't, in the olden days.

'Hello,' said Tom. A small worm of worry, the first he had

felt for weeks, uncurled in his stomach. Granny Babs wasn't coming to the wedding, he knew that. Aunty Joy had phoned to say her mother wasn't well enough to travel all the way from Bridgetown. Yet here she was, looking quite well.

He asked her to come in and she stepped into Marte's newly tiled hall, clopping in her high-heeled shoes across the big green and white squares, looking at herself in the mirror tiles on the wall. She was fiddling with her hair when Mummy came out of Marte's spare bedroom.

'Hello,' said Mummy. 'This is a surprise.' Tom knew from Mummy's voice that she didn't mean it was a *nice* surprise.

'I believe there's going to be a wedding,' said Granny Babs.

'Tom,' said Mummy. 'Would you mind going into the kitchen and making Granny Babs and me a cup of tea?'

Tom went into the kitchen and put the kettle on but he kept his ears open, as Jemma used to say. He wanted to know just how big a worry this visit might be.

'I was wondering,' said Granny Babs, 'whether Jemma ever gave you the letter from that fellow. That tramp you claimed was Tom's father.'

Tom held his breath. So, from the silence, did his mother.

'No?' Granny Babs was saying. 'I thought not, when I heard you were marrying her husband. Luckily I kept the original.'

Tom listened to the silence again. The worm of worry wriggled more deeply in his tummy.

Mummy's voice was very croaky. 'He wrote to me? And you kept the letter?'

The kettle began to whistle and Tom trotted over to turn it off. When he peeped through the door again, Mummy was clutching the envelope.

'. . . so I thought you'd better have it,' Granny Babs was saying. 'Just in case.'

'Just in case what?' whispered Mummy. 'Just in case there is a danger I might be happy?'

'Just in case Tom ever wants to know anything about his real father,' said Granny Babs. Well, thought Tom. That was fair enough. There were lots of things he wanted to know about his father.

'What a sweet little old lady you are,' said Mummy. 'Always trying to help.'

Tom wasn't sure whether his mother was being nice or nasty. There was something in her voice that reminded him of Caitlin. The way she spoke to all of them.

Granny Babs didn't seem to think Mummy had said something nice. She said: 'It won't work, you know. Marrying a man who was never meant to be yours.'

'All this time you've had my letter, but you waited until today to give it to me,' said Mummy very softly.

'I told you,' said Granny Babs, 'Jemma had a copy. I warned her about you preying on her husband. But it looks as if *you* couldn't trust *her*, seeing she never showed you the letter either. Perhaps,' Granny Babs' voice became soft, 'your dear friend wanted to make sure you never found the man who thought you were the love of his life.'

Mummy didn't say a word.

Tom peered around the door. Granny Babs was smiling her pulled-back smile. 'You're looking well for your age, Helen, but your skin could be better. I never *could* get you to wear a hat.'

Very softly, Mummy said: 'Sorry about that.'

Tom saw Granny Babs squeeze her red flaky lips together till you couldn't see them any more. She clip-clopped across the hall to the front door and went out, without saying goodbye or waiting for her cup of tea.

A few specks of powder hung in the perfumed air.

Tom went into the hall and touched Helen's hand. She looked down at him as if she didn't remember who he was.

'Are we going to read it?' Tom asked.

Mummy sat down on the floor and pulled Tom into her lap. She held him very tightly in her arms and rubbed her chin on his sprouty red head.

'We'll put it away until you're a man,' she said, after a little while. 'You'll understand him better then.'

'I wonder why Jemma didn't show it to you?' said Tom.

Helen sighed. 'It was her way of being kind,' she said.

After a while she let him go and got up, very stiffly, rubbing her bad arm. She took the envelope into the bedroom. She went to the window and pulled down the blind.

At noon the next day, wearing a dress the colour of clouds, Helen walked barefoot into the sunny garden and married John, the first boy she had ever loved.

She married him for the same reasons Jemma had. He was good, faithful, strong in word and deed, passionate and kind. She loved him very much, although she never called him her best friend. Jemma was too hard an act for any man to follow.

Tom lay along the branch of the jacaranda tree and watched from above. But for an instant, a blink, an eyelash of time, frozen in the frame the branches made, he saw a red-headed stranger, bending his head down to look into his mother's face, the way John was doing now.

And he wondered how it might have been.

ACKNOWLEDGMENTS

My sincere thanks must go first to the women who have shared the best and worst times with me, whose friendship, laughter, encouragement, sympathy, loyalty, small joys, large tragedies and unshakeable faith in me have provided the inspiration for this book. So thank you Maria Kelly, Maureen Thomas, Raema Anderson, Wendy Skogvold, Elizabeth O'Keefe, Prue Sky, Anne (Bear) Hickman, the late ML Parker, my lovely daughter, Anna Donaghy, my incredible sisters, Melanie O'Connor and Kristine Simeon ... and of course, Mrs Mole, one of the world's most extraordinary women, to whom this book is dedicated.

My life is richer through knowing you all.

I wish I could have included in this list all the other wonderful women friends, relations and colleagues whose friendship I have enjoyed so much. I hope you know who you are.

For their invaluable contributions to this story I am also grateful to the magnificent Frieda Terakes and the other courageous men and women who shall remain nameless, but who shared with me the saddest of stories during the years I spent researching the subject of child abuse.

Thank you to the men in my life, Francis, Aidan and Liam Donaghy, for keeping the faith.

I would like to thank Dr Danny Stewart for providing the medical material; my dedicated publisher, Linda Funnell, and my brilliant friend and agent, Jennie Orchard. And I would like to put on record my heartfelt gratitude to Dr Sally Greenaway and the nurses of the haematology unit at Westmead Hospital, for keeping me well enough to complete the book I have dreamed of writing all my life.

Bronwyn Donaghy
July 2002

Bronwyn Donaghy was an author and journalist who specialised in family issues for over twenty years, contributing regularly to the *Sydney Morning Herald, Parents Magazine, New Woman* and *Sydney's Child*.

In 1996 Bronwyn published her first adult book, *Anna's Story*, about the life and ecstasy-related death of Anna Wood. Now in its fifteenth printing, with over 100,000 copies sold, this book has impacted on students, parents and teachers all over Australia and beyond. Following the success of *Anna's Story*, Bronwyn was commissioned to write two further books on adolescent health issues in association with the Department of Adolescent Health at the New Children's Hospital in Sydney. These were *Leaving Early*, about teenage depression and suicide, and *Unzipped*, on teenage sexuality. She has also published a humorous collection of parenting pieces, *Keeping Mum: Secrets of Happy Parenting and Other Lies*, and a children's story, *Two and a Half Wishes*. As Bronwyn's writing career developed she became a successful public speaker, travelling all over Australia to speak about her life and her books.

Finally she found the time to fulfil her life-long dream — to write her first novel. Sadly she was never to see it in print. *Small Acts of Kindness* was completed shortly before she died, in July 2002, from a bone marrow disorder.

You can find further information about Bronwyn's life and achievements at www.bronwyndonaghy.com

WHITE GARDENIA

BELINDA ALEXANDRA

In a district of the city of Harbin, a haven for White Russian families since Russia's Communist revolution, Alina Kozlova must make a heartbreaking decision if her only child, Anya, is to survive the final days of World War II.

White Gardenia sweeps across cultures and continents, from the glamorous nightclubs of Shanghai to the harshness of Cold War Soviet Russia in the 1960s, from a desolate island in the Pacific Ocean to a new life in post-war Australia. Both mother and daughter must makes sacrifices, but is the price too high? Most importantly of all, will they ever find each other again?

Rich in incident and historical detail, this is a compelling and beautifully written tale about yearning and forgiveness. *White Gardenia* announces the arrival of a powerful new talent.

'captivating' — *Daily Telegraph*

'a passionate and powerful family saga'
— *Australian Women's Weekly*

'impossible to put down' — *NW*

ISBN 0 7322 7627 6

JOSEPHINE AND ME

BRENDA LITTLE

There seemed to be only two reactions to Josephine: vexation or delight. She delighted me.

Josephine and Emma had been friends for as long as they both could remember.

Emma's mother didn't like it much but there was something about Jo that made people look twice. Growing up by the sea, Jo and Emma spent their days making plans. They were going to go everywhere and see everything.

But sometimes life has its own ideas …

When Jo abandons all thought of travel and seems also to abandon her friend, Emma is forced to find the strength to act alone. Travelling through Europe and meeting new people help to distract her from missing home.

All it takes is one letter, and the situation for both young women changes. Lifelong friendship is about to be tested. Can the ties that bound so tightly stay intact?

Brenda Little crafts a story of friendship and how there are no choices when it comes to falling in love …

ISBN 0 7322 7556 3

TEARS OF THE MAASAI

FRANK COATES

In the aftermath of a bizarre mishap, Jack Morgan takes up a UN posting in Kenya, hoping to find obscurity on the anonymous streets of Nairobi. There he is befriended by the American 'Bear' Hoffman — a man equally at home in the city's racy nightlife as in the Kenyan bush.

Africa is a land of excitement, and Jack's hopes for seclusion are soon dashed as he is seduced by its adventure, the majesty of the landscape and by a beautiful Maasai woman named Malaika.

Malaika carries a dark secret, and when a warrior returns from her past, she and Jack are plunged into a world of ancient spiritualism and tribal curses. Caught at the centre of a gathering storm, they must fight for the survival of their love…

Rich with historical detail, *Tears of the Maasai* follows Jack Morgan on a flight from truth, and a Maasai family's journey through time, from Warrior supremacy, mysticism and magic, to the colour and drama of modern-day Kenya.

ISBN 0 7322 7920 8